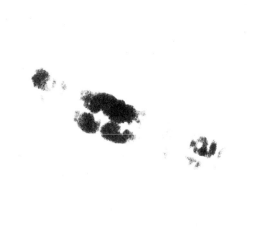

DANCER'S LAMENT

DANCER'S LAMENT

Path to Ascendancy
Book 1

Ian C. Esslemont

A Tom Doherty Associates Book
New York

This is a work of fiction. All of the characters, organizations, and events portrayed in this novel are either products of the author's imagination or are used fictitiously.

A Tor Book
Published by Tom Doherty Associates, LLC
175 Fifth Avenue
New York, NY 10010

www.tor-forge.com

Tor® is a registered trademark of Tom Doherty Associates, LLC.

The Library of Congress Cataloging-in-Publication Data is available upon request.

ISBN 978-0-7653-7944-3 (hardcover)
ISBN 978-0-7653-7945-0 (trade paperback)
ISBN 978-1-4668-6858-8 (e-book)

Our books may be purchased in bulk for promotional, educational, or business use. Please contact your local bookseller or the Macmillan Corporate and Premium Sales Department at 1-800-221-7945, extension 5442, or by e-mail at MacmillanSpecialMarkets@macmillan.com.

First published in Great Britain by Bantam Press, an imprint of Transworld Publishers

First U.S. Edition: May 2016

Printed in the United States of America

0 9 8 7 6 5 4 3 2 1

For Gerri and the boys

ACKNOWLEDGEMENTS

I offer my deepest appreciation to A. P. Canavan, pre-reader and editor extraordinaire. Also, thanks as always to Simon Taylor and everyone at Transworld for their support; and to Peter and Nicky Crowther, and Howard Morhaim.

'Quon Tali'

N

FALARI SEA

REACHER'S OCEAN

KARTOOL ISLAND
Kartool

MALAZ ISLAND
Malaz City

ICE FIELDS

WICKAN PLAINS

COLONNUS SEA

Baran
Hobal
Gris
Halfpen
Fools
Sentry
Unta
Nita
Jurda
Balstro
Athrans
Davig
Voron
Thade
Rath
Thade
Bloor

BLOOD SEA

Drim
Larent
Yellows
Estawn
Netor
Sheetry
Loyes
Satar
Halas
Bris
Marl
Nure
East
Ayhan
Carasin
Yor

NAPAN SEA

Nap
Then
Itko Kan
Pyl
Laeth
Wal Tes
Wal Fend

NAPAN ISLES

GENI

THE GREAT FENN RANGE

FOREST FENN

Ero Lake
New Seti
Tel
Telc
Ipras
Cawn
Askon
Fenya
Borid
Buld
Traly
Ijor
Nex
Fedah
Horan
Rynsen
Largen
Balk

DALHON PLAINS

FOREST HORN

NOM
PURGE
POR
SETI

Purage
Tellick
White
Lake Seti
High Postern
Quan
Tali
Dass
Attic
Cullis
Nadir
Bastial
En Krael
Ifaran
Idryb
Li Heng
Gar
Bylit
Aireck
Valan
Ebord
Destry
Korn
Panys
Arath
Seti

THE HORN

HORN OCEAN

DRIFT AVALII

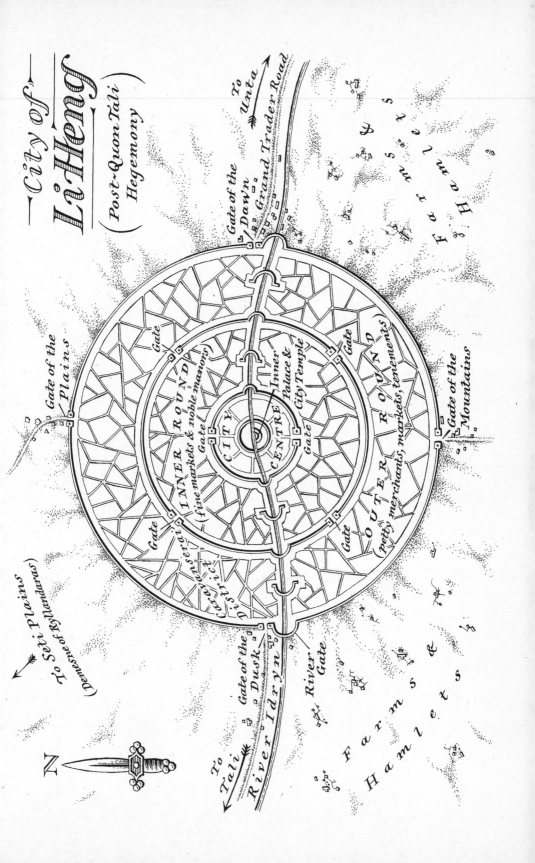

City of
Li Heng
(Post-Quon Tali Hegemony)

N

To Unta

Grand Trader Road

Gate of the Dawn

Gate of the Plains

Gate

INNER ROUND
(fine markets & noble manors)
Gate I

Conservatory District

CITY
CENTRE

Inner Palace &
City Temple
Gate

Gate

OUTER ROUND
(petty merchants, markets, tenements)

Gate of the Mountains

Gate

Gate

Gate of the Dusk

River Gate

River Idryn

To Tali

To Seti Plains
(Demesne of Ryllandaras)

Farms & Hamlets

Farms & Hamlets

DRAMATIS PERSONAE

Dorin Rav	A youth out of Tali
Wu	Pseudonym of a young Dal Hon mage

In Heng

Shalmanat	A sorceress, given the title of 'Protectress of Li Heng'
Silk	A city mage
Mister Ho	A city mage, also known as Hothalar
Mara	A city mage
Smokey	A city mage
Koroll	A city mage
Ullara	Daughter of a stabler, and a collector of birds
Pung the child-stealer	A Hengan crime boss
Greneth/Gren	Pung's lieutenant
Tran	One of Pung's underbosses
Urquart Rafalljara	A Hengan crime boss
Undath'al Brunn	A Hengan master thief in Urquart's gang, known as 'Rafall'
Rheena	A thief
Shreth	A thief
Loor	A thief

Of the Kanese Sword-Dancers

Hallens	Captain of King Chulalorn the Third's bodyguard
Iko	A new recruit to the king's bodyguard
Yuna	A member of the king's bodyguard
Torral	A member of the king's bodyguard
Sareh	A member of the king's bodyguard
Rei	A member of the king's bodyguard
Yvonna	A member of the king's bodyguard

Others

Ryllandaras	The White Jackal, also known as the man-beast
Sister Night	A powerful and ancient sorceress
Dassem	An acolyte of Hood, named by some the 'Sword of Hood'
Liss	A resident mage of Li Heng
K'rul	An elder god

Prelude

THE PRIZE WAS HIS AND NONE WOULD ROB HIM OF IT. A recent shudder of the earth had exposed it here on the Seti Plains, close by the Great Cliff, south of the river Idryn, near to where Burn herself is said to rest.

Uneasily, most obviously.

A small twinge, or minor itch, or passing flatulence from the Great Goddess had shaken the ground not more than a fortnight ago. And now this tunnel, or cave, revealed here in this narrow rocky cleft. His find. True, he'd only come across it because he'd caught a hint of movement out there on the plains and so had clambered down into the gorge out of prudent care. The plains curse, the man-eating beast Ryllandaras, was never far.

So it was his. Yet not his alone.

Someone else was lurking about: a sneaky fellow hard to pin down. And coming from him, from Dorin Rav, that was saying a lot. Not in all Quon or Tali had he met his match in stealth or murder. The so-called 'Assassin Guilds' he'd dug up these last years had proved themselves no more than gangs of brutes and thugs for hire. Not one true practitioner among them.

He'd been disgusted.

So much for the exploits of the thief queen Lady Apsalar, or daring Topaz, the favourites of so many jongleur songs. Petty greed, sadistic cruelty, and a kind of slope-browed cunning were all he'd found among the criminal underworld – if that was what you could call it. All of which, he had to allow, was at least the minimal requirement for extortion, blackmail, theft, and murder for hire.

Not that that had stopped him from profiting from their

1

ineptitude. A few well-placed thrusts and their stashes of coin rode tightly wrapped in a baldric across his chest – a baldric that also supported a selection of graded blades and lengths of rope.

He was of the opinion that one can never carry too much rope.

He passed the best of the night crouched on his haunches in a thick stand of desert tall-grass, patiently watching that dark opening, and saw nothing. A hunting snake slithered over one sandalled foot. Midges and chiggers feasted upon him. A lizard climbed his shirt, lost its footing on his sweat-slick neck and fell inside the padded, cloth-covered armour vest he wore next to his skin.

Yet he hadn't twitched. And still his rival had not revealed himself. Then, just as the sun kissed the lips of the narrow crevice ridge high above, a rock clattered close to the shadowed gap.

He ground his teeth. *Somehow* the bastard had slipped past. Very well. He'd follow. Dog the man until whatever lay ahead was revealed. The least the fellow could do was make himself useful by falling first into any hidden dangers.

He edged out to the mouth of the gap and, hunched, a blade ready, felt his way down. Just within, he paused to press himself against one wall of jagged broken rock. He listened and waited for his vision to adjust. A brush of cloth on stone sighed ahead. He felt his way onward.

A descending slope of loose broken rock ended at a narrow corridor of set blocks. Ancient, these, gigantic and of a dark stone he didn't recognize. He searched the gloom; where had the Hood-damned bastard gone? Then a dim ringing ahead as of metal on stone, quickly muted. He pressed himself to a wall – could he be seen outlined by the faint light behind? He darted forward.

The corridor ended at a wall that supported a door in the form of a slab of rock of similar origin. The slab stood at an angle aslant of the portal, a slim opening running top to bottom, at the foot a gap where a slim man or woman might just squirm within.

Damn the fellow for winning through first!

He knelt at the fissure, only to flinch away from the mouldy stink of things long dead. The still air was cold too, unaccountably so. Crystals of frost glittered on the rock. Wincing, he slipped one arm through. His other hand brushed the thick door slab. A nest of symbols carved in the naked rock writhed beneath his fingers.

2

Wards. Glyphs. A tomb. Or hoard. Out here? In the middle of nowhere?

Yet this had not stopped his rival.

He slid onward. Rising, brushing away the accumulated dust of centuries, it seemed to him passing strange that fine sand and grit should still choke the gap. Such speculations, however, were driven away by a wan golden glow coming from further ahead. *There's the bastard and now's your chance.*

He drew another blade and slid along the wall. His breath plumed in the oddly chill air.

It was a low-roofed chamber: a lost cellar or tomb, perhaps. Gloom swallowed its exact size and shape, which might have been circular. The low flame from a single clay oil-lamp provided the only faint light. Hoar frost glittered on what of the walls he could see. The lamp rested on a monolithic raised stone platform at the chamber's centre. A large figure, a near giant, sat at the block, slouched forward, arms resting on the surface. Its hair was long and iron-grey and hung in tangled lengths that obscured its features. Before it on the slab sat the remains of a mummified animal of some sort – possibly a monkey, Dorin thought.

Where was his rival? Hiding behind the stone? Must have nerves of iron.

He drew a breath to call the fellow out, but almost bit his tongue as the mummified animal moved. The thing reached out to sort among the dusty objects cluttering the stone. With a nimble long-fingered hand, it picked up what looked like a slim wooden tile and waved it through the air, showering dust and bright crystals of ice everywhere.

The corpse lashed out to slam the tile to the slab and Dorin grunted his shock.

'Don't meddle,' the corpse breathed in a voice like creaking wood. It raised its head, revealing outsized canines and bright gleaming eyes. 'I smell a breeze,' it said. 'That crack that lets in mice and cockroaches . . . and other pests . . .'

The tall figure shifted its head to fix those unnatural eyes upon Dorin. 'Come in, then – since you have already.' The being's gaze shifted slightly to the left. 'You too.'

Dorin spun to see his rival there just to one side.

Behind him all this time! A damned mage!

3

The fellow was short and young, dark-skinned – Dal Honese. *Young? Well, no older than I.* And he was an ugly lad with a scrunched-up face and a sad patchy attempt at a beard and moustache. He wore loose dark robes, dirty and tattered, and carried a walking stick – though he didn't grip it like a warrior. In answer to Dorin's scowl he flashed uneven yellow teeth.

Dorin shifted aside to face them both.

'You are Jaghut,' the newcomer called to their host, pleased with himself.

The huge man's expression remained unchanged. He lowered his head. 'I should think that obvious.'

Dorin took satisfaction from the fall of the smirk from the Dal Hon's face.

The creature – a Jaghut, or Jag, such as Dorin had heard of in stories – waved them in. 'Come, come. Make yourselves at home. We have all the time in the world.'

That gave Dorin pause. But not so his rival, who pushed in without hesitation. The youth bent over the huge block to study the scattered wooden tiles. 'You are doing a reading,' he announced.

'Another stunning deduction,' the Jag observed, acidly.

Dorin edged up behind his rival. *Why so bravely, or foolishly, offer his back now? Because he knows I'll not act in front of the Jag. Cheap courage, that.* He made a point of standing close to the Dal Hon's side. *Let him sweat.*

Squinting in the dim lamplight the young fellow was studying the dust-covered cards, tapping a thin finger to his lips. 'This casting has defeated you for some time.'

One thick brow arched ever so slightly. The lips drew back further from the sallow canines. 'Indeed.'

Dorin swept a quick glance over the wooden cards – artefacts as oversized as their host. The shadowed figures and images painted on their faces held little interest for him. His mother had once hired a reader to foretell his future . . . the woman's screams had woken all the neighbours. After that, there'd been no more readings for Dorin Rav.

The dark-skinned youth reached out for the nearest wooden slat but the animal – more than a monkey or diminutive ape, Dorin now saw; possibly, then, a nacht of the southern isles – batted his arm aside. It chattered something that sounded eerily like '*Doan*

4

medo'. The Dal Hon answered by hitting its hand away. The two then actually fell into a slapping fight there over the stone, until the Jag snarled his irritation and pushed the creature out of the youth's reach, from where it busied itself making faces at the lad, who responded with scrunched-up leers of his own.

Dorin mustered his courage to clear his throat and ask, 'What did you mean by "all the time in the world"?'

The Jag inclined his head as if acknowledging the justness of the question. 'This structure is my retreat. None may be allowed to know of its existence.' He raised a hand in a near apology. 'Now that you are here . . . you may never leave.'

Dorin did his best to keep his expression neutral – to hide his thoughts – but a smile crept over the being's wide mouth, entirely baring his canines, and he laughed, low and sardonic. 'You would not succeed, my friend.' He tapped a thick yellow nail, more like a talon, to the platform.

Squinting, Dorin examined the solid block of dark rock, some three paces in length. The surface was inscribed in an intricate pattern of swirls and those grooves were inlaid with silver. A humanoid shape lying flat, encircled by a series of complicated wards and sigils . . .

Dorin stepped away from what had resolved itself into a stone sarcophagus. *This one's?*

The Dal Hon meanwhile had set out exploring the chamber, poking his stick into the distant edges. 'Well then,' the lad mused from the dark, 'I suppose we should make ourselves at home.' He found a shelf along one wall, jabbed the stick at it, and objects tumbled, crashing loudly in the confined quarters.

The Jag scowled his annoyance. '*Must* you?'

'Sorry.' The youth raised a small pot fashioned of plain brown earthenware, now cracked. He held it out. 'Your most precious treasures, I assume?'

The Jag growled from somewhere deep within his throat. 'Grave offerings, I'll have you know.'

The Dal Hon returned to his explorations. The nacht had jumped from the sarcophagus and now stalked along behind the youth, mimicking his every move. Dorin put his back to one wall next to where the tunnel entered the chamber. *Should I try the door? Might as well.* He retreated up the tunnel. In the almost absolute dark, he felt along the door slab; the gap was there, but it now seemed far too slim for his shoulders. He'd slipped through *that*? How in the name of the Queen of Mystery . . .

Returning to the chamber, he found the Jag once more bent over the wooden cards. A frown of puzzlement now creased his long face.

'Is this your bed?' the Dal Hon called from somewhere in the darkness.

The Jag let out a long hissed breath and pressed his fingers to his temples, his elbows on the stone sarcophagus. He growled, 'I suppose I shall have to kill you now.'

The youth emerged from the gloom, his walking stick tapping. He spoke lightly, as if disinterested, 'But then you would just be alone again, wouldn't you?'

The fellow came alongside, and Dorin whispered, heated, 'What have you got us into?'

A vexed look from the lad – no younger than he, Dorin had to remind himself. 'I was following you.'

Dorin clenched his teeth. 'I thought I was following *you*—'

'Please,' the Jag rumbled, 'must I now endure your bickering?'

Dorin edged open his cloak to reveal his many knives.

The Dal Hon's brows rose. 'You could?'

'If anyone.'

'If you say so. Not my field.'

'And just what *is* your field?'

'Oh, a little of this, a little of that . . . Here, I found this.' He slipped a thin wooden box between them.

Dorin tucked it away. 'What is it?'

'I have absolutely no idea.' And he wandered off again.

Dorin found himself becoming just as irritated by the skinny fellow as their host.

The Dal Hon now gazed over the hunched Jag's shoulder, studying the cards. As Dorin watched, the nacht scampered up the young man's back until its wizened ugly hairy face peered over the youth's own shoulder. The sight of those three serried faces, each uglier and smaller than the one below, made Dorin feel dizzy, and rather queasy.

'The cards are unsettled,' the Dal Hon announced.

Massaging his brow with his fingertips, the Jag stifled his annoyance. 'Indeed.'

'You have ones here I have never seen.'

6

'My manufacture.'

'They appear not to be assigned.'

The Jag slapped his hands to the sarcophagus lid with a crack of bone on stone. '*Do you mind!*'

The Dal Hon flinched away, sniffed. 'Just trying to help.'

'*Jis trya alp,*' the nacht chattered.

The young mage tried to slap the creature away but it was far too quick for him, and it bounded off mouthing something that sounded entirely too similar to laughter. The youth now stalked the beast, his walking stick cocked like a club.

'What is to become of us?' Dorin asked.

The Jag had returned to massaging his forehead. 'A welcome diversion, I thought,' he said from behind his hands. 'Make the time pass more quickly. Already I regret it.'

Somewhere in the dark a hissing squalling fight had broken out.

The Jag lunged to his feet, gesturing. 'I'm trying to *think*!' A wave of power pounded through the chamber, slamming Dorin to the wall and squeezing the breath from him. The entire structure groaned and shifted. Dust flew up in a storm, obscuring everything. Dorin squinted into the haze, coughing and gasping. He held his aching chest, unable to straighten. *Ye gods! A mere fit of pique almost crushes me!*

Off in the dark, a wet coughing eased into a laboured bubbling moaning that faded into a last gasping death-rattle. The little nacht emerged from the swirling dust. It gave an almost human shrug. The Jag turned to Dorin and raised a finger. 'Excuse me one moment.' The huge creature stood, almost hunched double, his head brushing the shadowed stonework of the ceiling, and lumbered off. Dorin and the nacht watched him disappear. After a time came a gruff bemused growl: 'He's not here . . .'

A stab of anger, and envy, lanced through Dorin. *Damn the fellow! Playing with us all along! I'll have his head. No one does this to Dorin Rav.* The nacht happened to be standing just in front of him then, and in an instant he decided what he'd do. *And why not? I'm as good as dead anyway . . .*

He snatched up the beast by its neck and pressed a blade under its chin. 'Come out!' he shouted. 'I have your familiar, or pet, or whatever it is!'

The animal froze for an instant, perhaps in surprise, or disbelief.

Then it went limp. It hung in his arms as if dead already and Dorin had to hitch it up to steady it. *Damned heavy bastard.*

The Jag stepped out of the gloom. 'You have my *what*?'

'Let me out or I'll slit its throat.'

The same strange unreadable smile climbed the Jag's features and he cocked his head. '*You . . . kill . . . it*?' He laughed soundlessly. Returning to the sarcophagus, he set his elbows upon it then rested his chin on his fists. 'Very well. I will make you a deal. If you promise to take that *thing* with you, I will let you go.'

Dorin stared, utterly surprised. *What in the name of Hood . . . ?*

'We accept,' came the Dal Hon's voice from the darkness at his elbow, and Dorin flinched. The nacht came to life, wriggling and twisting, easily breaking his grip. It plucked the wooden box from his belt and launched itself upon the young mage.

The Jag studied them anew, his expression calculating. His bright amber gaze slid from Dorin to his companion, and he shook a finger at the Dal Hon. 'You – you move in ways I have not seen in a long time.' The blazing eyes shifted to Dorin. 'Is there nothing you fear? Nothing you would not dare?' And he laughed again, waving them off. 'By all means. Good riddance! At least now I shall have some peace and quiet. Though I predict that those without these walls will not!'

Dorin began edging backwards. 'The door,' he hissed to his— what . . . *accomplice*?

'Not an impediment, I expect,' the youth answered. The nacht rode his shoulders, a maniac's grin at its dagger-toothed mouth. Dorin leaned away. *Gods, what is this thing?*

The door was as before, the opening just manageable. The nacht scampered through first. It chattered and waved as if urging them on. Dorin squatted on his haunches, suspicious. Large, then small, then large once more? The Jag must have *let* them in. Must have been bored beyond reason.

The dark-skinned youth slid through. Dorin cast one last narrowed glance to the rear, as if expecting a quick attack after the lull, but saw nothing. *Very well. Back to your frigid gloom and brooding silence. Good riddance to you, I say.*

Outside it was dark – not the dimness of a coming dawn but that of gathering twilight. Much more murky as they were at the bottom of a narrow gorge. Dorin faced the youth who now stood waiting, his walking stick planted before him. He held the nacht curled up in one arm for all the world like a sleeping baby – the ugliest one in existence. 'So . . .' Dorin began, clearing his throat. 'What is your name, then?'

The Dal Hon's brows rose as if he was completely startled by the question. 'My name?' His eyes darted about the rocks. 'Ah . . . my name.' He smiled and raised a finger. 'Ah! Wu! My name is . . . Wu. Yes, Wu . . . and you?'

Dorin felt his lips tightening to a slit. *If you're going to use a fake name at least make it up beforehand!* He thought of a possible pseudonym for himself – his nickname from his youth? But *Beanpole* wasn't exactly the image he wished to project. No other name suggested itself and so he fell back on his own: 'Dorin.'

The Dal Hon – Dorin couldn't bring himself to think of the youth as *Wu* – gave a thoughtful nod. 'Good, good. Well . . . it has been amusing, but I must be going. Quite busy, you know. Much in demand.'

Now Dorin's gaze narrowed. He brought his hands up close to his baldric. 'Go? We have to decide how to split . . .' But the damned fellow was somehow fading away. Blasted mages! How he hated them! His hands flicked out and two blades darted to fly through the mage's dissolving form.

The Dal Hon's expression registered shocked surprise as he disappeared. 'Amazing! Those would have got me . . . had I been standing there in the first place . . .'

Mages! Blasted warren-rats! Dorin retrieved his knives, checked their edges. Only mages had ever escaped him. He scanned the dark cliff-sides. And yet . . . they were a long way from anywhere. Time remained. He'd find him. There was really only one place the fellow could possibly be heading for. Li Heng.

If he didn't track him down before then he'd find the Hood-damned thief there. Eventually.

*

Within the chamber, the Jaghut waved a hand and stone grated and shifted as the entrance sealed itself once again. He returned to studying the ancient pattern of the slats before him – one set out thousands of years ago. His tangled brows rose then, and he sat back, stroking his chin. 'Well, well . . . You would send two more upon your hopeless fool's errand.' He studied the darkness about him as if awaiting an answer. 'Why should these two fare any better than all those you have sent to their deaths before?' He waited again, head cocked, listening for a time; then his shoulders slumped and he hung his head. 'Oh – very well.' Grumbling, he rose and shambled off into the darkness beyond the lamp's glow.

The clank and clatter of rummaging echoed about the chamber before he returned to set an enormous battered full helm upon the stone slab, its grille facing him, and sat once more, sighing. He eyed the helm. 'So?' he demanded.

'Your problem, Gothos,' came a weak, breathless voice from within the bronze helm, 'is that you give up too easily.'

Gothos snorted his scorn. 'And what of you, Azathani?'

After a long silence the helm answered, sounding almost sad. 'Our problem is that we cannot.'

Chapter 1

Dorin Rav walked the dusty beaten earth of Quon's storied Trunk Road. It was an ancient traders' way that crossed the midsection of Quon like a narrow belt. From great Quon and Tali in the west, it stretched to the proverbial midsection clasp of Li Heng, and from there onward to the rich vineyards and orchards of wealthy Unta in the east.

Over thousands of years countless armies had trodden this route. They came marching out of both the east and the west: Bloor and Gris nobles convening to subdue the plains and the populace to the west of them; Tali and Quon kings emptying their treasuries to assemble vast infantry hordes, and eventually succeeding in subjugating the far eastern lands beneath their Iron Legions. Meanwhile, across the central plains, generation after generation of the Seti Wolf, Eagle, and Ferret clans raided all points indifferently.

He walked at a leisurely pace. He was not worried that his quarry might have struck out in any direction other than east. To the west and north lay the vast central grasslands of the Seti. To the south it was many days to any Dal Hon settlement or coastal Kanese confederacy. No, only to the east lay any nearby haven of civilization: the greatest of the independent city states, Li Heng itself.

The Trunk Road might be storied, he reflected as he walked, but these days it certainly wasn't busy. Pedestrians such as himself consisted almost entirely of local farmers. Long distance travellers tended to band together into large caravans for protection against Seti raids – and to discourage the attentions of the great man-beast, Ryllandaras.

When he'd come down out of Tali lands, he'd hired on as a guard with just such a band of traders, religious pilgrims and wanderers. Unfortunately for him, after more than a week without a sighting of the feared Seti, the caravan-mistress had let half her guards go. And so he'd found himself unemployed and cast adrift in the empty, dusty middle of nowhere.

Unlike his brother guards, he'd not been concerned for his safety. Being mostly of Tali extraction, they'd ganged together to strike back west. He'd continued on, quickly outstripping the caravan's rather disorganized, laborious pace. He did not fear any attack from the tribesmen, nor did he expect any attention from the legendary man-beast. Alone, he knew he could hide his presence. His opinion differed from his fellow travellers' regarding strength in numbers: the great clattering mass of banging copperware, shouting drivers, bawling donkeys, and rattling bric-a-brac was to his mind nothing less than an *attracter* of raiders and unwanted attention.

And so now he neared Li Heng, and somewhere nearby, ahead or behind, lay his quarry. A fellow who had dared to cheat him . . . Or, perhaps more to the point, had *succeeded* in cheating him. That was not to be borne. Not by Dorin Rav. Who had been beaten by no one.

The second day of travel revealed smoke over the prairie to the north, not so far off the trader road. He altered his path to investigate. After pushing through the tall-grass for a few leagues, he came to a wide swath of trampled and broken stalks. The first thing he found was a man's boot. When he picked it up, he found that it still held a foot.

It was a caravan, attacked and massacred in the night. By Seti tribesmen, probably. Old treaties existed – once enforced by the Tali Legions – that forbade predation on the road, but they were hardly honoured any longer. And there were always renegades and outlaws. Still, this was awfully close to Hengan lands.

Walking farther, he realized that it hadn't been the Seti at all, whether war-party or outlaws. Wagons and carts lay torn apart. Loot glittered among the trampled grass: ironware, clothes, broken chests. Corpses still wore their personal possessions. He paused and knelt at one body. A single swipe of massive claws had torn the woman across the front as deep as her spine. She had twisted as she fell, her hips no longer in line with her shoulders; her viscera lay tossed about, congealing in the dirt. The only reason the organs and intestines remained was that – for the moment – the wild dogs, jackals, and carrion crows had more than enough to eat.

Her wristlet, he noted, was of gold. This he unlatched and tucked away. Brushing his hands, he continued on. It seemed his earlier instincts regarding the curse of Li Heng, the man-eater's presence, were well founded. Ryllandaras had rampaged through this caravan like the predator of humans he was. Some named him a giant wolf, others a hyena, or a jackal. Such distinctions were meaningless as far as Dorin was concerned. Ryllandaras was a beast who ate people . . . what more need one know?

He kicked his way through the wreckage. At one point he stepped over a child's severed arm. The noise of movement brought him round and his hands went to his baldric. One of the presumed corpses, a man – soldier or caravan guard – was levering himself erect from where he had lain propped up against an overturned wagon. Dorin coolly watched him do so.

Weaving, stoop-shouldered, the fellow – dark, clothes and armour rent and bloodied – staggered towards him. He was a young man, muscular, half Dal Hon perhaps. His long wavy black hair hung like a curtain of night and Dorin felt a twinge of envy – *this one the girls must fawn over.* 'Ryllandaras?' he called to him.

The man gave a curt nod.

Something in that casual acknowledgement irked Dorin – too self-possessed by far. On a chance he asked, 'You didn't see anyone else come by, did you?'

The youth nodded again. 'Someone passed but I did not see him.'

Now Dorin frowned. 'You speak in riddles.'

'I speak the truth. I saw no one go by but someone did. He was humming.'

That's him. Humming! Fits all too well. Li Heng for certain. He gave an answering nod. 'My thanks.'

The young soldier lurched forward, suddenly animated. Something like a cross between disbelief and disgust twisted his mahogany features. 'You are not walking away, are you?'

'Yes.'

The youth opened his arms to gesture all about. 'But the dead . . . they must be seen to.'

'See to them, then. I'll not stop you.'

Another lurched step, the lad's face hardening. A hand settled on the longsword's bloodied grip. 'You'll stay and help, or greet Hood.'

Dorin's hands went to his hips where he carried his heaviest fighting blades. What was troubling everyone lately? Was it some sort of fog of animus carried by the man-beast? 'Reconsider, friend. There is no need to start a feud. The dead are dead. The crows and jackals will take care of them.'

The lad drew and Dorin flinched backwards, actually taken by surprise – *so fast!*

But the youth staggered sideways, gasping his pain, one hand across his chest where the torn mail and leathers hung in tatters.

Dorin eased his hands from his knife grips, began backing away. 'Perhaps you should just rest – or join them yourself.'

'The beast might return. He said we'd meet again.'

'He said—' Dorin froze. 'You duelled the Curse of Quon? The man-eater?'

The lad's gaze was on the horizon, shadowed, as he rubbed his chest. 'We fought all through the night.'

Dorin laughed outright, sneering. *To think he almost had me believing.* 'Learn to temper your lies, hick. No one has ever faced him and lived.'

A sullen glance from the other. 'I care not what you think. I know the truth of it . . . and that is enough for me.'

The truth of it? Smacks of religion. The lad must be an adherent. Dead on his feet now, in any case. Must have been cut down by another guard while fleeing the beast and is now trying for a cover story. Dorin continued backing away. *Well, he'll have to do better than claim that he faced Ryllandaras!*

'I will remember you!' the lad shouted after him. 'And this insult to the dead!'

Dorin had been pushing backwards through the tall-grass. His last glimpse of the guard was of him digging among the spilled cargo and raising a young girl to her feet.

He turned away with a shake of his head. Insult? Where was this fellow from? How provincial. He faced east. Two days' hike away lay Li Heng. Surely there, of all places, he would find a true assassins' guild where his skills would be appreciated.

And there also he would find this upstart Dal Hon mage and he

14

would have his revenge for this . . . for this . . . He slowed, cast a troubled glance back to the smoking fields behind. *For this insult?*

* * *

Dorin had grown up in Tali, and so was no gawking farm-boy. Yet while that west coast city was far larger than Li Heng, it was a loose and sprawling collection of distinct precincts and quarters. It, and its neighbouring city and sister state of Quon, might have pressed their names upon the entire continent – though many still refused to acknowledge the claim – but it did not possess anything like Heng's titanic famous fortifications. 'Strong as the walls of Heng' was a saying common across the land.

All through the final day of his approach up the trader road, those walls reared against the surrounding Seti Plains like a distant butte or outcrop of rock. Or like a wart, Dorin appended, reluctant to grant the city any unearned regard. To either side fields hung heavy with grain, and market garden plots lay ripening for harvest. Locals pulled carts burdened with produce, while sheep and hogs jostled Dorin on their way to be butchered.

Many of the fields boasted curious stone heaps that mystified him. After noting a few, he fell in with a girl swaying beneath a burden of large wicker baskets hung from a yoke across her bare, scraped-raw shoulders. Each brimmed over with bricks of cow manure.

'Those piles of field stones,' he asked. 'What are they?' The girl flinched, peered up with scared deer-like eyes through dirty tangled hair. Young, startlingly young, for such an onerous chore.

'The stones . . . ?' he repeated.

'Not from around here, are you,' she said, her vowels elongated in the Hengian manner.

'No.' He did not say where he was from; in fact, he was quite pleased to be hard to place, carrying a medium hue neither so dark as Dal Hon nor the olive of Tali or the Kanese confederacy, and not so burly or wavy-haired as to be Gris or Untan.

'Bolt-holes,' she said.

He cocked his head closer, wrinkled his nose at the stink. *The cow shit, one must hope.* 'Pardon?'

15

The girl glanced fearfully about the surrounding fields. 'Run there if *he* comes. Hide inside.'

Ah. *He*. The man-beast. Ryllandaras. An entire society living under siege. Thus the walls, of course. Nothing more than one big bolt-hole. That put things into their proper perspective.

'Thanks, child.' Child? Why say that? He was barely older. 'Pray tell, why the manure? What do they do with it, there, in the city?'

The girl's thick dark brows climbed in unguarded disbelief. 'Why, they burn it a'course. Don't see too many trees around, do you?'

Burn it? For fuel? To cook? Ye Gods, how disgusting . . .

He fell out of step with the girl. 'Child' may have slipped out in sympathy. He felt for her. For the dirty exhausting chore, and the probable buyer, a man he saw in his mind's eye as fat and old, leering down at her and murmuring that he'd throw in a few more coins if she'd just . . . cooperate. And she, desperate to bring in more wages to ease her parents' burdens, complying.

Should he not feel sympathy for such a plight?

But another, more cynical inner voice spun a different scenario: a calculating stone-hearted mother and father who knew full well what awaited daughter number four yet urged her on regardless, looking forward to the extra coins her winsomeness would bring. Who was to say which was the more accurate reading of the truth?

Or neither. Perhaps the child schemed for the chore, and once free of her smelly burden walked the busy city streets, marvelling, inspired, dreaming of one day remaining.

Who was to say? Not he.

Not so when a not too dissimilar young lad was sold from his village to Tali to enter into apprenticeship with a man who trained him to climb walls, squeeze into narrow openings, and spin knives. A skinny ragged child, who when chased into an alley turned his rage, ferocity, and tiny knives upon the two pursuing armoured guards and that night found his true calling . . .

But enough of that.

Hovels now crowded the trader way, as did corrals, market squares, and warehouses. All no doubt abandoned when night descended. The gates reared ahead, thick, three man-heights tall, and open only a slit, as if grudging, or fearful. He slowed to fall in next to a man on a wagon heaped with cheap blankets, brown earthenware pots, and copper wares.

As he expected, the two gate guards practically shoved him aside in their eagerness to extract their informal tithes and taxes from the unfortunate petty merchant. Past the guards, he helped himself to two pears from their baskets of confiscated goods and walked on, entering Heng unremarked and unmolested in the bright glaring heat of a late summer day.

He found himself in a crowded wide boulevard running more or less north–south, and bearing a slight curve to its broad course. Over the shop fronts and three storeys of tenements across the way reared another city wall. He realized he was within the bounded Outer Round, the outermost ring, or precinct, of the city proper. The air here was thick and still, redolent with cooking oils, but overlain by the stink of human sweat. Here he stopped for some time while making a great show of gawking right and left, as if having no idea where to go.

'Just in to the city, then?' someone said from behind.

He turned, smiling. 'Yes. I had no idea it'd be so . . . huge.'

The man was short and very wide about the middle. His black beard was oiled and braided. Gold rings shone at his ears and fingers. He answered Dorin's smile. 'Yes, I guess it is. Where're you from, then?'

'You wouldn't know it. A village near Cullis.'

'Cullis? Tali lands? Just so happens I know a lad from there.'

Dorin smiled again. 'That so? What's his name?'

The fellow glanced about. 'I'll introduce you. Listen, you must be parched after all your walking. How 'bout a drink? My treat.'

He frowned. 'I can pay for myself.'

''Course you can, lad! No offence, please. Just trying to be welcoming.' And the man pressed a wide hand to Dorin's back urging him onward, and he allowed it.

'What are your plans, then?' the fellow asked as he guided him down ever narrower and darker side alleys. 'You have a trade?'

'I thought I'd apprentice . . . weapon-smithing perhaps.'

The man pulled at his oiled beard. 'Weapon-smithing!' He whistled. 'Very difficult trade to enter, that. Start them young they do – younger than you.'

'Oh? That's . . . too bad.'

The fellow had manoeuvred him into a very narrow shadowed alley that ended in a naked wall. He turned, hands at his wide leather belt. 'Here we are, lad.'

Dorin peered about. *Quiet enough for my purposes as well . . .* 'Here?'

'Yes. Here's where you're stayin'.'

Steps behind. He turned to see four young men coming up the narrow way, all armed with short blunt sticks. *No edged weapons. Just theft, then.* He sidled up closer to the man while making a show of his confusion. 'I don't understand. There's nothing here.'

'You'll be stayin' here, lad, if you don't hand over those fancy leatherwork belts and those long-knives I seen. Where'd you come by them any—' and Dorin was suddenly behind him, one of those selfsame blades now pressed to his neck.

'Nobody move!'

The youths pulled up, surprised. The man raised his empty hands. 'Now calm down, lad. You've some moves, I see . . . maybe we can—'

Dorin pressed the blade even harder. 'Answer my questions and I'll let you live.'

'Questions? Whatever are you . . .' Dorin pressed so hard the man edged up on to his toes, hissing his alarm.

'I want names. Names of those who run the black market here. And any assassins, and where to make contact.'

'Killers for hire? So that's the way of it . . . Lad, you *are* green. The Protectress, she don't allow any killin' here in the city. An' now I'm sorry to say we're done.' The fellow waved one of his raised hands.

Dorin glanced at the four youths to ready himself for their move. But suddenly he was on the ground peering up at the clear blue sky through the narrow gap of the alleyway. The vision of one eye was a hazy bright pink. A face loomed over him – the fat fellow.

'You were watchin' the lads in the alley, weren't ya? A mistake there, my little blade. Should've been watchin' the roofs. Hengan slingers, lad. Deadly accurate. We'll have those belts and blades now. No hard feelings, hey?'

He tried to speak, to damn the fellow to Hood and beyond, but his mouth was numb and his eyes closed like heavy doors, leaving him in a black box, and he knew nothing more.

Itching and tickling woke him. That and a light rain pattering down on to his face. He blinked open his eyes; the thin slit of clouds overhead held the first promise of dawn. Something was

18

tickling his head. He pressed his hand above his ear to warm wetness, together with squirming shapes, and he yanked his hand away to see it smeared in blackening blood with a crowd of cockroaches happily feeding.

He next found himself atop a second-storey landing. How he got there he'd no idea. But the effort, and that image of his hand writhing with vermin, convulsed his stomach and he heaved over on to the alleyway. While he knelt on the small deck, gasping for breath, the insects below charged out to feed anew on the sprayed vomit.

Gods, but I'm developing a serious dislike of this city.

Still dazed, he wiped his mouth and headed off to try to find a place to hide and sleep.

Disjointed images came to him of narrow dark alleyways; hands rifling his torn shirt and he fighting someone off; running and smacking his head anew against a brick wall. Strangely, that impact cleared his thoughts the way a lightning strike at night allowed a moment of vision. He glimpsed a large wooden structure, some sort of barn, and he climbed its side, found a shadowed gable on the slope of the shingle roof, and squatted there, in the dark beneath the open sky. The barn, he noted, butted up against the tall stone wall of the Inner Round.

He did not mean to sleep; but his head kept drooping, and once he jerked awake to discover himself curled up on his side. Alarmed, he fought drunkenly for wakefulness, but failed to push away the cottony numbness of his thoughts and sank back into the dark.

The lightest of touches roused him to snatch a wrist. A yelp sounded at that; a high feminine squeak.

He opened his eyes, or rather, opened one – the other was gummed shut. He was grasping the slim forearm of a wisp of a girl who stared at him with wide, sable-black eyes. What impressed him was that the eyes held no fear. Only brief surprise.

'You are badly hurt,' she said.

'Nothing I don't deserve.'

'That's not the usual attitude among thieves.'

'I'm not a thief.'

'Ah, well. That explains everything, then.'

He released her arm; gingerly, he touched his head to find a cold damp cloth laid there. 'Thank you.'

'Manners? Also very unthief-like.'

Dorin felt his face scrunching up in annoyance. 'I told you . . .'

She waved her hand. 'Yes, yes. Here you are, wounded, hiding on our roof, yet you are not a thief. However, I believe you because you're clearly the one who's been robbed.' She gestured to indicate his full length.

Frowning, he roused himself to peer down. His jacket was gone, his shirtings were torn and blood-spattered, his trousers were likewise torn, scuffed and bloody, and his feet were bare. They'd taken his shoes? He didn't remember that happening. Now, his feet were blackened and filthy and oozing blood from innumerable cuts. At least he still possessed his laced inner vest of toughened leather lined with bone strapping.

By the beast gods, I'm a stinking wreck! One day in Li Heng and I've fallen to the lowest dregs!

All he felt was excruciating embarrassment and a rising dark fury. Embarrassment at his condition; rage against those who had thrown him into it.

'Come inside,' the girl urged. 'Soon it will be light enough for the guards on the wall to see you.' She pointed up.

He glanced up to the wall of the Inner Round, then peered about. He studied the surrounding shadowed maze of rooftops and the distant vista of the Seti Plains beyond, now brightening under a slanting pink and purple light; dawn was near.

Nodding, he eased himself up on to his feet, then winced and hissed, tottering on the blazing pain from his soles, and dizzy, his head pounding. The girl steadied him. 'This way.' She led him to the front of the gable where the shutters now swung open and guided him within. Here was a tall attic space, crowded with dusty chests and bales, with straw scattered about the wood floor. Birds fluttered their wings and flew about, disturbed by their entry.

She helped him ease down on to a heap of straw. 'Rest here. I'll bring food later.'

Dorin did not know what to say; he'd never felt so helpless. 'Thank you. You are . . . ?'

'Ullara.'

'Why are you . . . ?'

The girl blushed and looked away. Having sufficient clarity of mind to study her now, he noted the smudged dirt on her freckled cheeks, and how her sleeveless tunic was stained and much mended, as were her old faded skirts. Perhaps feeling his steady gaze, she edged away while motioning about the attic, saying, airily, 'Oh, I collect things I find on the roof.' And she swung her legs over an open trapdoor in the floor and disappeared.

Dorin frowned his puzzlement as he peered round. Perched all about on the trunks, bales, rafters, and roof-struts was a multitude of birds. All studied him with unblinking bead-like eyes. He was amazed as the dawning realization came that each one of them was a bird of prey. He recognized the common red plains falcon, the spotted hawk, owls large and small, and even two tawny eagles. Many, he noted, sported makeshift bandages on wings and legs.

He snorted into the swirls of hanging straw dust. *Greetings. Guess I'm the new wounded brother.*

*

Ullara was of course the shortened nickname of her much longer Hengan given name. She returned later that day with scraps of food and sat, her long thin legs drawn up beneath her skirts, to watch him eat. Dorin had to shake off his irritation at feeling like a rescued cat – or bird, in this case – and thus being in her care.

Finishing the crust of bread and mushed leavings of vegetables he set down the bowl and wiped his fingers in the straw. 'I should go now.'

The girl had watched him with an eerie sideways intensity, as if not really looking at him at all, her chin resting in one hand. She seemed to lack all the usual self-consciousness and attention to decorum of the Talian girls he'd known. 'You are not used to saying thanks after all,' she observed, matter-of-factly.

He forced his teeth to unclench. 'Thank you for all you have done.'

'You are welcome. You needn't go.'

'I might be found.'

'No you won't. No one else ever comes here.'

'What, then, is this place?'

'The upper garret of our business. We are stablers. Father allows me to keep my birds here – they help keep down the pests.'

He watched while one of the larger predators, a long-tailed hawk, glided away out of an open gable. 'Keep down the local dog and cat population too, I should think,' he murmured. 'Those are big birds.'

21

'That's true,' she allowed. 'It's the owls that really do most of the work.' She studied him anew, unblinking, tilting her head. Her unkempt mass of auburn hair was a matted dirty halo about her head. 'You, too, are a night-hunter.'

Dorin gave a small nod.

'You should sleep, then. I will wake you later.' He frowned at what sounded like a peremptory command. Noting his expression, she explained, 'You need to recover your strength for what is to come.'

Now he frowned even more deeply, his brows crimping. 'And what is that?'

She cocked her head, chin in her fists, eyeing him almost dreamily. 'Your hunting, of course.'

Later that day, though his head hurt abominably, he did manage to sleep, if poorly, starting awake a number of times, uncertain of his surroundings, his heart hammering.

The girl returned after dusk. She brought more table-scraps and a stoneware mug full of fresh rainwater taken from their cistern. The scraps, Dorin knew, couldn't have been intended for the birds, and so he surmised that even now hungry dogs watched a certain back door with sad, yet hopeful, gazes.

He thanked her again – which was indeed unusual behaviour for him, who so rarely had cause to thank anyone for anything – then slipped out of the open gable and climbed down to the alley below.

Standing at the open window, Ullara watched him go, then turned and hooted twice into the now darkened attic space. A gust of displaced air fluttered her tunic and layered skirts and a dark shape as tall as her hips perched next to her. Wood cracked as it sank its knife-like talons into the sill. Bending, she whispered into a great, wide, tufted ear. Large night-black eyes blinked twice, and the horned owl spread its wings, shaking them, and launched itself into the shadows.

She sat then on the still-warm shingles of the roof just outside the window. She drew her skirts tight about her knees and hugged them to her chest. She rested her pointed chin upon them and rocked herself while dreaming of straight black hair that peaked over a pale forehead and the sharp nose and thin lips of a very predatory profile. Most of all, however, she dwelt on the memory of eyes snapping open and the thrill of having found herself captured by the savage gaze of a raptor.

* * *

Rafalljara Undath'al Brunn, known on the streets of Li Heng by his nickname Rafall, should have been a happy man. The simple waylaying of that youth a week ago had netted him more than fifty gold Quon rounds. An amount worth four times its number in Hengan rounds. One of his larger hauls. All sewn into the lad's belts and baldrics. And the weapons – very fine indeed. Worth perhaps another twenty rounds.

But this troubled him.

The lad had asked after an assassins' brotherhood, or guild, such as existed in some cities; and the hoard he carried was just the sort one might net from such employment. Which meant he may have stolen from a killer.

And left him alive.

In his second-storey office, next to a window overlooking the cloth market square in the Outer Round, Rafall played with one of the foreigner's fine throwing knives, turning it round and round in his fingers. From below came the raucous calls and laughter of his own lads and lasses of the streets, eating, joking, and teasing one another.

But how was he to have known? Still, nothing to be done for it. What was done was done as the gods willed. It was simply his nature not to kill – if it could be helped. The Twins might have just played their last jest on old Rafall.

He touched the blackened knife's edge. *Fine enough to shave with . . . had I ever shaved.*

A knock on the door. 'Yes?'

Lee, one of his enforcer lads, pushed up the trap and handed him a slip of torn rag. 'An urchin lass, a dust-sweeper, was given this for you.'

He broke the crude seal of plain candle-wax that closed the folds. On the scrap, in the neat hand of a hired scribe, was the single word *Tonight*. Accompanying the message was a clumsy charcoal drawing of a knife.

So. I was right.

Rafall threw the rag aside to burn later. He studied Lee's puzzled lopsided face. 'I want everyone out tonight. All the clubbers rolling

23

drunks. All the pretty boys and lasses pulling customers. Everyone working.'

'Festival of Burn's still a long way off . . .'

'Just do as I say!'

The lad flinched, pulled at his wispy beard. 'If y' say so.' He slammed the door.

Good lads and lasses, all of 'em. Even the arm-breakers, clubbers, and enforcers. Even them. Beat anyone senseless, they would. But no knifing. No. That took another sort altogether. So the fellow wanted to talk. All right. They'd have them a chat. Got off on the wrong foot, was all. And if talk wasn't what the lad had in mind, he wouldn't have given fair warning, would he?

He spent the evening going over his accounts – a depressing enough exercise for any small businessman. His above-board 'import' business was haemorrhaging money. All the income from his street waifs, their whoring, theft, and mugging, even taken together with his fencing, barely kept him afloat. Too much uncertainty around the raids of the Seti, the terror of the man-eater, and unofficial 'taxes' and bandits in general. Overland commerce had pretty much fallen into ruin since the end of the last Talian hegemony. Why, the tithes Cawn levelled for portage were outrageous. Nothing better than thieves, those Cawnese.

What was a businessman to do?

He sighed, pushed away the books and looked up in the dim candlelight to see the dark-haired lad himself sitting opposite. His heart lurched and he dropped his quill. 'You're early,' he said in a gasp.

'Of course.' The thin youth made a show of peering about the office. 'No guards?'

'No. I took it you wanted to talk.'

'Good for you. I do want to talk – among other things. Now . . .' and he placed his slim long-fingered hands on the desk, 'I asked you a question a few days ago . . .'

Rafall swallowed hard. He edged one hand to his lap and there took hold of the grip and trigger of the crossbow he kept mounted under the desk. Talk was one thing – but a man'd be a fool not to have insurance. 'I know everyone, lad. If you're looking for work I can get the word out.' The youth's flat features turned down. So unremarkable, this one's appearance, Rafall thought. Bland, even. Unmemorable. But then that was all for the better, wasn't it? In this one's line of work only a fool would try to stand out.

'I thought you said there was no brotherhood in town. Something about your Protectress.'

'No, no organization. But killin', yes. Plenty of that. Accidents happen . . . you know how it is.'

The youth nodded. 'I understand.' He studied him, his eyes watchful, with a predatory air. 'Ask around. Bring me any offers. You know the inn down the street?'

'The Riverside? Aye.' Rafall didn't add that its owner was up to his bushy eyebrows in debt to him.

'I'll take a room there.'

'I'll make the arrangements and deliver the word.'

'Very good.' The lad leaned forward then, hands still flat on the desk between them. 'Now, about my possessions . . .'

* * *

In late summer the Favathalven family petitioned the Protectress to look into the death of their great matron, Denili Liejen Favathalven. 'Auntie', as she was known to her many customers, being a madam and one of the most important moneychangers in the city.

Ten days later a sleepy-eyed slave answered a knock at the brothel door. Opening the door a crack she curtsied, saying, 'Sorry, good sir, the house is not formally open yet. Perhaps you'd care for a— Oh!' Looking up, her breath had caught in her throat. Standing on the threshold was the most beautiful man she'd ever seen. Striking long blond hair fell loose about a lean smiling face; an exquisite white silk shirt was wrapped taut at a slim waist by a wide scarlet silk sash over black silk pantaloons. The man winked, and though the young slave had seen more than anyone her age ought to have seen, she blushed.

'I'm expected,' he said, his voice warm and gentle, and somehow so understanding of all her troubles and the unfairness of her life.

'This way,' she barely breathed, bowing him in.

The man paused in the entrance hall, peered around. The girl stared motionless, wishing he would glance to her again.

'Spivy!' a woman snapped from within. 'What're you doin' openin' the damned door? You useless— Oh!' The pinched woman who entered the hall also caught her breath, but not because of the beauty of their guest. She curtsied, then motioned to the stairs. 'This way, ah . . . good sir. I am Tapal – mistress of the estate.'

She led him to her dead aunt's offices above. Here the fellow ambled about, studying the walls, the windows. 'All windows sealed and barred,' she said, hardly able to take her eyes from him. The Protectress, she reflected enviously, didn't spare herself much, did she?

He nodded absently. Then he stopped before the broad stone fireplace. Kneeling, he held a hand over the hearth. 'Cold.'

'Not the season, is it? An' that's just a little pipe.'

'It's rectangular,' he said, peering up. He ran a hand inside then examined the black soot coating his fingers. He returned to pacing about the rooms, this time studying the scattered carpets and rugs. Eventually he stopped, turned to face her. 'A shame your mistress didn't keep a fire. She'd be alive now if she had.'

She gaped at him. *Surely not! How can that be possible?*

He bowed and headed for the stairs.

She would have followed but a stain on the rug right where he had been standing caught her eye. A black smear of soot. She stared at that offending mark until the sound of the man descending the treads pulled her back to herself. She hurried after him.

At the door Spivy curtsied, peering up at him fixedly. He smiled back down at her warmly. 'Goodbye, child.'

Tapal closed the door then immediately smacked Spivy across the side of her head. 'You keep your eyes down when greetin' guests!'

'Yes, mistress.' The girl rubbed her head, wincing, then dared to say, her voice low: 'May I ask, mistress . . . who was that?'

Tapal laughed throatily. 'You don't aim half high, do you, child? That, you ignorant minx, is Silk. A mage in service to the city.' She knelt closer, smirking as she enjoyed what she was about to impart: '*And* . . . most say . . . lover to our good Protectress herself.'

*

Silk walked the busy streets of Li Heng hardly aware of his surroundings. His mind was elsewhere, sifting the clues and hints he'd picked up from the Favathalven household, composing his report to his patron: the sorceress Shalmanat, Protectress of Li Heng.

Thus he failed to notice the many gasps from those he passed, both male and female; the many who froze in their steps, staring, some open-mouthed. He failed to hear the crash of dropped pots; the whispered invitations and admirations; the outright offers from women – and some men as well. Perhaps it was because his thoughts were so far away, but in fact he rarely noticed any of the stir he caused, as he'd grown used to it long ago.

He passed through the Inner Round and Central Round gates without challenge; the guards knew him for his rich finery, his rare blond hair, but mostly for the sudden shift in attention among any women nearby, including their fellow city guards.

Similarly, he passed unchallenged through the gates of the Palace Circle, crossed the broad cobbled marshalling grounds and was allowed through the main doors of the palace proper. These halls he ambled with his usual distracted air, his thoughts elsewhere. The vast majority of the palace functionaries he met in the hallways passed him by without any acknowledgement, other than fascinated sidelong glances, envious glares, or a curled lip, all depending upon the other's opinion of him: respected city mage, favoured lover of the Protectress, or mere fop no better than a male prostitute.

A footman directed him to the palace gardens. Here he found the usual crowd of scribes and higher bureaucrats gathered a respectful distance from a tall woman bearing a striking mane of bright white hair who wore a functional long blouse and trousers of plain undyed linen. Facing her was a squat fat fellow in glaringly bright blue and scarlet robes trimmed with rich brushed sable. Silk knew the man as Lakke Sumarkethol, High Priest of Burn the earth-goddess, official patron deity of Li Heng.

Beside these two, his thick arms crossed over an equally thick chest, his hair a greying tangled mop and his shirt and trousers in an equally tattered and unkempt state, stood the stolid figure of one of Silk's four compatriots: the city mage whom everyone called simply, Mister Ho.

'We ask that you act,' the High Mage was saying. 'It is against the law, after all. *Your* law, I might add.'

Silk met Ho's gaze and the man sent his eyes to the sky. Silk fought to keep a smile from his face as he stepped up into High Priest Lakke's sight.

The High Priest caught him from the corner of his vision and began to stammer, his voice catching, cheeks flushing. Silk merely crossed his arms, betraying no emotion. '. . . that is . . .' Lakke began again, clearing his throat. 'Protectress, the cult of Hood has long been outlawed here in Heng. We demand that you enforce the laws of the city.'

Shalmanat spoke, her gaze upon the golden flowers of a nearby shrub. 'Which is it?' Her voice was soft and musical, tinged by a strange foreign accent. As always, the sound of it ran like a warm hand down Silk's back and, as always, it was here, in *her* presence, that he understood the reactions he evoked in others.

Lakke's thick brows crimped as he paused, uncertain. 'I'm sorry? Which is what?'

The Protectress continued studying the heavy blossoms. She ran the back of a pale hand beneath one as if urging it to approach. 'First you ask, then you demand . . . I was just wondering which it was.'

The priest of Burn blushed furiously. He gulped rather like one of the fat catfish that inhabited the depths of the river Idryn. Silk and Ho shared a grin at the man's utter discomfiture. She could do that, the Protectress Shalmanat.

The man swallowed his embarrassment long enough to stammer, '. . . why . . . ask . . . of course, Protectress.'

She turned a brilliant smile upon him. 'Very good, Lakke. I thought so. Be assured. We shall look into it – as always.' She beckoned Silk and Ho forward – 'Come. Walk with me' – and started off without any farewell or dismissal of the priest.

As they walked away, Silk heard the man grind through clenched teeth: 'Protectress . . .'

He and his fellow mage took up positions just slightly behind the woman as she strolled the grounds. She walked with her long slim hands clasped behind her back. Her feet were bare, and silent upon the crushed gravel. Ho trudged flat-footed, like an ox. Silk struggled in his leather shoes to match the woman's noiseless tread.

'The blind fool,' Ho grumbled. 'He doesn't even know what's coming.'

'It's all over the market squares,' Silk observed.

'The merchants are always the first to know,' Shalmanat agreed. 'King Chulalorn the Third is moving. Kan is on its way.' She drew a hard breath, stopped walking, and stood still for a time, facing away, her hands pressed against the curve of her back. 'When?'

'Soon,' Ho answered. 'Within half a fortnight, I should think. His outriders and scouts are already on the plains.' He shot a glance heavy with significance to Silk. 'We will have much work to do.'

For his part, Silk fought an urge to take one of the woman's pale slim hands and press it to his lips – anything to ease the burden he felt settling now upon her shoulders.

'You have a report, Ho?' she asked after a time of silence.

The big fellow cleared his throat. 'There're rumours Pung has hired some kind of foreign magician.'

'Pung?'

'Runs the prostitution and black market in the Rounds. They call him Pung the child-stealer.'

The Protectress raised her gaze to study the clear blue sky for a time. 'Ah yes. Well, better than child-eater, I suppose.'

Ho cleared his throat once more, looking uncomfortable. Silk was relatively new to the Protectress's service while she and Ho went back very far indeed. Silk did not know all that lay between them and did not know whether to be envious or relieved that Shalmanat never teased him so.

'All talents are to present themselves upon entrance to Heng.'

'Yes, ma'am.'

'Well. He may be just another charlatan. Keep an eye on it none the less.'

Ho inclined his head. 'Yes, Protectress.'

Shalmanat then turned her luminous gaze upon Silk and he quickly lowered his eyes, if only to avoid the crushing embarrassment of blushing. 'And Silk? You are here to report?'

'There are indications that a new assassin is operating in the city.'

The brushing of her plain linen trousers betrayed that she had moved on and Silk raised his head. 'I see . . .' she mused as she walked. 'That is forbidden.'

He and Ho walked quickly after her. 'Yes, Protectress.'

'Stay on it, Silk. Persuade him or her to ply their trade elsewhere.'

'Yes, Protectress.'

She turned towards the entrance to the palace that led directly to her inner sanctum, the cynosure in this city of nested circles. The mages stopped as each understood the audience was at an end. Both stood for a time, watching her go. What his companion's thoughts were, Silk had no idea; the man never spoke of anything save their duties towards Shalmanat. In private he kept to his catacombs beneath the city, ever busy on this or that project or experiment – some sort of thaumaturgical research, Silk gathered.

And what did everyone think of Silk himself, with his suite of rooms in the most fashionable Central Round of Heng, among the apartments rich merchants held aside for their mistresses? Many might wonder whose lover he was. Well . . . it served as a cover, after all. And now . . . yes, well. Now . . . He shook his head.

Shalmanat climbed the marble stairs to the palace doors. Tall and slim, dressed all in white, to his eyes in the heat of the power she emanated she resembled an intense pale flame. Well could he sympathize with the Burn priest's agitation. For many in the streets of Heng were of the opinion that the city did indeed possess a new patron goddess who kept it safe from marauding bands of raiders, foreign armies, and even the man-beast Ryllandaras himself. They worshipped her at altars, street shrines, and temples: Shalmanat, patron goddess of Heng, whom some even named Queen.

When the tall double doors of the palace closed he and Ho turned away to walk the crackling gravel path back through the gardens. 'What of this Hood worship?' Silk asked. 'She gave no orders.'

'Give them a first warning.'

Silk nodded his agreement, pursed his lips in thought. 'Why doesn't she allow the Grey Walker? It is an established creed. Multitudes of other gods are welcome.'

The mage shrugged his thick knotted shoulders. 'Don't know. Never asked.' Silk felt a vague irritation at the man's myopic indifference to all except his arcane researches. 'Take Smokey and Koroll with you,' Ho added. 'Just to make our point.'

Silk nodded again; those two, and Mara, the other three of the city mages, handled the arm-twisting and day-to-day enforcement of the Protectress's will. Their presence would impress far more than his own rather . . . well, rather less than imposing appearance.

* * *

30

One night Dorin Rav returned to the gabled barn roof of Ullara's family. Nothing more than a whim, he told himself, and a plain errand of business: he owed her, after all. And he paid his debts. He found it as before, the wooden shingles creaking and ticking as they gave off the day's heat, and streaked in bird shit. And said birds roosting in rather alarming numbers along the roof crest and gables. He ducked within the vaulted attic. The bright amber eyes of more birds than he cared to count gleamed from the shadows of the beams and distant perches of boxes and crates. Distantly, from below, came the snorts and neighing of horses together with the jangle of tack. Men called to one another, their voices indistinct as they floated up from the streets: the night stalls were opening for another eve's business.

He took out a leather bag of coins – not so few as to be insulting, but not that many, as she was after all only a stabler's daughter – and hefted it. He decided, then, that he would hand it over in person together with his thanks rather than merely leaving it behind. He put it down and set to practising while he waited.

He snapped his wrists and twinned blued blades in sheaths hidden up his sleeves slipped into his palms. These he slashed about him as he spun, crouched, jumped and rolled between the heaped boxes and the narrow alleys of dusty crates. The raptors' fierce gazes followed him as he wove through the dark and they raised their wings, wary, whenever a dodge or a roll brought him near their perches.

Sweaty now, he straightened and pushed the throwing blades back into their sheaths. He grasped his leather belt, spun quickly, and a slim cord leaped from his hand to lash about a timber post. He yanked on it, testing the firmness of the hold. Then he walked up to the timber, rewinding the cord of woven black silk as he went. He fought for a time to unknot it from its grip upon the post, and when he finally freed it the many twisted ends clacked and clattered as tiny lead weights affixed there knocked among themselves.

'They use cords like that to capture birds,' said a girl's voice from the dark and Dorin flinched, startled.

He turned, raised a brow. 'You are quiet. There are few who could sneak up on me.'

Ullara approached from the shadows. She wore her same old dirty smock, her feet bare and dusty. She came quite close to stare

31

up at him and he was vaguely troubled to see how her eyes seemed to shine in the dark just like the birds that surrounded them. 'You came back,' she said.

He nodded, embarrassed for some reason. Her closeness made him conscious of his laboured breath and he struggled to suppress it.

'I was watching. You move so gracefully and effortlessly,' she said. 'Like a dancer.'

Memories of years of pain-filled training sessions enforced by blows slid across his mind and he smiled thinly, stepping aside. 'I've worked on it.' He retrieved the small leather bag. 'I have something for you.'

'Oh?'

He held it out to her. 'Payment. For your help.'

She did not reach for it. Instead, her steady gaze went from the bag to his face. For an instant he saw something there, hurt and a flare of anger it seemed to him, before she quickly turned away. She wrapped her arms round her slim chest and crossed to the open window. After a time she murmured, her voice low: 'Thank you, sir, for your consideration.'

He set the bag down on the wooden slats of a box. 'I just wanted to say thank you.'

'You have.'

He frowned into the dark. 'Don't you want it?'

'You can leave it there.'

'We're even, then?'

From the far gable, she turned her face to him, her expression unreadable in the shadows. 'Yes. Even.'

'All right, then. I guess I'll go.'

'Very well.'

He came to the gable's open window. Her face was lowered. 'Good eve,' he offered. 'My thanks.'

She looked away, blinking. 'Good eve.'

He paused, then, thinking he should go, yet something held him back. He felt that he ought to do something more, but didn't know what that should be. He cleared his throat instead, nodding, and stepped out on to the roof.

'Be careful,' she suddenly called after him and he stopped where he crouched at the roof's lip.

'Careful?'

32

'The rooftops are crowded these days,' she whispered.

'Crowded?'

'The Nightblades of Kan are here.'

He laughed – quietly – at that subject of song and stories. It was said that the fearsome Nightblades, servants of the kings of Itko Kan, flew through the dark at a word from the king, penetrated the very walls, and slew his enemies. He waved a hand. 'Those are just stories.'

Her warning gaze was fierce. 'No, it is true! Kan is coming. They are here. I have seen—' She stopped herself, glanced back within the attic and lowered her face once more. 'That is, I have – heard – in the market.'

Dorin knew he spent too little time listening to the talk in the streets below. He knew this was an unavoidable flaw deriving from his strengths – and weaknesses. By nature and preference the rooftops were his territory. And he was a solitary hunter. He shrugged, allowing, 'Well . . . I have heard nothing. But . . . my thanks.' He ducked over the lip and began lowering himself down the wall.

Knowing he would not hear, Ullara murmured, 'Have a care, my Dancer,' then retreated within. She tightened her arms about her chest as if fighting to keep some vast explosive force constrained. She fell heavily on a crate and rocked herself, her head lowered. Finally, as if no longer able to suppress a burgeoning eruption, she flung her arms outwards letting loose a great cry and at once every bird of prey leaped to the air, echoing her call with their shrill hunting shrieks, and sped off into the dark. Alone now among the churning dust she fell to the timber floor and curled herself up into a protective ball to lie panting and weeping.

*

Dorin traced the rooftops of the Outer Round. This was not as difficult as perhaps in other large cities such as Unta or Cawn, for space within Heng's walls was at a premium and every building pressed up against its neighbour – most, in point of fact, shared common walls. At one moment he ran the knife-edge of a lead-sheathed roof crest and here he paused, thinking he heard the call of a raptor. This troubled him, as most night-hunters, he believed, were silent. He studied the star-dusted night sky, the bright sickle moon, then ducked and hurried onward. He knew his path was taking him once more to his usual night-haunt: a compound a good third of the way round the walls, close to the north gate. Here, a large warehouse and yard carried out a seemingly above-board trade in timber, clay for bricks, and other such mundane building materials.

But this compound was the property of the black marketeer Pung the child-stealer. Here children captured from across the lands were held, and here they were assigned to their various fates: to work chained in mines where almost none would live to see their fifteenth year; to be cast among the poisonous chemicals of the leather-curing and dying vats where most choked out their lives even sooner – or to be broken to the sex trade where many met their ends in even worse manners.

This compound Dorin now overlooked from the flat brick roof of a three-storey tenement across the Plains Bourse, a sprawling smoky marketplace specializing in leather goods and metalworking that wound its course to abut the north gate.

He crouched behind the shallow lip of the flat roof and renewed his study of the compound's buildings and the comings and goings of Pung's guards and hirelings. Behind him, in piled rattan cages, pigeons cooed to the night. How to get in? That was the problem. Three times he'd tried an approach, and each time he'd been spotted long before getting close enough.

He edged forward to peer down into the torchlit crowded market below. The main warehouses were closed for the night, but food stalls lined the way, and inns and drinking houses were just now picking up business – most drawing trade from travellers who'd entered from the vast Seti Plains to the north. He settled in for another long watch. Eventually, one of these nights, his quarry would show himself. The bastard couldn't stay hidden in there for ever, surely.

For even he had heard the stories making the rounds of the taverns and corner idling-spots.

The news that Pung had hired the services of a new mage. Some had him a towering magus with eyes of fire; others, an aged oldster crippled and bent from the soul-twisting horrors of his wizardry; still others named him only a faint voice in the darkness whispering of things that made one's blood freeze. Some swore he could kill with a look, or a word. His Warren was variously speculated to be that of Rashan, D'riss, or Thyr; some claimed that he was a mystic shaman, or a necromancer with access to Hood's own paths.

Yet upon one feature all these differing accounts were in accord: the mage hailed from the sun-scorched savannahs far to the south, from Dal Hon.

It was his man – that slippery youth. The damned prick might disguise himself as an oldster but Dorin knew better. It was he. The one who'd laughed at him. Who'd cheated and stolen from him.

And no one got the better of Dorin Rav. Ever. It simply could not be allowed to stand.

So he eased down to his shins for yet another fruitless eve's watch, hoping to catch sight of his quarry out along the crowded bourse. The night darkened, the hours passed, his head drooped. Startled, glancing up, he noticed a tall shadow at the roof corner – a figure that had not been there before.

He watched while keeping himself absolutely still. Behind him the pigeons had all gone quiet. His hands slowly rose to cross his chest and close on the roughened grips of the slimmest throwing daggers pushed through his baldrics.

The big brass bell in the main temple to Burn began to ring out the mid-night hour. The shape stirred itself, broad wings unfolded, and it fell away to glide off in utter silence. He let out a long breath and relaxed his grip – what had that been? A mere bird? As tall as a youth?

The sight left him uncharacteristically unnerved. Was this the source of all the recent strange night sightings of unnatural daemons, spirits, and flying creatures? Some large predator, lost or imported? Perhaps Ullara knew of it; he'd have to ask . . . his thoughts shifted away, however, as a new sound reached him from the street below: the tapping of a thin sharp walking stick against stone flagging.

He jumped to his feet and ran down the length of the roof's edge, searching the shifting crowds below. Was it he? What might he be wearing now? He'd been a short fellow – but that stick! That stupid vanity of a walking stick . . .

He thought he caught the glimpse of a short dark figure far down the street before it disappeared from the flickering torch-light. He ran for the side of the building over a narrow alleyway and threw himself over the side to climb down.

In the market he walked swiftly – not too swiftly – yet resolutely towards the north gate. Weaving round wanderers and revellers, he congratulated himself once more on his personal choice not to wear clothing that would mark him outwardly as anything other than one more poor labourer in search of a night's entertainment: a hookah of d'bayang, perhaps, or the attentions of the lowest of prostitutes. Camouflage, stealth and deceit – such were the superior skills of his trade; only the failure ends up having to knife his way out of a corner. And only the fool advertises his vocation.

So he walked, deferring to the gangs of swaggering Hengan toughs who refused to yield any way, and to the entourages of baton-wielding guards clearing paths for their masters or mistresses in gaudy shaded litters carried by hulking bearers sweating despite the cool of the night. He passed a troop of down-on-their-luck Untan street performers: jugglers, musicians and child dancers. The sight of the painted boys and girls, the cheap bronze bangles ringing on their wrists and ankles, drew unhappy memories of his own training in similar circumstances – both for the punishing physical conditioning and the convenient cover. A smattering of lesser coins glinted among the cobbles before their bare shuffling and slapping feet.

Yet all the while he kept an eye to the east where the swirl of the traffic betrayed a figure making slow progress – one too short to be seen. He moved on. A courtesan stood beside the open door to her quarters, the colourful gauzy scarves of her calling wrapped about her. She beckoned him with the supple twist of a wrist, 'Delights of the Perfumed World await within, O champion.'

Dorin knew this type: too old now to maintain a coterie of steady clients, or remain a mistress. Such ones were reduced to eking out a living here on the streets.

Grinning, he motioned ahead. 'My sweetheart awaits beyond.'

The courtesan sniffed her derision. 'Sweetheart? Can mere sighs and blushes satisfy a stallion such as you?'

'The ways to pleasure are many.'

'Aye – and I know every one of them. Save your last coin, come back at dawn, and I will give you far more than a chaste kiss.'

Dorin bowed deeply. 'You shall not be forgotten, O Dispenser of Delights.'

All the nearby courtesans tittered at this epithet for a royal concubine and the woman chuckled behind her hands. 'You are a very rogue!' she called after him.

36

Dorin continued on his way, pleased with the exchange. Camouflage. Always camouflage.

He reached the broad open boulevard that was the North Way, or the Way of the Plains, close to where it led in from its namesake gate. Here he damned his luck, for the night was bright and the traffic nonexistent. He would stand out like a beacon crossing through the moonlight. Nor could he wait for some passing group to trail along behind, for with every heartbeat his quarry was disappearing ahead. Unhappy with the necessity of it, he struck out, hunched, slouching, disguising his walk into the stupefied shuffle of a d'bayang smoker.

He angled into the deepest shadows across the way, then sped along with the hope of catching a glimpse of the youth. He was in luck, as there the fellow stood, inspecting a torchlit stall front. Dorin eased back into the dark and waited. Presently, the youth walked on. He tapped and swung his walking stick jauntily as he went. Dorin followed. Coming abreast of the modest stall, he peered at the many amulets and charms. 'What are these?'

'Wards 'gainst the man-beast, good sir. Some blessed from the temples. You'd do well to carry one. Might I suggest—'

'I'm not leaving the city.'

'And what if the walls should fall?'

'Why should they fall?'

The old man shrugged his thin shoulders. 'There is talk of war – who is to say what might happen? Best to be prepared, yes?'

From the edge of his vision, Dorin watched his quarry amble on. 'There is always talk of war. Good for business, I suppose.'

The old man pursed his lips as if to say *Throw your life away, then*. Dorin moved on again. The road was narrow and contained no active night market or inns. Only isolated shops and stalls lit the mostly residential tenement fronts. He would have lost his quarry in the darkness were it not for the click of the walking stick from a flint cobblestone. He turned up a slim alleyway, and here he almost ran into the fellow, who stood motionless, his back to him, apparently studying the night sky above.

The man turned and Dorin was shocked to see the wrinkled aged features of an ancient – the disguise was masterful. The withered face screwed up even more as its owner squinted. 'So . . . a mere footpad, I see. A clubber, as I understand is slang for you

37

here.' He raised a warning finger. 'Well, have a care. For I'll have you know I work for—'

'I know who you damned well work for,' Dorin cut in savagely. 'Don't you recognize me?'

The fellow squinted his ferret-like tiny eyes. 'Did I perchance buy some shoes from you? Because if I did, I have a complaint—'

'No!' Dorin snarled. 'I did not – that is—' He wiped his hot slick forehead and saw that he'd already drawn his best dagger. 'All these wasted nights,' he murmured aloud in wonder. 'And he doesn't even . . .' He shook his head at his own foolishness.

'Is this a robbery or have you stopped me just to babble on?' The fellow set his hands atop the walking stick and rolled his eyes to the sky. 'Oh, please do not tell me this is about some god you saw in a stain on the tabletop. I really am quite busy.'

Dorin stepped away as if to go. As he did so he threw the dagger, which struck the fellow high in the chest and lodged there. 'You're no longer busy,' he said, and he watched the youth's eyes widen in shock.

The fellow slumped back against the wall. He frowned at Dorin, coughed and murmured, hurt: 'That was . . . unnecessarily . . . brusque . . .' Then he slid down the brick wall to settle propped up, as if asleep.

Dorin knelt on his haunches before him. 'This is to teach you that no one steals from me. Or thinks he's gotten the better of me – yes?' He studied the disguised face. A weak breath, wet with blood, eased from the lips. Dorin passed a hand before the beady eyes, which did not track. He sat back. 'Well, then, let's see what you've got on you.' He reached in under the cloak.

A sudden screech of rage and a sharp jab of pain jerked him to the opposite wall where he stood squeezing his hand, his heart hammering at the surprise. A monkey now occupied the fellow's lap. It glared its rage at him, waving him off; bared its curved yellow fangs.

Dorin shook his hand. Damned thing bit him! What kind of lunatic travels with a monkey under his cloak? But it wasn't a monkey, it was that creature from the tomb – the nacht. A kind of miniature ape from the wretched island of Malaz. He stalked out of the alley while sucking the gouges at the meat of his palm. Blasted creature could've taken his thumb! Then what would he do? At the alley mouth he paused, wiped a sleeve across his face.

Damned heat. It was too hot here on the plains, even though it was autumn.

He tied a handkerchief round his thumb, knotted it off. Then he turned to stare back up the deep shadows of the alley. His teeth slowly clenched hard enough to creak, and he hissed out a long breath of suspicion. With his off-hand he drew another blade and edged up the alley, crouched, sliding his feet forward silently on their soft leather soles.

He found the narrow way empty but for garbage, pots, and bits of furniture.

Later that night the city Watch received a call to subdue a madman who was howling and bellowing and smashing property in a lane off the Way of the Glaziers. When they arrived they found only garbage kicked and strewn all about, every resident's pots thrown against the walls, and furniture broken and trampled. They left, but not before demanding a fee, which the locals reluctantly handed over, lest the Watch arrive even later the next time.

Chapter 2

IN THE HONEY LIGHT OF EARLY DAWN THE PRIESTS AND ACOLYTES of Heng's uncounted temples walked barefoot through the lanes and broad ways of the city. Most carried copper begging bowls, the poorest holy men and women among them holding out mere upturned wicker hats. Shop-owners waited at their thresholds with small leaf-wrapped pouches of food that they deposited in the proffered begging bowls. Silk watched this timeless ritual while he waited for two of his fellow city mages, Smokey and Koroll, here on the main temple thoroughfare, the Street of the Gods. It was a curve of the Inner Round, hard against the wall on the outer side, given over to the many and varied gods, daemons, spirits, haunts, and otherworldly guardians of Quon lands.

At this early hour their devotees crowded the road. They brought offerings to the many temples, altars and shrines: leaf-wrapped pinches of rice or steamed vegetables; garlands woven of flowers, candles, incense of scented wood, tiny cups of cheap liquor; and prayer-scarves to be draped over shrines or tied to corner altar-pieces.

Towering over all, parting the mass like a man-o'-war, came the shambling figure of the inhuman Koroll. Half Thelomen or Toblakai, some said. A great forest of tangled unwashed hair fell about his shoulders. The slanting light cast strange shadows upon his face, seemingly all broken and rearranged in odd planes and angles; over these alien features swirled tattooed symbols and glyphs. Layers of cloth hung draped about him like tenting. And from this bulk extended a stone-like muscled arm and a hand gripping a staff fully as tall as he.

The half-human mage came to stand alongside Silk, planted the staff with a thump, and gripped its haft in both hands. Together they regarded the modest stained and aged stone building before them.

'Greetings, Koroll.'

'Good morn,' the giant rumbled.

Silk smelled smoke and turned, crooking a smile.

From up the other way came a young man in a long loose shirt of fine-brushed cotton over white linen trousers. His long dark hair was pulled back and braided in a neat ponytail, his goatee black and freshly trimmed. Silk gave him a nod. 'Smokey.'

'Silk.' The mage turned to the house. 'So, what have we here?'

'It was the custom,' Koroll began in his rough voice, 'generations ago, for noble families to bury their dead together in mausoleums. One such do we face now. The family name is forgotten, but the cult has chosen wisely, regardless.'

Smokey visibly shivered his revulsion. 'Hood,' he spat. 'Gives me the willies.'

Stone steps led up to twin open doors, possibly of siltstone, but carved to resemble panelled wood. Cluttering the steps lay a collection of offerings: drying foodstuffs, pot shards engraved with prayers, wilted garlands, and carved wooden dolls representing enemies marked for Hood's special attention.

Silk raised a hand, gesturing forward. 'Koroll – the honours, if you would . . .'

The giant strode up and thumped the butt of his staff to the threshold. 'Greetings!' he announced. 'In the name of the Protectress Shalmanat.'

They waited. The dark unlit hall paved in black marble remained empty. Smokey shot Silk a glance and rolled his eyes. 'Bloody cheap theatrics. You first, Silk.'

Silk's answering smile was tight and humourless. He entered, noting that the walls to each side bore alcoves, eight rows of them, floor to ceiling, down the entire length. Each held a dusty skull. Honoured ancestors. Silk tipped his own head to them, and advanced.

A short distance within, he paused as he came to three sprawled corpses – these far more fresh than the watching skulls. Smokey came to his side and crouched at the nearest. 'Enforcers,' he judged. 'Pung's, probably. Sometime last night.'

41

Silk raised his chin and called, 'Shalmanat's law. Murder is punishable by exile.'

A figure emerged from the shadowed gloom further in. A young man simply dressed in trousers and a loose shirt. He held a gleaming two-handed blade readied before him. 'They offended Hood,' he stated flatly.

'And how did they do that?' Silk enquired.

'They demanded a tithe upon the temple. I demonstrated Hood's tithe.'

'And who are you to judge?' Smokey demanded.

The lad's dark, almost blue-black eyes edged aside to Smokey. 'I am Hood's Sword.'

Smokey snorted a laugh. Silk, however, sensed something wrong; the youth had said the words not like a challenge or a claim, but as an obvious, uncontestable truth. As if he'd just observed that the sun rose or the land moved with Burn's exhalations.

'Well, *Hood's Sword*,' Smokey was saying, 'you'll have to face Shalmanat's justice. So come with us.'

The lad did not vary his ready stance. 'The only true justice is Hood's to give.'

Smokey held out a hand, fingers spread. 'Don't make me burn you, kid.'

'My life is Hood's to take or leave.'

Movement among a heap of blankets up against a wall drew Silk's eye and he distinguished a young girl asleep among the rags. Like the lad, she was mahogany dark – Dal Honese the pair of them. He placed a hand on Smokey's forearm. 'Wait . . .'

A faint blue flame – more like a weak aura – flickered and stuttered about Smokey's fingertips and the mage of Telas stared, his brows knitting. 'My Warren . . .'

A dry laugh echoed round the hall and Silk flinched. Koroll rumbled from the doors, 'We are not alone.'

'Indeed, friend giant,' came an old man's rasp. 'Though you carry the blood of the Thel Akai, it would be best not to press this matter.'

Silk squinted into the dark and could just make out the shape of a scrawny ancient, hunched cross-legged before a shrine at the far end of the hall – a shrine to the dead. He eased down Smokey's arm, murmured, 'Not now.'

The fire mage pointed to the lad. 'Later, friend,' Silk urged him back.

They stopped outside. The thinning traffic of adherents and worshippers gave the threesome a wide berth. Silk hugged himself, feeling oddly chilled from that house of the dead.

'What now?' Smokey demanded.

'These are no frauds peddling fear,' Koroll supplied. 'Hood is with them, whatever their other claims.'

Silk nodded his agreement as he stroked his chin, thinking. 'Pung can't let this insult stand. Let's leave them to him. See how he fares.'

The idea obviously appealed to Smokey who smiled, chuckling. 'That's a good one, Silk. Smooth.'

Koroll stamped his staff to the beaten dirt of the street. 'The mistress must be informed that the Dark Taker has indeed entered Li Heng.'

'I will inform her,' Silk answered.

Koroll nodded his great shaggy head ponderously. 'Very well. We are done here. I go to summon Ho from his labours within the catacombs.'

Silk inclined his head in farewell. The giant mage shambled off. Silk watched him go, trying to recall the words by which the old priest within had addressed him, but the foreign name escaped him. He turned to Smokey. 'And you? Care to join me?'

The fire mage brushed a hand along his oiled hair then pulled his long braid forward and examined the fine silver wire binding its end. 'Naw. I'm late for a manicure and massage with a big busty Purge gal.' He bowed, waved Silk off. 'I leave you to it.'

Silk answered the bow. 'Until later.' He turned and headed for the palace. Women, young and old, stopped to stare as he brushed by. Yet his thoughts were inward as he walked, and so he passed them by where they stood frozen in acts of laying garlands, or praying, or pouring milk over altars. He was off to see the Protectress of Li Heng. And thus, in his way, to offer up worship of his own.

* * *

North of Li Heng, a woman stood next to a smouldering campfire within a sheltered grove of poplars and alders. Her gaze was steady to the south. A frown of displeasure pulled her wide lips. She had been waiting within the grove for a full moon, and still each night she remained alone.

Turning, she kicked at the dying embers. Moments later the swelling beat of horse hooves announced the approach of a troop of cavalry. She waited, arms crossed; this was not the company she wished for.

The ten horsemen wore bright conical steel helmets and coats of mail beneath flowing robes dyed the green of the Itko Kan Southern League. Their leader dismounted, drew off his helmet, tucked it under his arm, and approached the woman, who had not stirred.

She examined the officer's youthful face – only recently bearing a wispy moustache – and saw no resentment or hostility in his gaze. Indeed, all she noted was a frank professionalism that was the hallmark of the academies of Itko Kan, and one explanation behind that city's domination of all its many neighbours to the south.

For his part, the officer took in her long wind-tossed black hair, the loose black silk pantaloons and shirt, her slim, strangely angled eyes and coarse wide cheekbones, and bowed deeply. 'M'lady. You are unescorted.'

'And what are the Kan Elites doing upon Hengan lands?'

The young man offered a modest shrug. 'The Seti have renegotiated their treaties with Kan.'

'Been bribed, you mean.'

Again, the modest shrug.

'And now the Kan cavalry commands the central plains round Heng.'

The officer bowed once more. 'Effectively.'

'Chulalorn the Third is a fool. He mustn't attempt to take Heng. Many lives will be lost – and all for nothing.'

'The king judges his strength sufficient.'

'Not even the Talian Iron Throne challenged the Protectress. Heng remained a centre of free trade during the hegemony.'

The officer nodded his agreement, but countered, 'The historian Gudaran suggested it served the throne to allow it to do so . . .'

'Gudaran was a creature of the court. A sycophant who kissed the Talian kings' arses.'

The officer coughed into a fist, reddening. 'Well . . . m'lady is far more of a scholar than I, I am certain. In any case, you will please accompany us.'

The woman hated coarse demonstrations, but understood their effectiveness, and so she indicated his helmet. 'That is a handsome piece – may I see it?'

The young man frowned his puzzlement, yet manners dictated that he must hand over the helmet. She examined it, turning it in her fingers. A turban of green silk encircled it and the sun gleamed from its polished iron surface.

She grasped its domed top in one hand, and, squeezing, crushed it like a fruit.

All colour drained from the officer's face. He weaved as if close to fainting. She extended the mangled piece. Mechanically, he took it from her.

'I choose to remain here for a time,' she said. 'You will tell your commanders not to harass me.'

The officer nodded, swallowing, then bowed jerkily and withdrew.

She dismissed the retreating officer and returned her gaze to the south. Behind her, the horses stamped the ground once more, and then galloped off. After a time she sighed and turned her attention to the remains of the campfire. She set her hands to her hips and glared about. 'I have observed all the rituals!' she called. 'I have sat at the fire all through the night!' She kicked dirt over the ashes. 'Why won't you come to me? What is it?' She glared about once more. 'Something's going on. I sense it! *Come to me, damn you!*'

* * *

Iko tried not to display her disapproval of all she saw revealed in the streets of Heng, but it was hard. *This* was the storied meeting place of all the lands? The last of the independent city states?

It was a pesthole.

She fought to stop herself from covering her nose against the stink of close unwashed bodies, the stale cooking oil, and the vile reek of excrement. Had they not heard of latrines in this benighted backwater? Kan carried its waste away in sanitary pipes of running water. Had they no such services here?

From her side, Yuna shot a dark glare and Iko returned her wandering gaze to the armoured back before her as they marched the streets in rank: twenty of King Chulalorn's legendary corps of Sword-Dancer bodyguards. All female. All virgin – though this particular detail Iko knew for a complete myth. All sworn to give their lives for his – and this Iko knew for a complete truth.

The fine mail coat of her sister ahead shimmered and glinted in the sunlight as they filed through Heng's jammed streets. The extraordinary slim length of their corps' unique weapon hung down the girl's armoured back, encased in its oiled wooden sheath, ready to be drawn free from over the shoulder. A blade whose secrets of manufacture were known to only a few mage-enchanters of Kan, and left the razor steel as pliable as its name: whipsword.

Reflexively, Iko reached up the worn grip of her own blade where it jutted up over her shoulder. A grip familiar from a near decade of intensive – some said brutal and inhuman – training that began when she was taken aged four.

A long drawn out snarled breath from Yuna brought Iko's attention to the opposite shop fronts where a crowd of local toughs were shouting out what they would do if they had their own set of female guardians – and demonstrating with thrusting fists and pelvises. Iko rolled her eyes. Certainly some of her fellows succumbed to desire for their patron, but most saw it as compromising their hard-won abilities. And the shameful dismissal of those weeping moon-eyed few was lesson enough.

Of course she knew the true reason behind her and Yuna's poor humour.

They were not at *his* side. *He* had sent them away on this political mission to the Protectress. A mission none of them wanted. Yet here they were, escorting some damned jumped-up Askan diplomat sent to deliver *his* terms to the oh so famous Protectress of Li Heng.

Iko wondered if perhaps this Hengan witch would prove as underwhelming as the city itself.

When they entered the gates to the palace grounds they acquired their own escort of Hengan soldiery. She and Yuna shared a knowing smirk at the puffed-up armoured fools; their banded cuirasses were antiquated, their shortswords effectively useless. Even their shields were rusty.

Not experienced campaigners, these Hengans. Good only for hiding behind walls. Not like the Kanese forces. When his father took an arrow in the throat at the siege of Nex, Chulalorn the Third came to the throne as a mere lad of fifteen. Since then, over nearly two decades of constant warfare, he'd completed his father's work of subjugating the wreckage left behind in the south by the collapse of the Talian hegemony. And so was an ancient political entity reasserted upon the face of the continent – Itko Kan.

The tall doors to the palace itself swung open before them – if one could name such a plain heap of stone a palace. Given the polished marble splendour of Chulalorn's own dynastic seat in Kan, Iko considered it an insult to the term.

They advanced up a reception hall, parting a crowd of gathered city aristocracy and richer merchants, all present to welcome the emissary. Iko remained stony-faced, glaring straight ahead. At the far end of the hall waited their real objective. She sat upon a chair so blindingly white as to be glowing. Tall she was, and slim. Inhumanly so, whispered many. Itko felt her superior certainty slipping away. There she was. In the flesh. All agreed her the mightiest sorceress of the lands, the Protectress of Li Heng.

Even from this distance the woman's calm gaze seemed to whisper *What need have I of armies?*

And arranged before her, the crowd a respectful distance from them, four city mages – each powerful enough to guide a kingdom yet gathered here in her service, as if to prove she feared no rival. Mountain-tall Koroll of Thelomen kind; wild-haired Mara whose magery could crush stone to dust; Hothalar in his bare dirty feet, who many claimed wielded the strength of a war elephant; and finely dressed Smokey, the mage of Telas, who burned the entire war fleet of Kartool as it approached Unta. And was paid handsomely for the service.

No indeed. What need had Li Heng of costly and hungry armies?

Like all of Chulalorn's bodyguards, Iko had been briefed on Heng's city mages, and so she wondered where the fifth was. The one who . . . and then she caught sight of him. Just now wandering in from a side door. Late on purpose perhaps? A half-smile played about his lips, as if to mock the pomposity of the occasion. He brushed a strand of stray blond hair from his face and Iko's own hand twitched as if wanting to be the one to caress that lock. Somehow she knew that he wished to be here no more than she; that, in fact, just like her, he would rather be outside these miserable confining walls walking the open fields. And, amazingly, his gaze found hers among so many, and the eyes held a strange sadness, a mystery that only she could solve if she just . . .

47

Iko bit her lip and tore her gaze away. Her heart was pounding, her face glowing hot. Gods! Such power! It was he. The fifth city mage. The one many considered the most truly dangerous of them all. Silk.

Blinking and struggling to steady her breathing, she focused upon the emissary. The man was babbling on about ancient pacts and alliances between Itko Kan and Heng and how that old order had served them both so well. The Protectress sat radiating a neutral reserve and patience.

Iko thought the audience a hollow pretence. If this woman did not bend to the Talian Iron Legions, she certainly would not yield to them. Yet the dance of diplomacy had to be allowed to run its course. Now she would thank King Chulalorn for his generous invitation to become his most favoured trading partner and ask for time to consider the documents.

All this Iko took in with half an ear while she studied the hall's entrances, its natural blind spots, the most defensible positions. Yet she could not keep her gaze from returning to the mages arrayed before the Protectress – skittishly avoiding Silk – for she understood that here was the real strength of Heng. A concentration of might few could match. What had Kan? Its Troika? Three mages? Not enough. Still . . . these could not be everywhere. It took soldiers to defend walls, to hold positions.

'Might we,' the Askan emissary began, unctuously, 'offer the court some slight entertainment?'

Iko groaned inwardly. A demonstration. How she hated their being trotted out like trained monkeys or dancing bears. She thought it frankly undignified.

The Protectress nodded her approval and the emissary sent a glance to Iko's commander, Hallens. 'A cleared ring at the centre of the court, if you would please,' the captain announced.

The assembled city nobles and notables yielded to the request, shifting backwards amid murmurs of anticipation. The contingent of Sword-Dancers lined the border of the ring. To Iko's relief Hallens did not pick her this time. Instead, the woman selected two of the 'heavies', the largest and most impressive-looking of them, Yuna and Torral. These two started forward, bowed to one another, and unslung their long whipswords, evoking a ringing, high-pitched note from the man-tall wavering razor-sharp blades.

They began their dance. Each spun like a top, gathering speed.

The blades began to flex, arcing round the women like whips indeed. Even as they spun, the dancers curled round each other, seeking openings. Now and then, utterly without hint or warning, their blades lashed out, snapping and whistling, but of course neither was touched as she leaped and ducked in this precisely choreographed set of attacks, counter-attacks, feints, and remises. The only sound now, other than the brush of the footwork across the polished stone floor, was the rising, ringing hiss of the keen blades themselves as they seemed to cut the very air.

Iko had seen it all before of course, and was trained in this particular set. Instead she watched the faces of the onlookers. Their fascination and fixed attention satisfied her, for such a show was rare; one had to be a guest of the palace in Kan to even hope to witness it.

The display ended very abruptly as in complete unison the two women suddenly knelt facing each other, one hand on the floor, bowing. The audience was startled for an instant, but then applause began as Hallens circled the ring handing out long scarves of silk. She nodded to Yuna who stood and began to turn, slowly, the long blade extended, one-handed, at shoulder height.

Hallens gestured in invitation to all. 'Please, throw them in, if you will.'

Chuckling, a noble threw his and as the cloth floated downward Yuna's blade snapped out, whipping, slicing the scarf in two. Everyone applauded, marvelling at the demonstration. More cloths came floating out and Yuna's blade snapped in all directions, each time unerringly finding its mark to multiply the falling scraps into multicoloured snow.

'All at once!' Hallens invited.

Every remaining scarf came billowing in from all sides and Yuna spun in a blur, the blade hissing in circling arcs that parted every drifting scrap no matter how tiny, and Iko knew that one could spend the afternoon sorting through the litter and not find one cloth untouched.

The hissing halted as abruptly as before as Yuna bent at the waist in a deep bow to the Protectress and held it, head lowered, the fingertips of her left hand touching the floor. In the silence following, the Protectress raised her hands and offered her gentle applause. The assembled nobles joined in, offering polite cheers as well. Yuna straightened, inclined her head in acknowledgement of

49

the applause, and backed away to re-join the circle. Hallens signed for the Sword-Dancers to re-form their ranks.

The Protectress applauded, Iko noted, but not her city mages. Not one of them clapped, or even altered their expressions throughout. Iko even thought she detected on Silk's face a sort of bored resignation of the kind one might feel when forced to endure a child's clumsy recital. The assumed superiority grated upon her. Were they truly so invulnerable?

The Askan emissary's bowing and fawning informed her that the audience was at an end. She and the other nineteen Sword-Dancers came to attention, offered a brief respectful bow, and began backing away. When they reached a proper distance they halted, parted to allow the emissary to pass between them, then turned and exited.

At the last possible moment Iko shot a glance to Silk with his charmingly rumpled finery and boyish mussed hair and she saw that his gaze now rested upon the Protectress herself. She glimpsed in his expression the wistfulness that had touched her before, and she thought she now understood something more of it.

*

Silk returned to watching the glittering Sword-Dancers exit and sighed in half-longing. So pure. So vibrant.

So . . . earnest.

He shook his head. Too shallow, those pools, to captivate beyond a brief dalliance. Although a few gazes had held a real fire betraying surprising depths . . .

And Chulalorn the Third's offer? Nothing Heng did not already possess.

Shalmanat inclined her head to the spectators who bowed deeply in response, familiar enough with her ways to know that the audience was at an end. They began filing out, talking loudly of the famous Kanese swordswomen, some hinting roguishly at the heavy duties involved in keeping such an extended harem of young women satisfied. Silk shot a glance to Shalmanat, but the Protectress's features remained as composed as ever. She was, of course, above all such profane matters. Otherworldly, many named her. A queen. Even a goddess.

Silk, however, did not want a goddess.

Once the court had emptied, and the guards pulled closed the outer doors behind them, the other four mages bowed to Shalmanat and walked to separate exits. Silk alone remained before the throne of brilliant white stone.

Shalmanat descended the steps of the dais. He noted that her feet were bare and that as usual she wore no jewellery with her plain linen trousers and long loose shirt. As she passed it struck him once again that she possessed a good hand's breadth in height beyond his own – and he was considered tall.

He bowed deeply from the waist, not coincidentally keeping his gaze hidden.

She paused, turning on the balls of her feet, and he smiled inwardly; she was trained in the ways of fighting. 'Yes, Silk?'

'News, m'lady.'

'Yes?'

He straightened, keeping his gaze on her feet where her toes peeped out from beneath the hem of her trousers. Unbidden, the thought assaulted him: judging from the effect of those bare toes, would he faint at the glimpse of a whole ankle? Swallowing to clear his throat, he coughed into a fist. 'We met the priest of Hood and his acolyte earlier.'

'Yes?'

'Koroll and Smokey and I agree that he is legitimate.' Silk dared raise his gaze to the shirt over her torso beneath the outward brush of her modest chest. 'The cult of Hood, it seems, has returned to Heng in truth.'

And then the impossible happened as the Protectress staggered. She tilted to the side, her feet tangling, and she would have fallen had not he, darting forward, caught her in his arms – *his arms!* – to gently lower her to the steps of the dais. His amazement at her reaction did not stop him from quickly yanking his guiding arm away, for the Protectress's body burned with a vicious heat. The inner flesh of his biceps and forearm stung as if he'd brushed a kiln and he gasped, half in surprise and half in pain.

'M'lady!'

Recovering, the Protectress waved off the episode. 'It is nothing. My thanks. I was merely . . . taken unawares.'

He found it unseemly to be standing over her and so he dared sit at her feet, on the cool polished stone flags of the floor. 'By what, may I ask?'

The woman looked away, blinking. Her fine long white hair fell over one shoulder like a cascade of frost. 'I had hoped the man was just another travelling impostor or swindler, trading on the natural fears of the populace.' She sent him a quick glance and this close he thought her pupils dusted in flecks of shimmering gold. 'But you say he is not.'

He forced a breath deep within his vice-tightening chest. 'Yes. Koroll judged that Hood was with them – and I concur.'

She sighed. 'Koroll would not be mistaken on such a matter.'

'You fear him, then? Hood? Is that why—'

Her raised hand silenced him. 'Not Hood . . . as such. No.' She let out a long low breath. 'Long ago I was young and foolish, as all youth is. I was desperate to know my fate and I sought out the greatest reader of futures of the time – the power that some say created the means of reading in the first place. The Tiste Andii had given her a name, then. They called her T'riss. You know her by another name now. The Enchantress – the Queen of Dreams.'

A shiver of wonder took hold of Silk's spine. This woman had spoken with a goddess! The mistress – some say ruler – of a Warren. To others, the patroness of sorcery itself. He steeled himself to dare ask, 'And . . . what did she say?'

A thin smile haunted the Protectress's lips as she gazed off across the hall. 'At first she refused. Said it would be too great a burden. But I was insistent.' She nodded to herself in wry memory. 'And so did I learn how my death would come to me . . . it would come carrying the very face of death itself.'

Silk surged to his feet. 'We will fall upon the temple tonight. All five of us. It will be nothing but a smoking pit by morning.'

The Protectress snapped up a hand. 'No! I forbid it. There is nothing to be done. There is no stratagem, or trick, or flight to be made. One cannot outrun one's fate. It is inevitable. You will not interfere.' She turned her golden eyes directly upon him and he lowered his gaze. 'Do I have your word?'

He unclenched his jaws. 'You do.'

'Very good.' A small gesture from one slim pale hand. 'We are done.'

He bowed and backed away, head lowered. Nearing the doors, he dared one swift glance. She remained upon the steps of the dais, now hugging herself, her hair a curtain of snow across her face. Silk turned to the doors and yanked one open. Very well. *He* might be forbidden to act . . . but there were others in this city. Others who might be persuaded by a bag of coin, or a bit of arm-twisting.

There was even that assassin he had heard of . . .

* * *

Dorin walked the northwest arm of the Outer Round. It was dominated by a bourse specializing in animal trading, with associated markets in fodder, tack and hides, corrals, abattoirs, and shops. He was ambling slowly, to all appearances merely one more labourer kicking about looking for work, but in actual fact he was tracing the building rooflines and windows, scouting routes for night-time hunting – or lines of retreat.

The way was quite crowded, the traffic of townsfolk and herded goats and sheep slowing him considerably. Squinting ahead through the dust, he glimpsed the multitude lining the parapets of the outer wall, together with further crowds jamming the stone stairways leading up. Many were pointing out over the wall. Dorin wondered if perhaps fighting had broken out between some lost Hengan foraging party and the Kanese forces spreading about the city. Then all standing upon the defences threw their hands in the air and gave vent to a great roar of delight such as one might hear from the spectators at any games or horserace. This did not sound like any sort of battle – especially one featuring Hengan infantry being run down by the glittering Kanese cavalry.

A lad came threading his way along the road towards him, flushed, his eyes bright, and Dorin grasped his shirt as he passed, yanking him to a halt. 'What is it? What's going on?'

'Bouts!' the lad enthused. 'Horsemen duelling!'

'Who? Who is duelling?'

The lad struggled to free himself. 'Don't know. The reds and the greens!'

Dorin released him and he scampered off. Reds and greens? Green would be the Kanese, of course. But reds? Who in all the Quon lands could that be? He headed for the stairs.

The walls of Heng were of course a byword for strength. The parapet of the outermost round stood broad enough to support a crowd some twenty people thick. Now the crenels were jammed with men and women, while braver souls perched on the tall merlons of the projecting machicolations. Dorin slid easily through

53

to the front and pulled himself up atop a merlon to stand with two boys and a girl – all making great show of their daredevil contempt for heights and their precarious exposure to the buffeting winds.

On the fields of the gently rolling plain two lines of cavalry had formed on opposing hilltops. One of them shone and glimmered as the slanting amber beams of the late afternoon light reflected from polished Kanese mail coats and helmets. Forest-green pennants and flags rippled and danced over tents where Dorin supposed the officers and commanders of this particular regiment were encamped.

The opposing hilltop was nowhere near as colourful or bright. The force occupying it wore surcoats of red, but it was a carmine so dark as to be almost black. Two large field tents of plain canvas dominated this hill. Raised before one stood a pole supporting an odd downward-hanging pennant that tapered to a narrow whipping tail. It was of similar red and featured a sinuous snake-like emblem of silver or white. The other tent boasted a more conventional flag that bore a yellowish design on blue. This sigil Dorin knew: the gold flame of Gris.

What was a member of the royal family of Gris doing here?

While Dorin watched – together with thousands of Hengan citizens – a single Kanese horseman rode out to the empty, well-trodden field between the troops, reared up in his saddle, and began to harangue the opposing force. Dorin was much too far away to hear the words, but he had no need. He recognized a challenge when he saw one.

So too did the reds, evidently, as after a brief rustling among the far fewer cavalry there a single horseman came cantering out to meet the challenger.

Dorin had been raised in Tali lands, and red livery brought one particular possibility to his mind, but he couldn't really believe it possible. 'That's not the Crimson Guard, is it?' he asked.

Without turning her shaded gaze from the field, the girl spoke. 'Who else in the name of Sleeping Burn might they be? Gods! Where do these hicks come from?'

'Under rocks,' the younger boy opined.

'Mummy's skirts,' offered the other.

Dorin found his forbearance under severe strain. But pushing the three to their deaths just wasn't an option in front of hundreds of witnesses.

The Crimson Guard – the legendary mercenary company that had opposed the Talian hegemony on almost all fronts. How his fellow citizens in Quon and Tali cursed them! Even after all these years. And they didn't even have a kingdom. The D'Avore family held a few tiny isolated fortresses in the mountains of the northern Fenn range – where, it was said, they honed their unmatched skills in constant battle against the monsters, giants, and even dragons of those wild mountains.

So surprised was he to actually see the company that he murmured aloud, 'What are they doing here?'

The girl turned on him, glaring. She was pale-skinned, and boasted a mane of glorious red hair. 'Gods, you're dense! How should I know?'

The younger lad shouted, 'They've come to fight with us against the Kanese!'

The girl now lowered her ferocious scowl upon the boy. 'Ass! They'd hardly be duelling in that case, would they?'

'And they're too few,' Dorin added.

The girl's gaze flicked to him. Her scorn softened to mere lofty disapproval. ''S true.' She raised her chin to the distant hilltop. 'They're probably escort for that fancy nobleman.'

'Makes sense,' Dorin mused. 'That's a member of the Grisian ruling family.' He studied the blue and yellow flag more closely and thought he distinguished a thin dark circlet over the flames. More of his heraldry came to him then and he added, 'If that's a crown over the flames, then that's the designated heir.'

The three, he noted, now regarded him quizzically and he cursed inwardly. *Never reveal more knowledge than you ought to have, fool!*

Out upon the field the two horsemen were speaking. Exchanging pedigrees, Dorin imagined, or some such pompous shit. Then, an accord reached, the two turned their mounts a short distance apart, readying weapons. The Kanese cavalryman drew a slim curved blade and raised a broad shield. The Guardsman, a mace. A susurration of anticipation rippled up and down the crowd.

'Is that Oberl?' Dorin heard someone ask. Oberl of Purge was one of the most famous champions of the Guard.

'No,' another answered, 'Oberl carries two swords.'

'Must be Petra!' came a shout. 'At the siege of Athrans she swore a vow never to kill.'

Dorin choked back a laugh. Never to kill? No, she just breaks every bone in your body. This was all just so much idiotic extravagance! It seemed to him that if you were actually going to fight, you hit hard and fast. Get it done. Like a cutter lopping off a limb.

The duellists heeled their mounts and charged. They met and passed in a quick single exchange. The mace struck a solid blow to the shield while the slim sword flashed over a ducking back. Having dropped their reins, the two urged their mounts round with their knees.

Dorin heard murmurs of awe from the crowd at such a display, but he could not keep a sour scowl from his brow. Privilege and money was all he saw on show. The privilege of being born among the class that possessed the resources and tradition for such training – and the money to sustain it.

In a flurry of kicked-up mud and torn grasses the two charged once more. A thousand breaths were drawn and held at that instant. The mace slammed high, thrusting, while the slim sword cut down the back of the Guardswoman. The two thundered on, parting. The Kanese officer's shield now hung low, that shoulder slumped. A great roar burst from a thousand throats.

'They have won every bout so far!' the younger boy shouted in Dorin's ear.

With a sweep of his sword the Kanese officer saluted his opponent, and turned his mount to his gathered fellows. Petra, if it was indeed she, bowed in acknowledgement then waved to the walls – eliciting a rapturous roar – and trotted back to her hilltop.

Dorin did not cheer. It seemed to him that that Kanese had been a fool to take on such a heavily armoured opponent while armed with such a light blade. Still, to be fair, perhaps he had no choice in the matter.

A new challenger emerged from among the Kanese cavalry. Instead of yelling his history or insulting the Guard, he merely drew his curved blade and swept it in downward salute then waited, point aimed at the ground.

The Guard answered swiftly as a slim figure all in armour enamelled a deep carmine rode out to meet the new opponent. At this one's appearance a great sussurus of anticipation rose among the massed onlookers. Dorin looked to the girl. 'Who is it?'

This girl actually had a hand pressed to her mouth, the other shading her gaze. She breathed, awed, 'The Red Prince!'

Dorin couldn't help his own eyebrows rising in amazement. The son of the Guard commander himself? He'd heard stories that the lad had led armies even before coming into his beard. Such a one would ride out to fight in single combat? Dorin was impressed, but then he considered that these bouts were quite formalized, and rarely resulted in any permanent maiming or wounding. He found himself scowling once more. A cheap opportunity to impress the populace and burnish his image. Of course he took it! Even if he lost – how brave of him!

Already he disliked this lad for such sly calculation.

The two met halfway. They appeared well matched, both carrying sword and shield, but the much larger Kanese officer obviously held the advantage in weight and reach. The two kneed their mounts and began circling one another – no charging this time.

At some silent sign or signal, the horses lurched together, slamming their shoulders. The shields smashed, grinding and sliding. The blades wove and flashed overhead. The horses kicked and pushed, churning up a cloud of dust.

When the dust dispersed the crowds gasped. The Red Prince was on the ground. The Kanese officer circled him, gazing down. After a moment, the lad stirred, rising. Straightening, he shook off his shield and drew a second blade. The officer saluted him and swung down from his mount.

The crowd went wild with delight. They roared, slapped the stones of the wall, and stamped their feet. Dorin could only scowl harder. What a damned show-off! He hadn't even been hurt by that fall! He tried to recall the youth's name: something odd. The names out of the north followed some sort of strange old tradition, he remembered. K'azz. Yes. K'azz D'Avore.

Now they circled afoot. The youth carried two slim blades, the officer his broad shield. Personally, Dorin gave the edge to the officer. But then, in a real fight, he wouldn't have dismounted anyway. He would've simply ridden the lad down.

Well, at least that's what *he'd* have done.

They met in a high ringing of iron that was audible even upon the walls. Watching, Dorin had to give the lad his due: he was fast, and had obviously fought many times before. The two continued to circle; the officer constantly pushing, the lad giving ground to bring both blades into use.

Then sunlight flashed as the lad's blades moved in a blur and the officer was down on one leg. K'azz set a sword next to his neck and the officer dipped his head in submission.

The crowd exploded into rapturous approval. They waved favours, even threw tokens from the walls. Dorin merely crossed his arms. The three with him were cheering and waving and howling. Out on the field, K'azz helped his one-time opponent back up into his saddle and saluted him as he went. Then he mounted his own warhorse – which was trained well enough not to run off – saluted the crowds with a wave, and returned to his camp.

The Hengan populace continued to roar their delight. Entertainment, Dorin reflected sourly, must be pretty thin on the ground here in Heng. The cheers had been abating, but suddenly they redoubled in volume and Dorin returned his attention to the Guard camp. It was breaking up and the Guard was forming a column, three abreast, and heading across the fields straight for Heng's north gate, the Gate of the Plains.

The horde of townsfolk lining the walls now stampeded in a crush for the stairs, intent on reaching the main way to give the Guard a triumphant greeting. From atop the merlon, Dorin watched them struggling to force their way down the steps. He looked to the sky. Gods! Should he?

'Good pickings tonight,' the girl announced, now close at his side.

He shot her a glance. She was watching him with a knowing, openly mocking grin. 'What do you mean?'

'Don't play all coy. I seen the blades you got hid. You can use them?'

Dorin allowed a wary nod.

'You with a crew?' He shook his head. She sighed at his monumental ignorance. 'Gotta join a crew, man. You're a nobody otherwise. Me, I'm with Tran. Me 'n' the lads. Can you keep a lookout? Think you can manage that?'

Tran. A minor street boss associated with . . . Pung. A plan – one so very elegant and simple – suddenly appeared to Dorin, and he mentally kicked himself for being so stupid as not to have thought of it before. He offered the girl a shy smile.

'Count me in.'

Iko listened to the roar of celebration out in the streets of Heng. She stood at the open latticework window of a covered walkway. Even from this distance she could make out individual laughter, cheers, and drunken singing. The majority sounded as if it were coming from furthest away, the outermost round.

Some sort of religious festival, she imagined. Though she'd heard nothing of it through the day.

She tapped the carved latticework: gold-painted wood. Hardly the stuff of prison bars.

Why, then, her restiveness? Shrugging, she returned to her pacing. Down the way, four of her sisters were on guard over the Sword-Dancers' chambers – they had no need for reinforcements. Still, sleep would not come, and she had exited their suite of inter-connected rooms.

Guest chambers, the chamberlain had explained.

Iko had taken one look at the fountains, the many scattered carpets, the cushions and divans, and felt her lips tighten with distaste.

More like the concubines'.

The chamberlain knew; how he'd smirked as he drew shut the doors upon them. Their captain, Hallens, demonstrated her displeasure by promptly kicking them open. The Hengan servants had jumped, dropping trays and towels, but at least the doors hadn't been locked.

Now Iko walked a roofed path that crossed the gardens. Night birds called from ornamental trees and bushes bearing dark heavy blossoms. Frogs murmured and insects clouded round torches set about the trails. At the far end of the walkway, where doors led to the complex of the palace proper, a single man stood guard. Or perhaps was merely as restless as she. The slim, immaculately dressed figure of the city mage, Smokey.

Well. A single guard would be all that was required – if he or she were a mage of such a reputation. Steeling herself, she approached, and offered a slight bow of greeting. This the mage answered, only a touch condescendingly. Closer now, she saw that his shirt was of the finest brushed cotton, his footwear of the highest quality soft leather, and that his hair and beard were too evenly black – dyed,

59

in point of fact, to hide a premature grey. Vanity was what she read in this. Vanity and an underlying insecurity. 'A warm evening,' she offered. 'Is it always so warm this late?'

'The plains can get quite hot, Sword-Dancer.'

She gestured out to the darkness beyond the decorative lattice-work of the walkway. 'There is some sort of religious festival?'

The mage shook his head. 'The locals are feting the arrival of the Crimson Guard . . . rumours are flying that they have come to save the city from you Kanese.'

Iko considered the mage's words. 'But they have not.'

'They have not. They have come escorting a Grisian prince. He is keen to make a name for himself and has come to hunt the man-beast Ryllandaras. As so many have before – and failed.'

Iko grunted her rather shocked amazement at this.

'Indeed. He and the Red Prince, K'azz, are close friends, so the talk goes. K'azz grew up in the Grisian court.' The mage shot her a strange look. 'A hostage, you understand.'

'I see.' She shrugged. 'Well, they are only mercenaries. And the entire corps numbers only a thousand, yes?'

The mage inclined his head once more. 'Indeed. They only take in new members when one of their number dies. And then only the greatest of those vying to enter.'

Iko now wondered what it was the mage was truly talking about; she decided it was war. She returned to studying the dark. 'Mercenaries are untrustworthy and duplicitous allies. When it looks as though the cause is lost they will always betray or desert their employer. Sometimes they even offer their services to the opposing side.'

The mage nodded sagely. Iko thought she detected a hint of wood smoke in the air. It was not unpleasant; it reminded her of kneeling next to her family's hearth, her mother cooking.

'This is true – for most of the companies that have come and gone here in Quon. But not elsewhere. Have you not heard of the Grey Swords of Elingarth? The Guard are just as they. Can you think of a single reported incident when either deserted an employer? Or betrayed a contract? No?' She shook her head. 'Exactly. They dare not. It would destroy their reputation and none would hire them.'

'Yet, in the end, war is not a profitable business.'

Iko waited, but the mage did not answer. She glanced to him

and saw him eyeing her with a new expression in his eyes – a new respect.

He finally spoke, nodding to himself. 'Indeed it is not – for those caught in it. And so I offer you advice, child . . . Urge your king away from this war. It will not win him the rewards he imagines. But more important, many southerners will die. And all for nothing. If he truly cared about the welfare of his people he would abandon this campaign.'

Stung, Iko faced him directly. 'I am disappointed, old man. So speaks a city mage of Heng. What is next – base threats?'

But the mage merely stroked his beard, shaking his head. 'It is I who am disappointed. Perhaps, in time, you will understand my words. I hope it will not be too late.'

Iko waved a curt farewell. 'It is already too late, mage. I bid you good night.' She turned away and stalked off. His last words came wafting through the darkness.

'Remember. All that comes he has brought upon himself . . .'

Chapter 3

T<small>HE RED-HEADED GIRL'S NAME WAS</small> R<small>HEENA</small>. S<small>HE AND HER</small> two loyal followers, Shreth and Loor – Loor being the younger – played thieves' games long familiar to Dorin. He recognized buttoning, fishing, and the crooked cross. Rheena picked the marks and usually served as the distraction. She sometimes asked for coin, or she'd catch a man's roving gaze and offer herself. During the negotiations the mark would get run into by Shreth, or the two lads would start a fight right on top of him. She also proved a shrewd judge of character as, after eyeing one finely dressed fellow, she immediately started yelling that the bastard had felt her up. Under the surrounding hostile stares the embarrassed mark practically begged her to take a quarter-round to go away.

But theirs was a dangerous game. The streets were crowded with revellers and she made a mistake with one big fellow, who snatched Loor's quick hand and twisted, sending him on his way with a kick. Shreth swung at him but was quickly laid out with a blow to the head. The man snatched Rheena by the arm and dragged her into an alley. Loor picked up a board but Dorin pulled him back, motioned for him to wait, and followed them himself.

In the narrow way the fellow had her up against a wall, one hand clutching her throat, the other holding her up by her crotch. Dorin cleared his throat. The fellow turned his head; his gaze was full of lazy confidence. 'Who the fuck are you?'

Dorin motioned up the alley. 'Put her down and walk away.'

The man dropped Rheena to the cobbles where she lay gasping for breath. He pointed a stubby finger at Dorin. 'Dumb-fuck kids. Shouldn't play with grownups.'

Dorin flexed his wrists to allow the thin blades he carried there to ease into his palms. The light in the alleyway was dim and flickering as revellers passed on the street waving torches and lanterns, but a change in the man's expression told Dorin he'd seen them and knew what they meant. 'Not worth it,' Dorin told him. 'Plenty of other girls out there. Walk away.'

A strange sort of knowing smile crept up the fellow's lips and he opened his arms wide. 'You gonna kill me, little man?'

'No.'

'No? Why not?'

'I don't kill for free.'

The other man frowned at that, stroked his chin with a wide paw. 'Hunh. Makes sense.' He kicked Rheena, who'd sat up. Shreth and Loor pressed up close behind Dorin, snarling their rage. 'You, girl,' the fellow demanded, 'who do you work for?'

Rheena was rubbing her neck. 'Fuck off.'

'It ain't Odd-Hand, I'm sure of that.'

Rheena started, surprised, and dropped her hand. 'Tran,' she spat, resentfully.

The big fellow grinned without humour. 'Thought so. Well, you tell Tran to keep his brats off our streets. Right?'

'Fine!'

'Good for you. Not so stupid after all.' He brushed his hands together. 'Now run along.'

Still unsteady, Rheena climbed to her feet. Shreth and Loor rushed forward and helped her limp away. Dorin did not move.

'You too, knife-boy.'

'What's your name?'

'Unimportant, lad. This is just business. Now g'wan.'

Dorin decided to let it go. He backed away, all the while keeping his eyes on the other man. The fellow – an enforcer? – watched him go, his amusement quite obvious.

Out on the street, Dorin asked, 'What was that all about?'

Rheena waved it off. 'Just a little border scuffle.'

'Who was he?'

'He works for Urquart.'

Urquart. Pung's main rival for control of all the city's black market and thievery. Rafall, he knew, worked for Urquart.

Rheena suddenly laughed uproariously. She tossed her flame-hued hair, the familiar fey light once more shining in her eyes. 'Forget all that!' She held out a fistful of coins. 'Let's get shit-faced drunk!' Shreth and Loor howled their enthusiasm, joining their voices to the surrounding roar of revelry and singing.

With dawn, Dorin slid out of the dive where Rheena and her small loyal crew had finished their drinking. As the coin dwindled, the quality of the dives had slid precipitously, until they'd crashed in this dingy basement among snoring drunks. Dorin didn't even think it a true business, just an abandoned room where you could find watered beer and the cheapest of narcotic chew and stale old d'bayang powder.

His head throbbed from the one tankard of disgusting beer he'd nursed and the smoke he couldn't avoid inhaling. He rubbed his stinging eyes and headed off for the main street of the Outer Round. He circled pools of spilt beer and vomit, and stepped over unconscious revellers. Shop-owners tossed trash and the contents of night buckets into the streets. Hengans walked the streets holding their heads and groaning. He overheard stories of one large gang of celebrants, overcome with alcohol and confidence, that sallied out into the field in the pre-dawn. They'd been armed only with what they could pick up, and made a charge for the Kanese camp. Cooler heads had prevailed, however, or perhaps it was the chill prairie wind in their faces, or rumours that Ryllandaras had been seen in the vicinity, but they thought better of the assault and retreated. The mounted Kanese pickets had kindly allowed them to go with only a few jabs of their lances to hurry them along.

What made everyone twice as sick was the news on all tongues of the Crimson Guard's being seen riding out of the north gate, the Gate of the Plains, that very morning. Evidently, as he and Rheena had deduced, they'd not come to rescue Heng but to escort a Grisian royal brat on yet another of those idiotic campaigns to hunt down the man-beast, Ryllandaras.

Walking the main way, Dorin found he was close to Ullara's family stable. He jiggled the few poor coins in his pouch – his share of the remaining takings, hardly worth his bother, but she could clearly use them.

Though it was light, he risked the climb up the side and ducked into the open gable window. Within, the usual crowd of birds of prey roosted. They stirred uneasily at his entrance, but soon calmed and returned to cleaning their feathers. The night-hunters among them eased back into sleep. Dorin peered about for the gigantic raptor he'd glimpsed on earlier nights but saw no sign of it. Not surprising, as he doubted it could even fit through any of the windows. He bunched up some straw and lay back to join the other night-hunters in their rest.

He awoke to the birds' muted mutterings and yawned, stretching. It was mid-day.

'Good morning.'

He turned over. Ullara was sitting on a box, feet tucked up beneath her, watching him.

'Morning.'

'You were working last night,' she said.

He nodded, then frowned; that hadn't been a question.

She jumped up. 'I'll get some tea.'

'Well . . . my thanks.'

'Thanks?' Her brows shot up. 'Again? Your manners *are* improving.'

He searched for a response but she was gone down the trap-door. Alone with the birds, he studied one stately russet plains falcon – the namesake of one of the Seti tribes. It returned his gaze with the cutting superiority that only a bird of prey can manage. Ullara returned with a cup of weak green tea, and a bowl of yogurt and bread.

'My mother makes the yogurt,' she explained. 'We have goats.'

Dorin sat cross-legged and scooped up the mix. 'It's very good.'

'Thank you, Dan—' She stopped herself, blushing.

'What was that? Dan?'

She plucked at her threadbare tunic, her head lowered, obviously mortified.

He cleared his throat. 'You don't have to say . . .' Her hair, he saw, had dirt and straw clumped within, and hadn't seen a brushing in a good long time.

She dared a quick glance up, her lip in her teeth. 'I . . . I name all my . . . rescues.'

It seemed to him that she was going to say something different there, but he did not comment. He waited, instead.

She gestured to the tall plains falcon. 'That's Prince.' She pointed to a savage-looking split-tail hawk. 'Keen.' A huge dozing tuft-eared owl, 'Biter.' Several more names followed: 'Swift, Watcher, Fury, Red, Cutter.'

Dorin nodded to each then returned to Ullara. 'And me?'

She hid her face once more, whispered, hushed, 'Dancer.'

He raised a brow at that; he had indeed been forced to train for a time as a dancer – for flexibility and speed. And his teacher had always treated duels as a dance as well. 'Well, thank you, Ullara.' His hand rested on his coin-pouch and he jumped, remembering. 'Oh, yes. This is for you.' He held it out.

She eyed it but made no move to take it. After a moment, he laid it on the boards of the floor amid the straw and bird shit. 'It isn't much . . . I just thought . . .'

'Thank you. My little brother is sickly, and we can't . . . my thanks.'

'I see. Well. I ought to be going.'

'Yes.' Again, so sad. How was it that he seemed only to make her sad? She reached to take up the bowl and his breath hissed from him in shock. 'Your hands!'

She tried to hide them but he was far quicker and took both, turning them over. The flesh of the fingers, backs and palms was cracked so severely that dried blood filled most of the deep crevasses and much of the ridged flesh was white – dead and hardened. 'You work with lye and other such chemicals?'

'It is my job to clean all the tack, and treat the leather for softness.'

'It's eating your flesh to the bone – you will lose your fingers.'

She yanked her hands away. 'I'll not let my mother do it! Nor my sisters!'

He raised his own hands in open surrender. 'No – I'm not suggesting. I'm just . . . Here.' From his shirt he drew another pouch and pulled out a packet wrapped in waxed parchment. 'Use this.'

'What is it?'

'A healing unguent. Here – let me.' He urged her to give him her hands. She extended them like a scared, wary animal, and he kneaded the honey-thick preparation into them. It softened with the heat, like a wax. He rubbed her fingers, careful to get it between.

'This is alchemy,' she said, her voice rising in alarm. 'You bought this.'

'Yes.'

She almost succeeded in yanking her hands from his. She hissed, 'We – I – cannot afford this!'

'Never mind. Consider it a gift.' He returned to rubbing her hands. 'Relax now.' He hardly had to say it, as her shoulders had fallen, easing, and her eyes slowly shut. A dreamy smile came to her lips as he worked the unguent into the wounds.

'This is infused with Denul magics,' she murmured, seeming half awake.

'Yes.'

'You are wasting it on me.'

'No. This is what it is for. Now . . . better, yes?'

'Yes,' she said, her voice barely audible. 'Better.'

'I've got to go. Will I see you again?'

She shook herself, blinking and straightening. 'Yes. Certainly.'

'Good. Now, take care of yourself.' He rose, and, peering down at her, fought an urge to take her head in his hands and press a kiss to her forehead and whisper *It will be all right. You will see. Everything will be all right.* He shook himself instead and retreated to the window, waved, and started down the side of the stable. As he made the alley, it occurred to him that perhaps their roles were now reversed – he the rescuer and she the wounded trembling bird.

Alone, Ullara remained sitting. She allowed her eyes to close once more and tucked her hands under her chin and held them there, rocking. A smile came to her lips again, only this time much more fierce. She curled up among the scattered straw and breathed in the scents rising from her oh so warmed hands.

* * *

Silk knew of three hidden entrances to the catacombs far beneath Heng. One was through the sewers behind the palace, another was via a tunnel accessible along the riverside, while the third was theoretical: a door barred and secured in the very wall of the Outer Round. He opted for the riverside. He owned several river crafts and selected the one he used for his more clandestine journeys; one little more than a long narrow dugout. He unmoored it and paddled out among the forest of pilings that supported the countless docks, wharves, and waterside businesses.

67

Since he was out on the Idryn, he decided to swing by someone, who, if not really a friend, could be described as a compatriot. For while all Heng knew there were five city mages in the Protectress's employ, what those five knew was that, in truth, there were far more than that. He idled for a time close to the shore of the muddy ochre course that was the Idryn here on its slow way to Cawn and the Bay of Nap. After tracing the flats among the shadows beneath the wharves high overhead, he spotted a hunched shape seated on a rock amid the mud, bare feet caked in the green-grey muck, hair a frighteningly tangled mass. The shape was hardly recognizable as female, but he knew her. She was holding up one of the exceptionally large Idryn crayfish by one claw.

'Ho! Liss!' he called.

The old woman peered up, squinting. 'Who's there? Is that that slick and smarmy fellow?'

Silk raised his eyes to the wood decking above. 'Must we, Liss?'

She made a show of addressing the crayfish. 'Why does he wear that hollow pretty mask?' She held the creature to her ear. 'No! Not that monstrous, surely!'

'Thank you, Liss. I'm sure the crayfish are full of insights.'

'They are full of Hengan citizens – I'll tell you that!'

He rubbed his chin. 'Well . . . I'll have to give you that one.'

'Come to drop the mask, Silk?'

Smiling, he shook his head. 'Just a greeting. On my way to see Ho.'

She shook the crayfish like a warning finger. 'Watch out for Hothalar, my friend. He is a haunted man.'

Silk bowed in answer to the warning. Liss, he knew, went far back here in Heng. The sluggish current dragged him onward.

'Have a care,' she shouted. 'I see trouble ahead.'

'What? The Kanese?'

'No. Send King Chulalorn my way and I'll squeeze the ambition out of him – along with all his seed! No, something else.'

'What?'

She called back, 'Don't know. Something sly, hidden. I see it in the corner of my eye.' Silk bowed again in answer to the warning as the figure disappeared among the forest of pilings.

Later that afternoon he found the gated access, magically disguised in the dark under the decking and raised walkways. He drew up his dugout, and, with extreme distaste, squelched his way through the muck to the entrance, and unlatched the iron grating.

Many tunnels and rickety ladders later, he was within the stone-walled catacombs. In the utter dark, he summoned his Warren and a tiny flame flickered to life upon his upturned palm. It gave no heat, of course, just illumination, as Thyr was his Warren. Many, he knew, assumed that he was a mage of Mockra – one specializing in what some named the art of glamour. But in fact his allure came naturally rather than deliberately. Or perhaps he did somehow innately draw upon Mockra. He didn't know. What he could do, however, through his years of discipline and study, was touch this one Warren of Thyr and even, in moments of his greatest inspiration, catch glimpses of a wellspring of might that lay beyond it.

The tunnel was a narrow semicircle of crudely dressed sandstone blocks. Narrow, but tall. Rats scampered from his light. He stilled, listening. All he heard was his heartbeat and water dripping. He picked a direction and followed it.

Beams of light streamed down here and there, illuminating short stretches of the anonymous stone tunnels. A stream of cascading water flooded one intersection. He stepped carefully through puddles for some time after that. At one point he thought he glimpsed a human figure moving among the shifting shadows and would have dismissed it as just such another but for a faint tapping that seemed to accompany the blurry disturbance.

'Hello?'

The rippling, shifting darkness that might or might not be an actual person turned at a corner. Silk found the junction and cast his sorcerous light beyond. The tunnel lay completely empty and utterly quiet. He snorted at his overworked imagination and moved on, coming at last to a gate of very thick iron bars. It was locked and there was no way he could open it. However, the bars were quite far apart and he was very slim. He almost tore an ear off, but he made it through. His shirt was now frankly ruined, as were his trousers of fine imported Darujhistani silk. He brushed at his clothes, cursing Ho, then carried on. A few turns later he came to a tunnel faced by a series of iron doors. He studied the flagged floor. The dust was disturbed. Someone walked here regularly. He listened at the nearest door. All was quiet. Eerily so, as he was so far underground. Yet he thought he heard *something*. Movement.

'Hello?' he whispered.

The door struck him in the side of his head as something rammed or punched it from within. He staggered away, holding his head, cursing again. 'Who are you?' he demanded, ears ringing and head throbbing.

'Lar!' came in an animal-like growl. Or some sound resembling that. 'Lar, Lar, Lar!'

'Lar? Lar who?'

'What are you doing here?' a new voice rumbled from far down the tunnel.

Silk spun, hunching, his Warren readied. A dark shape came shambling up. It filled the tunnel completely from side to side and top to bottom – the giant form of Koroll. Silk straightened, eased the knot of tension in his shoulders and neck. 'Greetings,' he offered.

'It is dangerous here,' Koroll murmured, his voice low. He waved Silk back up the tunnel. 'Come.'

Koroll unlocked the barred gate and had Silk shut it behind him. Then the giant led him on through the maze.

Another door, this one a stone slab two hand-lengths thick, opened on to a much wider and taller complex of stone-walled tunnels. Silk found that he could now walk next to Koroll as the Thelomen-kind giant slowly strode along, rather like a rocking shack. 'What was all that back there?' he asked.

'A prison.'

'Yes. I gathered that. For whom? Or what?'

'Things dangerous to Heng. Things that over the centuries Shalmanat has been forced to subdue.'

Silk felt the hairs of his arms and neck prickling as he considered this. Ye gods! *Centuries!* And what *things* might lie in those cells? Daemons? Creatures of other realms? Perhaps even murderous fellow mages . . . Silk shook himself as the cold subterranean air left him feeling chill and clammy.

Koroll led him into a broad chamber, round and dome-roofed, rather like some sort of ancient tomb. Silk was alarmed to hear chains – the reverberation of very large chains clunking and thumping in the dark. Reflexively, he raised the power of his light, revealing a tall block of stone at the chamber's centre and his fellow city mage Mister Ho at its side.

Ho crossed his thick arms. His scowl had turned even more wary than usual. 'What brings you down here, Silk?'

'The view,' Silk answered, absently. His gaze rose to where an equally large block of stone hung suspended over the first. It was held there by numerous thick chains all extending off into the dark where stone counterweights waited. A single chain led up into the gloom of the hidden roof, and there Silk thought he caught a faint glimmer of light. 'What is this?'

'A work in progress.'

The block was far wider and longer than any man. Silk rose on to his tiptoes to peer over the top. It was hollow, with thick sides. It resembled, to all appearances, an enormous . . . sarcophagus. As the thought came, Silk flinched away. What might it once have held? He shot a glance to Ho – one just as wary as his. 'What are you doing here?'

'Preparing a prison.'

'A prison? For whom?' And the answer came as he asked and Silk's hand went to his mouth. 'No . . . it will never work.'

Ho sent a dark glance to Koroll. The look seemed to say *Why did you bring this asshole here?* Koroll sighed and grasped his staff in both hands, resting his weight there. Ho cleared his throat. 'What do you want, Silk?'

Silk dropped his hand. 'Help. I want help tracking someone down.'

Ho grunted his understanding of the request. 'The assassin you mentioned?'

'Yes. He's good. Better than most who've tried to set up shop here.'

Ho brushed a hand along the glittering granite wall of the sarcophagus. 'Not my specialty. Nor Mara or Smokey.' He grunted a dry laugh. 'Something of a hole in our defences, hey?'

'I will help,' Koroll rumbled.

Silk raised a hand in thanks. 'With all respect, Koroll, you're not very . . . stealthy.'

'I will give you my nights,' Ho said.

Silk was quite surprised. 'You said it wasn't your specialty.'

The fellow shrugged his meaty shoulders. 'I'll pull something together.'

Silk tilted his head in cautious agreement. 'Very well. Tomorrow night, then.'

Ho nodded to Koroll. 'Make sure he gets out.'

The giant murmured a rolling laugh and raised an arm, pointing to the door. Silk was irritated at such a dismissal, but something in the strange mage's grim manner told him not to object. He bowed instead, mockingly, and followed Koroll. At the entrance, he paused, turning back. 'By the way . . . I thought I saw someone else down here.'

Ho stood motionless, his thick arms crossed, his gaze steady, almost suspicious. 'That's impossible. No one else could ever find their way down here.'

Silk gave a shrug, saluted, and headed out.

All the way back through the tunnels, he wondered whether he had discovered the truth of things. Was Ho simply Shalmanat's warder-in-chief? And this huge stone sarcophagus. Did they really imagine it could possibly succeed? After all, how could they hope to lure the man-beast down here?

* * *

A voice whispering from across the fire woke her. That and the sense of a presence – at long last. She started up from beneath her blanket, blinking, and wiping at her eyes. The fire was a mere orange blur of embers. The stars through the overhanging branches glowed much brighter. At first she thought no one was there, but then the faintest of ghostly waverings, as of a mirage, betrayed a presence. A very weak and tenebrous breath of one.

She recognized the unwelcome essence. 'Errant,' she growled, making no effort to conceal her distaste.

'Good to see you too,' came a wavering ghostly response. 'Sister. Cold night, isn't it?'

She smiled thinly. 'What do you want?'

The figure across the embers was of a man, seated cross-legged. Yet the bushes behind showed through quite clearly. 'Want? Why must I want something? Could this not be purely social?'

'No it could not.' Only the eyes, she noted, held any definite presence. They burned with an inner light. And the teeth gleamed where the lips were curled back in that familiar habitual sneer.

'Very well, sister. I am here for the same reason as you.'

'No you are not.'

A phantom shrug. 'Close enough.'

'And what is that?'

'Come, come. You sense it just as I have. You, who remain so very much of this *mortal* realm. And I, whose aspect could not help but take note of any play.'

Though she was resolved not to allow this one to bait her, she roused, annoyed. 'Play? This is no game, Errant.'

'Everything is a game, sister.'

'With you.'

'Your mulish mundanity bores me.'

'The oblivious arrogance of those who expect others to entertain them sickens me.'

The flickering ghost-image across the campfire smiled. 'Good to see you have not lost your edge, sister.'

She did not answer. Crossed her arms.

The Errant let out the faintest of sighs. 'Very well. I know when a throw is made. A gambit opened. It is my nature, of course. Our ... cousins ... have made another play. The enormous dusty wheels of fate are grinding into motion once again. What might this game bring? Who is to say?'

She smiled at his uncertainty. 'They worry you, don't they?'

'Of course they do! They have withdrawn. We no longer know what they intend.'

She made a show of shrugging her insouciance. 'I am not worried.'

'If you concerned yourself with the larger picture of things, you would be.'

'Do not condescend to me, Errant. You are not intelligent enough.'

The eyes glittered hungrily across the orange glow. 'And do not provoke me, sister. You are vulnerable. A nudge here or there and you could find yourself dead.'

'Says a pallid ghost with little to no influence.'

The sneering smile twisted into slyness. 'Oh, I have influence ... elsewhere.'

A new voice spoke at the dying fire. 'Making up, are we?'

The shade that was the sending of the Errant flinched and vanished.

She inclined her head in greeting to the hooded figure now warming his hands at the embers. 'Welcome, K'rul.'

'Sister. And what did our poor misguided friend have to say?'

'He has sensed it also. Ripples from the Azath. And the stone was cast here. I fear he will try to interfere.'

'It is true that he yet remains capable of meddling. Strange how those least fit to hold or wield power lust after it the most.' K'rul turned his hands in the warmth and she knew it as a gesture purely for her benefit. 'That is a mystery that remains beyond even me. However, another is in place to keep an eye on the Errant.'

'And what of our cousins?' she asked.

A tilt of the head. 'They, too, remain beyond me. Beyond us all. None have ever succeeded in penetrating their secrets.'

'Some may have,' she murmured, her gaze deep in the flickering glow of the fading embers.

'Possibly. But they have not returned to us, have they? They have disappeared within. The Azath are like black pits that swallow all.'

'Yet they repeatedly demonstrate this compelling urge to intercede. They have goals. And for that they require agents. Brother, I will try to plumb their intent.'

K'rul sighed, drew his hands back to clasp them across his lap. 'A perilous path for you, sister. And for me as well, I fear. That aside, is it not the case that only you, who yet remain free among us, could do so? Our brother lies imprisoned within the consequences of his own designs, while I remain enmeshed within mine. Very well, sister. I honour your intent and will do what I can to aid it.'

She bowed her head. 'Thank you, brother.'

K'rul raised a finger. 'Have a care. I foresee that this involvement could cost everything.'

'That is as it should be, else it would not be worthwhile.'

The hand withdrew. 'Very well. May you choose the wisest of all the many ways, Sister of Cold Nights.'

The hooded shape faded away into the dark and she was alone. Wincing, she stretched out her legs, arched her back, and threw more branches upon the embers. As the fire grew, she shifted to sit cross-legged, set her hands palm up on her knees, closed her eyes, and cast her awareness towards the city to the south.

She was searching. Searching for a flavour. The faintest of brush-strokes. Something . . . inexplicable. And through the darkness there came rumbling about her the creaking and grating of titanic wheels, such as Errant had mentioned. Only now, reverberating among the Warrens and Holds, these vibrations were not the cogs of fate's machinations but the wheels of a gigantic wagon accompanied by the rattling of chains. And stricken by a chilling dread, she shuddered.

Wheels. Wheels groaning in the dark.

Chapter 4

'HOW MUCH FOR PUNG'S HEAD?'

Rafall, who had been sipping his tea, spat all over the mass of papers on his desk. He dabbed a sleeve to the cheap fibre sheets and glared at the youth slouched in the chair opposite. *Hood forefend! He can't be serious, surely*? 'Let's not get ahead of ourselves, lad. We have a good thing going here. A fat purse for the old harridan. That grain merchant. Let's not ruin it.'

The lean youth appeared unmoved. His sharp gaze remained unreadable. 'It could be done. How much would Urquart pay?'

Ye gods – where to start? He opened his arms wide. 'Listen, lad. We – all of us – we're allowed to run our quaint little businesses because we keep our heads down and don't cause too much trouble. Understand? The Protectress and her pet mages, they could shut us all down if they wished.'

'You, maybe,' the lad muttered.

Rafall winced and bit his tongue to stop himself from cursing the youth as he would any of his usual lads or lasses. He took a deep breath. 'I'm going to do you a favour right now, lad. Here it is. With that little snipe there, you just effectively dismissed my life and therefore the livelihood of all those here who depend upon me for food and a roof over their head. Understand? Now, am I supposed to thank you for that? Or maybe I should now decide that you're a threat to me and arrange to get rid of you. There. See how consequences of words and actions work?'

The youth shifted in his seat. His mouth tightened and turned down in an uncertain frown.

Rafall was pleased. Maybe he'd finally made a dent in that massive arrogance. The problem with this one was he was too good. It had all come too easy. Too much early success. For his part, Rafall couldn't imagine what it must be like to see no one as a threat. But it couldn't breed prudence, of that he was sure.

The assassin suddenly lurched to his feet. 'You're forgetting who works for whom, Rafall. Get the word out. I want to know how much.'

Rafall pressed a hand to his forehead. 'You're not listening. Just . . . listen.' The lad had crossed to the window. 'Look around!' Rafall went on. 'There's a war on. Don't start another. You won't like it!' But the youth was gone out of the window into the night. Banging started on the trapdoor to his chambers.

'You okay, boss?' one of his guards called. 'Who's that you're talking to?'

Rafall moved to stand on the door. 'A nightmare,' he said. He could not take his gaze from the window. 'Just a nightmare.'

Dorin stopped to rest on a flat rooftop. He was panting and sweaty, but not from his exertions. It's nothing, he told himself. It means nothing. He's just searching for a hold on you. Like all the others. Trying to control you. Remember, you can't count on anyone.

He drew in the cool night air, felt the hairs on his neck prickle as they cooled and dried in the wind. And yet the fellow seemed genuinely kind to all the young pickpockets and cutpurses and clubbers in his employ. Like a father.

He scowled at that while he stared out across the dark rooftops. Yes. A father. Like the one who'd sold him. Pulled him yelling from his mother's arms and sold him off for a few coins that he no doubt squandered on drink.

So much for love. Or affection. Or any other ties, blood or otherwise. He drew out a coil of his best cord and yanked it taut around a forearm, round and round, biting into the flesh.

The only ties he could count on were those he tied himself.

A scuff on the sun-dried tiles of the roof alerted him. He spun, throwing daggers readied. A fellow who looked like a wrestler stood eyeing him. He carried no obvious weapons, but his thick arms hung loose at his sides, and they ended at the wide gnarled hands of a professional strangler.

'What do you want?' Dorin called. For some reason he felt wary, despite the distance between them and the brace of weapons he carried.

'We'd like to talk,' said a new voice, and Dorin spun again, to where another fellow occupied the far corner of the rooftop. This one was dressed like a godsdamned male courtesan. Dorin backed away to keep both in view. His feet in their soft leather slippers touched the lip of the roof behind him. 'I'm done talking.'

The fop smiled, hands held out and open. 'A brief word, that's all.'

For some reason Dorin paused before leaping off the roof. Why not? He was armed. Might as well hear this ridiculous fellow out. 'All right. Talk.'

The fop smiled his encouragement. 'Excellent. Thank you. We have a job for you.'

Dorin eased his ready stance ever so slightly. 'A job? What?'

The uncommonly handsome bastard shared a glance with his equally uncommonly ugly compatriot. 'The priest of Hood in town. We want him to meet his god.'

Dorin chuckled at the sentiment. 'How much?'

'One hundred gold rounds.'

It was an incredible price. Dorin raised an eyebrow. 'For one dead priest?'

A modest shrug from the man said that they had their reasons. 'As you see – an easy job. Shall we say you return here, this rooftop at mid-night, whenever the job is done?'

'Agreed.' Dorin hopped back off the lip and fell by lowering himself from one window to the next until he landed, a touch more heavily than he would've liked, in the alley beneath, and ran off.

*

Silk peered down over the lip of the roof into the darkness-shrouded alley. He couldn't see a blasted thing. He crossed his arms and tapped a thumb to his lips. 'Well . . . he's acrobatic. I'll give him that.'

'And if he fails?' Ho asked.

Silk shrugged again. 'Then we're rid of him.'

'And if he succeeds?'

Silk smiled. 'Then we'll be rid of him a few days from now.'

But Ho did not share the smile. He rubbed his grey-bristled jowls, frowning as if troubled by some vague unease.

Silk rolled his eyes to the night sky. *Gods! There's no pleasing some people, is there?* He waved Ho onwards. 'Fine. Let's take a tour of the walls. Mara says the Kanese infantry have finished their investment.'

'They will attack on all sides. Hope to overbear us.'

'Then we will be busy.'

Ho walked with a heavy tread, his hands clasped behind his back, his head lowered. 'I fear so.'

They reached a ladder and Silk allowed Ho to go first. 'You fear?' he asked when they reached the alley. 'What could you possibly fear?'

The big man sent Silk a puzzled look. 'Having to kill, of course.'

Silk resisted a scoff. 'You've killed – I know this.'

'Oh, yes. But not poor innocent soldiers. They're not responsible for this mess. They're forced to serve, you know. They don't even want to be here, I'm sure.'

Silk shook his head in wonder as he walked along. What a strange fellow! Could crush a man's skull in one fist yet disliked violence? Was he deluded? And as for soldiers – innocent? Please! Murderers and rapists all. Human filth. Eliminating them would be a favour to civilized society. Clearly his fellow mage was suffering from the romanticized image of the brave and honest soldier-citizen, or some such rubbish.

Soft-minded fool. The truth was, most people simply weren't worth one's attention.

* * *

Dorin walked the crowded night-time market streets that Rheena and her crew called their own. Eventually, he spotted her hanging about by an open-air tavern. She saw him as well and they met among the flow of people in the middle of the street.

'Where have you been?' she demanded.

'Eyeing some prospects.'

'Not without us you don't.'

'I have other work, you know.'

'Sidelines aren't allowed.'

Dorin crossed his arms. 'Oh? So, am I in or not?'

She pushed back her unruly bush of frizzy red hair. 'All right, all right. I'll take you to see Tran.'

He let his arms fall. 'Okay. 'Cause I can do more than keep a lookout, you know.'

'Oh, I know *that*!' And she hooked an arm through his, leading him on through the market.

'You can't browbeat me into being another of your loyal followers,' he said.

'I know that too,' she answered, shooting him a sly grin. She slipped her hand down his thigh and clenched there. 'Maybe I'll have to find another way to hook you.'

He felt his brows rising very high indeed.

She led him to the bourse of the hide merchants. Most of the shops were closed, though activity continued in warehouses and dye works where the hides were soaked, stirred and hung all through the night. The stench was horrendous, but in time he became able to tolerate it, just. Rheena's two loyal followers trailed behind. Neither looked too happy at the change in marching order.

Tran's base was one of these leather works. Two thugs lounged at the entrance. Rheena gave them a nod and sauntered in. One thrust out a truncheon, blocking Dorin's way. 'Who's this?'

'One of mine, okay?' Rheena answered, glaring.

'Tran's the judge of that.'

'Then we'll see, won't we?'

The fellow's lips quirked in a knowing way and he chuckled. 'Yeah. Won't we?' He let his arm fall. Dorin sent a glance to Rheena, wondering at the exchange, but she avoided his gaze as she hurried in. Even her loyal followers had laughed at the last comment, but they too quietened as he turned his eyes on them.

Inside, up a long hall, a great many men and women sat with plates and mugs before them, eating and drinking amid shouts and loud laughter. It appeared that Tran set a generous table – not surprising as his territory included several animal markets. Rheena kicked a fellow from one mostly empty bench and sat, elbows splayed on the crowded tabletop. Shreth and Loor were quick to sit to either side. Dorin slid in opposite.

Rheena raised her chin and shouted, 'Drink here for those out working hard!'

Someone shouted back: 'You're in trouble, Red.'

'Story of my life,' she answered.

A boy brought round a tall tankard and filled the nearby cups.

Dorin let his sit on the table while Shreth and Loor quickly emptied theirs. Shreth then elbowed Loor behind Rheena's back and the lad got up to hunt down more. Trenchers of hard bread arrived followed by a slab of grey meat. Dorin eyed it dubiously while the others set to with gusto, gnawing and pulling apart the greasy flesh. Dorin found that he had no appetite. He picked up a pear – one barely ripe – and chewed on it, waiting. Soon, he knew, it would come. The assertion of command. He wondered what form it would take this time. Benevolent ruthlessness? Bluster and glad-handing? Or perhaps the automatic – and ignorant – assumption of superiority?

The laughter in the room quietened and Dorin set down the core, bringing his hands under the table. A dark short fellow had entered, his slit gaze fixed upon Rheena. He marched for their table and she straightened as he came, a grin coming to her lips – a grin Dorin knew already as the one she used on marks. 'Tran!' she greeted, enthusiastic. 'Good to see you.'

But Tran had switched his attention to Dorin and did not answer. He stood at their table, glaring, and the room became very quiet. Dorin gazed back, as placid as he could manage, his hands ready under the table. The fellow – a minor boss – was youngish, perhaps in his twenties. Slim and wiry, and short. Already Dorin surmised that he carried quite the attitude.

The eyes slid back to Rheena, who lowered hers. Everyone, Dorin noted, now studied their cups. He, on the other hand, continued to study Tran. He decided that behind the hot slit eyes hid fear. Fear of any challenge to his power – and thus the mask of belligerence.

'Who said you could bring anyone in?' Tran demanded.

Rheena's attempt to laugh off the question was edged with nervousness. 'He's not *in* yet. He's here for you to check out. Name's Dorin.'

Dorin said nothing. He understood his place in this dance. He was a nobody right now, without even the standing to speak.

The gaze, as if reluctant to acknowledge Dorin's existence, now slowly edged to him again. 'Dorin, hey? What kind of name is that?'

'Talian.'

Tran grunted. 'And you want to join Pung's gang, hey? Why should we take you in?'

Dorin gave a modest shrug. 'You guys are always on the lookout for talent, yes?'

The tightening of the lines around the man's glaring eyes told Dorin he'd said the wrong thing; that this fellow was of the kind who hated talent – in others.

The lizard eyes blinked, slowly, as if clicking; swung to Loor sitting opposite. Tran tousled the lad's thick kinky hair. 'Here's a rogue ready to run with the big dogs, hey, Loor?'

'You bet!' the lad laughed, grinning. Dorin, however, caught the silent warning Rheena shot Loor's way.

Tran urged him up. 'C'mon, this way.' He walked Loor over to a narrow timber post, stood him in front of it. 'Here's your initiation, boy.'

Laughing again, Rheena called in a wheedling way, 'Tran . . .'

'Shut up, bitch.' He motioned Dorin to him. 'I hear you know how to use knives. That you even stood down Breaker-Jon.'

Dorin glanced to Rheena – Breaker-Jon? Must've been the big fellow in the alley. Rheena cast him a pleading look. *Oh, girl. You've done me no favours with your talk . . .*

'So let's see how good you are, hey?'

Loor's eyes now goggled with dread and he slouched from the post, mumbling, 'Another time, maybe . . .'

Tran took a fistful of the youth's hair and dragged him back to the post. 'I say now. You want in or not?'

The lad was on the verge of tears. 'Yeah, sure,' he managed, his voice breaking.

Dorin glanced about. None of the gathered crew appeared ready to step in. Most weren't even watching; their gazes hadn't risen from the tabletops. Cowed. Thoroughly beaten down. He'd seen it before, unfortunately. The rule of brutality and malice.

Tran now sent Dorin a gloating, twisted smile. 'Let's see you put one right next to his ear, there. Hey?'

Saying nothing, Dorin drew out his best throwing dagger. For a moment, he considered burying it in Tran's throat but thought better of it. He wanted to get close to Pung, or at least that damned Dal Hon he kept as a mage. And killing the man's lieutenants wouldn't help him do that.

He hefted the flat blade, raised his gaze to Loor. To his credit the boy was quiet, though he was crying. Tears were wet on his cheeks. No blubbering or fainting. Bravery and dedication – and to what? A monster who cared not one whit for his safety or life.

Dorin raised the blade to his eyes, sighted. It was a mystery to him why anyone would follow such a fool. Unfortunately, as he'd found in Tali and elsewhere, the rule of the most violent was often the norm. He tried not to meet Loor's pleading terrified eyes, but couldn't avoid them. He gave what he hoped was a calm reassuring nod, and drew back his arm.

Everything froze for him as he brought the arm forward, the blade flat against his fingers. He took in at that moment Rheena's horrified eyes-wide stare, her fingers white on the table edge; Shreth's almost comic gape-mouthed incomprehension; Tran's lips climbing into a grin of triumph; the rest of the crew now watching – and many of them already wincing.

He released. Loor flinched his head aside, yelping, and slapped a hand to his ear.

He'd overcompensated for the too narrow post and nicked the lobe.

Tran's grin fell. Rheena jumped from the bench, whooping her joy and relief. Shreth ran to his friend's side and slapped his shoulder in congratulations. Many of the crew gathered round as well, welcoming him to their gang.

In the noise of the celebrations Tran closed on Dorin and brought his pock-marked face up to his. 'So you can hit a post,' he murmured, unnoticed by anyone else. He brought a finger alongside his nose in warning. 'Posts don't fight back.' He turned away, crossed to Loor, and made a big show of slapping his shoulder and tousling his hair once more.

Dorin reflected that if he were Loor, he'd deck the bastard.

Tran eventually raised his arms for silence and the teasing of Loor fell away. He nodded to Rheena as if he were some sort of king granting his noble dispensation. 'Okay,' he admitted, 'maybe I do have a job for you.'

Rheena forced a smile – the most false and sickly one yet.

* * *

This first night of the investment of Heng, Silk was assigned the north wall. His personal preference during such shifts was to pace the length of the walkway throughout the night, always on the move, and thus never at any one predictable location. Since he was

83

no soldier, nor possessed of the least interest in that profession, he left it up to the commanding officers to make any such preparations or accommodations as they deemed necessary for communication.

This time the officer seemed most dutiful. A party of Hengan infantry met Silk at the top of the tower of the north gate. One young fellow doffed his helmet and bowed. 'Lord Silk, I am Captain Glenyllen. Welcome.'

'Thank you, captain.' Silk set off walking at once and though the fellow was startled, he was quick to catch up. The rest of the party – Silk's bodyguard for the evening – trailed behind. 'Any activity?'

'Nothing of note, yet.'

'You'll let me know if there is any, yes?'

'Yes, m'lord.'

'Thank you. No doubt you have responsibilities to attend to. Do not let me delay you.'

The captain swallowed hard, nodding. 'Of course.'

Silk inclined his head to indicate that the meeting was at an end yet the captain continued along beside him. 'Yes?' Silk asked.

The fellow cleared his throat. 'Sir – you were here for prior campaigns, were you not?'

'Yes.'

'The Protectress . . . have you ever seen her, ah, intervene?'

Silk stopped his rapid walk, faced the young man directly. 'No, captain. And pray to all the gods you know that she will never have to.'

The captain bowed again. 'Yes, m'lord.'

'You will use runners.'

'Yes, m'lord.'

Silk set off once more. The captain did not follow, though the bodyguard did, tramping heavily in their armour. Silk knew that before dawn he'd have worn out three or four sets of the footsore troopers.

He kept an eye on the surrounding fields as he paced. They were black as night, as the farmers had burned them all under orders of the Protectress. The Kanese campfires glowed like an arc of stars just outside crossbow range. He wondered what they were burning – had they carted their firewood with them? But Smokey was no doubt far ahead of him on that.

84

The movement of the soldiery was no secret to him. Through his Thyr-enhanced vision every warm-blooded creature out there glowed like a night-worm. This advantage was often interrupted, however, when he came abreast of the torches and lanterns set to light the defences. For the nonce, he was content to watch and wait, wondering what the Kanese king Chulalorn the Third intended for this first night.

His thoughts turned to considerations of hubris and overreach. Not even this one's grandfather, Chulalorn the First, had dared move against Heng. What new advantage or secret weapon might this grandson now possess that he should make the attempt?

Perhaps it was overconfidence. He was fresh from success. All the southlands lay within his grip, and he possessed an army of some thirty thousand veterans flush with victory at his back. Why not reach for the richest prize of central Quon Tali? Why not dominate the centre of the board, able to strike east or west at whim?

Or was he merely testing his limits, as young men were wont to do? Greedily reaching for more and more until their hands were finally slapped aside. And this one had yet to be slapped down. Silk hoped Shalmanat would not be forced to be the one to do so. Not because of the massive loss of life it would no doubt require, but because at present the people of Heng loved and even worshipped her.

He did not want them to fear her.

The probe that Silk knew had to come eventually appeared just after the eighth bell of the night, two before the brightening of the coming dawn. To his vision, its preparations were painfully obvious. The Kanese soldiers, believing themselves unseen, came massing together as all good troopers should. Silk had plenty of time to reach their intended section of wall.

Here he found the highest ranking officer and waved her over. 'Put out all the torches,' he ordered.

The woman's heavy mouth, so typical for a Hengan, drew down. 'What?'

'Put out all the torches here along this reach of wall.'

'Why?'

Silk sighed to calm himself. 'Because an attack's coming.'

'I don't see nothing.'

'That would be because of all the torches, wouldn't it?' Silk said through clenched teeth.

The woman shifted her weight to one hip and cocked her head to study him anew. 'You know,' she drawled, 'you're really cute when you get all huffy like that.'

Silk realized he'd met one of the women – and there were a few of them – who weren't the least bit impressed or mesmerized by him. He let out his breath and relaxed his jaws. 'By order of the Protectress – for whom I speak. Douse the torches.'

The officer slowly nodded. 'Well, when you put it that way . . .' She waved to the guards nearby. The torches and lanterns and braziers started going out all around. 'Whatcha going to do?'

'Stand up on the wall in full view of the entire Kanese army.'

'Ah. You gonna take a dive?'

'No, I'm not going to— Listen . . . what's your name?'

'Lieutenant Veralarathell.'

'Well, lieutenant, you don't seem to be demonstrating proper respect for command.'

The woman nodded her understanding. 'Ah. That's because I'm an engineer.'

'An engineer?'

She leaned closer and lowered her voice, 'A sapper, saboteur, miner—'

'I know what an engineer is!' Controlling his voice, he continued, 'I mean, I didn't know the two were conjoined.'

'Ah. Certainly are, sir. Comes with the papers.'

Silk pressed his fingertips to his brow. 'Well. Fascinating as all this is, I have an attack to thwart and a lesson to give.'

'I am all attention, sir.'

'Very good. When I give the word, order all your command to duck down and close their eyes.'

'Strange way to repel an attack – if I may say so, sir.'

Silk, who had been climbing a merlon, paused, his shoulders hunching. 'Just do it,' he hissed, and carried on. Atop his rather precarious position, the cool night wind buffeting him, he reflected that he had actually rather enjoyed that byplay. At least it was far preferable to the toadying – or contempt – most officers gave him.

He scanned the field and found the Kanese formation. It was close enough. Importantly, he could see them, which meant that they could see him – should there be enough light. And there certainly would be in a moment. More than enough.

He pressed his hands together and concentrated, summoning his Warren. He took his time to gather and amass all the energy he could. The assault force was closing even more slowly now, wary because of the change among the torches and braziers high atop the wall. Silk could barely contain the intense power he held at bay, yammering to burst forth. To wait much longer would mean the consumption of his own flesh to ash.

'Now,' he grated to the lieutenant through his gritted teeth. He gave them three heartbeats to comply then thrust his hands palm out towards the field before the wall.

A burst of white light brighter than any day flooded the field like a solid flow of water. Screams rose from leagues around, and rising calls of panic. He must have blacked out momentarily as hands pulled him down, supporting him. Blinking, he found himself peering up at the lieutenant, who was pressing her forearm to her eyes and blinking as well.

'Could've warned us,' she growled.

'I did.'

'Not too organized in the follow-through, either.'

Silk nodded his rueful acceptance of that. 'Yes, well, I was delayed by an officer who wouldn't shut up.'

'And who saved you from that dive.'

'Do I owe you a date?'

'You owe me a bottle of Untan cherry brandy.'

'Done.'

The officer inclined her head towards the wall where, beyond, cries and panicked shouts continued. 'They won't be back tonight.'

'Nor ever.'

The woman's broad face hardened. 'Never? You mean . . . ever?'

He shrugged a negative. 'No. I'm not that strong. Maybe in a few years some should start getting their sight back.'

Lieutenant Veralarathell's hardened mouth now turned down in distaste. 'Gods, man. Years gone blind?' She studied the dark out beyond the wall. 'Who'll take care of them? How will they provide for themselves?'

For the second time that night Silk raised his gaze to the night sky. What was everyone's problem with expediency these days? 'Please. They're enemy soldiers. They can all stumble into the Idryn and drown for all I care.'

The woman shook her head, now in open disapproval. 'You can keep your brandy, mage. Drink it. Maybe you'll find some human feelings there at the bottom.'

Silk was practised at hiding his feelings. He was insulted to his face every day by those who took one look at him and developed an instant dislike. But for some reason this woman's condemnation stung far deeper than most. As nonchalantly as he could, however, he tipped his head and offered a friendly grin. 'You are dismissed, then, lieutenant.'

The woman gave him her back and walked away.

The urge to report the woman to the commander of the Hengan forces gripped Silk for a moment, but then it passed. Not least because Lord Plyngeth despised him and would probably promote her just for insulting him. Mostly, he simply didn't want her to know she'd gotten under his skin.

Perhaps, instead, he'd tease her about it. When he was once more assigned to the north wall. Which he deemed unlikely to be in the near future. He cast a glance over the crenellations as he walked. His Thyr-enhanced vision revealed the chaos of the stumbling red glow-worm shapes milling about the fields like an overturned anthill.

No, he did not think they would be assaulting the north wall again any time soon.

* * *

After her first night's walk, and her conversation with the city mage Smokey, Iko made it her habit to take the air every evening, sometimes as late as long after the mid-night bell. She was thinking ahead to when it might be helpful to have these Hengans used to her being out wandering the grounds late at night. She'd even struck up a courteous familiarity with the palace guards.

This eve, however, she was not alone. Yvonna was with her. And the sister's grating presence reminded her of another reason why she so often sought the clean fresh air of the night over their crowded quarters with their heated rumours, rivalries, backbiting, and wearying eternal gossip.

And this night the mood of the city surrounding them was different. She'd sensed it immediately. It was, as the saying went, far too quiet; as if by some unspoken agreement all three hundred thousand or so of the city's inhabitants had decided to retreat indoors.

Iko paused on the gravelled garden walkway and strained to listen. Yvonna, meanwhile, was prattling on: 'There's talk about you and your walks, you know,' she announced in her ridiculous, falsely ingratiating way.

Iko frowned – was that a distant roar coming from the south? 'Oh?'

'Yes. Some say . . .' Yvonna paused, waiting. When Iko said nothing she continued, 'Well, perhaps I shouldn't say anything . . .'

Yet you have, you idiot. Iko sighed, rising to the bait. 'What do they say?'

Yvonna leaned closer as she warmed to the subject. 'Well, some . . . and I really shouldn't say who . . .'

Because you're one of them.

'. . . say that you've taken a lover here among the Hengan guards!' The girl laughed gushingly. 'Can you believe that?'

Gods, you're enjoying this, you petty bitch.

'And that your walks are a mere excuse for your assignations—'

'I get it,' Iko cut in. She was squinting off to the south. That was definitely the sound of an attack and the great voice of the giant Koroll answering it. Their brothers and sisters were dying in an assault on the walls of Heng even as this vapid fool twittered on pushing her ugly rumours. For Iko's part, every muscle ached to cut her way out of this palace and storm that wall herself.

'You're not even listening to me!' Yvonna complained. Her revelation was obviously not having the desired effect.

'Is he well hung?' Iko asked.

Yvonna wrinkled her nose in disgust. 'What?'

'My lover. Is he hung like a horse? Because I'd really like it to be worth it.'

Now the nostrils of Yvonna's pointed nose flared angrily. 'Don't you care what everyone thinks?'

'I don't care what idiots think. And we have to report to Hallens, now.' She ran without waiting to see whether her sister-at-arms followed.

She found their quarters a riot of activity. Armed sisters guarded every access and the rest were finishing readying their gear. She crossed to Hallens and bowed. Scanning the preparations, Hallens nodded to indicate that Iko had her attention.

'An attack on the south wall,' Iko reported. 'Do we join them?'

An indulgent smile quirked the tall woman's lips. 'No, Iko.'

'But an unexpected assault from the rear might turn the tide – or we could take a gate and hold it until a relieving party arrived.'

The smile broadened even as other nearby sisters gaped or smirked their astonishment. Their commander merely shook her head. 'These are mere probes, Iko. Chulalorn must test the walls – no . . .' she paused, as was her habit when correcting herself in mid-flow, 'rather, the king must test the Hengans. He must measure the degree of their readiness, yes?'

Iko, who had been clenching her lips against a flow of objections, jerked her head in protest. 'Why then do we prepare to fight?'

Now the older woman's thin lips drew down. 'Other news, Iko. Our sisters found the emissary's chambers empty and went to demand his whereabouts. Word has come that he has gone over to the Protectress. Bought by Hengan gold, no doubt. He has betrayed the trust of the king.'

'We must bring his head to Chulalorn!'

Hallens nodded. 'In time. In time.'

'Why then the preparations?'

'Because we have also been informed that we are now hostages against the siege.'

Iko laughed her scorn. 'We will easily cut our way free!'

Hallens raised her hands for calm. 'Yes. But not now.'

'Why ever not? Now is the time to strike. Before they have adequate guards in place!'

The sisters around them smirked anew at this, some hiding their mouths while others did not even bother. Iko felt her brows crimping in a ferocious frown. What was going on? Had Hallens turned as well? Was she the only one ready to fight?

Hallens invited her aside. 'Let us walk, Iko.'

She now felt the blood drain from her face: dear gods above! She was to be disciplined. In front of everyone she had virtually accused her commander of cowardice and now she was to be kicked down to the lowest of the low.

She hung her head, bowing. 'Yes . . . commander.'

Without, it was quiet. The attacks – probes, as Hallens had it – were over. The air was cool and its touch revived her spirits . . . slightly. 'I apologize,' she murmured once they were alone on the gravel path.

Hallens, so much taller, now cast another of her smiles down upon her. 'For what? For being a Sword-Dancer? No, Iko. You show proper fighting spirit.' She paused, sorting among her words, and Iko braced herself: *Here it comes* . . . 'But you are impetuous. You do not consider the broader strategic picture.'

So her sisters were right to laugh at her! What a fool she must've seemed! She felt her throat clenching in sick self-loathing. 'You will send me down,' she gasped. Her heart burned in her chest with the shame of it.

The woman suddenly turned to her and grasped her shoulders. 'No, Iko. Not at all. If that were true, I would not be out here with you now explaining our situation.'

'You owe me no explanation.'

'But I do.' Hallens released her shoulders to resume her slow measured walk. 'There is a sickness among us, Iko,' she began, haltingly. 'It comes from too much time in the palace, I think. Too many among us now value status and prestige over service, I fear. Who has Chulalorn's momentary favour versus who has not. Or worse – who has the support of the palace functionaries.' She shook her head sadly and her bunched auburn curls brushed her shoulders. 'The bureaucrats, Iko. They will be the death of us . . .' She pinched her eyes as she walked along. 'But I digress. My point is that you seem immune to this political sickness and for that I am glad.'

Iko found she was frowning once more. 'I'm sorry, commander, but I do not understand . . .'

'You will. What bell is it?'

'The second past the mid-night sounding.'

Hallens pinched her eyes again. 'I am not used to these late-night vigils. But you are, yes? How old are you, Iko?'

'Sixteen years.'

Her commander smiled fondly in reminiscence. 'I remember my sixteenth year. When Chulalorn the Second travelled to Dal Hon

91

for the treaty negotiations. I stood guard for two days and nights without relief when all the others fell sick. I fought off seven attempts upon his life.'

'It is legend among us,' Iko answered, hushed.

The woman waved it aside. 'Well . . . Sometimes I wonder whether we shall ever see such days again.' She cleared her throat and scanned the night sky for a time. 'Anyway. They are late.'

Iko was surprised. 'I'm sorry, commander. Who?'

'Those whom I brought you out to meet. The attack must have delayed them.'

Iko peered round at the shadowed gardens. 'But . . . we are in the palace grounds . . .'

Hallens raised a hand for silence. 'Regardless – ah! Here they are.'

Iko peered round once again but saw nothing. Then her hand reflexively flew to the grip of her whipsword as something shifted in the dark. A night-black shape rose before her as if stepping out of the murk itself. Then another dropped from the sky on her left. Stunned, Iko let her hand fall, for she knew these shapes that now surrounded them, or had had them described to her – the way their black clothes seemed to shift and blur. The narrow slits of their eyes. And those eyes as flat and black as deepest night.

Their hidden companion order. The Nightblades of Itko Kan.

One stepped forth. She, or he, inclined a head all wrapped in obscuring layers of jet-black gauze. Hallens answered the small nod as one equal to another. 'What does Chulalorn command?' she enquired.

'You are to remain in place,' answered a man's voice, soft, yet firm.

'How goes the hunting?'

'There is nothing to hunt. The Protectress places too much faith in her mages and has cultivated no other assets. The rooftops are ours to travel as we wish.' The Nightblade extended a hand towards Iko and she was unnerved to see a long thin blade in his grip, its metal blued against any betraying glimmer. 'This was to be a private meeting. Why bring another?'

'This is Iko,' Hallens answered. 'You are to regard her as my second.'

Iko jerked, stunned, only just managing to keep her mouth from falling open. The arm fell. 'Very well. We will bring any further orders.' The Nightblade moved to go.

Iko blurted, 'And Jerruth? The emissary?'

The Nightblade did not even turn round. 'He is nothing. He will be found when the city falls.' Then the man was gone; it was as if he'd dissolved into the night. Many in Itko Kan speculated that these servants to the Chulalorn dynasty were all sorcerers and mages, but Iko had heard that in truth few were, and that plain gruelling training lay behind their rare skills and abilities – just as with hers.

She turned to Hallens, whom she found eyeing her with a playful half-smile pulling at her lips. 'I cannot be your second,' she exclaimed.

'Nonsense. You are my choice. We need your ferocity and dedication. We are trapped behind enemy lines, after all.'

'And what if they should try to disarm us?'

Hallens barked a raucous laugh and started back to their quarters. 'They would be fools to try. No, they dare not touch us. And they believe we wouldn't throw our lives away in an attempt to cut a path through the city. Or that we would be stupid enough to make an attempt upon the Protectress.' She regarded Iko sidelong. 'That's not our job. But,' and she clasped her hands behind her back, 'your point about the gate *is* a rather good one.'

Iko said nothing, understanding the unspoken promise – they would see action. Eventually, they would be unsheathed.

Chapter 5

WORD ON THEIR FIRST JOB CAME TO RHEENA AND DORIN the next night. They were hanging around the corner of an alleyway, lounging and eyeing the touts, marks, courtesans, clients, and those simply out enjoying the night air as they passed back and forth in this section of the Outer Round. It was what Dorin could only describe as 'loitering'. Truth was, they were of course advertising their presence, and, more important, keeping any other crew from moving into that section of territory.

He reflected that much of this belonging to a gang consisted of standing about waiting for something to happen. Very different from his previous apprenticeship. That sour old man hadn't allowed him one hour of time to himself. Here, it seemed that just showing up counted for much of what was expected of them.

Word came via one of Tran's young street beggars. They were told to get down to the riverside straight away. The wording implied that they were already late; Rheena raised her eyes to the night sky and pushed herself from the wall. She waved Dorin onward. 'C'mon. Mister high-and-mighty's all testy tonight.'

Shreth and Loor followed along. Dorin noted that the mutual teasing and joking was gone between them, along with any resentment towards him. Both now carried themselves with a serious watchful air, as if they were bodyguards, or hired muscle.

'Why do you put up with him?' Dorin asked as they threaded the crowds of the night market.

'Who? Tran?'

'Yes.'

Her shrug was fatalistic. 'He's Pung's chosen man. No going against Pung. He'll boil your balls, that one will.'

94

'Will we see him?'

She shot him a disbelieving glance. 'Pung? Whatever for?'

Dorin kept his features flat. 'I want to show him what I can do.'

Rheena laughed. 'You can be sure he's heard! Everything gets reported. He has informants everywhere.'

Dorin was quiet for a time. In truth, he hadn't considered that. The man may even have paid informants and spies among Urquart's gang. Good thing none of them had ever seen him – except Rafall. Now that he was seeing more of the world, reflecting on Tran's leadership, or pathetic lack thereof, it occurred to him that such shortcomings might not be all that rare in every walk of life – especially those of the black market and thievery. Individuals who had failed at every other calling, or proved themselves appallingly unreliable, tended to tumble down into the alleyways of the night market as their last option: the addicts, the hopelessly indebted, the serial liars, the foolish, the deluded, the lazy, and the just plain dim.

The grim reality on the street was proving far removed from the jongleurs' and troubadours' tales of roguish grinning thieves with hearts of gold. It was a calling, he decided, far too romanticized, and in actual truth full of damaged broken people. And, in the end, in no way admirable. Just rather shabby, seedy, sad – and violent.

And what did that say about him? Here Dorin clenched his jaws and let a hard breath out of his nose. *He* was no thief. He'd never stolen anything. He'd picked up a few things from that ruined merchants' caravan, but they'd been dead. He was paid for his talents. It was not a job or work. It was his calling. He realized, then, that he didn't even consider what he did business. Rheena and these others, he knew, were in it for the coin. They wanted to get rich. Preferably as quickly and easily as possible.

Money, however, held no fascination for him. He was a craftsman. He was interested only in the perfection of his skills.

In silence, they reached the wharf. Torches and lanterns on poles lit the waterfront. Rheena led, walking past barge after barge until she reached the one that not coincidentally was the boat with the largest gang of crew hanging about. Here an older, bearded and pot-bellied fellow sauntered over, pointing a finger. 'Late as usual, Red.'

'Busy, Bruneth,' she replied, airily.

'Busy my arse. You don't even know what work is.' The fellow cast an eye over Shreth, Loor, and lastly Dorin. He snorted his disbelief. 'If it ain't mister famous knife thrower. Where we're going none of your fancy-pants tricks are gonna impress anyone, okay?'

Dorin raised an eyebrow. Rheena waved Bruneth off and jumped down to the barge, sat back against a crate, and stretched out her legs. 'So let's get going.'

Bruneth grumbled darkly into his beard, but waved to the lounging crew. The lines were slipped, poles unshipped, and the barge started downriver with the slow current.

Shreth and Loor produced a set of dice and set to whiling away the time. Members of the crew, all Tran's men and women, drifted over to join them. Rheena had closed her eyes, apparently dozing, or making a great show of it to impress everyone. Bruneth had gone to stand next to the man handling the broad tiller oar at the rear of the barge. Curious, Dorin walked the narrow aisles between the piled crates and barrels of cargo.

Some had been carelessly broken open, perhaps by Bruneth's people, to verify their contents. Dorin looked in and was surprised to see bundled arrows, weapons, coils of rope, and military supplies and materiel. The barrels held salted meat and other such preserved foodstuffs.

Dorin went to Rheena, touched her foot. 'These are all taken from the city guard depot.'

She shrugged. 'Oh?'

'There's a siege on, you know. Food is already rationed.'

She hadn't yet opened her eyes. 'Look. If some crates fall off the back of a wagon, who's the wiser? We're gonna get paid for it, aren't we?'

'But you're undermining the city defences—'

Rheena cracked one eye. 'Gods, Dorin. I swear. Don't act like you just arrived with the turnip cart. Where do you think this stuff comes from? Everybody does it. Why shouldn't we get some of the action?'

He considered her answer. Yes, why should he care? Who was the Protectress to him? No one. Why then did this grate so? Then

96

he had it. It was not a question of one ruler over another, the Hengans or the Kanese. It was that right now men and women were putting their lives at risk to shield him and *this* was how he was repaying them? And for what? A handful of greasy coins? The meanness of it turned his stomach. He thought it . . . well, beneath him.

They passed beneath the arch of the outer wall over the Idryn. No city guards called down and no crossbow bolts flew. Either the guards didn't care if someone *left* the city, or they'd been paid to look the other way.

Downstream they came to a wooded turn of the river and here Bruneth ordered them to the southern shore. As they approached, a narrow light shone from among the trees, blinking on and off. 'Ready lines,' Bruneth hissed. 'Throw!'

The crew heaved the lines to the wooded shore. Dark shapes moved to gather them up and soon they were being drawn in. The side of the barge scraped up against the man-tall mud cliff that was the southern riverside.

'Who's there?' Bruneth demanded of the dark.

'No names, I think,' a man answered, letting himself down to the timbers. Amid the murk, Dorin glimpsed a flash from metal armour and the fittings of a sword sheath. Other shapes moved amid the cover of the treed cliff-top.

By the sleeping goddess – they were selling to the Kanese! Well, he decided, mentally shrugging. Who else would be in need of military supplies?

'Start unloading,' the newcomer called up to the trees.

Bruneth huffed his objection. 'Payment first.'

'Of course,' the fellow – an officer? – answered smoothly.

Over the rush of the river and the night wind rustling through the tree boughs, the sound of a crossbow being ratcheted touched Dorin's ear. He casually crossed over to Rheena and took her arm, drawing her to the barge's side. 'This looks very bad,' he murmured.

She shook off his hand, vexed. 'I told you – we're bein' paid for it.'

'I think we are,' he answered, darkly. 'At the first sign of trouble, jump over the side.'

She eyed him as if he were drunk. 'What? I can't swim.'

'Hang on to the side.'

'Where is it, then?' Bruneth grumbled again.

'Coming. Ah!' The dark shapes, armoured soldiers, handed down a set of saddlebags. The officer passed them over. They were obviously very heavy. Bruneth knelt to open them and the officer backed away from him as he did so.

Shit was all Dorin managed before multiple crossbow bolts slammed into Bruneth. Dorin pushed Rheena over the side and ducked as further bolts raked the barge deck. He dodged to where Loor and Shreth had leaped behind the cover of some barrels, their eyes white all round in the dark. Bruneth's crew started firing back. The officer had drawn his longsword and was calmly closing on the nearest crewman.

'Jump!' Dorin snarled.

'Can't swim,' Loor stammered back.

Furious, Dorin simply grabbed the two by their shirts and dragged them to the side and heaved them over. 'It's shallow here!' he hissed after them.

He turned round to find himself staring directly at the Kanese officer. He retreated up an aisle between piled crates, drawing his heaviest fighting knives. The man advanced, then lunged, swinging. Dorin edged aside the blow, sending the sword blade slamming into a crate. To the surprise of both, it jammed there. The officer yanked on the hilt. Dorin darted forward and sank his knife into the officer's neck just behind the chin-strap of his helmet. The man froze. Their eyes met. In the fellow's gaze Dorin saw the despairing recognition that he was dead and there was nothing he could do about it.

The officer sank to his knees. Dorin moved on past him. He rounded a roped heap of barrels, heading for the side, only to flinch down as a flurry of crossbow bolts slammed into the lashed timbers ahead. Cursing, he backed away to find cover on the side away from shore. The barge rocked beneath his feet as numerous soldiers jumped down to it. He sensed the odds slipping steadily away from him but kept his head, crawling behind cover to search for another way to the side. He pulled himself over dead and dying members of Bruneth's crew, all punched through by multiple bolts. The living called to him and he silently cursed them for giving away his position.

Soldiers rounded the aisle ahead, spotted him. There was nothing for it now. He charged, blades readied. Surprised, the lead soldier snapped up his crossbow. He shot too early and the bolt struck just ahead of Dorin's feet.

Then he was among them, knives swinging. He had the advantage in the constricted alley and went for swift killing blows, slicing exposed necks, faces, and throats. The fourth and last soldier of this group he held up as a shield between himself and the shore. The moment he stopped moving bolts began thumping into the corpse and the crates about him. He started shuffling clumsily towards the nearest side.

Before he made it, another clutch of soldiers reached him. These charged with longswords. He heaved the corpse on to the first, entangling him, and closed with the rest. Cursing him, the two at the back dropped their swords – useless in such close combat – and went for their knives. Dorin trapped the sword blade of the nearest and counter-thrust up into the groin. The man went down with a shriek. The second obviously fancied himself some sort of duellist as he held two longswords. Dorin lured him into crossing them then pushed forward, trapping the blades between them. He whipped a knife across the fellow's throat then turned away just in time to parry knife attacks from the last two.

These proved experienced veterans. Each fought with two gauches. Dorin found himself on the defensive, parrying four blades. They forced him back down the aisle and out past his cover. Crossbow bolts smacked into the barrels and crates about him.

Snarling, he pressed forward against the far heavier and armoured soldiers. This would not do. He'd trained in fighting up to eight opponents at a time. Two would not get the better of him! Feinting, he tricked one into committing ahead of the other and this one he kept busy and in the way of the second. He knew he could take him but the question was how best to do it.

There was no time to be pretty about it – even now the barge rocked beneath new boots – so Dorin took the first opening he had to thrust a blade straight in the throat and kicked the man backwards on to his friend. The two went down in a tangle. Crouching, Dorin stitched the second at groin, stomach and neck in quick succession then ran for the side.

Soldiers yelled behind. Bolts hissed the air. He jumped, rolled, and tumbled over the edge into the murky warm Idryn.

The Kanese fired into the water for some time before eventually giving up. Torch-wielding search parties scoured the nearby shore, but by then Dorin had pulled himself along through the mud and weeds and grass at the river's edge until he resembled just another heap of muck.

He moved slowly, sliding himself along by tugging at the roots of the stalks about him. Once he judged he'd gone far enough he slithered up the mud slope and entered the woods, confident that his training would allow him to avoid detection. At a sound he paused, listening. Bracken and dry branches broke to the north. He closed on the noise, knives readied.

It was Loor, stumbling through the dark. Dorin moved quickly, before the lad's fumbling could alert any Kanese. The lad jumped as he appeared and he barely had time to slap a hand across his mouth before he shouted his surprise.

'What are you doing?' he hissed into Loor's ear. He released his mouth.

'Looking for you,' the lad answered – not quietly enough.

'Make for the river gate, you fool.'

'Shreth's wounded. Rheena's with him.'

Dorin clamped his lips shut. *Damn this night to Hood's dark laughter! Oponn must be howling.* 'Lead the way,' he snarled.

Allowing Loor to go ahead, Dorin soon realized, was a mistake. The lad was completely lost. Dorin finally took hold of his shoulder and forced him to a halt. Loor drew breath to speak but Dorin silenced him, listening.

It had surprised him how easily the Kanese had given up the search. Now that he listened to the night noises of the woods, chilled to the bone as his sodden clothes wicked away his body heat, it came to him that perhaps they weren't supposed to be here any more than he. That possibility allowed him to relax just a touch, and let himself breathe more deeply.

'Where did you leave her?' he asked, his voice low.

'The river bank.'

'Okay. This way.'

After reaching the river's edge he doubled back, thinking that the wounded Shreth hadn't gotten this far. They found them lying in the water. Rheena was holding Shreth's chin up above the surface as he lay on top of her. Dorin drew him up the mud slope. He was awake but weak with blood loss; he'd taken a bolt in the leg and another had gouged his scalp. Both wounds still bled badly. Dorin set to binding the leg then wrapped the youth's head. He and Loor walked him through the woods, an arm over each of their shoulders. Shreth kept blacking out but there was nothing they could do for that.

Dorin kept finding Rheena staring at him. 'What is it?' he finally asked.

'You killed them soldiers,' she said, awed. 'All of them. I saw.'

'Not all of them.'

She turned away. 'Stupid Tran and his dumb deals. Pung's going to hear about this, I tell you.'

'I'm sure he will,' Dorin said grimly. Who else arranged for the theft of those goods, after all?

'What're we gonna do?' Loor whined, breathless.

'If we can make it to the river gate before dawn, I can get you in.'

'Okay,' Rheena answered with a fierce nod. 'We'll make it. Let's go.'

In the last hour before dawn, Dorin swam them one by one through the river gate. Shreth was now unconscious, his breathing shallow. Dorin eased him into the flow and drew him along on top of him, swimming on his back, a hand under Streth's chin. If the Idryn had had any stronger current it would have been impossible to manage.

Pre-dawn fishermen on the easternmost dock were astonished that morning as three bedraggled, filthy and sodden figures climbed up the bank, lifted a fourth member of their party, and staggered up the dock leaving behind clots of river mud and a trail of wet tracks.

Being such a sight, they kept to the back alleys as much as possible, Dorin and Loor carrying Shreth between them. As they neared Tran's territory, Dorin slowed, wondering just what he should do. The idea of entering the man's headquarters and being surrounded by his crew did not appeal. It would be too much like surrendering – especially after such a disaster.

Rheena cast him an irritated glare, hissed, 'What is it?'

He stopped, and Loor had no choice but to stop with him. 'I don't think you should go back to Tran.'

She gaped at him, peered round as if asking for witness to his idiocy. 'Why ever not?'

'He'll have to blame someone for this failure, Rheena. And if

101

none of Bruneth's people got away, you're the likely candidate.'

She laughed. 'He can blame me all he wants. Truth is, he's the one in charge. It's on his head.'

Dorin frowned a negative. 'He'll offer you up in his place – make up some damned lie. Accuse you of cutting a deal with the Kanese. Anything to squirm out of the blame.'

She was shaking her head now, her muddied mass of frizzy, mud-streaked hair hanging lopsided. 'Don't do this. If you run, you're the mark. Pung will hunt you down.'

He gently lowered Shreth. 'You can blame me. Say I blew the deal.'

'We'd never—' Loor began, but Dorin cut him off.

'You'll do whatever you have to do to live! Okay, Loor?' The lad actually looked hurt by Dorin's vehemence, but he nodded, biting his lip. Dorin turned to Rheena. 'See you around.'

She was glaring, hands on hips, but her eyes were wet. 'Fine. Go ahead. I *will* blame you, then. You dumb asshole!'

Dorin bowed, dipping his head. 'Take care.' He jogged off the way they had come.

From behind him, up the alley, came a last shout, '*Damn you!*'

* * *

Silk had never before been asked to attend the Protectress during one of her interviews, and so when the request came he was quite surprised, and a touch curious. As ordered, he entered the audience chamber only to find it empty. Nonplussed, he halted, staring about. Did he have the hour wrong?

A palace retainer came padding up the hall towards him and bowed. Rather distracted, Silk hardly gave him any attention. 'Yes?'

'The Protectress requests your presence at the Inner Focus.'

Now Silk turned. The Inner Focus? Truly? He'd only been there once before. Since when was Shalmanat interviewing within her most private sanctum? He started at once for the doors that were guarded day and night.

As he approached up the hallway the guards stamped their spears and opened the door. Bright white daylight glared, momentarily blinding Silk as he advanced. The door shut behind him. Blinking, he was just able to make out the broad circular chamber, unadorned, and the figure seated at the very centre. He started forward; the heels of his fine leather boots resounded rather loudly on the white marble floor. Reaching the middle, he bowed to Shalmanat who was seated on her private chair – not the white stone monstrosity of the audience chamber meant to impress the gullible. Rather, the slim woman was seated on a plain leather camp stool. The sort that might stand next to any fireside across the Seti Plains.

She was dressed as usual in her long linen shirt and trousers. But there was a sternness about her eyes this day. Silk bowed. 'M'lady.'

She gestured to her right. 'Stand here, please, Silk. I will be interviewing a very . . . special . . . sorceress today. I would like your impressions afterwards.'

Silk bowed once more, now very curious indeed. 'Of course, m'lady.' He moved to Shalmanat's right. The woman brushed back her long pale hair in a gesture Silk would almost have named nervous, then clapped her hands. The door grated open.

A single unprepossessing figure entered the chamber. Silk was first struck by her very plain unremarkableness. If Shalmanat had not described her as special, he would have passed her on the street without a second glance. Yet he noticed that she did not pause or blink as she entered the glare of the chamber, but walked forward unhesitatingly.

As she closed, Silk's earlier impression was reinforced. Her clothes were cheap and rumpled, and her night-dark hair was poorly cut and in a tangle as if she'd been camping roughly these last days. Her feet and sandals were caked in dried mud. It seemed to him that she was strangely negligent of her appearance, especially for such an important audience. But it was her face that caught his attention. He would have thought her ugly were her features not so very odd indeed. The face was broad and flat, the eyes strangely far apart, the lips thick and downturned, as if always clenched in a grim line.

The woman halted a discreet distance off and bowed to Shalmanat, as was proper. 'Protectress,' she began, 'my thanks for this audience.'

Shalmanat answered the bow with the slightest of nods. 'It is my duty.' She indicated Silk. 'One of my city mages: Silk.' The woman flicked her dark eyes to him and the power of her gaze struck him

103

like a hammer blow to his brow. He swallowed, quite shaken, and inclined his head. Shalmanat asked, 'And you are?'

As if caught off guard by the question, the woman tilted her head, pursing her lips. 'You may call me Lady Night.'

Shalmanat nodded graciously. 'Very well, Lady Night. What can we in Heng do for you?'

'I ask permission to reside here for a time. Pursuing my . . . research.'

'We welcome all scholars and magi. May I ask as to the nature of your research?'

She tilted her head once more, quite obviously searching for words. At last, she allowed, 'It involves the nature of the Warrens.'

'How very esoteric.' The Protectress leaned forward ever so slightly. 'Such as?'

Shrugging, the woman reached into the folds of her shirt and produced a card that was about the size of her hand. It was of the sort one might find in any set of the divinatory Deck of Dragons. She let it fall to the polished marble flags between them, face up. It was blank.

The Protectress raised her gaze. 'A blank card. How very interesting.'

Lady Night invited her to take it. 'Feel it.'

Shalmanat gestured to Silk, who picked it up. He pressed a hand to it, summoned his Warren powers, and was astonished when the card answered, turning chill to his touch. He turned his wondering gaze to Shalmanat. 'It is awake – yet unresolved.'

The Protectress's brows rose, impressed. She looked to Lady Night. 'There has been chaos among the talents of late . . .'

Silk had heard of no such disquiet, but the cards and readings held no interest for him, so he would be the last person to know of it.

Shalmanat had extended a hand to the door, indicating an end to the audience. 'You are of course welcome to pursue your research, Lady Night. Good luck in it.'

The woman bowed, and, in an odd mistake of etiquette, simply turned and walked away. Silk watched her go, one eyebrow raised.

When the door shut behind the sorceress, Shalmanat turned to him, cocking her head. 'Well?'

Silk blew out a breath. 'I don't know what to make of her. For the life of me, I can't even place her background. Is she of distant Genabackis?'

'She is from very far away indeed,' Shalmanat answered, as if speaking to herself. Studying the door, she murmured, 'I will not fool myself into thinking that she has failed to take my measure. But what I will suspect is that she is not aware that I know of her.' She swung her gaze to Silk. 'Keep an eye on her, but on no account must you confront her, you understand?'

Silk bowed. 'As you so order.'

'Very well. I could hardly refuse *her* entry, but I'll not remain ignorant of her intent.' She stood abruptly, started for the door. 'And what of the siege?'

Silk stumbled after her. 'Ah – settling in for the long game. Spies report steady convoys of resupply from the south.'

'And their mage corps?'

'Thin, at best. Which surprises me, given Itko Kan's reputation as a breeding ground of talent.'

Shalmanat nodded her thoughtful agreement. 'Yes. It may be that our King Chulalorn the Third is holding out on us.'

Silk considered that. With the walls effectively stalemating the military, Kan would have to have another option, else would not have come at all. The obvious choice would be a cadre of mages to match Heng's own. But none of them had sensed any such gathering. 'Perhaps some secret gambit,' he offered.

She was nodding. 'Yes. You will look into this?'

Silk bowed. 'Yes, Protectress.'

As for their new visitor – she hadn't reacted to him in the least. Indeed, after that first glance, it had been as if he hadn't existed at all. As they exited the Inner Focus, he wondered whether he was losing his touch.

* * *

Not knowing what to do, or where to go, Dorin wandered the streets as dawn's light came crawling down the inner walls and hawkers began shouting their morning meals. His feet eventually led him to Ullara's family establishment, and, having no better option, he climbed hidden from sight in the back alleyway and ducked through the open gable.

105

At his entrance, the usual crowd of predatory birds shifted uneasily and shook their wings. A few let out piercing calls as they studied him from over their curved razor beaks. Perhaps they knew his scent or appearance, for they quickly settled back down again – at least not one of them went for his neck.

He sat heavily on a box, sank his head into his hands, and considered weeping.

Tears would not come. But the self-loathing would not stop. *Failure! Idiot! Even imbecilic Tran has managed to advance! What have you accomplished?*

Escaped an ambush, yes – while emerging as the prime candidate for the failure. And now he was no closer to Pung . . . much further away, in fact.

The trapdoor opened. Dorin recognized the sounds of Ullara's movements. The scent of tea and fresh-baked bread made his mouth water. Sighing, he raised his eyes past his fingers.

She sat on the box opposite, her feet tucked up under her skirts, regarding him, chin in hands. A tray with tea and bread rested among the straw on the boards between them.

'How did you know I was here?' he asked.

'The birds – that is, I heard them.'

'Well . . . thank you.' He studied the steam rising from the tea.

'You look terrible.'

He examined his mud-streaked hands, his torn and filthy shirt and trousers, now stiff and stinking of the river. 'Yes. I do.'

'What happened?'

He rubbed his hands over his face. Flakes of dried mud fell like tears. He sighed again. 'Nothing's going the way I imagined it would.'

'Nothing ever does.'

Words of wisdom from a child. Well, isn't that the old saying?

He picked up the cup of tea, sipped, regarded her over its rim. 'Why are you being so kind to me?'

The girl blushed furiously, looking away. She reached over and ran a hand down the chest of a tasselled eagle, one far from its home on the south savannahs. A bird big enough to consider her a meal. 'I take care of all my orphans.'

'Well, my thanks.'

'What isn't going the way you expected?'

'Everything. These small-minded locals! No one seems to want my talents. There's no room for me. Everything's taken or spoken for.'

She shrugged her bony shoulders. 'Of course all the good roosts are taken – that's why they're taken. No one's going to give one away.'

A half-smile pulled at his lips from this bird-logic. But he supposed it was true. He took a mouthful of bread. 'Well . . . I tried to take one and it went poorly. Now this town's ruined for me. I'll have to move on. I think I'll try Unta. They say the pickings are rich there. At least the wine is better.'

'What makes you think it'll be any different there?'

He slowed in his chewing, swallowed hard. 'I suppose I'll have to go and find out.'

She said nothing but he saw how tightly her thin pale lips were clenched. He motioned to a nearby brown falcon, its right wing obviously broken. 'What happens to your orphans after they are healed?'

At first she would not look up, but her lips quirked and she rolled her eyes. 'They fly away.'

'Yes, they do.'

'But not all!' and she buried her face in the eagle's chest, wrapping her arms round it. Over her head, it seemed to glare down its beak at him. He was amazed to see her lack of concern for the murderous scimitar-like weapon poised directly above her.

'I have one last job to do tonight. Money for the journey.'

'Then you will come to say goodbye?' she asked from within the downy white chest feathers.

'Yes.'

'You swear?'

'Yes. I swear I will say goodbye before I go.'

She pulled away from the eagle's breast, wiped her nose on her arm, sniffing. 'All right, then. Tonight.'

He stood, finished his tea. 'Thank you.'

'You could sleep here – I mean, if you wished.'

'Thank you, but I need to prepare. I will see you later.' He crossed to the gable.

'You promise?' she called, and he nodded as he let himself down.

Alone, Ullara turned to the eagle. She set her hands on her slim hips. The fierceness of her gaze matched the bird's. She pointed to another, larger, gable opening. 'Gather them all,' she told it.

The great eagle raised its beak and let go its shrill hunting call, then spread its wings and swooped through the aperture, disappearing.

*

Dorin washed in a public bath on the river shore, then rested in one of the small rooms he'd rented around the city – rents he could no longer afford to maintain. He drew out his gear and dressed very slowly and deliberately. First went on his lightweight armoured vest, which now bore loops for more than twenty weapons, then a dark padded undershirt and thin dark trousers. He selected twelve matched daggers of various weights and dimensions, and coils of graded weights of wire and cotton rope. Some of these he wrapped round his arms, others round his waist. He pulled on lightweight leather shoes, soled in hemp cord, then wrapped his legs in cloth swathings and leather strapping. Through the leather went half the daggers; the rest he sheathed in his two baldrics. Into tiny pockets hidden about his shirt and trousers and vest went small vials and packets of various chemicals and unguents. Pitch for his fingertips; charcoal for his face; dust that could be blown into a pursuer's path to sting their eyes, and another that caused uncontrollable coughing.

Throughout, his old master's scornful impatient voice battered him: *Should've stretched first, boy! When's the last time you practised with those knuckle-blades? You're right leg's stiff – took a hit last night, did you? Remember to compensate. Why not the climbing hooks? Too good for them, are we?*

He could almost feel the beating of the bamboo switch across his shoulders and back. Of course the strikes had hardly hurt at all, the ancient fellow had been so infirm. It was his pride that was wounded.

Yes, I should've stretched, and yes, I shouldn't go out on two consecutive nights. And yes, I haven't been practising enough lately . . .

Resting on his knees, he tested the edge and ease of draw of each weapon. Satisfied, he threw on a loose shapeless overshirt and a hooded cloak, then went to the open window and swung himself up on to the roof. The sun was just setting. Its amber beams still struck the city's single tall tower, above the central palace.

Crouched, Dorin padded off for the section of the Inner Round known as the Street of the Gods.

When he neared the precinct, he took to the narrow back streets. These proved mostly residential, peppered with the occasional temple or shrine to some foreign or lesser known god or spirit. Shops catered to the worship and upkeep of the temples: candle-makers, funerary houses, dealers in rare aromatic woods and spices for incense and embalmment.

After some searching, he found a vantage point on the decorated roof of a temple to the hoary old beast gods. He knelt between the tall stone boar of Fener, god of war and ferocity, and a rough like-ness of Togg, the wolf god of winter. Across the way and up a few decrepit buildings lay the plain run-down abandoned mausoleum that everyone in Heng knew held a newly consecrated temple to Hood, the ancient god of death himself.

Its door was open, its threshold dark and empty. Even the street before it lay empty of all traffic. This surprised Dorin, as dusk was a traditional time of worship for acolytes of Hood. Then he had his answer as he spotted a gang of thugs turning away anyone heading in that direction.

Intrigued, he went to the back of the roof, let himself down, and circled round to approach the main street from an alleyway. Here he waited until one such person passed by, when he called from the shadows: 'Friend! I am come to bow before the Great Hooded One, yet I find myself turned away. What is the meaning of this?'

This fellow halted, gestured back up the way. 'Hunh. The fools. Criminals feuding with the true servant within. Imagine! Picking a feud with Hood! He will visit them for their irreverence, I tell you.'

Criminals? This is Pung's territory . . . 'Thank you, friend.' Dorin circled back to his vantage point and settled in for the night to deepen.

Shortly before the mid-night bell, the gang, carrying torches, came up the street and faced the mausoleum. Swords out, four tentatively edged their way forward into the dark opening. A moment later came the sound of blows taken and four bodies rolled out, one after the other, on to the street.

'Come out, y'damned coward!' shouted the leader of the gang.

Not bloody likely. Not when you have to go in to get him.

'Fine!' The gang leader gestured curtly and his crew threw

objects that crashed on the threshold. After this came torches, and flames flickered to life in the open doorway.

What good is that, Dorin wondered? It's made of stone. Maybe they mean to smoke him out.

The leader then browbeat more of his gang into charging the doorway. They leaped the dying flames and in the light the defender met them. His blows were clean and efficient. All went down. Two fell in the flames and caught fire, screaming before unconsciousness took them.

All this Dorin watched with care, especially the man's astonishing speed. But what truly surprised him was the fact that he knew him. The firelight had revealed a slim dark lad with black hair. It was that caravan guard who claimed to have fought Ryllandaras out upon the Seti Plains. Dorin now wondered if perhaps he truly had. In which case, he supposed he'd have to be damned wary of him.

The thugs pulled their fallen fellows out of the remains of the fire and beat out the flames. Their leader cursed and stamped about. More flammables were thrown at the mausoleum, to similar non-effect. Dorin eased himself down to sit them out. They yelled insults, threatened the fellow, cursed him up and down, threw rocks, fired arrows, and finally resorted to heaving garbage into the dark opening.

Silence answered them. *The silence of the grave*, Dorin mouthed to himself, smirking.

Pung's siege appeared to be proceeding as successfully as that of the Kanese.

Finally, tired and frustrated, the useless street muscle wandered off. Dorin gave it a few minutes longer, then rose up to study the stone door, now soot-blackened. Nothing moved that he could see. Considering that, he drew out a slim packet of greased paper, opened it, and touched a fingertip to the balm within. He dabbed the fingertip to his eyes, blinking at the sting of it. Slowly, the night brightened about him. The effect would linger for about two hours. He moved to the rear and let himself down.

The problem with mausoleums, he reflected, was that they had only one entrance. The dead, it seemed, had no use for windows or back doors. Because of this, he was forced to come sidling up one wall and edge along the front to approach the opening. At least his enhanced night vision showed the threshold empty of any lurking swordsman. Still, the fellow could be waiting just inside, sword raised. Unhappy with the necessity of it, Dorin drew his two heaviest fighting knives. Holding one to parry high and the other low, he slipped round one jamb to hug the wall just inside.

No figure lunged, swinging. He slid along until he reached the inner corner of the main hall. He felt the openings of funerary sconces against his back, each sporting a grinning ancestor. The balm allowed him to see more lining each wall. Of the lad, he detected no hint. At the far end of the hall he could just make out some sort of shrine. Distant pillars there looked to provide the only interior cover. A figure sat slumped up against the shrine – not the swordsman, though: too old and skinny. The priest no doubt. His target.

A quick in and out, then. Dash in, strike, dash out. He silently exchanged one of the knives for his longest and thinnest stabbing dagger. Crouched, he edged forward one careful step at a time, silently cursing the tiny shards of ceramic his foot accidentally brushed, and the tossed debris he had to take such care to step round.

He reached the figure without hearing any betraying noise of movement elsewhere in the mausoleum. The old man's head hung in sleep. He knelt to thrust the blade straight in through the chest, then paused. His breath left him in a long exhalation of wonder and he let his hand fall.

From behind, a longsword's blade kissed the side of his neck. 'You do not strike,' the lad said.

'I see there is no need.'

'You see truly.'

With great care, Dorin sheathed his blades then extended his arms, hands empty. 'I am done, then.'

The blade held firm, cold, and so sharp Dorin felt it cut his neck with every slight move he made. 'You are not here for me?' the lad asked.

'The priest was my target.'

'So you claim now.'

'Were I after you, I would have edged round the sides to flush you out.'

The weapon held for three more heartbeats, then withdrew. 'True. That is what I would have done.'

Hands still straight out, Dorin very slowly turned to face the lad who held his blade readied between them.

111

The youth scowled, recognizing him in turn. 'You. The one who cares nothing for the dead.'

'The dead care nothing for me.'

'How would you know?'

'How would you?'

The blade's keen point lurched forward a touch, but stilled. 'You are lucky, little back-stabber, that I have a use for you.'

'I've stabbed no one in the back.'

'Yet that is what assassins do.'

'Back-stabbings, betrayals, ambushes and poisonings are many. Some call these assassinations – we do not.'

'Hunh. A discriminating murderer. You also deal in trivial hair-splitting, I see.'

Dorin looked to the ceiling. 'Kill me or let me go. But please do not torture me with your chatter.'

The blade was once more at Dorin's neck, and he blinked. *No one is that fast.*

'You will return to your pathetic masters and give your report. Perhaps then they will leave us alone.'

Dorin realized that the fellow assumed he worked for Pung. Disgusted, he drew a sharp breath to deny the charge but then clamped his lips against saying anything. Naturally, he was not allowed to betray any confidence regarding his employers. So he merely tipped his head in a stiff nod of agreement.

The fellow smoothly slipped aside to allow him out.

Dorin circled round, keeping his face to the swordsman, and keeping his arms out. He backed towards the entrance. As he retreated he glimpsed a dark bundle of ragged blankets up against one wall, and, from within, the face of a small girl, her dark eyes watching. The child from the caravan.

Surprising, and damned macabre, but what else might this fellow do with ... what, his sister? Daughter? He returned his attention to the swordsman. 'You have quite the rich scam here, friend. Good luck with it.'

'Scam? There are no scams, lies, or deceits when one stands before Hood.'

Dorin slipped outside. Jogging off, he raised his eyes to the night sky once more. *Gods, the fellow actually seems to believe the patter. But then, maybe that's what really sells it.*

In the darkness of the mausoleum the swordsman eased out of his ready stance, released a hissed calming breath. Too good by half, that one. Hard to let him go.

The rubbish and flakes of ash scattered about the flags stirred then, a wind hissing among the lingering embers, raising a glow. A noise that might have been no more than that wind murmured, *I saw your temptation. Your forbearance is noted, servant. That one knows it not, but he serves as well.*

The lad fell to one knee before the slumped figure. 'As you say, master.'

'Who are you talking to?' the child asked.

'No one. Try to sleep. It is safe now. I promise you.'

*

Dorin reached the appointed rooftop after the mid-night bell but paced there anyway, hoping his employers would not care too much for punctuality. After waiting two bells his patience was rewarded by the brushing of cloth from one side of the flat expanse, and the fop straightened up. The fellow adjusted his shirt and trousers.

Dorin stilled himself, listening for any others.

Tiles shifted from the opposite edge and the wrestler reared up there. Dorin noted they were on either side of him. He drew two mid-weight throwing blades, called, 'Close enough.'

The fop bowed. His smile glimmered bright in the moonlight. 'What news?' he asked.

'The priest is dead.'

The fop brushed at his silk jacket. 'Really? What proof do you bring?'

This threw Dorin for an instant until he waved a hand in dismissal. 'No one takes the heads any more.'

'Then how can we know?'

'Because I say so, and my word as a professional should be good enough.'

This maddening fellow now studied his fingernails. 'Do you have any references?'

Dorin extended a blade to each of them. *Should've taken half in advance.* 'I'm not the thief here.'

The fop just waved to his cohort who started forward, hands

out, in a wrestler's advance. Dorin was puzzled once more. Did this fellow really think he could just walk up and grapple him? Unsettled, he shifted, retreating across the rooftop. 'What is this? I'm the one who should be stalking you.'

'Your time in the city is over, little night-blade,' said the fop. 'We're here to send you on your way. Go, and live. Stay . . . and die.'

Run? Run from these two? He could take them. Still, their manner unnerved him. He started angling his retreat over towards the fop. The man raised his hands as if straightening his jacket, but Dorin's teachings from his old master included typical preparatory gestures from the main Warrens, and he recognized a Thyr summoning of power. He threw up an arm over his eyes.

Blazing pink-tinged light struck him almost physically. For a flash of an instant he thought he glimpsed the length of his ulna through the flesh of his forearm. Then starry shimmering darkness. He was blind.

He spun, but not quickly enough, as burly arms closed round him in a crushing embrace, yanking him from his feet. Mages! Damned mages always caused him such trouble! His arms were clenched to his sides but a number of hidden pockets remained in reach. He chose one, twisted, and drew his arm up between them, then tore the packet in his fingers and blew the last of his breath straight out in a great gust of air.

He was tossed aside in a roar of coughing and spluttering. He staggered off, blinking, his eyes watering uncontrollably. He was blind – but not utterly so. He could see shadings now: blurry slabs of light and dark.

The wrestler was gasping and coughing off somewhere. 'What is the matter with you?' demanded the fop. The side! Where was the roof's edge! If he could just reach the lip . . .

Someone tripped him from behind and he fell sprawling.

'Would you *get* him?' the fop sighed, exasperated.

'Dried powder of the essayan flower,' the wrestler grumbled in his far deeper voice. 'Been a long time since I've felt that.' And he coughed anew, gasping.

'Get him!'

'Couldn't we just break his arms and throw him out of the city?'

'Fine. Do it.'

'Okay. Come here, little man.'

Dorin shuffled away on his back to buy time, as already his vision was returning. He'd had just enough warning to prepare for that blast of Thyr-summoned light, and now his eyes were recovering. The wrestler was closing. His tread was heavy on the tiles, his hands extended to either side.

'I am sorry, little man,' said the fellow in his gravelly voice, 'but m'lady will not tolerate assassins in her city.'

City mages! He was facing *two* blasted city mages! But why then the contract?

Showing startling speed, the wrestler closed, snatching his ankle. Dorin readied to cut through the fellow's entire forearm and wrist in what would normally be a mortal wound.

Three crossbow bolts thumped into the man's chest and he staggered backwards, releasing Dorin's ankle.

Dark figures fell one by one to the rooftop and straightened. Their black gauzy wrappings rippled and blew about them like clouds of obscuring murk.

Nightblades. A full flight of them.

The Kanese had arrived.

Dorin tensed to run but, rubbing his eyes, he saw that not one of the Kanese assassins was focused upon him. Now that the big fellow was down, all were closing on the poor wretched fop who surely wouldn't last an instant. Yet, somehow, a veritable storm of shot bolts and thrown blades blew past the skinny mage as he calmly turned his shoulders and tilted his head in a dismissive, almost lazy, dance of avoidance.

The man was not running from a full flight of Nightblades, Dorin realized, almost in awe.

Then the mage raised his hands.

Dorin spun to press his face into the tiles and cover his head. But it was not light that washed over him. What came instead was a furnace roar and wave of kiln heat that blew agony across his back. He turned over to see an arc of smoking heaps. And in the centre stood this fop city mage, smiling. The slate tiles of the roof glowed red in a circle about him, hissing and crackling. As Dorin watched, amazed, the fellow pulled off his jacket, which was aflame, and calmly began rolling up his sleeves as if preparing for a very dirty task ahead.

This was war, Dorin realized. A mage war. One he was woefully unprepared for. He began crawling for the roof's edge.

115

More Nightblades landed to his right, drew back their arms to throw at the fop mage. Then, incredibly, the other one rose anew, the wrestler, bearing his forest of crossbow bolts. He smashed two heads together and they burst like ripe grapes, spattering wet mulched fluids across the glowing hot tiles, hissing.

Dorin kicked himself to his feet and jumped to the next roof. In his still blurry vision he misjudged the distance and landed hard. He straightened slowly, winded.

A Nightblade landed ahead of him. He crouched, drawing a throwing blade. Yet even as he did so the words of his old master came to him and he realized his mistake: *Nightblades never work alone.*

Something stabbed into his back, just over his right hip. He staggered to a chimney, let his arms fall. The Nightblades closed.

Dorin snapped up his hands in twin throws, then instantly readied two more weapons. But he did not need to. His aim had been true. Both lay dead.

He limped off, a hand pressed to his side.

A crossbow bolt bit his arm. Another actually passed between his fingers as he staggered. Perched on a steep roof of red ceramic tiles, he turned to confront his pursuers.

Four Nightblades landed about him. He feigned flight, rolled, threw, and straightened. Three now moved in a circle about him while a limp figure tumbled from the roof. He edged his head aside as one gestured. Something kissed his neck in passing.

Close on any fellow practitioner! came the words of that damned wiry old man, and Dorin faked losing his footing, tumbling, and leaped upon the one slightly lower than him. They fell, exchanged a flurry of blows and blocks, forearms locked against each other, then Dorin braced one foot, skidding, and the other continued on to fall over the lip of the three-storey roof, leaving a smear of bright arterial blood behind.

The remaining two exchanged glances, and slowly edged away from one another, twin blades readied.

Dorin tried to steady his breath but his side was screaming. Cold wetness smeared his leg. He felt at his back and came away with a naked razor-thin blade that he threw at one, who blocked it.

Rage and fear combined were keeping him on his feet. Yet there was also something more. *This* was what he'd been yearning for all these years. *This* was what he'd trained for all his life.

These were his peers. Now was his time to finally prove himself.

He struck a ready stance, blades reversed, hidden behind his wrists, and charged the one on his right, who met him with a spinning defence. A kick struck his shoulder sending him down towards the left and he accepted the impetus, accelerating it, dragging his blade across the man's front as his feet flew over his head. He landed on the tiles as the fellow curled round his midriff, shrinking into a knot and sliding down the steep roof.

Dorin drew breath, steadied himself. A blow struck him exactly at his wound, eliciting a grunt of savage pain, and he staggered, almost losing his footing. He spun to face his last opponent.

This one regarded him from knife-fighting range. He, or rather she, raised the bloodied blade to her face, saluting him.

He answered the salute, but weakly, hardly able to remain upright, his vision dimming.

'You are good,' she said. 'Do you work for the Protectress?'

'No. I'm independent.'

'There are no more independents. Those days are gone. Your style is very old, classical. Who was your teacher?'

In answer, Dorin raised both blades and closed. He struck and blocked a series of blows, none definitive. Knowing that he would faint at any moment, his opponent freely gave ground, skidding across the tiles. Enraged, Dorin threw himself at her, but his weakened leg gave and he slipped. She reversed a blade above him for a thrust.

A shocking piercing shriek sounded then, jolting Dorin. The Nightblade screamed as something struck her face, latched hold, and dragged her backwards in a flurry of beating wings. She tumbled off the roof still clutching at her face and howling her agony.

Weaving, his vision darkening, Dorin struggled to blink back the night. He took hold of a ledge and let himself down the side of the building, hand over hand, barely aware. He thumped to the littered alley below and staggered off.

He knew he was almost delirious with shock and loss of blood. He limped on, sliding along the brick walls. Faces gaped at him then disappeared. Narrow alleyways tilted and swam in his vision. Waves of darkness pulled at him. Yet he fought to remain upright, a hand pressed to his side, his leg numb.

A girl took his arm, whispered, urgent, 'This way . . . come.' He

117

had no choice but to submit to her pull. A set of plain wooden stairs reared before him like a fortification. Small hands pushed at him. A voice was begging, weeping, 'Come, come!'

A final insurmountable barrier: a ladder. He pressed his face against the wooden upright, slurred, 'Could you make this any harder?'

A burst of choked laughter. Then, fierce, 'Climb! Don't you know how to do that?'

He managed to say in a very slow and measured manner: 'I'm not having my best day.'

'Get up there! Or you are dead!'

'I met Hood already. He was dead.'

'Just climb. Yes, that's right.'

'He had a sword.'

'Yes. That's what everyone's saying.'

Dorin slammed his head into some low crossbeam, blinked. 'What?'

'Hood's Sword is here,' explained the voice behind. 'Everyone says so.'

'I haven't heard.'

'You don't have a mother or a grandmother here.'

'That's . . . true.' He was crawling now on a dirty floor of wooden slats. Why was he crawling? Easier to sleep. So he laid his head down and went to sleep.

Chapter 6

A SHAKE OF HER SHOULDER WOKE IKO. SHE FOUND HERSELF staring up at a dishevelled Hallens.

'We must go,' the woman demanded. 'Now.'

Iko rose, dressed swiftly. 'What is it?'

Her commander glanced sideways to the other sisters in the sleeping chamber and Iko understood; she clenched her lips tight and followed as the woman hurried out.

It was not yet mid-night. Beyond the high walls of the palace compound the noises of the surrounding city were loud with the crowds and carts of the distant night markets. Voices raised in song and in drunken anger reached her. The grounds, however, were deserted as always. Iko caught up with her commander and whispered again, 'What is it?'

'Word from the Nightblades. We must meet immediately.'

Iko accepted this and refrained from any further bothersome questioning. Hallens led her to the wildest, most remote section of the gardens and here they waited in silence.

Though Iko was expecting the Nightblades, and strained her senses to listen and to watch, even so they rose about her like shades emerging from the night. Fear of such sorcery shuddered through her; in the south, all were frightened of the witches and warlocks whose powers only worked ill.

Hallens started forward. 'What has happened?'

Her commander's urgency shocked Iko. Then it came to her: sudden word from the Nightblades, this unseemly haste. By the countless forgotten gods! *Not the king!*

'There is no threat,' one assured her. 'For now.'

Hallens straightened as if slapped. 'Meaning?' she demanded.

'A flight of our Blades engaged city mages. With them was another. A young man. An obvious trained assassin.'

Iko's breath left her in a clenched hiss. An assassin! Then . . . *Gods, no!* She took Hallens' elbow. 'We will cut our way out at once!'

Her commander's voice was clenched and fierce as she demanded, 'The king?'

The Blade raised a placating hand. 'We think not.'

'You *think* not?'

'While we were observing the city mages, they tried to kill the assassin.'

Relief flooded Iko – a falling-out! Of course! There would be no honour among such filth.

'We believe it a dispute over payment.'

'Well? What of it?' Hallens said. 'You are a hundred or so. Why are you not hunting him down even now?'

The fellow shifted uncomfortably. He began, carefully, 'Our master happened to be present to witness the engagement. He saw the youth's style and later examined the wounds delivered by him. He is of the opinion that we are facing a student of Faruj.'

Iko choked down a scoff of disbelief. Faruj! The legendary master assassin of the Talian Iron Crown himself? *Hood!* The power behind the crown, many said. 'Surely he must be dead by now,' she let go. 'He served, what, three Talian kings?'

'Some believe he died during the wars of independence. Others are of the opinion that he fled west. Probably to Tali itself.'

Iko was amazed. A student of Faruj himself! The man whose name made kings tremble on their thrones. And the student might carry all those ancient teachings lost in the fall of the Iron Crown . . . Iko's gaze sharpened upon the Nightblade. 'You would offer him a place.'

The Kanese assassin inclined his head in assent. 'Our master would pursue the possibility.'

'And you wish our help,' Hallens finished for him.

He nodded again. 'We and the city mages are both hunting him now. If we can reach him before they do, we could force him to the ground and there we would need your help in subduing him. Or perhaps you may negotiate – as a non-practitioner.' The man's obscured shoulders rose and fell as if in mild embarrassment. 'Trust is not something cultivated between those of our . . . vocation.'

'Failing this, you will kill him, of course,' said Hallens.

'Of course.'

She gave a curt nod of agreement. 'Very well. However – should there be any hint that he is moving upon Chulalorn you will alert us immediately.' She raised a finger in warning. 'Otherwise, I shall hunt you down and flay your flesh from your bones.'

The Nightblade merely backed away, whispering, 'He is our king as well.'

Once more they were alone with the wind through the tree boughs and the surrounding murmur of the busy city. As they walked back to their chambers, Iko took the time to reconsider the news with a cooler head and it struck her as almost inconceivable that Shalmanat would actually plan on assassinating a king – any king. She couldn't think of any historical precedent. Such a step would surely be a dangerous threat to any ruler. She cleared her throat. 'Do you really think this Protectress would actually hire such a one?'

Hallens slowed and halted. 'I do not believe so. But prudence dictates that we prepare. It would be a serious escalation. All the attacks I have faced have been soldiers and hirelings of Chulalorn's cousins and rival clans and families. None were true professional killers. These royal families are all related and intermarry. They take each other hostage, as Chulalorn has. And the old Talian rulers as well. A Grisian king was held for ten years once, and even continued ruling the entire time – as was his right, of course.' She shook her head, frowning. 'Yet Shalmanat comes from no such shared aristocratic family background. And she is a sorceress . . . who knows how she might think?' She motioned Iko onward. 'No word to the others, please. I do not wish panic or worry.'

Iko nodded, relieved; such an evaluation meshed with her own. In war it was always the practice that nobles be held and ransomed. Few were ever killed, except perhaps in single combat. And she had heard before that the Talians held their conquered kings hostage rather than murdering them. All the better to control the many royal houses, of course. The ugly truth was that rulers usually had more to fear from their own relatives and peers than any stranger.

* * *

121

It had been a week since Silk and Ho cleared the rooftops of an incursion of Kanese Nightblades. Of the young assassin, nothing had surfaced. Silk imagined that the Blades must have taken care of him. He himself suffered no injury in the ambush other than the loss of his favourite jacket, while Ho had handily proved the truth of all the many stories Silk had heard of him. Stories he had always dismissed.

Namely, that the other mage was impossible to kill. And so it seemed, as bolt after bolt hammered into the fellow while he crushed the throats and broke the backs of every Nightblade he could catch hold of. It had been an astonishing display of prowess, and Silk was still quite impressed, even though he was of the opinion that he'd performed none too shabbily himself. He thought that between them they had, rather dramatically, given King Chulalorn the Third something to think about.

This night he stood on the west wall. The officer had proved an unctuous fellow with the annoying habit of winking as he made vague intimations regarding Silk and Shalmanat. In the end, Silk had silenced the oaf by suggesting he go hump a goat. The man went white and his hand clenched his sword grip, only to hold there, shuddering. In the end, he had spun and marched away. Silk knew he'd made a blood enemy. He'd shrugged internally. Such was life.

It was past the mid-night bell when a runner came dashing up to him, exhausted, bloodied, and cut. 'The south,' the woman gasped, near to collapse. Silk climbed a nearby merlon for a look. All was dark. Cursing, he jumped down, waved to his bodyguard, and ran. Smokey had the south. And normally, wherever that man was stationed a firestorm of boiling flames blazed throughout the night.

As he neared the southern curve of the Outer Round, he heard a much louder roar of battle than he was used to. The Kanese had reached the fortifications, he realized, astonished. He bounded up the nearest stairs only to find his way blocked by a squad of Hengan regulars crouched behind a barricade they'd assembled. 'What are you doing?' he demanded of the nearest ranked guard.

The man saluted, clearly surprised to be facing a city mage. 'We'll stop them here, sir,' he assured him.

Silk barely managed to refrain from slapping the fellow across the face. 'Charge them now, man! That's an order!'

The sergeant gaped at him. 'But . . . they've taken the walk.'

'Sweep them off. Now. Go!' And he pointed, waiting. 'Well?'

Swallowing his unease, the sergeant gestured his troop up. 'And you are with us, I suppose?' he commented quite acidly, forgetting in the heat of the moment whom he addressed.

'I will be behind you, sergeant. And if you wish to ever see again, do *not* turn round. Is that clear?'

The fellow paled, now understanding his position. 'Yes . . . sir.' He drew his shortsword. 'Up and at 'em!' he roared, and kicked his way through the barricade.

In the fury and press of the battle, Silk did not discriminate. Anyone facing his way received a full blast of Thyr scorching straight in their faces. Many howled their agony and threw themselves from the wall. Silk followed the detachment of guards in a steady advance, and none dared slow him or turn round.

In this manner they recovered one full stretch of the curtain wall. They relieved a half company of guards surrounded and besieged within a tower. When Silk ducked within – the Kanese archers were now definitely targeting him – a runner summoned him to the small dorm at the top. Here he found the reason why the guards had not abandoned the tower. On a bloodstained cot lay Smokey, his shirt torn open round the shaft of a crossbow bolt to the right of his heart.

Incredibly, the man was conscious, just. Silk knelt next to the cot. 'Everything's gone to the Abyss in your absence.'

'It would, wouldn't it?' the man answered in the barest whisper.

'What happened? I've seen you burn every arrow and melt every bolt that ever came your way.'

The mage of Telas gestured weakly to the shaft. 'Some kind of unburnable fibre. A damned mage-killer.'

Silk flinched from the black shaft. 'Really? Well, you're not dead.'

'Getting there.'

Silk squeezed his shoulder. 'I'll take over.'

'That's supposed to comfort me?'

Silk straightened, waved guards to him. 'Take him to the healers. Immediately.'

'And us?' asked the sergeant from where his men and women defended the doorway.

'We return to the fray.'

The man winced. 'We can hold here till reinforcements arrive.'

Silk was tiring of the 'always defend' mentality of the man. But it was not his fault. These Hengan guards knew only how to hide behind their walls. 'We can't allow the Kanese to secure their hold. We continue the advance. Ready your troops.'

To his credit, the sergeant saluted – if wearily.

They preceded him out on to the wide parapet. He pressed them onward. They picked up a few Hengan trailers and survivors, but the Kanese were too many. Soon those facing Silk saw through his best trick and advanced with shields or armoured hands raised across their faces. He was reduced to heating their shields and weapons and that took time, and much more energy. His shirt clung to him, sodden in sweat, his heart felt as if it were being crushed and his vision swam with the strength he was draining from himself. Yet the Kanese shock infantry were still spilling over the wall on countless ladders. They had a foothold and wouldn't release it. His guard was being beaten back despite their natural dread of the city mage behind them.

Arrows nicked him in passing – a sure sign he was slowing. Soon, one would take him.

Then panic disturbed the ranks pressing in upon his men. Many turned to face the rear. Screams of fear and agony came in waves like an onrushing stampede. Something suddenly threw the attackers against the crenellations as if swept aside by a giant's hand. Armour scraped stone and blood burst from gasping open mouths as Kanese were smeared up the crenels and out over the wall the way one might drag wet laundry.

A girl in a long black dress, of darkest Dal Hon descent, her hair a cloud a black frizziness about her head, now commanded the entire section of the wall alone. Hengan guards came rushing up behind her. Silk straightened his shirt and bowed. 'Always a pleasure, Mara.'

'Shut the fuck up, Silk.' She went to the parapet, and, completely ignoring the smeared blood and gore there, leaned far out, and cursed anew. 'Stay out of the damned city!' she bellowed, and gestured fiercely.

Silk felt the surge of power actually sway the stones of the wall. He glanced out, careful not to let any of the blood get on his shirt.

All the ladders now lay scattered on the ground among writhing fallen soldiers. 'Subtle as always, Mara.'

'Where's Smokey?'

'Took a bolt. I had to rescue the situation.'

'You? Rescue the situation? That's a laugh.'

'You are too harsh, Mara.'

'Kiss my arse,' she replied. But off-handedly, without heat.

Not a bad idea, he reflected. Maybe that would settle her down a little. Then he recalled the many stories regarding the grisly fates of her lovers. Perhaps it would be best if he avoided being found crushed flat as a crêpe. He adjusted his cuffs. 'Well, thank you all the same.'

'I'm not here for you.'

No, you are not. You are here to serve Shalmanat. And why? Not because of any regard for her. No. I know you, Mara of some nameless squalid village in the Dal Hon provinces. You worship power alone. The biggest fist. And the Protectress is the most powerful you've found yet.

That wins no respect from me, girl.

He tipped his head. 'Well . . . seeing as you have everything in hand, I'll go and get some sleep.' And he ambled off.

'Do you even have a prick, Silk?' she called after him.

Over his shoulder he offered his most boyish grin. 'You couldn't afford to find out, dear.'

She cursed him out after that, but he walked off ignoring her, knowing that always infuriated her. Coming to the tower, he found Hengan guards tossing bodies out over the wall. He watched for a time, his head tilted, intrigued. Then he ordered them away. Alone, he searched among the fallen, thinking to himself *There ought to be someone my size . . .*

With the dawn, a lone Kanese soldier was found wandering the trampled burned fields, his head and face a bloodied caked mess, clearly dazed from the blow. He was of no rank, a lowly impressed infantryman, once probably a town-dwelling artisan or craftsman from the look of his soft hands and pale complexion. Pickets escorted him to the crowded tents of the infirmary quarter and he was set down among the many wounded lying unconscious or sitting hunched, awaiting treatment.

Once Silk's rescuers had left, he wrapped his head and half his face in a rag and ambled off. He avoided any command quarters, where security would be tightest. Instead, his path took him to the rear of the lines, to the disordered tents of the camp followers – the cooks, servants, petty merchants, harlots, and attending wives, husbands, and children. A veritable roving city that had dragged itself up from the south, trailing the Kanese ranks.

Here he wandered, nodding to people, striking up brief conversations, and moving on as he searched for his bright-eyed Ahn, who had followed him all the way from Laeth. He fell in among the loudest, most raucous gambling and drinking crowd, lost all his coin in games of cards and troughs but held no grudges, then settled in for the rest of the late afternoon and evening to listen.

He heard much complaint of the privations of a march so far north into foreign territory. He heard of shortages of everything, from arrows to food and wood to cook with. He heard himself described in the most uncomplimentary manner, along with Ho and the rest of the city mages. When he casually mentioned the Kanese mages, the dismissal was unanimous. None of this generation, it seemed, were of the stature of the old terrifying ones, such as A'karonys, or the murderous Jadeen of Traly.

He remained at the camp for the rest of that night, listening and evaluating. Exactly what he was listening for, he did not know. He knew only that he would sense it when he heard it – that odd note, strange detail, or fact that did not make sense. He heard no such thing. This first foray into the Kanese camp had uncovered nothing. And so he casually pushed himself to his feet, nodded his farewells to those nearby, and walked off into the pre-dawn glow.

His path brought him past a knot of the lowest of the low among the camp followers, the manual labourers, infirmary cleaners, and cesspit diggers – who were also, not incidentally, the grave diggers – and at last, in passing, he overheard a strange thing. One old fellow was heatedly claiming that a friend of his had seen a monster in camp.

Silk halted and joined the small group hunched round their meagre fire. 'You mean Ryllandaras?' he asked, careful to use a friendly and curious tone.

The old fellow puffed up at the question as he'd been receiving only smirks from his companions. He bobbed his head in deference. 'Oh, no, sir. Not the man-beast. No sir. Kela said it was like a man only all twisted and bigger.'

'Perhaps your friend merely mistook what she was seeing.'

'Can't say, sir. Only know what she said. Works in among the private tents where no one's allowed. They keep it chained and hidden away, she says. Talks to itself all day and night in a language no one understands.'

The fellow was clearly very eager to glow in the status such secrets brought their bearer and so Silk allowed himself to appear suitably impressed. He lowered his voice, whispering, 'If it's a secret then we'd best not talk of it, hey? Who knows who might be listening.'

The old man's bushy brows rose and he touched the side of his nose, nodding his appreciation. 'Right you are, sir. 'Course. Might be important.'

Silk gave them a friendly nod in farewell and continued on. They may, or may not, pursue the matter. But if he knew his human nature, they'd have ten times the information and gossip on this thing when next he came through. In any case, he had a lead. *Like a man, only twisted and bigger.*

He angled for the city walls. Now, just how in the name of the sleeping goddess would he get back in without being seen?

* * *

The day-hunters and the night-hunters, Dorin decided, were very much of two different breeds. The night-hunters, the owls mainly, kept to the darkest and most shadowed corners of the broad dusty attic. If disturbed during the day, they would merely crack open one disapproving eye, peer about, then slip back into their slumber.

On the other hand, the day-hunters, the hawks, falcons and eagles, when disturbed by some night-time noise or commotion, would rear up in a startled manner as if half taking flight. They would then complain and grumble for a long time, adjusting their perches and preening, resentful of the intrusion.

Dorin had time to make such observations while he lay with his torso tightly wrapped, regaining his strength under Ullara's care. That had been a close call. His closest yet. If not for the two remaining Denul-enhanced unguents he possessed, it might have been the end for him. As it was, he believed he accounted for some six or eight Nightblades himself – not a bad total.

He vowed to do much better should there ever be a next time.

Ullara was pleased to be once more in the role of caregiver rather than receiver. At first he ate hugely to regain his strength, until he noticed that she did not appear to be eating at all. He eventually managed to coax from her the truth that the entire family was enduring a shortage of foodstuffs. He handed over coin then and demanded that she buy for everyone. That day she went to the market and returned with more than the family ever normally bought. Which, she later admitted to him, had been a mistake. Her father had questioned her and she'd had to make up the lie that she'd sold one of her 'pets'.

At least her father was now more supportive of what he'd always dismissed as a useless waste of her time.

This day Dorin walked about the attic, easing into his usual practice routine – not that he was up to it. But he was approaching it. Each evening he questioned Ullara about the news. A fortnight had passed since that night upon the rooftops and as far as he could tell nothing had changed in the stand-off of the siege. Ullara, however, reported dire shortages in the markets. Surging prices for staples such as flour. The disappearance of fresh vegetables from every stall. Dorin wondered how long the Protectress could hold out.

Noise at the trapdoor sent him dashing to cover he'd erected to shield himself from discovery. Though Ullara had claimed no one else ever came up here Dorin had been shaken to discover she was wrong when the door lifted one day and an older woman emerged. Her mother, he'd assumed.

She had rooted among the boxes then descended, completely oblivious of the screaming signs of his residence in prints among the dust and his rumpled bedding. Not her area of expertise, he supposed. And people tended not to see what they did not expect to see – a tendency he'd been trained to exploit.

This day it was Ullara. Dorin was surprised to see her carrying a bottle of wine. He gestured to the bottle. 'A special day?'

She blinked, momentarily confused, then blushed, embarrassed. Everything he said seemed to embarrass the poor lass, Dorin thought. She offered it. 'Oh, no. We're out of drinking water.'

He took the bottle, sat. 'But you have a huge river running through the city.'

'Everyone thinks the Kanese have poisoned the water.'

He found that hard to believe – wouldn't the poisons merely wash away downstream? 'Do you think they'd do that?'

'Who knows what those evil southerners might do?'

There it was again – that strange bigotry against those who lived beyond the next valley or mountain range. It was a common prejudice Dorin did not share. Perhaps because he'd been trained to view everyone equally. As potential targets.

He took a sip, welcoming the fluids. Though it was late in the autumn, the heat the attic collected could be blistering. At such times he hid out on the roof in the shade of a gable.

'How goes the siege?'

'The same. Stand-off.'

'I understand these things can last for years.'

'Surely that can't be possible.'

Dorin gestured with the bottle. 'It's a question of wills. Theirs or—' He was about to say ours, but stopped himself. 'The Kanese's or the Hengans'. If you are running low on food, then they must be as well.'

Ullara fiercely shook her head. 'Oh, no. They're receiving regular convoys up from the south.'

Dorin lowered the bottle to stare at her quizzically. 'How would you know that?'

She blushed once more, her gaze fluttering about the attic. 'I . . . heard. In the market.'

'That's just gossip. Wild rumours and talk.'

She pressed her lips tight and squeezed her hands between her knees, saying nothing.

He handed her the bottle and cleared his throat. 'Well . . . Ullara. Thank you so much for all you've done. You saved my life – you really have.'

She hung her head. 'You're going.'

'Tomorrow, I think.'

'You're not fully healed!'

'I won't be for some time. But I can't stay here any longer. I might be found.' He lowered his head to catch her eye. 'Then there'd be some awkward questions for you.'

She turned away, hunching further.

'I'm sorry, but I have to go. I can't stay for ever. You know that.'

'Just a little longer,' she whispered.

'Tomorrow, Ullara,' he answered, just as softly. He wanted to soothe her, perhaps hold her to comfort her, but that did not feel right to him and so he took her hand – so calloused and rough for one of her tender age – and kissed it.

She burst into tears then and ran from the attic.

He was left wondering whether he'd done the right thing. Or the wrong thing.

She did not return with the dusk, nor with the next dawn. He waited into the morning and then, reluctantly, swung out of the gable that offered the most cover, and descended to an alley.

He slipped into the street. It was surprisingly empty for the time of day; the ongoing siege must be taking its toll on business. He would search out his stashes to see if any remained, then strike east for Unta. Perhaps downriver to Cawn then onward by ship. Best to avoid the long dreary overland route.

He was heading north, along the Outer Round, wondering just how much barge traffic there might be downriver from Heng, when someone stepped out and called, 'Dorin! What a surprise to see you.'

He damned these last weeks of inactivity – they had obviously dulled his senses outrageously – loosened his shoulders, and looked up to see Rheena. The girl gestured, inviting him into a narrow side street. 'I think we should talk.'

'I agree.'

Once round the corner of the street she surprised him once more by lunging in close and planting her mouth on his. She said through their lips, 'They just want to talk, Dorin. Just talk.'

He flinched away, stunned. She glared. He glanced out to the street to see two obvious specimens of street muscle closing. 'Rheena . . .' He backed away, drew his blades.

'Just talk!' she repeated, pleading.

'So he may have told you, girl.'

Four big fellows now blocked the alley mouth. Dorin didn't even have to look behind to know it was a dead end. Rheena had chosen well, damn her.

He readied himself, adjusting his footing. He may be weakened, but he was certain he could still take these plodding amateurs.

Then they raised their hands, empty. 'Just a word,' the leader called.

Dorin continued backing away. 'Say it.'

'A meeting. Pung might have a proposition for you.'

Dorin spotted a repeating course of raised brick high in one wall. He sheathed his blades and leaped all in one motion. His fingertips caught the course. His side flared with pain. Grunting, he heaved himself up to a higher course and yet another. He paused there, glanced down at the five upturned faces, Rheena included. 'Sorry, don't trust your boss enough to come along.' With the tips of his feet on the courses he made quick progress to the third-storey roof.

'Name a place, then!' came a last angry call from below.

Dorin peered over the edge. 'There's no place I'd feel—' He stopped himself. Actually, there was one place in the city where he would feel quite safe from the damned man. He crouched at the lip. 'Okay. There is one place I'd be willing to meet your boss – should he have the guts to show . . .'

Chapter 7

'I DO NOT WANT YOU HERE,' SAID THE BLACK-HAIRED DAL Hon swordsman, practically pouting.

Dorin was leaning against the doorjamb of the mausoleum, watching the empty night-time Street of the Gods. He said, distractedly, 'I'm really not interested in what you want.'

'Leave now.'

Dorin cupped a hand at his ear and made a show of listening to the rear of the chamber. 'I don't hear the priest objecting.'

'He only talks to me,' the youth ground through clenched teeth.

Dorin crossed his arms, shot a quick glance to the street. 'You mean like an imaginary friend?'

The youth jerked forward, a hand slapping to the much-worn grip of his sword. Dorin imagined he could hear the wire, horn, and tang creaking in that white-knuckled clench.

He remained calm – outwardly, at least. He'd guessed that the youth slew only those who threatened the temple, or his god, or something like that. In which case, the lad's own bizarre self-imposed strictures protected him. He'd just have to be careful not to overstep some stupid obscure religious law like eating horse on a new moon, or wearing a pointy hat indoors.

The youth subsided into sullen silence after that, which suited Dorin fine. He kept watch without being further accosted. His one remaining concern was the child – she lay as before amid rumpled old blankets against a wall. Asleep this time, at least. Yet kept in a mausoleum? What was this lad thinking?

'Yours?' he asked, pointing to the girl.

The lad's jaws hardened. 'My ward. Why?'

132

'Just wondering why you haven't passed her along to some family.'

'She is safest here with me. None shall harm her here. I've sworn it.'

Dorin raised a hand in surrender. 'Just wondering.'

As the night hours passed, the street emptied of legitimate devotees while a crowd came to gather on the street in either direction from the mausoleum. A rather burly crowd for this particular thoroughfare; not one black-shawled grandmother among them.

Some ten of the sturdy fellows detached themselves from the crowd and advanced. Dorin slipped further into the cover of the stone jamb. 'Far enough!' he called. 'No sense continuing with this unless the man himself is here.'

The street enforcers parted, revealing another figure among them, this one far shorter and broader. The fellow padded forward with a slow rolling gait. His round bald head gleamed with sweat even in the cool night air. His body was just as round, with a great protruding pot belly and thick trunk-like arms. If this was Pung himself, then Dorin wondered why he wasn't known as Pung the bung. He was dressed rather conventionally for an underworld boss, in plain wide trousers, a dark blue silk shirt and dark green jacket.

'Are you Pung?' Dorin called.

'What is this?' the black-haired youth hissed from the hall. Dorin ignored him. The man nodded his shiny bullet-like head, then advanced up to the mausoleum's stone threshold.

'You wanted to talk?' Dorin asked.

The man raised a hand for silence, then knelt. 'First things first,' he said in a thick, wet voice, like molasses. On his knees, he crossed his arms at his chest and bowed, then extended his arms in front of him. 'May Hood preserve me,' he murmured and stood, grunting with effort.

Meaty hands on his hips, he studied Dorin up and down. 'So. You're the fella causing all the ruckus.'

'Depends on the ruckus.'

Pung rubbed his heavy jowls, cocking an eye. 'Well, let's see now . . . There's a baker's dozen or so on a barge south of the city that included an officer of the Kan Elites. Then there's a near equal number of Kan Nightblades gutted across roofs and spattered on streets.'

'What's that got to do with me?'

Pung shook his head and gave him a disgusted look. 'Lad, I got eyes on the roofs. I see the Nightblades comin' and goin'. There's nothin' that moves in this town that I don't know about.'

'That include the city mages?'

'I'm smart enough to stay out of their way.'

Dorin sensed, rather than felt or heard, the youth come up behind him. 'Leave our threshold,' the young man demanded.

Pung raised his wide hands, empty, palm outward. 'I come offering worship.'

'You are no devotee of Hood.'

'Oh, I am, lad. I am.'

Dorin looked to the ceiling and crossed his arms. 'Is this what we're here to talk about?'

Pung's lips drew down in disapproval of such rudeness. 'I'm thinking you've been doing a heap of free killin' for someone who claims to do it only for pay.'

'And?'

'Want to get paid?' One edge of his heavy mouth crooked up with that question.

Dorin did indeed want to get paid. However, now that he saw which way things were going, he decided to try a little fishing instead. 'I'm wondering why you need me when you have such a deadly mage.'

The squat fellow's hairless thick brows clenched in confusion, then he burst out with a harsh guffawing laugh. 'Oh, yeah! That guy. My fearsome mage. Ha! I'll drag him out for you if you like.'

Dorin was puzzled by the reaction, but made a show of waving it off as unimportant. He said, 'Well, I would like to get paid.'

Pung inclined his blunt head. 'Good. We should talk. But not here. Private, don't you think?'

'I'll pay you a visit.'

The man's small eyes narrowed in their deep pockets, then the edge of his mouth curled up again in appreciation of the comment. 'Soon.' He backed away. As he did so, he raised a finger to the youth. 'Your time will come, lad.'

'Not before yours,' the young man answered with what Dorin thought a strange tone of certainty.

The two watched Pung's guards encircle him once more, and

all move off with many glances back over their shoulders.

Once they were alone, the youth's blade was suddenly across the threshold, barring the way out. The speed of the move shocked Dorin. 'Do not follow this man.'

Blinking to recover, Dorin grated, 'Or . . . you will do what?'

'I will do nothing. It is what I see.'

'And that is?'

'Death. There will be death.'

'That's the general idea. Or do you mean mine?'

'No, not yours.'

'Whose?'

'Hood commands my silence in this.'

Dorin pressed a hand to the flat of the blade and edged it away. 'Then stand aside. And never interfere with me again. Or I will kill you. Is that clear?'

'It is very clear.'

The way the youth spoke disturbed Dorin, but he could not pin down the reason. He nodded to emphasize his point and walked out, slipping round the side of the mausoleum to head in the opposite direction from the toughs. Frankly, the lad's entire manner made him uneasy. He had to wonder whether the fellow was actually sane. Perhaps he wasn't just pretending to hear voices to delude the gullible. Perhaps he was hearing them, and he was the deluded one. Or, far scarier, perhaps he was hearing them and they were real.

* * *

Just because they were hostages didn't mean that Iko and the rest of the Sword-Dancers neglected their training. Their daily routines had even become something of a local attraction as city aristocrats and members of the rich merchant families made a point of gathering to watch, as if the display were some sort of sport. Sitting after a long run of twelve katas, Iko worked on recovering her breath and watched as well. It occurred to her that one reason for the crowds might be that many of the girls chose to exercise in a tight chest wrap and loincloth only. Because they wished to soak up the last of the sun, they would say. But Iko knew some enjoyed showing off.

Hallens, sweaty herself from recent sparring, came and sat next

135

to her. Her eyes were on the ongoing matches, but she said, beneath her breath, 'I have word the king is becoming impatient and that tonight the Blades will see employment.'

'Who?'

'The one herself.'

Iko sat back, surprised and, for a fleeting instant, a touch disappointed. Chulalorn would order such a move? Still – it wasn't as if she was nobility. 'We will be on alert all through the night.'

'No. Nothing out of the ordinary. We must not be seen as complicit.'

'Then . . . what?'

'Take one of your midnight walks. Take someone with you. One you trust. Watch for any alarm.'

'I would chose Rei.'

'Good choice.' Hallens stood, stretching, and Iko sat back, now quite distracted from the bouts. He is the king, she reminded herself. The Nightblades serve him as they served his father. It was not her place to judge. She was also a mere servant sworn to serve.

Still, the idea that the Protectress would stoop to such a dishonourable deed had earlier disgusted her. Now she must serve as a near accessory when the king orders the same thing? She clenched her lips tight and eased her shoulders. He was the king. His was the right, as ruler. Hers was to obey.

She could not help being rather subdued through the day and later as they sat together for the evening meal. This they took cross-legged on the floor of their quarters, serving one another; in Itko Kan, and many other southern cities, chairs were looked upon as rather odd and awkward contrivances.

After, she waited aside, quiet. This too was easily accomplished, for in the eyes of her sisters she was Hallens' new whipping-girl, unable to do anything right, and constantly in need of correction.

When the appointed hour neared she rose and approached Rei where she sat among the sisters, talking and laughing about gods knew what. Iko couldn't fathom how anyone could still have anything to talk over after living together for so many years.

'Walk with me, Rei,' she said.

The tall sister – almost all were taller than Iko – waved her off. 'Find another chaperon.'

'I choose you.'

Rei made a face and peered round for Hallens. Iko pointed. 'She's over there.'

Rei went to her and Iko watched while Hallens waved her off in turn. She stalked back, picked up her sword, and marched off. 'Fine!'

They walked the grounds. Or rather, Iko walked the grounds, while Rei shambled after, sighing and huffing her annoyance. Iko tried to keep her gaze from the tall dome of the Inner Focus, which some named the temple, with its single tall tower behind. But she kept glancing that way, wondering just what was transpiring behind those stone walls.

After a time Rei ceased her complaints. Then she said, 'You won't see one.'

Iko jumped. 'See what? What are you talking about?'

'A Nightblade. You won't see one.'

'Of course I won't! Whatever made you think that?'

Rei glanced to the walls. 'I see you watching the roofs and such. But you never see them. Not that you'd want to anyway. They're not what the songsters make them out to be.'

Iko studied the slim woman, who was pushing back her long straight bangs as was her constant habit. 'Have you seen them?'

'No. Not that I want to. They're just murderers. Romanticized cowardly back-stabbers.'

Iko was almost shocked. 'Cowardly?'

'They won't face anyone honestly. So they come in the night, from behind.'

Iko cast another quick glance to the dome of the Inner Focus. 'I don't know . . . I imagine it must take courage to enter enemy territory all alone, without retreat, and know you are dead if you are discovered.'

The woman was unmoved. 'I hear their graduation test is to strangle a baby.'

Iko stared. 'Strangle—' She laughed nervously. 'Now who is the one listening to stories?'

'This is what I hear.'

Iko turned away, hugged one shoulder against the chill of the night air. What an absurd claim. Chulalorn would employ such monstrous creatures? Still, after such an act, the only thing left to cling to would be the service that demanded it . . .

137

She kneaded her shoulder, wondering, could there be similar stories circulating regarding them?

For a time neither spoke, then Rei drew a breath that might have been a sigh. 'It is . . . pleasant, out here, Iko. The air is welcome. One can almost imagine . . .'

'That we are not prisoners?'

A laugh. 'We can escape from here whenever we wish.'

'So we like to think.'

'Don't be ridiculous. Of course we could.'

'But we haven't yet.'

'You are always worrying. Don't worry.'

'I was just considering—' Iko stopped herself because she saw a shadow. She glimpsed it clearly as a long drawn out lance thrown across the ground in a flash. She spun to see the dome of the Inner Focus dimming like a fading ember.

Behind her, Rei's breath caught.

'Did you see that?' Iko gasped, wondering whether she'd imagined it.

'I can hardly see now. We should report this.'

'You report. I will take a look.'

'Be careful.' Rei dashed off.

Iko headed to the nearest doors leading to the inner chambers. Two palace guards stood watch. She didn't know if she should be relieved by this or not. Did it mean that the Nightblades hadn't made it in? She stopped a good distance beyond sword range and pointed up past them. 'Did you see that?'

'See what?'

'The dome. I thought I saw it glow.'

'You must be mistaken,' said one.

'We saw no such thing,' said the other.

Of course you didn't. She didn't know what to say to that and so shrugged. 'Well . . . I guess I was mistaken.'

'I suggest you stay in your chambers from now on, Sword-Dancer.'

'Perhaps so.' She bowed a farewell, and backed away.

She found the rooms a whirlwind of activity as her sisters dashed about, each asking what had happened and no one knowing. She pushed through the crowd surrounding Hallens and Rei. Hallens cast her a questioning glance to which she responded with a negative shake of her head.

The captain's answering frown was sour. She waved everyone away. 'Back to bed. Tomorrow.'

'What is it?' Yvonna demanded. 'What is going on?'

'Nothing,' Hallens snapped. 'Nothing happened and no one will say anything. Understood? Now back to sleep.'

Iko nodded her assent. She headed to her bedding. Yvonna grasped her arm and whispered, insistent, 'You were out there. What was Rei talking about? What did she see? You can tell me.'

'Nothing. Didn't you hear? Nothing happened.'

Yvonna glared down at her, then snorted. 'Of course *you* wouldn't know, would you?' Iko just damned her to the Abyss and went her way.

* * *

Silk was kissing the smooth stomach of the daughter of a very rich merchant family when a summons pierced his concentration. It came as white light of a purity far beyond any that a mage of Thyr could fashion. In fact, it came from that other realm that Silk had been privileged to glimpse twice during his most profound incantations. It came not in words, but as an image and a demand.

The Inner Focus – the temple – and his presence.

He flinched from the bed, wincing, and rubbing his temples. 'Sorry, dearest. Have to go.'

She stared up at him, utterly shocked. 'What?'

'I must go. City mage business.'

She pulled her silk robes about herself, sat up. 'Bullshit! It's as they say – you do prefer men!'

He drew on his trousers. 'If that will soothe your vanity, my sweet.'

'Or you can't perform!'

He squeezed his erection through the cloth, showing her. 'Not an issue.'

She heaved a pillow. 'Get out! My father will hear of this!'

'And what details exactly will he hear?'

She fairly shrieked, 'Just get out!' and hid her face.

He backed away as he buttoned up his shirt. 'I'm very sorry, dearest. You really were . . . most tasty.'

A perfume pot smashed into the wall next to his head. He ducked as he exited.

Reaching the street, he turned and made directly for the nearest gate. As it was the middle of the night it would be closed, but it would be manned, and he would be let through. He was confident the girl – what was her name? – wouldn't give any true account of the night. Rather the opposite, in fact. The truth would quite take away from the glow of her conquest, after all.

He jogged listening for sounds of any disturbance or attack, yet heard nothing out of the ordinary. Now he feared the worst. Could *she* be wounded? Surrounded? Had the others been summoned? He quickened his pace and wished he were a talent of one of those Warrens that allowed faster physical movement, such as Serc.

He charged up the stairs, waving at the guards as he came, and sprinted through the empty halls of the outer palace. Past these, he reached the more private rooms, then saw ahead the doors of Shalmanat's sanctum, the Inner Focus. Here a mass of guards milled, blocking the way, and he yelled, 'Make room!'

'The doors are shut,' one told him.

He waved them aside. 'Not to me.'

Fresh blood smeared the stone flags before the doors. Dread clenched his heart.

'Four dead,' one guard whispered.

Silk pressed a hand to a door, found it warm to the touch. 'What happened?'

'Don't know. People just report a blinding flash from the Focus. Then silence. No one can get in.'

'Are the other mages here?' The guard shook a negative. Mystified, Silk gave the door a push and felt it yield. 'Bar the way,' he told the guard, and slipped within, shutting the door after him.

Brilliance assaulted him. He blinked, squinting, his eyes watering, and shaded his gaze. Eventually, as his vision adjusted, he could make out one smear of lesser intensity and he headed towards it. He marvelled as his feet struck the white stone flags invisible to him. It was as if he were suspended within the sun itself. No adept of Thyr could marshal anything near this potency.

He realized that this manifestation transcended his Warren – and then he knew. He knew who, or more accurately *what*, Shalmanat was.

He found her sitting on her camp stool once more. Surrounding her lay eight smears of black ash – as if she had tossed eight handfuls of soot from where she sat. Ignoring these for the moment, he went to her and knelt.

Her eyes were shut and she was weaving gently in her seat, as if in a trance, or a dreaming dance. He reached out to touch her but reconsidered, and withdrew his hand. Instead he called to her, softly, 'Protectress . . . Shalmanat . . .'

The sinuous dance slowed, halted. The eyes fluttered, opening. Irises lay before him like twin open wells. Yet instead of darkness within, each pupil glowed a bright velvety crimson.

He knew for certain then. 'Shalmanat.'

The eyes found his, focused. A wan smile touched the lips. 'You heard.'

'Yes. And I came. What—' He started, seeing her shirt sliced open at her side. He drew on the cloth to see the wound along her ribs as a bright sealed gash. Healed as if cauterized instantly.

As if.

He lowered himself as before to one knee, gestured to each side in wonder. 'This is more than Thyr. This is Liosan. Kurald Liosan. Elder Light.' He bowed his head to her. 'And you are Tiste Liosan.'

Her exhausted smile lifted a touch higher. 'I am unmasked.'

He indicated the nearest tossed dusting of soot. 'And this?'

The thin-lipped mouth tightened. 'Chulalorn's childishness.'

'Childishness?'

She took a deep breath, straightened her back. 'Kings are like children. They expect to be obeyed, and throw fits when thwarted.'

Silk eyed the eight smears. *Light alone did this.* The power that moves all creation, some say. 'But how could they have gained entry?'

She lifted her thin shoulders. 'Who knows? A bribe? A threat? They need only suborn one guard.'

'You are not safe.'

The lips quirked upwards again. 'On the contrary, dear Silk.' She gestured to the streaks. 'I am very safe.'

Silk answered the wry smile. Yes . . . well. 'I mean, what will we do?'

'Yes. Good question.' She hugged herself. Her long arms reached far beyond each shoulder. 'Yes. Chulalorn poked the hornets' nest. Now he will find himself facing far more than he bargained for.

This is an escalation, Silk. And thoughtless. Overweening.' She was nodding to herself now. 'Very well. The child must be taught that there are far older powers in this world and that he is but an infant among them. The north, I think. Their grip is weakest in the north. We still get foraging parties in and out there. Tomorrow, Silk. You shall accompany me tomorrow night.'

'To the north?'

She was still nodding. Her gaze held somewhere far past Silk now. 'Yes. I will summon Ryllandaras.'

* * *

Dorin sought out one of his few remaining rented safe-rooms and lay back on the straw-stuffed pallet. Sleep, however, would not come. He wondered how to enter Pung's compound. Simply walk in the front door? No. He must not be spotted meeting the man. It was already regrettable that a few of the toughs had seen him. Unavoidable, he supposed.

He would pursue the best option he'd planned during those long vigils overlooking the black market boss's compound. He would gain entry to the larger open compound among the returning crews of street thugs, beggars and cutpurses. From there, he would try to push into the main quarters that held Pung's offices. Failing that, he would circle round and try for another entrance. And failing that, he would climb to the second storey or the roof.

Very well. That would have to do. If he was cornered, he would simply reveal that he was expected. Yes, much easier to enter a defended position if you didn't have to worry about how you would get out.

That resolved, he eased into relaxation and allowed himself to fall asleep. The last thought that came to him was what Pung had meant regarding his old acquaintance – that Dal Hon mage. It sounded to him as if the fellow was not sitting quite as comfortably as he'd imagined.

With the sixth bell of the next day the shift of returning crews came trickling in through the doors of Pung's compound. With them came a well-dressed lad, walking straight in. A guard raised his truncheon to stop the fellow. 'Who're you?'

'Toben.'

'What do you do?'

'I take things from people.'

The guard gestured, inviting him to show what he had. The lad drew out a very fat bag and opened it. The guard took a handful of the clinking contents then urged the lad onward. 'Okay. You can go.'

The lad didn't move. Others pushed in past him. 'You can't do that.'

'Do what?'

'Just grab a bunch of my coin.'

'Got no idea what you're talking 'bout, kid. G'wan.'

'I'll complain.'

'You do that and I'll beat the crap out of you every time I see you – okay?'

The lad tossed a rude gesture and marched off. The guard turned to his fellows. 'Did you see that? The nerve of some people, I tell you.'

The nearest guard held out his hand and the first looked to the sky, groaning, and began portioning out shares.

Inside, Dorin turned away from the main stream heading to what looked like the largest of a series of dormitories. He angled towards the open-fronted warehouses and great piles of gravel, bricks, and other building materials, throwing off his jacket as he went.

He was reaching behind his back, in the process of moving the weapons he'd brought to more accessible places, when he turned a corner of piled lumber and almost ran straight into a guard.

Inwardly, he cursed. He'd known Pung kept four wandering compound guards – just his bad luck to run into one here. He slapped a hand to his forehead, jumping. 'Gods! You frightened me!'

'What're you doin' here?' the older fellow grumbled, his mouth turned down beneath a huge moustache.

'My girl's waiting for me at the back. It's our only chance to . . . you know . . . get together . . .'

The guard snorted, peering round. 'Got a hot date, hey?' The moustache drew down. 'How hot?'

Wincing, Dorin held out a single Hengan round.

The guard sneered. 'Not so hot. What do you get? Just a stroking?'

143

Dorin added three. The guard looked mildly impressed. 'Lookin' better – but not quite all the way.'

Letting out a hissed breath, Dorin added one more. The guard swiped them into his hand. 'There you go. Worth your while, I'd say.'

Dorin forced a nervous laugh. 'Oh yeah! That's for sure.' He edged past the guard and jogged onward. That had cost him dear, but it was worth it as the plan was to wait into the night and come upon Pung in the pre-dawn hours. A slain guard would've forced his hand.

He found a ready hiding spot among the odds and ends of piled wood, sat cross-legged, and dozed, waiting for the appointed time.

The sky glowing the rosy pink of imminent dawn was his sign to straighten his legs and rub the circulation back into them. Once that was accomplished, he rose and readied the gear he'd brought. First he reversed his shirt and trousers to their inside lining, which was a dull pewter grey. Then he finished moving his weapons and gear to ready-at-hand positions and set off for the main building. The west wall was the least overlooked and here he spotted several possible means of ingress – all windows. He took a running leap and reached the lowest. Its shutters proved too corroded to open. He propped his feet on the sill and launched himself up to the window above. This one had bars, but very far apart. He slid between them, landed on his hands, cartwheeled, and stood. He was in a hireling dormitory. Everyone was asleep. He padded between the bunks to the door. Peeping out, he saw that the hall was empty. He went to find the stairs up to the second floor where he assumed Pung kept court.

The stairs led up to a guardroom, or antechamber, which was empty. He gently padded forward to the inner door, lifted the latch, and pushed the door open. Across a room rested a broad desk behind which sat Pung himself, reading. The many other chairs in the room were all empty.

Pung glanced up from the sheaf of papers he was studying. 'It's about time. Everyone's fallen asleep waiting.'

Determined not to show the least disappointment, Dorin slipped in the door, walked up to Pung's desk, and sat in the nearest chair. He swung his feet up on to the desk. 'Seems private now.'

Nodding, Pung opened a drawer, pulled out a tall bottle and two tiny shot glasses and poured two drinks. Dorin ignored the one in front of him. Pung tossed his back, sucked air through his teeth, and regarded Dorin. 'Been hearing rumours for months now that there was a blade in town. Had to take it slow, though. You'd be surprised how many arseholes show up claiming to be shit-hot deadly knifemen – or women. Full of talk they are. And talk is cheap. The real thing, though,' he lifted his glass to Dorin, 'that's rare.'

Dorin waited, saying nothing; he'd yet to hear any offer.

Pung sucked his teeth once more, regarded him silently for a time. 'You gonna work for me you have to prove you're not all talk. Anyone can knife a person. All those I've met who like that sorta work are the kind of fellas high on my own list to kill out of pure self-protection – if you see what I mean. So . . . you're going to have to prove yourself. Kind of like an initiation.' And he smiled, his thick lips pulled back in a teeth-baring grin.

The word gave Dorin an ugly feeling. It reminded him of that night at Tran's place and he was taken by a chilling premonition that perhaps he'd made a mistake in coming here.

'There's a fella works for Urquart,' Pung continued. 'Works well with the young street thieves and such. Too popular. Makes my work harder. Can't have that.'

Dorin's feeling of unease grew.

'You kill him and you're in. His name's Rafalljara. But you might've heard of him by his street name, Rafall.'

Dorin kept his face flat, but inwardly he couldn't believe what he was hearing. Why not some other damned agent of Urquart? Did Pung know? Was that behind the assignment? He stared at the fellow hard, but the wide-jowled sweaty face revealed nothing. The man was far too experienced in hiding his thoughts. Not trusting himself to speak, Dorin nodded his assent. He suddenly felt as dirty as he had that night at Tran's.

Pung grunted his agreement and did something behind the desk – pulled a cord perhaps. A moment later the door opened and a tall bland-looking fellow entered and closed the door behind himself.

'This is Greneth,' said Pung. 'He's my second.' He asked Dorin, 'Anybody see you comin' in?'

'No one who would remember me tomorrow.'

Pung grunted again. 'Good. Gren, take this fellow down and introduce him around as a new enforcer – nothing more than that. What name?'

Dorin was startled. 'Danar,' he managed, stammering, and damned the stammer.

Pung's grin seemed to curl briefly. 'Okay ... Danar.' He motioned to Greneth. 'Oh! And show him our mage too. Danar here was curious about him.' Now the wide grin was definitely sneering. Pung gestured to the door. Dorin eased himself to his feet. Greneth stepped away from the door. Dorin cast one look back; Pung had returned to glancing through the sheaf of papers.

None of this had gone the way he'd intended at all. Pung hadn't even mentioned a sum – and he stupidly hadn't demanded one. It had all somehow twisted, and he couldn't pin down just when it had happened. He decided it was when he sat down.

Greneth introduced him around. They passed the guard he'd met yesterday and the man didn't even blink. Dorin could only shake his head: we all see what we expect, or want, to see.

Then Greneth took him out to the works. Here hordes of kids ran about making bricks, sawing wood, picking rope, twisting hemp, and feeding dried dung into kilns. They entered the largest of the great warehouses. Greneth unlocked a door to an inner room revealing stone stairs leading underground. He locked the door behind them, lifted a lantern, lit it from a torch, and started down the stairs. Dorin followed, intrigued.

'There're leagues of catacombs under the city,' Greneth explained as they descended. He had a very weak, almost wheezy voice. 'Our forebears buried their dead in them for thousands of years.' A gate of iron bars blocked the way at the base. Greneth unlocked this as well and pushed it open. Beyond, they came to an intersection of rounded, semicircular tunnels. Dorin was surprised to see a troop of young children slouching up out of the darkness, some no more than infants. They looked for all the world like dirt-smeared escapees from Hood's paths, except that they carried shovels and buckets, and all were manacled. He glanced up to see Greneth watching him, a sly grin at his lips. 'They buried them with the richest funerary goods they could afford.' He waved Dorin onward. 'This way.'

At last Greneth stopped at a door in the round stone wall, selected a key from the large ring he carried, and unlocked it. He pushed the door inward, and it grated and scraped over the ground from disuse. He extended the lantern for Dorin to take and waved him in. 'Our terrifying and fearsome mage.'

Dorin almost stepped into the chamber but managed to catch himself at the threshold. Lantern in hand, he invited Greneth to proceed him. The man's sly smile grew to almost split his face, and he inclined his head in acknowledgement of the delicate point. 'Of course.' He entered, hands clasped behind his back.

Dorin edged in and peered round. It was a large chamber, though very low-roofed. Thick pillars of brick took up most of the room's volume. The stink of excrement and sweat was appalling. The walls appeared to be decorated. He crossed to the nearest and raised the lantern for a better look. Charcoal drawings covered the brickwork, rectangular panels about the size of large tablets. He chose one and studied it. Some sort of animal was depicted bounding in mid-leap, its fearsome jaws agape. Some sort of . . . hound?

'*Noo!*'

Dorin spun, knife readied, but relaxed immediately as he took in the shape closing upon him. It was the Dal Hon youth, chained and manacled, his clothes tattered and filthy. The poor fellow was secured at the ankles with a chain leading up to cuffs at his wrists, but the length was insufficient and he couldn't raise his hands past chest height.

He shuffled over to put himself between Dorin and the wall. 'It's not ready yet,' he slurred, his voice sounding strange. Then Dorin saw that he held a burned stick in his mouth. Bobbing, almost shrugging in embarrassment, the fellow continued, 'Just some ideas I'm working on – nothing finished yet!' and he gave a laugh whose note of madness sent a shiver up Dorin's spine.

Greneth grabbed hold of the chain and yanked it so that the lad fell to the floor. Then he set to kicking him savagely in his side.

'Critics!' the fellow whimpered as he curled into a protective ball. 'Critics everywhere!'

Catching his breath, Greneth straightened, brushed back his hair. 'This,' he began, with a kick to punctuate every word, 'is . . . what . . . happens . . . when . . . you . . . lie . . . to . . . Pung.' He raised his gaze to Dorin. 'This fellow came to us promising the moon—'

'Yes, the moon . . .' the lad said, eagerly.

147

'Shut up!' Greneth kicked him again. 'But when it came time to deliver, what could he do? Nothing! Couldn't kill anyone. Couldn't conjure a damned thing. Turns out he's a charlatan. A fake.' Greneth straightened his shirt, eyed Dorin up and down. 'This is what Pung does to those who can't deliver.'

Dorin turned away to study the countless other panels sketched on the walls. What did the lad mean about the moon? It made him shiver. It seemed . . . insane.

'Pung took everything,' the lad groaned. 'Everything. Even something that wasn't mine.'

Dorin shot a look to Greneth, then crouched down over the Dal Hon. 'What? What was it?'

'A box. A box containing something incalculably important . . .'

'He carried no treasures,' Greneth said, dismissive.

Dorin straightened. Did he mean the box they took from the Jaghut? Did the lad even recognize him? Or had he been driven irredeemably mad? He couldn't question him with Greneth here. He'd have to return later. As to being a charlatan – he was sure the fellow possessed *some* sort of power. Certain of it. He'd done things Dorin had never seen anyone else do.

He turned to Greneth, shrugging. 'Serves him right, then.' He headed for the door. 'Let's go. Stinks in here.'

He pulled up short at the entrance as it was crowded by the child labourers. All peered in, their eyes bright on their dirt-smeared faces. Greneth waved them off. 'Get back to work!' They scattered, leaving something in the entrance – something small and furry with tiny eyes. Greneth sent a kick after it and it scampered off, chattering. 'Damned monkey!'

'I don't think that was a monkey,' Dorin said, amazed.

'It's the mage's pet. No one can catch the damned thing. Now it has the run of the tunnels beneath the city. We'll poison it yet.'

A slight wind brushed Dorin. It blew hot and dry in the doorway and he frowned, casting a glance to Greneth who seemed oblivious, or simply uninterested. Where could it be coming from? There were no other entrances that he could see. Behind him, the lad had shuffled over to a wall and returned to his sketching, humming and murmuring to himself – even though there was no light at all within his cell.

Dorin felt all the hairs of his arms and neck stand on end. There was something very strange here. Something of the Warrens, but Greneth seemed blind to it. Dorin allowed the man to swing the door shut and lock it, then handed back the lantern. Glancing over his shoulder as he followed Greneth back up the tunnel, he noticed the many child miners edging in from the dark, closing once more on the mage's cell.

He'd return as well. Sometime. But first he had his own promise to Pung to fulfil.

Chapter 8

GETTING OUT OF LI HENG PROVED FAR EASIER THAN SILK imagined it ought to be. He received orders to join a foraging party assembling in the pre-dawn hours on a north section of the Outer Round. Here he found Shalmanat, cloaked, her head wrapped in cloth and veil, awaiting him among a crew of their regular scouts and scavengers.

They were let down the wall by rope then jogged off through a maze of burned hovels. 'What of the Kanese?' he asked as they ran.

'They do not chase these parties. I believe they hope to encourage deserting.' Then Shalmanat raced off, and proved a tireless runner. Silk struggled to keep up. The path she chose took them past the churned dirt of one-time market gardens to surrounding burned fields, and then on to the open plains. Here the land lay gently rolling – uncounted leagues of unbroken grasslands dotted with copses of trees, small streams, and modest lakes stretching all the way north to the Fenn mountains. The country of the Seti horse clans, Ferret, Wolf, and Eagle. And the warrior society of the White Jackal who worshipped Ryllandaras, the Elder Hero himself. Brother, some said, to Treach, the tiger god of summer.

They jog-trotted through the heat of the day, Silk suffering terribly. He was no soldier. His namesake shirt hung from him soaked in sweat, and no doubt ruined by the salt stains to come. His feet in their heeled boots screamed in pain; he was certain he'd scoured all the flesh from his ankles.

Late in the day he commented, 'We have seen no war bands.'

'The Kanese have bribed them to hunt elsewhere.'

'And Ryllandaras? What of him? How will you call him?'

'He knows already that I have stepped on to his lands.'

'You make him sound like some patron god of the plains.'

She cast him a long look. Only her dark eyes showed between head-wrap and veil. 'He is. Of a sort.'

That silenced him. For a time. In the late afternoon she slowed her pace, perhaps out of consideration for him. He was only mildly chagrined – he had not the training, and she was not human, after all. Side by side they pushed through the tall sharp-edged grasses. 'And what will we eat?' he asked, by now quite hungry.

'What did you bring?'

He laughed, a touch uneasily. 'No one said anything about bringing food.'

'There are no wayside inns or taverns out here, dear Silk.'

'You are teasing me.' At least he hoped she was. She handed him a strip of some fibrous dark material that resembled old burlap. 'What is this?'

'Dried meat.'

He sniffed it. It smelled of nothing. 'What does one do with it, pray tell?'

'Hold a bite of it in your cheek for the rest of the afternoon.'

He made a face. 'Gods forgive me, what a disgusting thing to do.'

She laughed. 'You are an urban creature, Silk.'

'And urbane.' He examined the desiccated strip, sniffed it again. 'What was it?'

'Horse.'

He put it away, grimacing. 'I think I'll wait.'

She laughed again, high and sweet-sounding, and Silk was pleased to hear it.

Towards dusk, however, he began to feel a little worried. No one ever travelled the Seti Plains in such a small party. It was tantamount to suicide. Even the Seti kept to war bands of twenty or more armed warriors. When the sun finally fell below the western horizon and the midges and other such biting insects multiplied into clouds surrounding them, he asked, 'Should we not start a fire for the night?'

'I will start a fire,' she answered, and, peering round, pointed out the tallest of the modest hills about. Silk felt a growing unease; it seemed she was truly determined to invite a visit from the man-beast.

Atop the hillock, she searched about then selected an area and sat cross-legged. He sat next to her, wrapped his arms about his aching knees. 'Why choose me – to accompany you, I mean?'

She nodded at the question. 'I could not bring Ho. He and Ryllandaras have fought before.'

Silk's brows shot up at this casual revelation. 'Really? They've fought?'

'Yes, once or twice. He and Ryllandaras . . . well, they have much in common. I could not bring Koroll, as the man-beast would take his presence as a challenge. Likewise Mara or Smokey.'

Silk observed, rather drily, 'You are saying that he will not judge me a challenge?'

'You are offended?'

'Just my pride.'

She cast him another long look. 'I did not think you so easily dismayed by the opinions of others.'

He offered a reassuring smile. 'I am not.'

'Good. That is one of the things I value about you, Silk. Your . . . independence of thought.' She turned her attention to the ground before her then, and Silk said nothing as he recognized the beginnings of ritual preparations – though the exact ritual itself was a mystery to him, as it was of Tiste Liosan. Her slim pale hands danced in graceful designs and her breathing laboured in precise increments. Then she leaned back, her breath levelling in a long exhalation, and rested her hands on her knees. 'It is done.'

'I see nothing.'

'Look through your Warren.'

It was a chill night as the sky was almost completely clear. The stars shone hard and bright. The constellation of the Mariner was high in the east, while the Weaver curved now towards the western horizon. He summoned his Warren. What was revealed drove him backwards like a glimpse into a furnace. A churning pillar of puissance spun before him. He bent his head back but could not glimpse its top. 'What is this?' he yelled, awed, though the spectacle was utterly silent.

'A beacon few can see.'

'More than he will see this.'

'And they are welcome to approach – knowing he will be coming as well.'

He shivered despite his patron's complete confidence. 'What now?'

'Now we wait.'

He nodded, accepting this, though unhappy about it. He'd detested the dried meat, but now found himself wishing there was more of it. Or at least a drink. He'd brought nothing of the sort himself. He drew breath and asked, 'Have you any—'

Shalmanat held out a curved goat-hide waterskin, such as the Seti carry. Now definitely chagrined, he took it and pulled out the wooden stopper and drank. It was plain water, but warm from having been carried next to her body. Perhaps hung over her breast, or her stomach. He savoured the warmth.

Stoppering the waterskin, he handed it back and regarded her, now sitting within his arm's reach. Her silver hair hung about her shoulders, blown lightly by the weak night winds; her face was long – too long by contemporary Hengan standards of beauty. The eyes too far apart, the lips too thin. But he knew her secret now. She was of the Tiste. An ancient race with a sad history, if he recalled the songs he'd heard correctly.

He cleared his throat and asked, 'Why Li Heng? I mean, what brought you here? If I may ask.'

She nodded absently at the question and leaned back, setting her hands to the earth behind her. 'A fair question, Silk.' Then she was quiet for a time, gathering her thoughts. 'I fought in the wars, you know.'

'What wars?'

She turned to him, surprised. 'Why, the wars of light and darkness, of course.'

His breath was punched from him in stunned amazement. *Oh, of course . . .*

She continued, perhaps unaware of his astonishment, 'I was a staff aid to – well, to one of Osserc's officers. They used to call them the Daughters of Light, unofficially. The Andii never did become accustomed to war, you know. But we did. We had the tradition of an older legion to guide us. Yes, we Liosan took to war far too well.' She clenched her lips then, and lowered her gaze. 'I, however, lost my taste for it. I came to . . . admire . . . one of the leaders of the Andii. In time I came to see the struggle as . . . self-defeating.'

Her gaze rose, perhaps tracing the height of the invisible pillar

153

of Liosan magery before her. 'I fled the bloodshed,' she murmured, almost dreamily. 'Found these crossroads. And here I set my seat and tried to establish a peace. Tried to build something rather than destroy. And,' she lifted her shoulders in a shrug, 'there you are.'

Silk had no idea what to say. What could one say to such a confidence? He cleared his throat once more. 'Well . . . we are grateful for all that you have done.'

She smiled, wistfully. 'Thank you.'

Unable to set his fears to rest, he asked, 'And Ryllandaras? You do not fear him?'

'Fear him? Yes, I fear him greatly. However, I know that he will not harm me.'

And what of me, Silk wondered? Perhaps she assumed her personal safety extended to him – in which case he hoped it was more than mere assumption. Nevertheless, he recalled how she had stressed that it was all about challenge with the man-beast, so he resolved not to draw any weapon, and to work on projecting his utter harmlessness, a particular specialty of his.

Was this why she'd brought him? Because of this rather unusual talent? Well, he supposed he would find out soon enough.

The night darkened as they waited. Eventually, it became too much for him, exhausted as he was. His eyes kept drooping, his head nodding. Despite his dread and the cold, he gave in and lay down. He tucked his head on one arm, and slept.

A stink woke him. A pervasive animal musk penetrated his uneasy dreams until it made him wrinkle his nose and nearly cough. The shortage of breath choked him and he started up, making a face. 'What is that—'

A curt wave from Shalmanat silenced him.

She was standing, facing the west. He clambered to his feet with an effort, kneaded his numb legs. It was light, but the sun had yet to rise above the eastward rim of the world. Thin streamers of clouds high above glowed pink and gold. The wind pulled at his shirt and vest, uncomfortably chill.

Something was approaching. It walked with a slow heavy gait, swinging from side to side, its heavy arms hanging forward, ash-grey in the dim light. While Silk watched – aching to draw a weapon – it paused, raising a black snout to scent the air, warily.

The man-beast wary? This was a new revelation for Silk. But

then he considered all the many stories relating the countless hunts that had set out against this one. All of which had come to singularly messy ends.

Evidently satisfied, the beast continued onward, climbing the hillock. Silk could not help but sidle over a touch closer to Shalmanat. As the beast closed, it reared taller and taller until a daunted Silk realized that even hunched over as it was, nearly on all four limbs, it yet stood twice the height of a man; should it straighten fully it would no doubt reach thrice. Its tangled pelt of sandy-yellow fur lightened to creamy white down its throat and chest. Muscles knotted its thick wiry limbs and its long fingers ended in amber claws the length of fighting knives. Its blackened muzzle was long yet thick, carrying something of the jackal, or hunting dog. However, the obvious intelligence in its pale blue eyes suggested wolfishness to Silk. Ryllandaras was an embodiment of the canine-human melding in all its various manifestations.

The creature closed upon them until Silk almost shouted his alarm and shrank away. Then, just as Shalmanat raised a hand in greeting, it halted and, astonishingly, sank to one knee.

Silk thought he had reached the limits of horror until the beast spoke, when it stirred his hair to hear intelligible words issue from such a monstrosity.

'Shalmanat, I greet you,' it ground out in a slurred and distorted voice. 'My enemy . . . and my love.'

'I do not seek your regard,' she answered, 'but I thank you.'

Straightening, the creature now loomed over them like a pale thundercloud. It motioned one clawed hand to Silk. 'Is this your trap, then, my love? Am I to dismiss this one to my peril?'

The Protectress shook her head. 'No. No traps. Merely someone to watch my back out here upon these plains. For I hear it is dangerous to travel them.'

Something like a cross between a growling bark and a laugh from the beast answered that. 'Indeed it is. And as I have said before – no trap is necessary for you have already captured me.'

The Protectress's answering smile was warm, though tinged by sadness. 'Is this to be yet another tale of star-crossed lovers? The old story of the terrifying monster captivated by beauty?'

'To me you are terrifying, this is true.'

Shalmanat laughed so freely that Silk felt a knife-blade of

155

jealousy twist his gut. Her smile fading, she crossed her arms. 'I invoke our agreement,' she said. 'I would have you fall upon these Kanese invaders.'

The creature rumbled a low growl that set the ground beneath Silk's feet vibrating. 'There are far easier prey upon the plains,' it answered, reluctant.

'It is my request. Would you deny it?'

The beast did not answer. Only its low panting breath sounded in the night. It scanned the nearby grounds as if searching for enemies.

It fears something, Silk realized. Some hold Shalmanat has over it.

'Shall I withdraw my prohibitions upon travel and trade across the plains?' she asked. 'Shall I allow trading posts to be built at every seasonal camp? Every butte or river fork? What will become of the Seti then? What will become of you when towns rise round those posts? When game grows scarce and the ground is broken to the plough? Where will you run then?'

The creature waved a heavy clawed hand, growling and hissing. '*You* are the monster here, Shalmanat. You know my answer.'

She raised her chin, her mouth set. 'Very well. Obey, then.'

'So it shall be. So my love remains my greatest enemy. And the one who has chained me.'

A vision came to Silk of the subterranean chamber, the stone sarcophagus, and the chains bumping and rattling in the dark. Was this beast prescient? Perhaps some gift of foresight was afforded it as it was to some, after all, a god.

Shalmanat nodded curtly. 'We are done, then. Drive them from the north shore.'

The beast inclined its great mangy head. 'It shall be as you command.' And with that it turned and loped off on all fours, quickly reaching a pace Silk was certain no horse could hope to match.

The two watched it disappear between the rolling hills as the sun broached the east. Shalmanat let go a long sigh and rubbed one arm. Silk thought her mood certainly melancholy, perhaps even regretful. And he, who had never known the emotion in regard to anyone, found himself jealous of a monster.

* * *

156

She stood on a rooftop in the quiet of night, overlooking a large compound in the north of the outermost precinct of the city. The strange phenomena disturbing Kurald Galain, the Elder Warren of Darkness, seemed to emanate from there.

She wished to solve this mystery, but she was wary as well. Was this a renegade priestess of Elder Dark? Or a gifted thaumaturgic researcher, a sorcerer out of Jacuruku? For all she knew it might even be one of her brothers or sisters. Not all were accounted for. Barging in would force a confrontation . . . one the city surrounding her might not survive.

And K'rul would disapprove.

She lowered her gaze to her hands, turning them over as if examining them for the first time. So clumsy, so ineffectual, these instruments. How hard it was to be the last. The last to give herself over to a role, persona, or manifestation – call it what you would. Not that any choice remained even if she wished to abandon her path. The High King's curse had seen to that.

The mortal's realm yet remained open to her. And with it – a mortal's fate.

She clenched her fists. Felt the slide of the ligaments pulling the bones together; felt the pulse of the blood within. Such a fragile vessel. It was a wonder anything could be accomplished by them. And yet, wonders had.

It was a mystery beyond her kind's ken. How could this be? Were they missing something? Was there some flaw within them? This was the mystery she had given over her life to solving.

She felt, rather than heard, the light footfalls about her and let her head sink in frustration. 'I thought your masters and I had reached an agreement,' she said.

'We acknowledge only one master,' a voice responded from her rear.

She turned, took in four black-clad figures ranged about her. 'Go back and ask him if this is his will,' she answered.

'We do not take orders from you,' said another.

She turned to the second speaker. 'That was not an order. That was a way out. I suggest you take it.'

'We suggest you leave the city. We grant no special privileges.'

She drew a hard breath to control her annoyance, then said, slowly and deliberately: 'I neither have, nor want, any part in your little dispute.'

'You force us to act, then,' the second answered, and the four shifted, readying fighting daggers, their blades as dark as night.

She merely stilled momentarily and in that instant the tiles beneath her feet gathered a layer of frost and the air around her crackled. Mist now ran from her in rivulets, curling and streaming. She reached out to a Nightblade and he gasped, clutched at a throat now choked by crystals of frost, and toppled.

The other three rushed at once.

She brushed aside the first's thrust. The wrist froze and shattered as she blocked. The blade of the second burst into shards as it slammed against her, while the body of the third fell one way and the head another when the woman's hand brushed through the neck as if it were thin cloth.

The first two tore at their throats, unable to produce a sound, and fell.

The woman knelt over one, considered the man's cowled upturned face. Ice glittered on the cloth. She watched as a wave of crystals swept over the eyes, turning them into frosted milky orbs as hard as stone. 'I am Sister of Cold Nights,' she told the corpse. 'Do not try my ire.'

Straightening, she examined her hands once again and cursed under her breath. This was not, she knew, what K'rul had intended. She crossed the rooftop and descended to the street, still irritated; that had been one of the best overlooks she'd found.

* * *

Hallens had everyone on full alert in the days and nights following the Nightblades' intimation of an attack upon the Protectress. Nothing, however, changed at all. No alarms, searches, attempted arrests, or condemnations. No tumult or confusion showed itself among the staff and functionaries of the palace. Food was delivered as before; laundry taken away for cleaning without dispute.

It was, Iko had to admit, the strangest house arrest she'd ever heard of. The only change of behaviour was enforced among the Sword-Dancers themselves: none walked alone during the day; twice the normal numbers stood watch through the night; and a self-imposed curfew was in force.

Questions raised by these new orders were met by silence from Hallens. Iko's personal status as the sisters' whipping-girl remained.

She found no opportunity for any private conversation with her commander.

The situation was almost more of a trial to her patience than she could bear. Her sisters' disdain and superior airs galled her more than she ever imagined it would have. Was status among her sisters so important to her after all? She was, she decided, a disappointment to herself.

All this time she'd been so certain that common opinion meant nothing to her. That she knew her value and those who could not see it were fools. Now, staring out of a barred window, her arms crossed fiercely, fists knotted beneath her upper arms, she wondered who was the fool after all. When all those around you considered you a fool, so you were, by all accounts. And thus to history as well. For when people were questioned regarding the past they would say, 'That little fool? She was no use.' And so it would be recorded, and so is history shown to be as accurate as those consulted in its compiling.

To add to her foul mood the worst of the offenders among her sisters, led by Yvonna and Torral, now came crowding around her. 'Is this your doing, then?' Yvonna sneered.

Still facing out of the window, and knowing full well what they meant, she answered, 'Is what my doing?'

'All these new rules. The curfew.'

'What do you care? You never went out anyway.'

'Did you try running off?' Torral taunted. 'You a traitor to our lord king?'

Iko rounded on this one – not the best swordswoman of them, but one of the stronger, and certainly the most gleefully brutal. 'Don't push me today, Torral,' she said, sounding tired even to her ears.

The woman's eyes lit up with the chance to deal pain. 'I wouldn't even break a sweat.'

'Just take your stupid games elsewhere.'

Torral pursed her full lips into a moue of petulance. 'Oh, poor little Iko. Poor little baby girl. Run to Hallens now, won't you?'

Iko raised her eyes to the roof and hissed a long-suffering breath between her teeth. 'Fine.' She waved Torral to follow. 'C'mon. Let's do this. I'm bored to death anyway.'

Torral's one-sided smile climbed even higher. 'You're stupider than I thought.' She pushed on ahead to the main hall of their rooms, trailed by her gaggle of hangers-on. 'Practice blades here!' she shouted.

Iko followed, alone.

All the sisters gathered round. Furniture and rugs were hurriedly pushed aside. Iko stripped down to loose trousers and a tunic, slipped off her sandals. One of her sisters, Rei, crossed to her carrying a wooden practice blade.

'She'll go for the ribs,' Rei warned, speaking low.

'I know. And thanks.'

Rei just gave a sour smile. 'Better win, or she'll be unbearable afterwards.'

'Don't I know it.' Iko glanced about, saw Hallens among the crowd, her arms crossed, looking on with barely concealed disapproval. But not interfering. No, better to let them vent a little steam, Iko imagined. Not that that would help her when she was lying on the ground with a broken skull.

Torral's gang urged her on and laughed at muttered comments too low for Iko to make out.

No one offered her any encouragement. Most, however, were quiet.

Torral stepped out quickly, making the air hum with cuts from her blade. 'Let's go, little one. No chance to run away now.'

Iko couldn't believe how infuriating the woman was; she decided to come out fighting. 'Does it look like I'm running, you stupid cow?'

Torral's brows shot up and her hard smile widened. 'Oho! The kitten's trying out its claws! Have to slap her down, I think.'

Iko stepped out and struck a ready stance, her body sideways, the blade extended, its tip resting at just over the height of her nose. Torral bowed mockingly then responded. She eased forward until a single sword-length separated them – they were now, effectively, committed to a mutual kill zone.

Iko waited, her attention on her opponent's chest – her centre of gravity. At the same time, however, she took in the wider picture as a sort of flowing commentary on where that centre of gravity might be headed.

Torral shifted into an overhead ready position, blade held downward in a vertical line bisecting her shoulder.

Iko ignored the invitation to enter into the dance of stance, pose, and counter-pose. The dance might be stylish and impressive to onlookers – especially the ignorant ones – but in her view it had no place in a real fight. Torral, she knew, wanted the fight. And so she would wait; Torral would have to come to her.

Iko was a counter-attacker by instinct. She tended to wait for her opponent to commit herself then responded in the most deadly and efficient manner. She also knew that her waiting suited Torral; the woman loved to rush in to overbear and punish her opponents. In short, Iko had the advantage of knowing Torral better than Torral knew her.

After a series of pretty stances – all technically very well executed – meant to impress her lackeys and admirers among the Sword-Dancers, Torral turned serious. She struck the forward ready pose, a power stance, her favourite. Iko noted the tensing of the shoulders, the flaring nostrils as Torral drew in extra air for the rush.

The flurry came so fast she had no chance to think. At this level everything moved beyond conscious thought; the body ran on muscle memory, moving instinctively, while the mind . . . well, the mind *floated*, attempting not to interfere just yet. No one this proficient planned what to do. You did not plan . . . you waited. Waited for an opening.

The staccato clack of the training swords rang like an avalanche of clattering rocks within the chambers. Torral would have driven Iko right across the great main central plaza if Iko were not so true to the rule of always stepping sideways, always circling round. Torral followed raining blow after blow that Iko slipped and parried while she watched . . . waiting.

Iko almost felt sorry for her sister. For they were in truth dancing now.

And she was leading.

Her opening came when she was piqued to see Torral employ the same series of cuts twice in a row. Was this how low her opinion was of her, she wondered, that she should be so careless? Or perhaps it was a measure of how sure she was of winning. In any case, Iko had one possible key and waited, watching.

Torral continued in her relentless attack, ever swinging, her blade clacking from Iko's in an unremitting display of aggression. Another would have bided her time, waiting for the woman to pause out of utter exhaustion, but Iko knew better. This was Torral's natural pace – she could maintain it all day. Keep and hold the initiative was the woman's credo.

161

And so Iko circled, ever watching for the first of that repeated series of cuts. It appeared, and in that instant Iko's body twitched in muscle memory. She slipped the second cut to ride over the extended blade and strike the woman across the left of her face with the crack of wood against bone.

Torral staggered backwards, more in shock than pain. She pressed a hand to her mouth and came away with blood. Her dark pupils, fixed upon Iko, grew wide in outrage. 'You little shit,' she breathed, nearly in disbelief, and charged once more.

The bout should have been over at the moment of that killing blow. But none intervened as Torral's blade was a blur against Iko's, hammering and thrusting in a dizzying display of fury and technical brilliance.

And still Iko circled, giving ground, leading her opponent in another dance.

Until she saw a chance to counter, this time across the gut. Winded, the other woman fell to her knees, gasping for breath. Iko considered the bout finished then.

Yet Torral struggled to rise once more, gasping and spitting, slurring curses.

Iko had had enough. She stepped in, sword raised, meaning to strike at half-power across the back of the skull to knock the fool out, when a shout of command from Hallens froze her arms.

'Enough!'

She backed away from where Torral still struggled to rise. The swordwomen parted for Hallens. 'We will need all swords for what is to come,' she told Iko, waving her off. She yanked Torral up by the arm, shook her. 'A good bout. A good lesson – yes, Torral?' Wiping the spit and blood from her chin the dazed woman gave a curt resentful nod. 'Yes. Very good,' Hallens answered for her. She pushed her into the arms of her followers among the Sword-Dancers then walked off without any acknowledgement of Iko's performance.

Across the way, grinning like a cat, Rei mouthed a silent *Well done.*

Iko handed over the battered wooden blade and stormed away. What stupidity! What a useless unnecessary waste of time and effort. None of this was bringing them any closer to an answer to their current predicament.

She returned to the barred window, crossed her quivering, numb arms. She didn't even feel good about winning. It could be bad for the unit's cohesion. Torral might just be dense enough to be resentful of the beating, though she'd brought it upon herself. Iko feared she might have made an enemy among her sisters. Better, perhaps, if she'd simply taken a hit and gone down. Then it would be over. Everyone would be satisfied and leave her alone as not worth their time.

Now she had yet one more stupid thing to worry about.

* * *

He decided he would do it before the striking of the mid-night bell. Rafall usually stayed up far into the later hours going over his books. He would not expect a visitor. It would be routine; no different from all his earlier visits.

Rafall would be alone, as he almost always was. He'd enter, strike, and leave with none even being aware of his arrival. Rafall would even greet him as a friend. Invite him to sit. Offer a drink. It would be simple. Comically so. Not a test of his abilities at all, he reflected.

No – this was intended as a test of something very different.

Something Dorin was not certain he wished to succeed in.

He yanked on the cord wrapped round his forearm, tested the tiny collapsed grapnel snug there against his wrist and wondered, why this hesitation?

The test was straightforward, surely.

Yes. A test of his dependability. His degree of, dare he say . . . pliability? Or perhaps . . . *prostration*?

His teeth were clenched now, and he clasped his hands to either side of his neck, where a hidden iron lip, a slim collar, rose from his armoured vest. It was meant as a channel that could possibly catch a blade – a light one, of course. Something he'd yet had to test, though a compatriot in Tali swore by the precaution.

He ran his thumbs along the cloth-disguised iron ridge and the memory came to him of that prick, Tran, yanking Loor by the hair to a pillar for his test. His *initiation*, Tran had called it. His initiation into humiliation, degradation, and meek submission in order to belong.

Pung, he believed, suspected some sort of prior patronage or business relationship between him and Rafall. And thus the test. This *initiation* into Pung's ranks.

163

Was this to be his test of submissiveness and self-degradation?

Yet what did it matter? He'd trained as a killer. It was his job. Nothing more. Why then the distaste for this one? It was not a question of morality. No, he'd dispensed with any such artificial external measures of right or wrong long ago. It was internal. It had everything to do with his own self-measure.

The problem was, he'd sworn a vow to himself. More than a vow, really. A pledge to what he considered himself to be. To his integrity. His pride.

He might kill any man or woman . . . but he would bend to none.

There. It was out in the open. Now the question was what to do about it. He let go a long hard exhalation and grasped hold of the edges of the window before him and leaned there, breathing loudly into the night. His arms trembled, rigid. As if ready to yank him out instantly – or to hold him back. He felt as if he were drowning.

He'd agreed. He had to go through with it. Yet he'd already decided not to join any crew or gang or party where any sort of submission was the condition of entry. He was too stupidly proud, he supposed, to compromise himself. That's just how it was.

The answer, it came to him, would be to leave it to Rafall. The man had done right by him so far. Certainly, he'd knocked him down the day he'd entered the city – but that was business, before they'd struck any agreement or professional understanding. He held no grudge for that. It had been a rather bracing lesson, in fact.

There. He would put the point to Rafall. Yes. And the argument would be very pointed indeed.

*

The yell rang through the rooms in the early pre-dawn hours. Rafall's guards bolted from their chairs where they dozed before the only access to their boss's rooms – the base of a steep ladder up to the garret chambers. They bashed and hammered the closed trapdoor, but found it blocked by some weight above, and so dashed down the stairs and out to the street to climb up from the outside.

Yet Rafall's headquarters had been deliberately designed to be near impossible to access from without, and so it was some time before the nimblest and lightest of his boys and girls managed the tricky ascent. Along the way, up gable and overhang, they encountered splashes of fresh drying blood and signs of a struggle in broken slate shingles, scraps of torn cloth, and a dropped bloodied knife – one of Rafall's.

Within, they levered the furniture from the trapdoor and allowed the guard's entrance. They searched, but amid the clutter of the struggle found no sign of Rafall himself. Blood lay everywhere, quite liberally so. One girl discovered a crossbow bolt driven into the soft wood panelling of the wall opposite the man's desk. Their patron's last ditch defence, missing its mark.

Suspicion immediately fixed upon Pung. The ugly toad had long been envious of Rafall's ease and camaraderie with the street youths – a touch wholly beyond him. Many were for going after him themselves. But Gremain, Rafall's long-time lieutenant and eldest among the thieves and clubbers, reined in the hotter heads, cuffed a few, and ordered them to clean up while he and a few others took word of this to Urquart. It would then be up to him, the man Rafall answered to, to decide on any course of action.

This settled the matter and everyone set to clearing up – simultaneously pocketing whatever they could lay their hands on and searching for any hidden cache. Gremain nodded to a few of his most trusted lads and they came down the ladder after him. He knew that if Urquart were true to form, then all Rafall's old territory should come to him in an orderly straightforward descent. In the meantime, he'd let the others ransack the man's quarters. It would serve to help smooth over any resentment among those who might otherwise consider the job theirs.

*

At noon the next day, a battered half-sunk open boat loaded with refugees fleeing Heng pulled up on the south shore of the Idryn. Kanian soldiers met them there and searched for any weapons, while confiscating any valuables they could find. Their captain then read aloud from a prepared document stating that it was solely by the grace of the good King Chulalorn of Itko Kan, head of the Southern League, that the refugees were granted freedom from the Hengan yoke, and that from this point onward they were to consider themselves subjects of said Southern League, and legally owed their allegiance to King Chulalorn.

Among the rag-tag mass of refugees was one rather overweight Hengan with a full oiled beard, his fingers bearing indentations where rings had been yanked away by the soldiers, and bleeding earlobes where other rings had been just as brutally removed. He wore a torn and bloodstained shirt and trousers of fine buff leather. He'd obviously taken a head wound recently as the cloth wrapped there was still red with fresh blood. Long after most of the others had gone their way this fellow stood peering westward, to where the distant walls of Heng were just visible through the trees lining the shore. He sighed, his thick rounded shoulders rising and falling, and he tucked his hands into the belt that held his wide belly and frowned pensively. Then he too turned away, shaking his head, and started on the long walk east downriver to Cawn.

Chapter 9

Now that Dorin had secured the patronage of Li Heng's black market boss, he was, truth be told, damned bored. Pung wouldn't let him out of his sight. He had to remain within the compound; couldn't leave without permission. It was as if the fellow didn't trust him.

Perhaps Pung was only now realizing that it might not have been a good idea to order Dorin to murder his previous employer.

Certainly there were occasional jobs accompanying regular muscle on routine assignments to collect debts. But these were drying up as the siege dragged on. Indeed, even the thieves now came back empty-handed; it seemed the markets were now almost entirely empty and deserted. Yet Pung had him still remain close, unnamed, the lurking ominous threat. Nothing challenging. No real work. He was beginning to feel like a caged exotic pet. The sneaking suspicion now nagged that perhaps Pung had hired him – if *hired* was really the right word – just to take him out of everyone else's hands.

In which case he'd sold himself far too cheaply. In fact, he was beginning to think that he'd made a very serious mistake in accepting anyone's patronage at all. It just didn't feel right. It wasn't his style.

Still, his hobby remained: his pursuit of the mystery that was the Dal Hon mage.

Everyone, it seemed, knew he was down there, chained and locked in the dark. All the children forced to work about the compound, cleaning and running errands, seemed to know; certainly all those looting the tombs did. But none would speak of it. When he put the question to the dirt-faced kids, most looked frightened. A few, however, shot him narrow gauging looks. As if the prisoner were a secret they possessed and he was not to be trusted with it. An odd reaction, that.

His casual request of Gren to be allowed to go below was met with a similar silence and a long, measuring stare. And that was it. Not even a denial. That Gren ignored the question said everything. And of course Dorin couldn't raise it again; to do so would look . . . suspicious.

So he was powerless. For a time. Then he noticed how many kids were smeared in the greenish silt and clay of the underground tombs. Too many to be accounted for by the few he watched using the one main entrance Gren had taken him through.

So he kept watch. Very carefully of course, from the most distant vantages available. And soon enough he noticed how many of the child labourers disappeared around certain woodpiles yet didn't emerge. How many appeared from certain run-down storage huts without being seen to enter.

Pung and his crew of dim thugs didn't seem aware of what was going on. But then they had nothing but contempt for the children, kicking and beating them at will. Why should they suspect them to be capable of their own deceptions?

One evening he started following them. Eventually one girl in filthy baggy rags, or at least what he thought was a girl, slid into a gap between piled logs and disappeared. It was a tight fit but he was quite lean and had trained for such narrow passages himself.

The gap led to a hole and a choice. Dive in headfirst and see what might await? Hadn't the girl? Yet who knew what might lie in store for trespassers below? A pit? Sharpened stakes?

Lying there in the dark he decided that perhaps he was letting his imagination get the better of him. They were, after all, only kids. He sidled forward, lost his grip as his palms slid and slipped on clay, and was taken by the slick wet slope.

He thanked the gods he didn't yell. He landed in utter darkness amid a litter of trash that he recognized by feel as rags, sandals, torn shoes, wooden slats and rope. Reflexively, he gathered his feet beneath himself and stood, only to bash his head on a timber. He ducked, biting back curses and biting his lips as well. Stars danced in the blackness of his vision.

He knelt in the dark, bent forward, gripping his head, and waited for his vision to adjust. Slowly he made out that he occupied a crude room, or cellar, hacked from the dirt. What glimmers of natural light there were shone down from the chute above, while the weak flickering yellow of lamplight glowed from a tunnel ahead. He tried walking hunched over, but found that the roof was still too low and so was reduced to shuffling forward on all fours.

He crawled for a time, cautiously, wary of detection – though why he should be wary of a pack of children he wasn't certain – and was surprised to find a veritable warren of tunnels running beneath the compound, and no doubt beyond. At one corner he detected the murmuring of a voice and paused, listening, then followed the sound.

The raw dirt tunnel ended at a junction with a much larger, properly excavated and stone-lined one. He straightened, carefully, and padded forward to another corner. Here the voice was much stronger, amplified perhaps by the semicircular stone walls. He peeked round the corner and so confused was he by what he saw that it took him a moment to understand that he was looking at a horde of kids all sitting in a crowd before one door, all leaning forward, straining to hear the voice that Dorin now realized was coming from within.

He cocked his head as well, listening. 'Gather round, gather round, my pretties,' the voice was murmuring. 'Listen to me and none will dare raise a hand against you, I swear. But we must stay together. United. A family.'

Dorin's brows rose as he identified the voice as that of his Dal Hon rival.

'So you always say,' objected one boy, 'but they still beat Jawan and came for little Rill and did those icky things they do to her.'

'But they don't enter our tunnels,' answered the voice from beyond the door.

'They're too damned small for them!'

'Exactly. Those are ours. How goes the digging beneath the main house, Deel?'

'They don't suspect nothing. But Gren's poking round – he's sharp, that one.'

'Listen,' objected the first youth again. 'No more digging till you deliver on our protection. I say that's fair.'

Many of the matted mops of dirty hair bobbed as the children nodded and murmured their agreement.

The voice behind the door was silent for a time, then the Dal Hon spoke again. 'Very well. I was hoping to wait longer before having to resort to such measures. But I will summon a daemon out of the darkness . . . if I must.'

The kids' eyes glowed brightly as they shared awed glances.

'Really?' one whispered in amazement. 'You c'n do that?'

'Of course!' the Dal Hon snapped, quite annoyed. 'I am not to be trifled with. As I shall demonstrate.'

Dorin decided he'd had enough of this ridiculous shadow-puppet show and stepped into the open. 'That seems to be your problem,' he said. 'You promise more than you can deliver.'

The gathered diggers all gaped up at him, then, as one, let go shrill shrieks and ran pell-mell up the catacomb tunnel, disappearing. All that was left behind was the nacht. It eyed him malevolently and bared its fangs, hissing.

He ignored the beast, leaned up against the curved wall opposite the door, crossed his arms. 'I'm right . . . aren't I?'

After a long silence, the lad answered, grudgingly, 'Maybe . . .'

'You promised Pung too much and now look where you are.'

'Maybe I'm right where I want to be.'

'I don't think so. But at least you're making the most of where you are, anyway.'

'True. That's what I believe I'm best at. This locale is rife with possibilities. Something you can be part of . . . if you wish.'

Dorin rolled his eyes in the dark. 'Partner of a lying charlatan chained in a cell. Very promising.'

'I'm no charlatan!' came the answer, quite heated. 'And I can prove it if I have to.'

Dorin pushed himself from the wall. 'You're good with shadows and images and throwing sounds maybe – illusions and delusions out of Mockra and Thyr, perhaps. But that's it. You can't even magic yourself out of a cell, let alone summon some daemon.'

'Don't make me! I swear!'

Dorin made talking motions with his hand as he walked off. 'I know, I know. *You'll be sorry* and all that.'

'You *will* be sorry. What's to come is on all of you, then. Listen – whatsyourname – our box. The one from the crypt. I believe it contains the key to incalculable power. Really. It does. Are you listening?'

Dorin paused, shaking his head. This lad's tenacity knew no

bounds. 'Gods. You really are crazy, aren't you? Completely Oponn-taken mad.' He waved an unseen dismissal and ducked into one of the hand-dug tunnels.

'You'll regret this!' the lad yelled after him, his voice breaking. 'All of you! Your lack of vision! You'll regret the day you turned your back on me! You'll see!'

The words receded into unintelligible noise, muted by the yards of dirt as Dorin shuffled along. He was furious with himself. He wanted to strangle the damned Dal Hon for piquing his interest to begin with. Yet another mistake in judgement. He couldn't believe the time and effort he'd wasted on that useless fake. This town kept wrong-footing him somehow. But no more. Even though the lad did seem to be up to something here below. Stealing his share of the catacomb's funerary loot, no doubt. Still, there had been something about him. His illusions had been amazingly real – he must have *some* talent, if only for that.

Dorin stopped as he came to a fork in the tunnel. Now, how to find his way out of this damned maze . . .

* * *

It surprised Iko that she was now being treated with a new measure of respect among her sisters. Grudging, in some cases, but a new respect all the same. The change in attitude seemed very strange to her; all she'd done was beaten one of the corps' hotheads. Then the new thought came that prior to this bout she'd kept her distance from the sparring matches, choosing instead to watch and gauge weaknesses.

What hadn't occurred to her before was that others might interpret this as weakness. As if she didn't wish to expose her own incompetence. Stupid. She wouldn't have been chosen for the corps if she couldn't fight.

So too were her walks with Hallens being viewed in a different light. Some sisters even came to her to ask what their plans were, as if she and Hallens were discussing strategy.

The resentful and evil-minded among the sisters, however, did not relent. Iko caught a hint of the rumour that it was Hallens she was busy seducing now, instead of the guards. To this she could only shake her head. Those who delighted in insulting or working to smear others would not change their ways, even after repeatedly

171

being proved wrong. It was the only manner they knew to deal with the world, warped, bitter, and pathetic though it was.

This day her commander was even more quiet and reserved than usual; she walked slowly with her hands clasped at her belt, her head lowered, perhaps studying the patterns in the gravel path. Iko was careful to allow her some distance, and remained quiet as well. The weather was cool with the autumn, fat clouds passing overhead. Shadows were chill, though the sunlight yet held a summer's heat.

Hallens paused, raised her flat profile to the sky – her nose had been crushed in a fight long ago – and said, 'You have heard the news regarding the north?'

'Yes.' The Hengan palace servants hadn't been shy about reporting Ryllandaras's progress in slaughtering the Kanese forces across the north.

'Chulalorn must answer this,' Hallens said, 'or the siege is lost.'

'Yes?'

Hallens nodded at the implied question. 'I fear the struggle has entered dangerous new territory. There are those who say the Protectress controls Ryllandaras and it was she who unleashed him upon us. Whether that is true or not, Chulalorn must answer in kind or retreat. Escalation, dear Iko. I fear it.'

'You mean sorcery – battle magics? But we cannot match the city mages.'

'True. Our king's resources are stretched thin. A'karonys is engaged in the south, and Ghula-Sin rarely leaves Horan. His presence there keeps the Dal Hon in check, after all. Yet pacts have been signed. Agreements that go back to Chulalorn's grandfather's time. Our king did not come out of the south empty-handed, Iko. He brought with him . . . things. Things that I fear he may unleash upon Heng, should he be pressed too hard.'

Iko stared in wonder at what almost sounded like criticism, even near infidelity, towards their king. 'Such as?' she barely breathed.

Her commander glanced to her, softened the exchange with a smile, albeit a sad one. 'I do not know, Iko. Let us just say that in the columns were covered wagons and sealed carriages that even I was not allowed to search.'

Iko nodded her understanding. 'I see. But it may not come to that.'

'It may not. Though I fear it already has.'

'How so?'

'The emissary is dead. Slain last night.'

Iko was stunned for an instant, then recovered. 'Really? Here? But the city mages' protection . . .'

'They obviously didn't give a damn about some Kanese turncoat.'

'Ah. But . . . we've heard nothing.'

'They wouldn't announce it, would they?'

'No. I suppose not. It was the Nightblades, then?'

'They let me know. But curiously, they did not take the credit for the execution. I suspect some third party. A hired killer.'

Iko shivered at the thought of someone brought in to take on work not even the Nightblades could accomplish. 'Escalation,' she said, affirming Hallens' fear.

Gravel crackled as her commander walked on. 'Yes, Iko. And we may no longer be safe.'

* * *

Dorin sat slouched in the common room of Pung's quarters. He'd been doing a lot of that lately, slouching. Unfortunately, it also meant having to listen to Pung's assembled thugs, enforcers and bodyguards as they talked. If their dumb grunting could be named talk. Of this or that tough guy who wasn't so tough after all, was he? Or the girls they'd had, willing or usually not at all willing. Or last night's dog fights and the great bags of coin won or lost. It was all so very trivial and astonishingly repetitive, when one examined it objectively.

If the toughs addressed him, which was rare, they usually called him 'knife-boy' or 'little killer'. They seemed to think that their size – and they were large fellows, mostly fat – somehow meant that he was no threat to them. He ached to show them the error of their thinking. The second type of thug was the short and bony tiny rabid dog sort; these Dorin thought a far greater danger as they seemed especially resentful of his status. They had fierce defensive glares that intensified if he happened to glance their way. Often before he knew it his gaze would be caught by one's bulging, daggers-drawn unblinking glower, and he would have to break the implied challenge by shifting his gaze to the ceiling and rolling his eyes. The owner of said glare would then settle back into his chair, snorting, or mutter some comment to his fellows who would guffaw on cue.

But they all worked for Pung. And Pung would be displeased if he cut them open. He was frankly finding it more and more difficult to conform to the narrow rules and expectations that came along with working for someone.

He was sitting in the common room, trying to avoid catching the eye of any of the short fierce thugs, wondering just what he got from throwing in his lot with Pung. Room and board, obviously. But as yet no pay. No coin. No wages. A cut of the proceeds, he supposed, not that he'd seen any distribution among the rest.

What seemed to be offered by being in Pung's gang, or any band or organization, was security – and perhaps a crude sense of belonging or identity. One could lay one's head down to sleep in the reasonable expectation of not waking up with one's throat slit. You could, well, if not *rely* on your companions, at least turn your back on them with some measure of security.

All except him, of course. This minimal shared companionship didn't seem to extend to him. Not yet, in any case, and not that he wanted or needed it. He considered his fellows no better than ham-handed amoral bullies good for nothing more than intimidating shopkeepers and twisting the arms of any fools desperate or stupid enough to borrow money from Pung.

The novel thought then occurred to him that perhaps they saw this completely open and frank evaluation in his gaze, which might tend to put their backs up.

He may need to work on filtering his contempt.

Or perhaps not.

And speaking of a sense of belonging, he'd seen Rheena once or twice. In the back of a few large gatherings of the crew. She'd made no special effort to approach him. Had rather made a show of her indifference, actually. Loor, though, hadn't been shy about coming over and leaning against the wall near him and sharing the nod of an experienced operator. He was lonely, perhaps. Shreth had never fully recovered from his wound and was now working in a felt-maker's shop.

If Rheena wanted to make it plain that there was nothing to talk about, then fine. He'd make no effort either. It wasn't as though he needed –

An earthquake struck.

At least it felt like an earthquake. An avalanche-like roaring punished Dorin's ears. Everyone in the common room surged to their feet; chairs were overturned; glasses vibrated off tables; the tables themselves shuddered across the floor while dust came billowing up in clouds that drove everyone outside, waving and coughing.

From all the compound buildings more of the strong-arms and toughs came running as if fleeing impending collapse. All except, Dorin noted, the hordes of digger youths. As the overpowering crashing and thundering roaring faded, it resolved itself in his ears as the earth-shaking guttural braying of a titanic beast.

Pung came staggering out, glaring right and left. 'What in the name of Burn was that?'

'Sounded like some kinda monster,' said one of the toughs.

'Right beneath us,' supplied another.

Pung's wild terrified gaze roved the compound till it lighted upon Dorin. 'You! Take a look.'

'Me?'

'Yes, you. Go below. Look around. What do I pay you for?'

Dorin clenched his teeth so as to not point out that he'd yet to be paid. He would have looked to the sky in exasperation, but he saw the smirks of the assembled enforcers and this calmed him like a spray of cold water down his neck, reminding him to keep his professional neutral mask in place. He offered Pung the slightest inclination of his head. 'Very well. If there are no other takers . . .' He pointed an invitation to one of the bony, belligerent thugs.

The man laughed, quite nervously, and shook his head. 'Your job, sneaky boy. Not mine.'

Now it was Dorin's turn to offer his own snort of superior contempt, and look away. 'Gren!' he called.

Pung's lieutenant jumped where he was still peering fearfully into the darker corners of the compound. 'What?'

Dorin motioned to the warehouse. 'The door . . .'

Gren's hand went to his keys. 'Oh. Right.'

Gren's hands were shaking as he unlocked the door in the warehouse. He hesitated, peered anxiously down the murky lamplit stone stairwell. 'Is that it?' Dorin asked into the uncharacteristic silence surrounding them.

The man jumped again, flinching at the noise. 'What?'

'What about the gate below?'

The man stared at him, swallowing. He fiddled among the keys then silently handed over a large bronze one. Dorin took it and started down.

'You're really . . .' Gren called after him in his hushed hoarse voice, 'you really are just gonna walk in there?'

Dorin turned, made a show of shrugging casually. 'It's my job.'

The skinny lieutenant, so scornful of him earlier, now shook his head in disbelief and shut the door behind him. Motionless in the lamp's dim light he considered the man's expression. He didn't know him well enough to read him easily, but he hoped that it had been more than a dismissive *what a damned stupid fool.*

He took a breath, loosened his shoulders, and listened to the dark. Silence, save for the ticking and creaking of wood above. Where were all the children? Dead? Torn to bloody pieces by some monster? He turned to face the darkness below. Grit slid and crackled beneath his sandals. He eased them off and continued down barefoot.

The barred gate was closed. He unlocked it, wincing at every click and grating of metal on metal. He edged it open and slid inside. In either direction lamps flickered along the semicircular stone tunnels. No bodies lay as humps on the floor, no signs of any struggle. But the lamps were far too weak to fully light the tunnels, and so the majority of the lengths held absolute dark, punctuated by flickering pools of inadequate amber glow. He eased into the tunnel, daggers out, and headed for the Dal Hon's cell.

He suspected he knew what had happened. He'd heard stories of such things recounted many times. Had once even studied the messy aftermath. A mage, driven by desperation – or recklessness – reaches into Warrens far beyond his or her abilities and loses control of the forces thus summoned. It was not that uncommon, he understood, as often the only way new talents could practise was in that very manner: testing the waters, so to speak, and the surety of their grip and skill.

He believed this was what had happened. The Dal Hon youth, taunted and tortured, really did dare what he'd boasted of and the daemon had come. And of course shaken off the lad's feeble attempts to compel it.

As for all the kids down here digging for tombs, they were probably still running.

He slowly felt his way forward along the stone-flagged tunnels, ready at any moment to find his bare foot sinking into something warm, wet and yielding. He peered round an intersection of the semicircular catacombs, spotted the length of tunnel that he believed held the youth's cell, and edged forward, daggers readied.

By this time his vision had adjusted enough to make out the wreckage of the cell's sturdy door of adzed planks scattered across the tunnel, apparently by an explosive force from within. He padded up as silently as possible and slid into the cell, put his back to one of the brick pillars, circled it, blades out.

Nothing. Empty. Emboldened, and a touch intrigued, he dared to search the rest of the cell as well as he could in the darkness. He found nothing; not even a mangled corpse or splash of blood.

Mysterious. Not at all like the other unravellings he'd heard described. He stepped out into the tunnel and listened to the quiet of the earth. Yet, not absolutely. Something . . . He stalked into the deepest of the dark and edged forward, hunched and ready.

In night blackness he heard it while seeing nothing: light panting breaths. Terror? And close – just beyond. He sensed a corner ahead and reached round it, hand open. His fingertips brushed something, cloth, and there came a quick intake of breath.

He snatched his captive and yanked the body to him, a blade to the neck. Backing up into the light he found that he held a young girl. One of the diggers. 'What are you doing here?' he hissed.

She straightened and raised her chin, defiant. 'Who're you?'

'What happened?'

She snorted. 'What happened? Our mage summoned a monster and loosed it here in the tunnels. That's what happened.'

Our mage? 'Then why are you here?'

The girl sent him a superior glare. 'Because we're working together, that's why. You tell your boss, Pung the Toad, that if he so much as sets foot down here . . . then the beast'll eat him.'

Dorin couldn't help raising an eyebrow. 'Really? A beast. Will eat him.'

The girl wasn't bothered by his tone. 'Him'r anyone else comes down here!' She raised a hand and pushed against the blade he held tucked under her chin. 'So you better run while you can – ya hired knifer.'

Dorin was more surprised by her brashness than the threat of some monster. Smiling, he drew away the blade. 'So you have your mage hidden somewhere, then.'

'I ain't saying.'

He sheathed the knife, took hold of her arm and twisted it to the angle where the joint could turn no further without tearing. 'Where?'

The girl winced, but bit her lip.

Dorin, he said to himself, you're twisting a kid's arm.

He quickly let go and rubbed his hands on his thighs as if to clean them.

Now it was the girl who was surprised, but she recovered quickly, scowling. 'The monster's loose down here, so you better go.'

He backed away, still smiling. 'You'd better go as well. They'll come to look, I'm sure.'

She laughed her youthful derision, but he heard her quick footfalls as she slipped away.

So. Either they really are hiding him, or he's gone and they're bluffing to get out from under Pung's yoke. Either way . . . He shrugged mentally. Didn't matter to him.

He headed back to the entrance. He passed the wreckage of the door and paused, troubled by a suspicion. Too often this Dal Hon fellow had gotten the better of him. He collected a lamp and returned to the cell. Ignoring the scattered wood for the moment, he crouched down on his haunches and brought the lamp to the dirt-covered stone flags. He swung the light back and forth, searching.

Not a one. Not a single print other than human ones. No paw, or otherwise inhuman spoor. Straightening, he swept his bare foot across the floor, brushing the dirt and obscuring all record of who had or had not passed.

He turned to the broken door frame. It hung drunkenly, a ruin. Yet . . . He brought the flickering gold flame closer to the wounds scouring the wood.

These scars were not those of claws or teeth. He knew the difference, having been trained in how to counterfeit such marks. Edged blades made these gouges and scrapes. He straightened, smiling even more broadly.

Well, well, well. A good gambit, my friend. I salute you. Might even work. Threaten to loose a monster, whip up a fearsome noise . . . and slip away.

He returned the lamp to its niche.

Exiting the cavernous warehouse, he stood blinking in the light for a time. Gren was there, with a handful of the toughs, and Pung. The thugs all looked surprised and rather annoyed to see him. Coins changed hands.

Pung curtly waved him over. 'Well? You see anything? What is it?'

'Your mage's gone.'

'Gone? What d'ya mean, gone?'

'How do you know?' Gren demanded.

Dorin offered the man a lazy blinking look. ''Cause something crashed through his door.' Which was true – technically.

'Have a look,' Pung told Gren. The lieutenant turned on the toughs, pointing. 'You three – have a look.'

These three were now even more annoyed. 'I want a lamp,' one complained.

'So take a fucking lamp, then!' Pung snarled, jerking a thumb.

Dorin tossed the key, warning, 'I wouldn't stay down there too long. If you know what I mean . . .'

They sneered back, but looked even less happy.

He walked away without one glance back, not even to Pung. He returned to the common room, poured a glass of the cheap wine Pung supplied, and sat in his usual place. When he glanced up, none of the handful present would meet his gaze.

More damned like it.

*

Silk was with his tailor, examining his figure in a tall mirror of polished bronze, turning to left and right, and frowning. 'The cut of your trousers makes my stomach look large.'

The tailor ducked his head, hunching abjectly. 'I am sorry to do that, sir.'

Silk waved a hand. 'Never mind. A wrap or sash perhaps. Black Darujhistani silk, of course.'

The tailor bowed once more. 'My apologies, good sir . . . but I am very sorry to say that we have no more Darujhistani cloth available.'

'No more—' Silk turned on the fellow, blinking. 'How could that be, man? You are a tailor, are you not?'

The bony old man bowed once more, wincing. 'Disruption in overland trade from Unta, I'm told. The siege, perhaps . . .'

Silk eased the frown from his mouth and half turned away. He fussed with his collar. 'Ah. You are right, of course.' Strangely enough, it hadn't occurred to him that the siege would have interfered with such mundane matters as cloth imports. Things were getting quite out of hand.

'I do have some fine Talian brushed satin in sunflower yellow . . .'

'Gods, no. What do I look like? A Bloorian bumpkin?'

'Perhaps some—' the tailor began, but Silk heard nothing more as a noise crashed inside his head like pounding hammers and he staggered into a stack of piled bolts of cloth. He leaned against it, nearly double, gripping his fractured skull. '. . . a physician, sir?' the old fellow was saying, bending next to him and peering anxiously.

Silk straightened. He wiped the tears from his eyes with a sleeve and caught the pained wince from the tailor as he did so. 'What on this side of Hood's paths was that?' he asked, blinking and still dizzy.

The old man peered about the shop. 'What was what, sir?'

'You heard nothing?'

'No, sir.'

Just the Warrens, then, Silk thought, amazed. Like a gargantuan tearing, or shattering. He pulled off the samples and kicked away the pinned trousers. 'I must go.'

'Shall I start with the suit, then, sir?'

'No!' Silk snarled, pulling on his own trousers and hopping for the stairs.

Threading his way through the crowds on the street – none of whom appeared to have noticed the disturbance – he hurried for the palace.

'Just the white shirt?' came a distant reedy call from above, the tailor at a window. 'The one with the fine tapering at the sleeves?'

Silk waved an angry negative and ran on, but two steps later he halted, hands going to his head. He turned, yelled, 'The aqua blue!' and raced on.

Palace functionaries waved him to the Inner Focus. Here the guards opened the door as he approached and shut it behind him. He crossed the gleaming bright marble floor to where Mara stood next to Shalmanat, who sat, uncharacteristically slumped, head in hands.

'Are you well?' he asked as he came. Shalmanat nodded. 'Is it Ryllandaras? Has he entered the city?'

She shook her head. Her hands were clutched in her fine long hair.

'That was my thought,' Mara said, crossing her arms and scowling.

'No . . .' said Shalmanat, her voice weak and hoarse, 'not Ryllandaras.'

'Then what?'

'Something else.' The Protectress yanked at her hair as if frenzied.

Mara caught Silk's eye and offered a helpless shrug.

Silk nodded at this. Okay. So, what now? 'Ho and Koroll?'

Mara brought her head close to his, whispered, 'Out searching the catacombs. They think it's beneath the city, whatever it is.'

'It could be anywhere!' the Protectress yelled. She tore her hair as if she would yank it from her skull.

He knelt before her, tried to meet her gaze. 'What is it? Shalmanat – help us.'

Her eyes were fixed upon some distant vista only she could see. 'It cannot be,' she said, her brows knotting. 'How could it be? It was broken. Sealed away.'

'What? What was sealed away?'

Her wild gaze met his, but it was empty of any recognition. 'Our shame,' she breathed.

Over Shalmanat, Mara tilted her head to the exit, suggesting it was time to go. Silk nodded his agreement.

Outside, in the hall, once they'd left the guards behind, Silk indicated a side chamber. Mara looked to the ceiling, but followed.

'We have to decide what to do,' he began, shutting the door.

She crossed her arms across her substantial chest. 'Looks like we underestimated these Kanese. Cute trick, hey? We loose a monster on them outside the walls, and they retaliate by releasing one inside. But Koroll and Ho will track it down.'

Silk struggled to keep his face empty of the irritation he felt. 'I mean, regarding the summoning.'

'What of it?'

'Officially, we make a point of ignoring it.'

Now she winkled her handsome features into a scowl. 'What d'you mean?'

He couldn't help pressing a hand to his brow. 'We can't let them know they've unnerved us.'

'Us? *Her*, you mean.'

He bit back a few choice insults at that shortsightedness, pulled his hand down his face. '*Her* resolve is *our* resolve. The citizens would panic. Then we're finished.'

Mara frowned now, eyeing him sidelong, considering this. Then she snorted, nodding, and paced the small meeting room. 'Hunh. Not just a pretty face, hey Silk?'

His answering smile was brittle. 'We wait for word from Koroll.'

She brushed past, waving her dismissal. 'Fine. Okay.' She yanked open the door, paused on the threshold. 'And don't try any of this pulling rank shit! 'Cause you got none, right?' She stormed out.

Silk arched an eyebrow at the empty doorway. *Gods! Co-workers! What* can *one do?*

* * *

Fanah Leerulenal, a leather engraver, did not consider himself an aficionado of fortune-telling. His mother, however, bless her departed soul, had been quite the devotee. She consulted a talent once a week, and always before making any major decision. This siege, however, with its uncertainties and anxieties, left him wondering whether perhaps it would be better to flee the city, as so many of his friends constantly threatened.

He paused, therefore, that day on his way to work – not that there was any work, just a few remaining scraps of poorest quality hide. The market was mostly empty now but for a petty merchant's wheeled street stall cluttered with charms, amulets, bones of noted local witches, and various decks of the Dragons. *This* fellow was of course doing a roaring business. Fanah picked up one boxed set – a too-expensive Untan edition done on ivory tablets – and set it back down.

'I can see you have an expert's eye,' the fat stall-keeper announced, rather too eagerly.

Fanah merely cast him a disbelieving glance. He noticed one large wooden slat hanging from the twine that ran above the stall's crowded counter; the face of the card appeared to depict empty moiling smoke. 'What is this?'

The stall-keeper leaned out, arms akimbo. 'Ah!' he said, knowingly, 'the new House. Shall I wrap you a set?'

'No,' Fanah answered, annoyed. 'The damned thing's blank.'

'Not at all, good friend,' the merchant responded, completely undeterred. He plucked it down and offered it. 'Look more closely.'

Fanah had given the errand all the time he could spare, but he paused as his eyes caught movement on the face of the card. He peered more closely. 'The House is undefined as yet,' said the stall-keeper. 'The talents say the new manifestations are searching for their final form.'

Fanah watched, fascinated, as the painted face seemed to coil and shift under his gaze. Rather like clouds, or fog, he thought – or shifting shadows. Yet as he bent closer, a shape did persist behind. Low, and broad . . . running?

'My compliments to the artist,' he said. 'The light seems to move across the—'

A guttural, growling snarl like stones grating yanked Fanah up straight. The stall-keeper peered up and down the street, startled. 'That's a damned big dog,' he muttered, annoyed, and a touch worried.

The growling rose to an avalanche roar and the stall began to vibrate. Charms and amulets clattered to the cobbles. Fanah backed away. A few people nearby paused, searching for the source of the noise. The rest simply ran away.

The stall erupted skywards as if the beast had somehow sneaked under the wheels and leaped up. Boards burst; the stall-keeper was thrown backwards. Fanah backpedalled beneath a shower of the cheap trinkets until his buttocks hit the opposite building's wall. A creature the size of a pony shook itself, snorting and growling, among the wreckage of the stall. Huge it was, yet recognizably a hound, though of monstrous size. Its scarred hide was a tawny brown, going to cream towards its chest. Its sides and legs twitched and bunched in cables of muscle. Amber claws scratched and grated across the cobbles as it shifted left and right, sniffing in a great bellows-like testing of the air. Then, to Fanah's horror, its pale glowing gaze lowered to him. One great lunge of its powerful back legs shot it over the street and Fanah fell to his knees, hands over his head, awaiting an agonizing death under its enormous maw.

And he waited. Yet nothing happened. He dared to lift his head for a look. Charms and trinkets rattled as the stall-keeper sat up from among the litter of his wares. 'Where . . . where is it?' Fanah breathed.

'It's run off,' the stall-keeper offered, none too sure himself.

Fanah tottered to his feet. 'Gods . . . what . . . who would . . . I'm late for work.' He patted himself as if to ascertain that he was all there, then staggered onward.

'Hey!' he heard the merchant shouting to the empty street. 'Whose was that! Who owns that monstrous thing? *Who's gonna pay for my stall!*'

*

Ganoth Amtar lay drunk in an empty looted building that had once been a temple to some long forgotten god or cult. How appropriate it was too, he reflected, that he should occupy such a ruin, seeing as he himself had once been a priest in the cult of the Enchantress here in Heng. But he had fallen away from the order, or rather the order had moved away from him. Too complacent, he thought his fellow priests and priestesses in their comfortable sinecures, warming their wide bottoms next to fires and eating far too well. And he had not been discreet in voicing his disapproval and contempt. Where, he'd demanded, was the fire that drove proselytizing the faith? Where was the passion of their convictions? Nowhere that he could find. More effort went into vying for promotion and prestige than into care of the flock . . . and he had not been discreet in voicing his contempt of this too.

And his reward? Demotion to the most degrading of duties. This was his reward for his concern over the welfare of the order? Well, damn them to the mysteries they claimed to worship, then, he'd decided, and walked away from it all.

Though it broke his heart to turn his back upon his faith.

He tipped the tall earthenware jug to his lips once again, spilling much down the front of his already stained robes. So does the derelict lie within derelict precincts, he told himself, and lifted the jug in salute to the far murky corners where the moon's slanting light failed to reach.

Yet he was not alone. Other shapes huddled in the dark; some his fellow casualties of life's vicissitudes, others refugees or rendered homeless by the siege. All starving and freezing in the cold of the coming winter.

Ganoth saluted them as well; the needy, the flock that any true priest should tend rather than padding his own nest. He drank again, almost choking on the vile sour dregs.

And something shifted in the darkened gloom of the old temple's far corner. As an ex-priest, he recognized it for what it was. The hairs on the nape of his neck stirred in recognition of the phenomenon. Only in the highest ritual invocations had he seen it, and then as a shimmering across a still pool, or a flickering on silvered glass: an opening to a Higher Realm.

He stood, tossed the jug to crash among the broken building stones. His neighbours grumbled their complaints. Across the moon-dappled mosaic floor, shadows stirred and spun in a chiaroscuro dance. *Show me!* he implored the darkness, throwing wide his arms. *Give me revelation!*

The shadows shifted then, seeming to retreat, revealing a half-glimpse into a murky desolate landscape of a rocky plain, and a gigantic creature leaped into the temple and howled to the sky.

Stones fell in that brassy roar. Every other occupant of the abandoned building jumped to their feet and ran amid screams and shouts that Ganoth barely heard over the great rolling braying.

Beautiful it was, and horrific. A hound of unearthly size, its pale sides much scarred by battle, its flanks quivering in anticipation and bloodlust. Ganoth recognized its attitude as well: the beast was tensed, on the hunt. It lifted its blunt muzzle, larger than Ganoth's head, and sniffed mightily, peering this way and that.

Its pointed ears pricked then, and it growled a thoaty rolling of tumbling rock, and started across the mosaic floor where its claws scraped and gouged the stones, and leaped high into the air as if to clear a wall but disappeared instead into the stones as if passing through a window.

In the silence Ganoth stood panting, his heart drumming. *Thank you!* he breathed, transfixed. *Thank you.* He fell to his knees, arms wide to the dark, his face lifted to the shifting shadows above. *Thank you!*

In the next few days sightings were reported all over Li Heng; nearly every ring of the city's nested circles experienced its share of the panic. Silk was kept busy investigating each encounter. There seemed no logic nor purpose behind the visitations. Witnesses spoke of the monster crashing through walls and disappearing into alleyways. Several deaths were blamed on the beast. Yet when Silk investigated he found that not one of the mortalities was directly caused by the creature. One old man's heart gave out in fright; an old woman fell down a set of stairs in her panic and died of her injuries; a child was kicked by a terrified mule; a wall collapsed on a family. Not one citizen had been bitten or torn apart – at least none that had yet been found.

The sightings were separated by great distances. No trail of wreckage could be traced between the encounters. It was as if the thing were popping up randomly all over. Or, Silk was now coming to suspect, people were simply jumping at shadows.

It seemed even to be becoming fashionable to have caught a glimpse of the monster. Descriptions varied wildly. So-called 'witnesses' swore the thing was a daemon with blazing furnace eyes, or a shaggy furry beast with jaws that could tear the head off a horse; a prairie lion mated with a daemon; a monstrous jackal; or Ryllandaras's cousin Trake himself.

At the scene of the most recent appearance Silk was bemused to find the floor of the house littered with cards – the sort talents used for their divinatory readings. Curious, he plucked one from the litter of shattered glass and fallen bric-a-brac, broken candles and goose down from a torn cushion. It was wrinkled and thin, of cheap pressed plant fibre paper. On a dusk-shrouded hillside a muscular figure, naked from the waist up, worked hunched over the construction of a stone structure of some sort. He knew enough of the Dragons to recognize the Mason of Darkness.

He went to where the witness, the owner of the establishment, waited under guard. He showed the woman the card. 'You had these out?'

The terrified woman nodded, clutching at her throat. 'Yes,' she managed, hoarse. 'Was doing a reading.'

'A reading? For whom? Have they fled?'

She shook her head. 'Oh, no, sir. Was no client. Just looking ahead. Querying the future.'

Silk lost interest and turned away.

Stepping over the remains of the door he paused, tilted his head. He remembered another meeting involving a card of the Deck of Dragons; that visiting mage, the haughty one with the poorly kept hair. What was the name she'd given? Lady Night? She'd claimed to be investigating some manifestation involving the deck. Obviously, she'd brought this about. He'd lost track of her. But now he'd keep a lookout. If this thing hadn't eaten her already.

Later that day he gave up hunting down reported sightings and went to find Koroll. Tracking the inhuman mage proved far easier in the intent than the reality. In the end, he was driven to the embarrassing expedient of shouting down the tunnels for the half-Thelomen giant.

He waited in the darkness beneath the city. The torch he held sizzled and popped as its resins burned. He cocked his head, trying to listen. The silence was profound. Such a contrast to the streets above. Movement made him start at the dark. But it was just rats scampering along with their fat rolling gait as they ran up the tunnel. Their eyes reflected the torchlight like lamps in miniature. He ignored them as he would ignore anyone else sharing the passage with him.

Heavy steps announced the approach of something large. It occurred to him that perhaps he ought to raise his Warren, just in case. He was about to when a low, powerful voice spoke from the dark: 'You needn't yell.'

He eased his shoulders, lowering his Warren. 'I was calling.'

The entire circumference of the tunnel ahead seemed to shift as something filling it closed upon him. It resolved into the walking hut that was Koroll. 'Well, I am here.'

'Any luck?' Silk asked.

'In what?' Koroll seemed genuinely puzzled.

Silk looked to the ceiling just above his head. 'In locating the beast.'

'Ah. That. No.'

Silk struggled to stifle his annoyance. 'Then what are you doing down here?'

'I have been listening to the darkness.'

Silk's brows rose in open irritation. 'Really. Listening. Amazing. And what does the dark tell you?'

'That we are not alone down here.'

'Fascinating. I never would have suspected that.'

'Really? You should open your mind, friend Silk.'

Silk clenched his teeth, granting Koroll the point on that exchange. 'And the location of this presence?' he asked, his voice tight.

'Ah!' Koroll gestured, inviting Silk along the tunnel. 'That is the problem,' he said as he shambled along, ducking arches and timbers. 'My considered opinion is – everywhere and yet nowhere.'

Silk wondered whether the giant had struck his head on these obstructions once too often. 'That's no help, Koroll. Sounds like cheap mystical claptrap to me.'

The giant peered down at him, perhaps frowning, though his facial tattoos and the strange lines of his angular features made it hard to tell. 'Really?' he said, wonderingly. 'Well, it is the best I can do.'

Silk looked to the arched ceiling. *Gods help us.*

Koroll brought him to Ho, who was kneeling, examining a pit where the floor of one catacomb tunnel had collapsed, opening on to yet another beneath.

'Poor workmanship,' Silk sniffed.

Ho straightened. He dusted his dirty torn trousers and shook his head. 'This is new.'

'The creature?'

'Perhaps.'

'What word, friend Koroll?' Ho asked.

As this section of catacomb was taller than most, the giant crossed his thick arms. He nodded as he considered for some time. Silk fought the urge just to walk away. 'I've decided,' the other announced, 'to tell a story.'

'Wonderful,' Silk muttered into the dark.

Ho, he noticed, shot him an annoyed glare before turning back to Koroll. 'Please do,' he invited and he squatted, arms crossed over his knees, to listen.

The giant pursed his thick lips as he searched for where to start. Silk felt his shoulders falling in despair, but he remained.

'Know you the wars of Light and Night?' Koroll began, eyeing Silk.

Silk nodded, even opened his mouth to tell them Shalmanat had confessed that she'd been an officer in the Army of Light, serving one of its champions. But he stopped himself in time; these two, having been with her for so long, must be aware of that already.

'Well,' Koroll continued, 'what few know is that there was a third party in the wars. A third tribe of Tiste.'

Silk nodded at this as well; he'd heard rumours of such.

'They were the Edur,' Koroll said, 'the Tiste Edur. For a time they formed an alliance with the Andii but there was a falling-out, and in a great betrayal the Edur slaughtered many Andii. In turn, they themselves were hunted down and driven into the wilderness. Their homeland was shattered and broken in a great struggle. That homeland, or place of their power – the translations vary – was known as Emurlahn. Into it were exiled all the daemons, beasts, and horrors of that great war and it was irrevocably sealed off, and a guardian was set upon its borders to keep watch over them. A champion who could not be defeated. And so has it been inaccessible to all.'

Now Silk felt the hairs on his forearms stir and his breath shorten. *Broken*, she'd said. *Sealed away*. 'Are you saying . . .' he began, hesitating.

The giant was nodding his agreement. 'It may be that someone has found a way in.'

Silk discovered that he was shaking his head. 'No. This is preposterous. Too much. There must be some other explanation. Why go to such lengths . . .' He could not stop shaking his head. 'A hundred other more mundane explanations could suffice here, surely. Some rogue summoner, for example.'

'Perchance,' Ho murmured, sounding completely unconvinced.

'In any case,' Koroll rumbled on, 'all the stories are in agreement that this realm, or homeland, possessed guardians. Heralds, one might even name them. Freely running creatures that attacked any and all who dared trespass or meddle in that place. And invariably,' Koroll now glanced about at the murky tunnels surrounding them, 'they are described as a pack of monstrous hounds.'

Silk felt almost dizzy as he remembered the character of that explosion in his mind. A bestial howl emerging from the Warrens and sending them shuddering with their power. Yes, bestial. But unlike anything he'd ever heard before. Monstrous and utterly terrifying. He licked his cracked dry lips and breathed into the dark, 'Shalmanat fears this to be the case . . . What must we do?'

'Find the one who has done this,' Ho said. 'Find this mage and get rid of him. Or, failing that, destroy him.'

'But anyone with such daemons at his beck and call—'

'I do not believe these things answer to anyone,' Ho interrupted, sounding even more grim. 'And are all the more dangerous for it.'

'So we will search out this mage,' Koroll said into the silence that followed Ho's last comment. The giant raised his jagged profile and stared off into the dark. 'And he is canny, this one. Good at hiding.' He tilted his head then, as if struck by a thought. 'Good at hiding in shadows.'

Chapter 10

PUNG CONTINUED TO KEEP DORIN CLOSE. HE WAS VIRTUALLY confined to quarters in the rooms beneath Pung's personal suite on the upper floor of the main building. Perhaps, Dorin reasoned, it was a precaution against any assassination attempt; or perhaps it was just to keep an eye on him.

Yet disturbing rumours and stories of the state of the city under the siege continued to come drifting in from the pickpockets and toughs who patrolled the streets. Stories of the markets closing one after the other. Of empty stalls. Of citizens being willing to sell anything for food – even themselves. Such stories turned Dorin's thoughts to Ullara and her family. How was she faring under such terrible conditions? One morning he'd had enough of sitting about while the entire city seemed to be sinking around him, and he straightened from his chair and headed for the door.

The creaking of wood announced that one of the biggest enforcers had roused himself to peer up from his tankard of beer and perpetual game of tiles or dice. 'Where're you going, knife-boy?'

'For a walk,' he threw over his shoulder as he exited.

He headed for the main entrance. No one called or chased after him. He stared down the two truncheon-carrying fellows at the wide double doors and kept on walking on to the side street that led up to one of the Outer Round's main avenues.

On this boulevard he took immense pleasure from simply being out and taking in the sights. Yet the streets struck him as very different from the ones he had made his own not so long ago. As reported, they were disturbingly empty. Shop fronts were closed and shuttered. No one was out hawking any wares at all. The few

191

people he spotted were hunched in dirty cloaks, their gazes wary and frightened, their pace quick as if fearful of being chased.

His wandering brought him close to the base of the north curtain wall and here a gang of youths crowded the battlements. They were taking turns slinging stones at some enemy. They groaned at apparent poor shots while cheering lucky ones. Puzzled, Dorin stopped at the base of the first stairs he came to and called up, 'Who are you shooting at? I thought the north was clear.'

A very young lad, no more than a child, ragged and looking near feral, stopped for a moment to eye him as if he were an idiot. 'The godsdamned turncoat Crimson Guard is what! Where you been lately?' He returned to his slinging.

Dorin rubbed his chin, surprised by the news. *Where have I been? Where no one has any curiosity, obviously.*

He peered round to find someone to ask for news but found no one. The main avenue – utterly deserted. Amazing. And alarming. He picked a nearby shop at random and banged on the door. 'Hello? Anyone there?'

After a long moment, rattling and shaking announced the unbarring of locks and bolts. The door cracked open a slit. A man with sunken hooded eyes gazed out at him sadly. 'We have nothing for sale,' he said, sounding exhausted yet frightened at the same time.

Dorin gestured to the wall. 'I hear the Crimson Guard are here.'

The man nodded tiredly. 'They have come chasing Ryllandaras.'

'Then he has fled?'

The man shook a negative. 'No. The monster has not fled.'

'Really? That is . . . unusual, is it not?' The fellow merely stared, blinking heavily. Dorin cleared his throat. 'Sorry. Have you no bread? It is past noon and I could use a bite.'

The man blinked anew, as if flustered. Then, disconcertingly, he laughed, swinging shut the door. 'Bread,' Dorin heard him repeating in disbelief from within. 'A bite . . . noon.'

Dorin moved on. He didn't consider it so funny that he should ask for something to eat when it was long past mid-day. His thoughts turned again to Ullara and he headed for her family's barn.

In the alley beside the large three-storey structure he looked through slats and was surprised to see all the paddocks empty. Not one mule or horse in sight. All was quiet, the straw dust hanging motionless in the thin beams that came slanting down. He climbed to the roof gable.

Within, the birds roosted as before, but far fewer now. Tall owls slumbered in shadowed corners while much smaller hawks and falcons eyed him with their distrustful bright yellow gazes. And asleep, curled on the straw, lay Ullara. She appeared so bedraggled, so defenceless, that for an instant he feared the worst. But as he stepped on to the slats of the floor she stirred and blinked up at him.

'Am I dreaming?' she murmured, smiling vaguely.

'No, I don't think so.'

Her eyes snapped awake and she started up on her elbow. 'You should not be here!'

'Yes, I know. Your father would kill you.'

'No – that is, yes. But not him – they're searching for you, don't you know? All of them.'

He sat on a crate. 'Who?'

'Everyone!'

He raised his brows. 'Really? I haven't been out recently.'

'Obviously,' she muttered darkly, and drew her feet up under her. She regarded him quite sternly. 'You're supposed to be gone,' she accused him.

He kept his brows raised. 'This is the welcome I get?'

She surged forward to thrust her thin hands against his chest as if she would push him away. 'This is serious!'

He caught her hands, then stilled as he saw how drawn and pale she was. He studied her more closely. She was, he saw, more than just thin – she was emaciated, haggard, her eyes yellow with jaundice. 'You are not eating properly,' he said.

She burst out with mad laughter at that, almost frenzied, then tilted as if the effort cost her too much. He caught her, drew her on to his lap and held her close. Her head fell against his neck and rested there. 'When did you last have food?' he asked.

'We are doing better than most,' she breathed against his throat. 'My beauties bring me gifts.' She waved to the slats of the floor. He squinted there at a scattering of tiny white sticks – bones. The strewn bones of countless small rodents and other animals.

He felt his throat tighten almost too much for words, his eyes

193

stinging. 'I see,' he managed, hoarse, and rocked her on his lap. 'I see.'

It was late in the afternoon, close to the evening, when he gently laid her back down among the straw. Before he left he set down a bag of coin, all he had on him, though he knew it a useless gesture. What use were coins when there was nothing to buy?

Back on the street, he headed for Pung's compound. The damned siege, he'd decided, had to stop. It was killing her. Certainly, it was killing many other people. But he didn't give a damn about any of them. All that mattered was his debt. A debt he could pay by ending things . . . were he willing to take the risk.

He stormed into the common room to find Pung himself there, which was unusual as the man usually kept to his private chambers above. The black market boss turned at his arrival, pointing. 'There you are.'

Dorin affected disinterest, crossed to the table that held the beer and wine. 'What of it?'

Pung addressed all the toughs at their tables, his tone aggrieved: 'Man takes my coin, eats my food. Then, when there's work to do, where is he?'

The table was also heaped with cured meats, cheeses and hard breads. The siege was obviously not hurting Pung. In fact, business had probably never been better. The thought came to him: when the host weakens, the parasites fatten. Dorin picked up a cut of cured ham and forced himself to eat it, unable to put Ullara out of his mind. The meat was ash in his mouth. 'Sightseeing,' he said round the mouthful.

'Sightseeing,' Pung repeated, mocking. 'Well, work's come for you.'

'What kind of work?'

'Your kind. A contract's been opened. To all comers. They want the head of whoever's behind these monster visitations.'

Dorin poured a glass of the watered wine, sipped it. 'Who does?'

'The powers that be.'

'Well . . . he's dead, isn't he?'

Pung pulled in his chin and scowled as if insulted by the suggestion. 'No body was found. There was no blood, no carcass. Obviously the bastard used his pet monster to smash the doors then strolled out.'

Dorin considered why he'd bothered covering for the wretched Dal Hon; he guessed he just felt sorry for the poor fool. Nothing, it seemed, ever went the pitiful fellow's way. He shrugged. 'If you say so.'

'Yes I say so.' Pung pointed a thick arm to the door. 'So you're gonna track him down and bring me his Burn-damned head!'

Dorin finished the sour wine, sucked his teeth. 'And the price?'

'Five hundred rounds.'

Dorin grunted, impressed. Five hundred was a fair lot of gold. 'And the cut?'

'My usual. Eighty-twenty.'

'*Eighty?*'

Pung opened his arms, shrugging. 'Hey, look at all the overhead I've got. You, all you need is a knife.'

Dorin was tempted to show the fat bastard just what he could do with that knife. But he was surrounded by near a hundred of the fellow's sworn men, so he eased up from leaning against the table and ambled to the door.

The band of rabid-dog toughs all grinned at him, teeth bared, panting their silent laughter.

He decided then and there that this was the shittiest deal he'd ever cut. But then, it was his first, so of course it would be lousy. It was the beginner tax, he remembered his old teacher telling him. When you're new to a field, or a region, everyone's going to rip you off or dump on you. It was only natural. That is, until you established your presence. Your staying power. Only after that would anyone take you seriously.

Of course, that means you have to live long enough . . .

Halfway across the compound, he turned and shouted: 'Gren! The godsdamned key!'

*

He wasn't troubled by the assignment to track down the renegade mage because he figured the skinny wretch must be halfway to Unta by now, what with all the heat that was coming down on him from all sides. So too the youths who haunted the tunnels as well; no doubt they'd all run off.

But he didn't get far into the catacombs before he started coming across signs that they were still about. Fresh tracks, parted cobwebs, scuffed dust – all marks of recent passage. It angered and puzzled

195

him. Why were they hanging about? Pung's thugs will round them up once they'd convinced themselves the beast was gone and it was safe to look for them.

He carried a torch for light, lit from the lamp at the entrance. It was difficult to gauge the time underground, but he knew it shouldn't take him all that long to track down the youths' hangout. It was a good thing for them that Pung's muscle were not trained trackers or hunters. All those thugs had going for them was the typical dull brute indifference to the suffering of others. And that alone only gets you so far. They were also probably damned scared of coming down here into these dark narrow tunnels where their size was no longer an advantage.

He avoided the lesser travelled tunnels, always choosing the turn that looked the most recently taken, until his route brought him far down among the lowest of the catacombs. The torch was an absolute necessity; no light at all penetrated this far underground. He hated having to carry the damned thing, as it announced his presence down the long tunnels, but it was utterly black otherwise. Eventually he slowed, as all the tracks appeared to be converging on one particular chamber ahead. Footsteps behind him confirmed just how busy this section of catacomb was. He hastily jammed the torch into a gap in the stones of the wall and ducked into the nearest archway.

A troop of the digger youths passed, the lead one carrying a lantern. Dorin noted that they now boasted a mishmash of weapons and armour that looked to have been looted or stolen from all over. The effect of the oversized helmets and hauberks would have been comical were it not all so preposterous. What were they thinking? Pung's boys will collect them and beat them senseless, perhaps even killing, or at least maiming, a few of the ringleaders as a lesson to the rest. He felt his teeth clenching at the stupidity of it.

Once the tunnel was empty again, he collected his torch and padded as quietly as he could to the open stone archway of the chamber. The portal led to what was obviously a tomb, one of the largest. He stood blinking in the entranceway as the amber light of flickering lamps within revealed the astounding sight of heaps of glittering funerary goods: silver and gold figures of the gods – Burn, Fanderay, Togg, Fener – along with cups and masks and great piles of necklaces, wristlets and brooches.

A fellow in dirty robes was hunched over the stone top of a sarcophagus, furiously sketching away with charcoal on a sheet of curling parchment. The damned Dal Hon mage.

Dorin eased in, edged round the stone coffins. He was about to reach out to grab the blasted fool by the neck when the fellow suddenly spoke up. 'Have a drink! Won't be one moment.'

Dorin let his arms drop, straightened, and let out a clenched breath. 'You saw me coming.'

'Saw your shadow. Have a drink!' Without looking up from his work, the fellow gestured to another stone sarcophagus, this one cluttered with tall crystal decanters and ceramic jugs. Also piled there on silver platters – more funerary goods – lay apples, dried pears, and cuts of smoked meats.

Dorin examined the bounty, amazed. 'You are not doing too shabbily . . .' Thinking of Ullara, he pocketed two apples.

Charcoal stick in mouth, the mage held up the drawing, examining it critically in the lamplight. 'So many fully stocked cellars and buried hoards and storerooms – and so many tunnels to dig,' he said round the stick, sighing.

Dorin squinted at the drawing. It looked like a typical landscape – a village on a lakeshore – but the sketched shapes inhabiting it did not look at all human. The mage rolled up the parchment and set it aside. Still curious, Dorin asked, 'Why the drawing?'

The little fellow pursed his wrinkled lips, studying him for a time as he had the sketch. He shrugged. 'Kind of like a map. But I can't make sense of it. It's not adding up.'

Closer now, Dorin was annoyed to see that the fool still carried the disguise, or illusion, of an old man. He waved to indicate the fellow's features. 'You can drop that with me.'

A long slow shake of the wizened, monkey-like head. 'No. Not an appearance. I inhabit all my disguises now.'

Dorin frowned, vaguely puzzled. *All?*

'Appearances,' the Dal Hon lad continued. 'That's what's working against us.'

'Us?'

The fellow nodded, suddenly now irritatingly sure of himself, almost cocky. 'You are young, slim, lithe. You do not look like a threat. The dumb muscle don't take you seriously, do they? Neither of us looks the part, do we? This is proving an impediment – though admittedly a temporary one should we survive long enough.'

197

We? He leaned back against the cold hard limestone of the sarcophagus. He felt as if the fellow were running along ahead in an argument he wasn't even aware of – and somehow winning. He waved the words aside. 'Listen . . . you know why I'm here.'

'Oh yes.' The lad seemed strangely unconcerned by the knowledge. 'And I know why you haven't struck.'

Dorin crossed his arms and resisted raising his eyes to the stone ceiling a bare hand's breadth above his head. 'Why's that?'

The lad tapped an aged and bent finger to his temple. 'Because you can think. Any fool can pick up a knife and stab people with it. That's what the Pungs of the world want – a mindless blade cast to do their bidding. And in the world there is no shortage of those who fit that role. But not you.'

Dorin was beginning to feel insulted. Who was this lad to make such claims? He didn't know anything about him. He glanced about and his eyes caught the glitter of the numerous decanters. He poured himself a glass of red wine. 'Not me, hmmm?' he asked, and sipped, and immediately spat out the vile sour fluid. Gods! Sour as rat piss! He raised the glass to examine it then set it back down. How many years had that wine been sitting down here?

The lad appeared eager to explain his case, so Dorin raised a hand to forestall him. 'Listen. You should clear out. But if you're not going to run, then at least send away the kids. Pung won't be gentle. There's talk of cutting tendons so they'll never run again. Think about that – on your head.'

'They're free to choose and they've chosen to stay with me.'

'Of course they have.' He cast about for a container of clear liquid. He found one, sniffed it, smelling nothing, then drank. It was plain water and he winced, hoping he hadn't just poisoned himself. He cleared his throat. 'You've filled their heads with your crazy plans and fantasies, haven't you? Of course they've swallowed it all.'

The lad looked offended, raising his chin. 'Not all of it is fantasy.'

Dorin nodded. 'Oh, yes. Your beastie. You got lucky once. Don't let it go to your head.'

'There's more to it than that. The box . . .'

But Dorin was shaking his head, refusing to listen any more. He waved for silence. 'Listen. This is the deal – I'll say I couldn't find you. That should give you a couple of days.' He pointed off into the dark. 'Use that to clear out. Soon Pung'll be down here with his crew and it will be on your head.' He gave what he hoped was a warning glare and crossed to the archway. A gang of the youths crowded it now, boys and girls. He waved them aside.

'I have glimpsed something grand, Dorin,' the lad called. 'A wonderful possibility – and I think you can get us there! You have the talent we need. Together we can get there!'

The young ones peered up at him with eyes startlingly white against the dirt caked across their faces. He brushed past them and strode on up the tunnel.

Throw in his lot with some pathological liar hiding in a rat hole? Who in the gods' own creation does he think he is? Still, all those wide eyes staring up at him . . . He shook his shoulders. Idiots. Should've run off long ago. Cleared out. That was the only smart thing to do.

He paused then as his hand found the two apples in his pocket and he drew them out. The air was chill and damp in the tunnel about him as he stood contemplating the wrinkled fruit and the echoes of another's, similar, words.

* * *

Silk was not always officially on duty, but since the town had very nearly entirely shut down there was little else for him to do. The constant rounds of parties and gatherings once thrown by the richer families were now all cancelled; the clubs where tasteful dancers teased and skilled musicians played were now boarded up, the entertainers having all melted away, perhaps travelled on to Tali, or Unta. All that were left open were the lowest of the inns and taverns where soldiers collected to swill watered beer, vomit it back up, and pick drunken fights. The sort of place where one couldn't tell the difference between the common room floor and the latrines. He shuddered at the thought of even setting foot in such a place.

And so this day saw him walking the southern parapets of the Outer Round in an uncharacteristically chill wind that blew out of the west, from over the plains. In his fine silks he was not appropriately dressed for such weather, without jacket or cloak, yet it was too far to walk to retrieve one and so he paced stiffly, his arms tight at his sides, shivering.

Inside the walls, just beneath him, a crowd hammered and sawed at a platform in preparation for the coming festival of Burn's Sleep. At dusk in two days' time a great procession of these platforms, each carrying a recumbent statue of the Great Goddess, would wind its way along the circles of the city rounds, gathering before the Inner Temple. And so would Burn be sustained in her long sleep.

He was surprised that the festival was still going ahead, given the terrible conditions under the siege. But then, it might be that such rituals were just what the citizens needed in such times: to be reminded of who they were, what their values were, and what made them a people.

And, to his taste, the so-called festival was a damnably sombre one in any case.

He moved on from the edge of the parapet. Hengan regulars gave him nods as he passed. He knew they did not feel that he was one of them, nor even like him particularly, but his presence reassured them. And at this point in the siege maintaining morale was everything. It was perhaps a sad comment that things were so bad that even his slim, effete figure could help bolster confidence among the soldiery.

He shivered anew as he paced and clasped his hands behind his back to warm them. Hengan winters could be chill, but this was unusually cold for autumn. And firewood was at a premium as high as food. He spotted ahead the familiar profile of Smokey, his hair neatly pulled back and tied in a long oiled queue, a thick wool cloak tight about him. He was peering out over the ravaged southern fields, the siege lines, and dotted tents beyond. Silk came and rested his forearms on a crenel next to him.

'Good to see you up and about.'

The mage of Telas blinked in his reverie and scowled anew at the reference to his wound. He reflexively rubbed his chest. 'A little higher and that would've been the end of it.'

Silk noted a touch of grey in the man's slightly ragged goatee. Standards of personal grooming were falling everywhere, it seemed; or perhaps it was new – the shock of the near-death experience. He gestured out over the fields where low white scarves of smoke from the many campfires rode the slow winds. 'Quiet today.'

Smokey scratched his goatee. 'Yeah. For now. But they're cookin' up something. I can smell it.'

Silk nodded his agreement, shuddered, and wished he'd brought a damned cloak of his own. 'Can't just call it a bad job and walk away, I guess.'

'Sadly no. Too much invested. Can't be seen to be broken here. Outer provinces might start getting ideas, hey?'

'Chulalorn was stupid to have committed as much as he did.'

The older mage gave a small shrug. 'All in, hey? Full of confidence, he was.' He ran a speculative eye over Silk. 'I hear the monster's wandered off.'

Silk nodded once more. 'So it would seem. A few reports of sightings to the east. Just word of mouth, mind you. Rumours, nothing more. Everyone has gone to ground. Our vagabond mage. Even the assassin when Ho offers a real damned contract. Crime is at an all-time low.'

'Except for smuggling, hoarding, extortion, price-gouging, war profiteering, and black marketing.'

'Unless you call all that shrewd marketing,' and Silk smiled winningly, winking.

Smokey turned away with a sour expression. 'Sometimes I wonder, Silk. I really do.'

'I am merely a product of the times, friend Smokey.'

'So you tell people – but don't start believing it.' Peering past him, the mage raised his brows and directed Silk's attention along the wall. Silk glanced over to see Mara approaching.

'It *was* quiet,' he murmured to Smokey, then, turning, said: 'Mara! What a pleasure!'

'Put a bung in it, Silk,' the woman growled.

He knew the mage possessed what artists would call a voluptuous figure, but she appeared even larger now as she was wrapped up in layers of robes and a thick cloak. She noticed him eyeing her dress and scowled. 'Fucking cold.'

'Not like the plains of Dal Hon, hey Mara?' Smokey commented.

'Not a bit. What are you two plotting about?'

'Our escape,' Silk answered. 'We're thinking of running away. Joining the Crimson Guard.'

Smokey looked surprised. 'I was thinking 'bout that, actually. Some time. Like to travel. Sick of squatting in the same place. They have a standing invitation for any mage to join, you know.'

Mara hunched her shoulders against the wind, shivering. 'All that riding. I hate riding. Chafes my arse.'

Silk clenched his lips tight against a number of possible comments.

Mara noted this, growling, 'Wipe that stupid smirk off your face.'

Smokey cleared his throat, glancing about. 'How is she doing?' he asked Mara, his voice low.

'Better these days. Must've been some kind of shock or something. Strange, anyway.'

'Her past . . . I think,' Silk said.

Mara eyed him sceptically, then shrugged. 'Maybe. Who's to know? Word of her craziness didn't get out, thankfully. Would've been a bitch.'

'Perhaps she has reason to be afraid,' Silk said, rather impatiently.

'That thing – whatever it was?' Mara answered, sneering. 'A no-show if you ask me.'

'Koroll has a theory—'

'Hot air,' the woman cut in. 'I don't see the connection.'

Silk was angered at the dismissal, but took a moment to calm himself and responded, neutrally, 'Don't just reject our considered opinions.'

Mara snorted, eyeing Silk dismissively. 'I got no time for the hand-wringing of lightweights.'

'Maybe that's enough for now,' Smokey said with an edge of warning.

Neither spared the man a glance. Silk faced Mara squarely. He felt strangely elated by the confrontation and realized he'd been waiting a long time for it – though it was arguably foolish and utterly reckless. A smile now touched his lips, and he looked her up and down the way a patron at a bordello might evaluate the merchandise. 'Lightweight, is it?'

'You know it.'

'Not the place for this,' Smokey hissed.

Silk tilted his head as if puzzled. 'You've never had any time for me, Mara. Why is that?'

She laughed. 'You disgust me, that's why. Seducing everyone. Playing with people's emotions. Ever thought about all the hearts you've broken?'

He nodded his understanding 'Ah, I see. You think I manipulate people's affections. Well, I have to tell you that what I do has nothing to do with the heart. I seduce no one. Innocence doesn't interest me. Quite the opposite, I assure you. Such concern for others' feelings does surprise me, though. Especially from someone who doesn't even have a heart.'

Fury darkened Mara's face even further. Silk noticed the stone floor of the parapet vibrating now beneath his feet. Smokey stepped between them and faced Mara, barking, 'We're not alone!'

The woman's shoulders relaxed slightly. She took one step back, as if from a precipice, pointed to Smokey, hissed, 'Keep this shit out of my sight,' and marched off.

Smokey turned on Silk, glaring. 'Coulda got yourself killed, you damned fool.'

'She's just a bully,' Silk remarked and was surprised to find himself shaking uncontrollably.

'A bully?'

'She damns me for playing with feelings, but all she worships is power and strength. And she has the bully's contempt for those who don't have it. She steps over the people starving in the streets without seeing their suffering.'

'And you see it, do you?' Smokey asked, sharply. 'Not like the old Silk I remember.'

Silk blinked, frowning. *Yes. Now I do.* He realized that when these people had been fat and content he'd had no time for them. But now that he'd seen their misery and privation he felt a strange sort of closeness with them. He nodded to Smokey. 'Yes, I do.'

'Hunh.' Smokey leaned his forearms on the crenel. 'Sieges are like being thrust into the fire . . . they have a way of changing people.'

For some obscure reason Silk felt insulted. 'I've not changed one whit,' he objected, bridling.

Smokey sent an amused smile. 'Sure, Silk. Sure.'

* * *

Dorin knew he was good at moving quietly and secretly but there was little anyone could do when someone was lying in wait. And so he was startled when he climbed down into the alley at the side of Ullara's family establishment to find Rheena rising from cover to confront him.

He jerked backwards a step, his hands going to the rear of his belt and remaining there. She also didn't move, a scowl on her face and her arms crossed, her gaze narrowed in a disapproving glare.

They faced one another in this manner for a time until he relaxed, letting his hands fall. He brushed past her, leaving the alleyway. 'Yes?'

She followed, arms still crossed, her scowl deepening. 'Just this one warning,' she murmured, her voice low.

On the street, he turned to her once more. 'Yes?'

She moved her head in an almost imperceptible negative then brushed back her unruly mane of fiery red hair. 'Stop coming. Others might see as well.'

He had to stop a smile from reaching his lips as the sudden realization came. 'You're not jealous, are you, Rheena?'

Her eyes widened in shock – or embarrassment, he wasn't certain which – and her face turned almost as red as her hair. 'You stupid fool,' she grated. 'I'm trying to protect the both of you!'

He thought of the meagre gift of food left above; what could be the harm? He waved her off and turned away. 'I'm careful.'

She hurried to keep pace. '*I* found you!' Around them, up and down the avenue, banners now hung from second-storey windows, bunting decorated shop fronts, and a few sparse pots and bouquets of flowers sat out before doors and windows. All, he was told, in preparation for the coming festival of Burn's Sleep.

'Well, don't tell anyone.'

'Of course not! But others have eyes too.'

'Fine. Like I said, I'm being careful.'

She muttered, darkly, 'Not careful enough.'

He looked at her, and remembered that this was the second time he'd come upon her this close to Ullara's home; she must have known for some time now. So far she seemed to have kept it to herself. He nodded to her then, granting her the point. 'Well . . . thanks for the warning.'

She eyed him for a time, as if unsure he wasn't mocking her, then just sniffed and tossed her hair.

Dorin smiled at that, thinking of the old Rheena. He started walking again, but slowly, strolling. 'So you're Tran's second now, yes?'

'Yeah.' She sounded singularly unimpressed by the responsibility. 'Someone has to tell him what to do.'

'Well . . . you be careful too.'

She snorted a grim laugh. 'Yeah, the stupid shit.'

Next to them, an old woman wrapped in a black shawl knelt before a small altar that held a clay figurine of the recumbent sleeping goddess herself. They watched while she lit an array of votive candles and bowed her head. From beneath the black lace headscarf came the sound of muted, stifled weeping.

Dorin urged Rheena on. 'So they're going ahead with it despite everything.' He motioned to encompass the banners and flags.

'Of course. It is more important than ever to have her favour now.'

He eyed her sidelong. 'You think she notices?'

She sighed, her gaze lingering on a bouquet of dried wild flowers nailed to a door. 'Once,' she began, sounding uncharacteristically wistful, 'my mother took me on a pilgrimage to the Idryn Falls. There, it is said, the very earth itself was cracked and shifted by *her* restlessness . . .'

'Yes?'

She shrugged, looking embarrassed. 'A great spout of water shot up from the pool beneath the falls. The very exhalation of the goddess, they said.'

Dorin wanted to smile but stopped himself. 'Maybe.'

She shook herself, scowling anew. 'Yeah. Maybe.'

He motioned to a side alley. 'I should go.'

She nodded. 'Yeah. See you around.'

'Take care.'

'Sure.'

He lingered a moment, feeling awkward, but finally jerked a nod and crossed to the alley. Glancing back he saw her still there, watching after him, and he raised a hand but she had turned away.

Chapter 11

ORIN KNEW – AS DID JUST ABOUT EVERYONE ACROSS Quon lands – that the procession of icons and shrines celebrating Burn's Sleep was the main religious festival of Heng. Preparations had begun long ago, the siege notwithstanding, when the official date was set by the Grand Temple. Pilgrims usually began congregating long before.

But not this year. This year the Kanese forces turned away all comers. Even those travelling by river had been intercepted and warned off. All this despite the High Priest of Burn's hurrying by litter out to King Chulalorn's compound south of the city to plead the case for the festival.

When the evening of the appointed day came, curiosity drove Dorin to take a look; as he left the common room the toughs glared but said nothing. They were not the least interested in the festival. It struck him then that perhaps it wasn't that they were particularly irreligious – every one of them was certainly superstitious – it was that they simply lacked all curiosity and imagination. The shallowness of such a life made him almost pity them.

All the pickpockets and prostitutes were out, of course. Tonight should see the richest shifts of the last month. And thinking of work, he'd come very near to being called out to stick a knife into a few recalcitrant debtors today. Fortunately, the mere threat of his appearance had done the job. Again, Dorin wondered whether he wanted to be the mad dog in the cellar whose presence kept everyone in line.

The main streets were crowded with more Hengans than Dorin had seen in the last three months. They gathered round the many broad platforms that supported effigies of Burn aslumber, together with a number of lesser entities such as the Enchantress, also known as the Queen of Dreams; D'rek the Worm of Autumn; Poliel, who was the Lady of Pestilence and Corruption; and Mowri, Lady of Slaves and Beggars. All similarly sombre entities who shared aspects touching upon fate, futurity, and the struggle of life and death.

The Hengans, it seemed to him, currently shared a rather solemn and sober reflection on mortality; understandable, given their current grim circumstances. The crowds of men and women, even children, took turns supporting the massive pallets while the rest filed behind, waiting their turn. Many carried shaded candles or lamps. Dorin leaned up against a wall, arms crossed, and watched the long slow panoply pass.

In the wavering amber light he saw the final icon making its tottering way up the main avenue. It was the smallest of the lot by far: slim but tall, an effigy of a hooded figure. As it neared, Dorin's surprise grew as he recognized the young man leading its supporters up the street. It was the dark, half Dal Hon youth from the mausoleum. And the severe looming effigy, carved of wood and stubbornly plain and unadorned, was of the Hooded One himself.

His first reaction was to steel himself for a riot. Yet the crowd of Hengan citizens did not react as he'd anticipated. True, many halted, just as startled as he, and glared or muttered their disapproval, but a few actually stepped out to join the group as it passed. Most, however, merely accepted this manifestation as just one more god in the procession. One which was also true to the spirit of the festival; for if any god could lay claim to sharing in concerns of mortality and fate, it was the master of the Paths Beyond.

Some dropped to one knee offering their obeisance and their prayers as this new effigy rocked by on its way up the avenue. On an impulse, Dorin went up to walk beside the youth leading this gathering procession. The swordsman shot him a dark look, but did not object. He wore loose worn leathers, his two-handed blade at his side, its grip high. His long black hair was unbound and lightly curled, and again Dorin knew a twinge of envy for the youth's looks. Then he reflected that in his own calling it was always best *not* to attract attention.

As they walked along, he asked, 'What is your name?'

'Dassem,' the fellow forced through clenched teeth.

'Dorin. Not still angry, are you?'

'Yes.'

'But you do not send me away.'

'Because while I may not approve of you, this is where you belong – walking with this icon.'

Dorin raised his eyes to the night sky.

They completed their circuit of the Outer Round and now passed through the roofed gates to the Inner Round. A thought struck Dorin. 'You are comfortable leaving your temple unprotected?'

'They have given up the siege,' the youth answered. He sounded disappointed. 'Things are rather dull now.'

'I can offer you work,' said a new, familiar voice from just behind. Dorin glanced quickly back to find a short fellow, cloaked and hooded, following. The figure might be hidden in a shapeless cloak too big for him, but Dorin recognized the voice – and the manner. 'What are you doing here?' he hissed. 'We can't be seen together. I'm supposed to be hunting you!'

The squat Dal Hon mage raised a finger to his lips. 'Shh. I'm in disguise.' Dorin resisted the urge to slap the fellow.

'What work?' Dassem asked.

'Don't listen to him,' Dorin warned. 'He's an utter liar.'

'Murderer,' the Dal Hon rejoined.

'Thief.'

'Incompetent.'

'No fighting in the god of death's presence,' Dassem warned sternly.

Dorin scowled down at the little fellow. 'Incompetent? What do you mean incompetent?'

The mage opened his arms wide. 'Well, you were hired to kill me, weren't you?' He wrinkled up his wizened face, squinting at him. 'Not much of an assassin, I'd say.'

Dorin raised a hand to cuff him, but Dassem stepped between them. 'He is a bringer of death,' he assured the mage. 'He walks at the side of Hood.'

'Says who?' the little mage asked, cocking his head and still squinting.

'My master.'

The Dal Hon – Wu, Dorin now remembered – raised his brows

and nodded as if enlightened. 'Oh!' he said, drawing the word out. 'Well, in that case, I yield to such indisputable authority.'

'Just so,' the swordsman agreed, either deaf to, or choosing to ignore, the sarcasm.

They walked in silence for a time after that. Dorin kept sensing eyes upon him and glanced once or twice to Wu; the Dal Hon was studying him thoughtfully. Uncomfortable beneath the steady regard, he demanded, brusquely, 'What?'

A shrug from the youth. 'So, an assassin. But not for hire . . .' The lad, who only looked like a greying elder, raised a crooked finger as if in an 'a-ha' moment. 'Or. Should I say one who cannot be bought?'

Dorin merely waved a curt dismissal. He told Dassem, 'Don't listen to him. He's as mad as a cross-eyed rat, I tell you.'

'They say madness is a gift of the gods,' the young acolyte answered gravely.

Dorin threw up his hands in frustration.

They were reaching the end of their circuit of the Inner Round and were approaching the covered gatehouse that allowed access to the Central. 'What sort of work?' the acolyte asked the mage again.

The fellow airily waved a hand. 'Oh, bodyguarding, you could say.'

The youth nodded his understanding. 'I see. I will ask my master and see if he objects.'

'Your master?' Dorin protested. 'That priest? He's a cadaver.'

The young lad peered at him intently. 'Yes. He is.'

Dorin studied the two, peering back and forth. Insane, the pair of them. Well, they were welcome to each other.

As they passed from beneath the gloom of the tunnel twin halberds fell, barring their way. They, the effigy supported by its crowd of adherents, and the following file, all came to a bumping halt of crowded bodies. The cowled head of the statue of Hood scraped and grated against the tunnel's stonework arch. A squad of Hengen soldiery marched out across the avenue, blocking it. Two men strode forward and to his discomfort Dorin recognized one. It was the ragged, burly city mage from the rooftop ambush.

'All worshippers may proceed,' this city mage announced, 'but Hood is not welcome within the central precincts of the city.'

'He is present none the less,' Dassem answered, and he pushed forward until his chest touched the crossed hafts of the halberds.

'In spirit only,' the other city mage answered. He bore a neatly trimmed goatee and his long hair was pulled back in a braided queue.

'Do not make a scene,' the first one continued. 'You've made your point. Participated in the procession. Now go in peace.'

The swordsman raised a hand, gesturing to encompass the city ahead. 'You cannot keep him out.'

The city mage shrugged. 'None the less – go your way.'

The Dal Hon, Wu, pushed forward from Dorin's side. He pointed at the heavy-set dishevelled mage and called out loudly: 'If Hood be forestalled, Shalmanat shall fall!'

Dassem turned on him, '*What?*'

The city mage's eyes widened and he pointed back. '*You!*'

Wu glanced shiftily right and left. 'Me?'

'Arrest that mage!' the big fellow yelled.

Wu retreated to Dorin, who nearly flinched away as everyone's attention followed. The city mage's gaze found him and widened even further. 'You as well! Arrest that one next to him!'

'And that swordsman!' the other city mage shouted.

As one, the guardsmen drew their blades and hiked up their shields. Dassem raised his empty hands. 'This is a religious procession honouring the gods. I offer no violence.'

Dorin muttered to Wu, '*I'm* not going so peacefully.'

'I predict we will not have to,' Wu answered. 'I sense . . . ' He threw up a hand, pointing skyward, shouting, 'Look out!'

Heads snapped upward. Out of the night sky came dropping a file of black-clad figures who lit lightly on the street cobbles. They straightened with knives readied and glinting. 'Get the city mages!' the lead one ordered, and charged.

Utter panicked chaos exploded across the entire avenue. Citizens screamed their terror, ran in all directions, crashed against one another and surrounded the two city mages. The halbardiers rushed to join the guards who now pushed through the terrified crowd to close with the Kanese Nightblades. The metallic tings of thrown blades striking stone echoed all about the avenue. Someone shrieked in pain, while another yelled something that sounded like a loud death rattle.

Dorin, along with the swordsman and the Dal Hon mage, now stood completely ignored. He found it nearly impossible to keep track of the Nightblades through the shifting, pressing crowds. He glimpsed one or two dark figures dashing off into murky unlit alleyways. Meanwhile, the city mages fought to escape the horde of clamouring citizens pressing against them, all begging to be saved.

The worshippers of Hood hastily set down the effigy and retreated down the tunnel. The tall statue effectively blocked the way out of the Central Circle, rather like the grimmest of guardians. The complete panic and confusion now escalated into a riot as benches and barrels went crashing into shop fronts and a general pillaging began.

Dassem turned to the other two, crossed his arms, and cast a gimlet eye on Wu. The little mage peered nervously right and left again and opened his hands meekly. 'What?'

The swordsman gestured to invite them down the arched tunnel. 'Shall we go?'

'Indeed!' Wu answered, and he edged round the effigy. 'I do like these night outings,' he enthused. 'So invigorating. And the locals. So energetic.'

As they descended the empty street, Wu in the centre and Dorin and Dassem to either side, Dorin offered, 'Something to remember. When the Nightblades attack, they don't take the time to shout "Get this fellow" or "Get that fellow". They already know their targets.'

The little mage, moving in a sort of crouched monkey-like shuffle, and with a walking stick now – where had that come from? – sighed the tired impatience of a long-suffering teacher. 'It's all about the *perception* of reality, my friend. Not the slavish recreation of a true reality. *That* is boring beyond belief.'

* * *

A ferociously cold wind buffeted Silk where he stood next to the Protectress on a narrow ledge atop the palace tower. He hugged himself for warmth; he longed to raise his Warren for a touch of heat, but that would only advertise his presence and perhaps invite a sniping crossbow bolt, or an assassination attempt from the Nightblades. Shalmanat, at his side, wore a thick fur-trimmed cloak bunched about her shoulders; her long frost-white hair whipped and lashed about her.

It was a bright clear night, and they watched the smoke rising from various quarters of the Outer Round. Silk shivered and hugged himself more tightly. The riots had been long in coming; can't have a long siege without the citizens erupting in a riot or two. Usually over food. This one might have been triggered by the high emotions of a religious festival, but it was really all about fear – fear and hunger. The terror over the nightmare beasts had kept the populace in check for a time, but that was wearing off.

The high winds whipped all sounds away, but Silk fancied he could hear the shouting of the rioters, the snap of the flames, and the crash of breaking wood. 'Not a very quiet send-off for Burn,' he observed.

The Protectress's answering smile was thin. 'Good thing she's already asleep.'

'At least the Kanese haven't attacked,' he offered, trying to find something reassuring to say.

'They wouldn't dare. Not during the festival. The entire city would rise against them.'

Silk reflected that this was probably so. Though many now turned to the Protectress as a patron of the city, the Hengans' love for Burn remained deep. He watched Shalmanat closely. She appeared to have recovered from the shock of whatever it was that had assaulted her with the visitation of the beasts, but to his eyes not nearly fully. Her pensive gaze on the riots now, she didn't seem able to muster anger or outrage. No, she appeared hurt, with-drawn, resigned even. That resignation frightened him. He was, he realized, frightened for her.

Footsteps sounded on the circular stone staircase behind and they turned. Smokey emerged, soot-smeared, his hair dishevelled, a sleeve torn, and a bruise on one cheek where someone had punched him.

'I've suppressed the fires,' he announced, sounding exhausted and hoarse.

Shalmanat inclined her head to him. 'My thanks, Smokey.'

'We've announced a curfew,' he continued.

'And the instigators?'

'They got away. We assumed you didn't want us to use force against the populace . . .'

Her answering nod was firm. 'Yes. I'll not have that. Thank you.'

'We'll have his head yet,' the mage of Telas muttered, ferociously.

'Not his head,' Shalmanat answered quickly. 'I want all of him. I have . . . questions for him.' She turned away to lean once more on the stone ledge enclosing the narrow terrace. Smokey shot Silk a glance; Silk fought to keep his concern from his face.

'His magery is strange . . .' Smokey allowed, slowly. 'Something of Mockra, a whisper of the Enchantress's touch, something like Rashan. Yet something else as well.'

'Yes,' the Protectress agreed. She leaned far out over the ledge, as if tasting the wind. 'Something else.'

'If we all committed to the search . . .' Smokey began.

'No. Your job is to defend the city. I cannot have you from the walls.'

Smokey bowed his head. 'Very well. However, if he *can* access Rashan, then we'll never flush him out of the catacombs.'

'Yes,' the Protectress sighed. 'You are right in that.' She lifted her head to the north, her hair snapping like a banner. 'The plains are open to us. Why are we still short of food?'

Smokey grimaced as if pained. 'We're hunted out, and the foraging parties won't travel more than a day's journey . . . They fear the man-beast,' he added, reluctantly.

'But they have my assurances . . .'

The mage nodded his agreement. 'That is so. However, when it's night and you're all alone out on the grasslands, assurances don't count for much.'

Shalmanat sighed as she studied the ravaged fields. 'I see. Very well . . . Silk, you will accompany them.'

'Pardon?' he asked, rather startled.

She turned to study him with her odd inhuman eyes; this night they seemed to hold a touch of amber brightness in the dark. She tilted her head, still studying him. 'It will do you good to get out, I think. To assume some responsibility. Take a large party.'

Silk was now truly frowning his confusion. 'Protectress,' he began, tentatively, 'is this really necessary?'

'It is.' She shivered then, pulling her cloak tighter about her. 'It's too cold.' She passed between them and headed down the stairs, murmuring irritably to herself, 'Why is it so cold?'

In the silence following her departure Silk cast a significant glance to Smokey and waited. After a brief moment the latter shrugged and waved a hand in disgust. 'That shifty mage? I don't know. Maybe it's true. I saw some strange things this night. But what does it mean? Cuts too close to religious history for my liking.'

'The wars of Light and Dark,' Silk recited. 'I used to think those just stories. But she fears these phenomena touch upon them. She fears it mightily.'

Smokey nodded sombrely. 'She does indeed.'

'What does Koroll say?'

Smokey crossed his arms and smoothed his goatee. 'Being of Thelomen-kind, he says he takes the long view in this. We must wait and see.'

Silk's answering laugh was without humour. 'Why am I not surprised?'

A wicked sly smile now quirked Smokey's lips. 'Good luck on your first command.'

'Oh, go to the Abyss.'

* * *

The next morning Dorin was summoned to the compound yard. Here he found Pung with a large party of his strong-arm toughs and enforcers, big and small. Two favoured bodyguards stood with the crime boss, truncheons in their hands. Dorin paused only momentarily, as behind him more of the thugs came lumbering out of the common room as if to urge him onward.

He moved forward before it would appear that he was reluctant. Everyone, he noted, was armed with clubs or sticks. They spread out in a circle as he approached. It looked to him as though they thought him unarmed. Indeed, he showed no knives at his belts, but in truth he was far from weaponless. And so he crossed the broad yard careful to maintain an unconcerned, neutral blandness of expression.

Before he got too close, the two bodyguards stepped between him and Pung. Dorin waved to them. 'What's this?'

Pung was glowering at him, rather like an angry thick-jowled dog. 'I hear you was with our damned mage last night.'

Dorin cursed inwardly; he'd taken a chance on none here knowing, but Pung, it appeared, had better informants than he'd imagined. He crossed his arms in a show of nonchalance – and took hold of the blades hidden up his sleeves. 'Yes. What of it?'

Pung's face darkened. 'What of it?' he stammered, almost too enraged for words. 'You're supposed to kill the bastard!'

Dorin nodded. 'And I almost had him too, except for the procession. There were hundreds out. Maybe you heard about that too?'

Pung let a breath hiss through his pressed lips. 'Yeah. So . . . you almost had him, hey?' A strange sort of smile crept up those thick lips, rather like a crude attempt at cunning. 'So, you won't mind if we head on in now and drag them all up, hey?'

Dorin shrugged. 'Go ahead – if you can find them.'

Pung opened his arms as if to embrace him. 'Good, good.' He waved Dorin onward. 'Come, then. I've something to show you.'

He headed for the warehouse that was the main entrance to the tunnels. The thugs pressed in behind Dorin, and Pung's two guards fell in step just ahead. They slapped their truncheons into their palms as they walked.

Inside the cavernous warehouse the only glow in the shadowed dark was one of the smithy forges. A youth was pumping the bellows and white and blue flames crackled with each gust of air through the coals. Another youth, a young boy, hung suspended by his arms from ropes; his toes just brushed the dirt floor. The bare chests and backs of both lads bore the ugly mottling of bruising together with dried streams of blood in shallow cuts from countless lashings.

For the first time Dorin's heart clenched, and revulsion twisted his stomach. But a dark cold fury also welled up within, hardening his mouth, and he decided then that no matter how this turned out, Pung had to die.

'Raise his foot,' Pung told one of his thugs. The fellow came forward and yanked up one of the boy's legs, gripping the shin. Gagged, the lad whimpered, stark terror in his tearing eyes.

Pung lifted a truncheon and tapped it gently into one meaty palm. 'I'm told this hurts like Hood's own touch,' he said to Dorin, arching an eyebrow. He nodded to the tough who tensed, steadying the foot. Pung stepped in, swinging powerfully, and the truncheon smacked into the boy's sole with a shockingly loud slap. The youth convulsed, shrieking into his gag, then sagged, almost faint, crying continuously.

Pung shoved his face close to the boy's. 'Going to take us to him now?' he demanded.

It looked to Dorin as though the lad was far too gone in agony to comprehend anything.

'The other,' Pung ordered. The thug switched legs.

Dorin started forward, only to halt as four crossbows swung up to cover him. Pung eyed him derisively. 'Got something to say?'

Dorin kept a tight grip on the blades sheathed under his sleeves. 'I'll take you,' he said.

Pung pointed the truncheon and waved it back and forth. 'Oh, no. Not you. I don't trust you.' He spun, the weapon swinging, and smacked again into the child's foot with an agonizing slap that jerked the poor lad like a lightning strike.

Dorin also flinched, and gritted his teeth in suppressed rage. Too many. Too blasted many right now . . .

Pung backhanded the dazed boy's sweat-streaked head from side to side. 'Well?' he demanded. 'Now? Going to lead us to him now?'

And the lad nodded, blearily, blinking, mouthing something behind the gag. Pung nodded to the tough, who let the foot fall. Another released the ropes. The child moaned, nearly falling, as his weight came to rest on his tortured feet.

'Okay,' Pung announced, tossing away the truncheon. He motioned to the crowd of his enforcers. 'You lot. Take this kid down and bring me back the damned mage. Whole or part. I don't give a fuck which.'

One of the short enforcers pushed the limping boy along. Gren, next to Dorin, gave him a leer and a wink and said, 'That's how you get things done.' He went to the door, keys jangling.

That's how you make blood enemies, Dorin answered him, silently.

Ten descended the steps, lamps in hand, pushing the lad ahead of them. Twelve now remained with Dorin inside the darkened cavernous warehouse, not counting Pung, who faced him. 'Now it's your turn.' He nodded to his men. 'Cover him. He's got blades hidden on him, I'm sure.'

The four crossbowmen steadied their aim at Dorin's heart. He opened his hands and slowly extended his arms to allow himself to be searched. Two toughs patted him down. They found short blades at his wrists, his collar, the rear of his belt, and the ankles of his soft leather shoes. When they pulled off his shoes he casually rested his hands at his waist only to have them slapped away, whereupon he held them out, hands open and fingers straight.

Hands grasped Dorin's arms from behind. They pulled him over to the same ropes and tied his wrists. Pung signalled and the toughs heaved on the ropes; Dorin's weight slowly lifted from his feet until only his toes just brushed the dirt floor. The ropes creaked and stretched. The toughs tightened them further then tied them off.

Pung had been poking at the sullen glowing forge. Now he came away lifting an iron bar whose end shone like a lamp. Smoke curled from its tip. He pointed it at Dorin, saying, conversationally, 'You know, I didn't like you the moment I laid eyes on you.'

'The feeling's mutual,' Dorin answered through clenched teeth.

Pung waved the bar's bent crimson tip so close before Dorin's eyes that he could feel its heat and hear it hissing. 'Good,' he continued, 'good. I'm glad we're finally clearing the air between us. Honesty's always best, don't you think?'

Dorin could bend his head back no further. 'I agree.'

Pung pulled the bar away. 'Thought you might.' He turned to his crew. 'What do you think, lads? Where should we start? Eyes, hands, or feet?' He held the bar straight up before him. 'Or maybe we should just lower him on to this and let him cook from the inside out?'

All the toughs had a good laugh at that – Dorin couldn't help but wonder how many times they'd actually done it. The crossbowmen now cradled their stocks in their arms. One had even set his down. Dorin clenched his fists and shifted the long thin blades he'd held pressed between the straight index and middle fingers of each hand. Then he grasped the ropes, holding them in his fists, and began sawing by edging his fingers back and forth.

Most of the answering catcalls were for Pung to burn the feet off first and the black marketeer raised a hand, acquiescing to the majority. 'Okay, okay. The feet . . . first. Panet – fill one of them brazier pots and bring it over here.'

One of the toughs went to the forge and started shovelling coals into an iron pot. The men were all chuckling now, and taking bets on how soon he'd start begging, or whether he'd piss himself, or whether he'd faint the moment they shoved his foot in.

'Grab his feet,' Pung ordered.

No one held a crossbow now; they'd all been set aside. The toughs closed in on him to take hold of his legs. Dorin kicked down a number of them, but they laughed at that, baiting him; they were too many. They piled on, pulled his legs straight. He knew this was what they really wanted and enjoyed: this fight – a damned unfair one – and wrestling a helpless foe, but he couldn't help but struggle to keep his knees bent and his feet high. At the same time, he sawed on the ropes with all his strength; hot blood ran as he slit his fingers in his fury.

They dragged the brazier pot over. Pung was pointing the bar, grinning as he gave orders. 'Okay, closer. In front. Bring the right one – that one – hold it steady.'

Raging heat seared Dorin's heel and he flinched, managing to yank it away.

'Aw,' said Pung. 'He moved. Hold him steady now . . .' His voice died away as he stared up at Dorin's hands, frowning. 'What's . . .'

The combined forces of the toughs' yanking and Dorin's twisting and pulling and cutting did the job, and one rope parted. Dorin fell sideways on to the crowd of thugs and they all collapsed together. He jabbed the thin blade into the eye socket of one, who whipped his head away, howling, yanking the blade from Dorin's blood-slippery fingers. He stamped the hardened outside edge of one foot into the throat of another, felt cartilage crush.

The second rope gave. A knife thrust into his side but he still wore his bone and leather vest and the blade skittered over it. He twisted his head away from another knife thrust, slit that wrist and took the knife away even as the hand reflexively opened. That knife then went straight across the nearest throat. An arm closed round his neck from behind. He punched up over his shoulder with the thin blade extended, exactly where one eye should be, and was rewarded by the scream of a hit; the arm yanked away in a slither of commingled sweat and blood.

None of them had even stood up yet. They grappled and twisted, heaved and wrestled in a slick hot heap. A kick from Dorin sent one into the brazier pot, upending it, and the fellow rolled away shrieking and batting himself. Greasy fingers groped and tried to gouge his eyes with broken nails; hands sought to twist and capture his arms. Sweat-slick, he slithered about, gasping and hissing his effort, and slid the knife down his side, opening up someone's stomach in a gush of hot blood and bile.

A blade entered his thigh and another licked his neck. He twisted again, panicked. His groping hand found the grip of a second knife in a corpse's belt. With both he slashed and thrust all about himself in a paroxysm of loathing and disgust. Then it was over – a bare four or five heartbeats was all it took. Yet already Dorin regretted it. He'd succumbed to blind fury and savagery in the moment. Now only he moved with any purpose among the piled bodies; all those who still lived clenched wounds, or spasmed in anguish.

No hands held him. All the limbs lying over him were flaccid. The bodies pressing against him were motionless or shuddering in the grip of fatal wounds. He straightened from the heap, pushed the slick limp arms from himself. Tottering, blood running in streaks down his legs and arms, he stepped over the dead and the maimed survivors. One fellow lay face up, gingerly fingering the blade standing from one eye as if he couldn't believe it was actually there. Dorin calmly made for the nearest crossbow.

Pung had backed away until his rear pressed up against the forge; his face held a mixture of disbelief, rage, and horror. 'Bastard!' he yelled, and threw the bar, which flew wide. Dorin turned to him, a crossbow in each hand, the stocks braced against his sides. Blinking, Pung seemed to come to himself. He ducked from sight behind the forge.

'You can't escape,' Dorin called. He raised the crossbows. 'I've got you covered.'

The black market boss straightened up then, but he was not alone: he held a squirming youth before him by the neck. It was the lad from the bellows.

Dorin cursed silently as the man now slowly edged towards a rear door. He dropped one weapon to steady his aim; he'd have a shot, but the kid kept struggling, kicking his feet and flailing his arms.

'Better run!' Pung yelled. 'I'll find you, and I'll have your head!'

Dorin advanced to keep a close shot, sighting carefully down the stock.

Then the ground shook and an enormous gust of dust and dirt came shooting up the tunnel mouth. The beaten-earth floor of the warehouse actually subsided in folds as Dorin staggered, blinking in the dust. He saw Pung similarly struggling to keep his footing. The roof groaned in a creaking and explosive snapping of thick timbers.

Dorin glimpsed the kid clamping his mouth on Pung's forearm and heard the crime boss's shout of pain and outrage. Then the boy was scampering away and Dorin snapped off a shot, but the earth was rocking and bucking and the bolt went wide. Pung darted out of the door.

A full section of the warehouse wall groaned, sagging, and Dorin spotted the lad. He was laughing and dancing some kind of jig amid the clouds of dust. Dorin snatched his arm and ran for the nearest way out.

'It worked!' the boy was laughing. 'Worked!'

'What worked?'

'His trap! Ha ha!'

'Trap? You mean this was deliberate? Not an accident?'

'A'course! They come down there and whoosh! Buried!'

Coughing, Dorin waved the suspended dirt from his face. 'What about the other lad?'

The boy stopped laughing, then shrugged. 'Pillip? He knew. Musta run.'

At the wide front doors, Dorin propelled the lad onward, then paused. He glanced back to the buckled dirt floor and snorted his amazement, together with a kind of grudging respect. He saluted the dusty air with the crossbow then threw it in. *Well done, you crazy bastard. Well done.*

More of Pung's people, youths, enforcers and thugs, had all gathered to stare at the canted warehouse. But as he limped between them, shedding droplets of blood, smeared in dust and dirt, none challenged him as he headed for the main gate. They only stared with wide eyes at what he imagined must resemble a corpse that had dragged itself free of the freshly opened earth.

Chapter 12

THE JOURNEY OUT OF LI HENG PROVED UNEVENTFUL. SILK sat on the lead wagon, next to a grey-haired veteran scout named Buell, who kept a wad of some gods-forsaken leaves and dark sticky resin tucked into one cheek. The habit had stained his teeth the colour of leather. The train of ten wagons was guarded by a column of twenty Hengan regulars commanded by a young lieutenant named Venaralan.

As representative of the Protectress, Silk was officially in charge of the expedition. But he did not participate in any of the organization or daily running of the train, leaving that to Buell, and sat instead wrapped in a cloak, with his legs extended straight, a wide-brimmed hat low over his face against the sun, and dozed.

He knew that, as lifelong Hengans, soldiers and scouts alike were profoundly uneasy to be leaving behind the walls of their city and venturing out northward across the plains. He also knew that despite the Protectress's assurances that they were safe from the predations of the man-beast, not one person with him today believed that he could defend them from the creature should it attack. He did not blame them for this lack of confidence in his abilities – not even he believed he could defend the column against Ryllandaras. No, what he chose to put faith in was the beast's self-proclaimed devotion to Shalmanat. After all, such dedication was something he understood quite well.

And so he affected complete indifference, and the implied – he hoped – self-confidence this projected to the men and women.

The wagon wheels screeched and creaked, the seat rocked beneath him, and the mules pulled with surprising eagerness, their eyes rolling all white and their ears laid back flat in terror of the lingering scent of the man-beast. Buell reclined lazily with Silk, only occasionally snapping the long-handled switch in his hand, now and then leaning over the side to eject a stream of the sticky brown fluid from his mouth, and keeping up a streaming conversation for both of them.

'Cold winter this year, neh?' he observed, then carried on without even waiting for a response: 'Bad for us. There's those in the city who say the Kanese mages whipped it up, hey? What say you? Don't think so m'self. After all, them Kanese must be freezing their peckers off, hey? What do you think of our fair-haired lieutenant? Sweet-cheeks I call him! Ain't even felt a razor yet I don't doubt, let alone the cheeks of a woman. Not that it matters if he was Greymane hisself should the beast come for us. I mean, it's not like we're gonna jump on to the mules and race to safety, is it?'

Uncomfortable with this topic, Silk tilted his head to cast the man a glance from under his wide hat. 'Don't you think ten wagons is a bit optimistic?'

'No sir. Them Kanese emptied the barns and lofts all right. But these villagers are under orders to keep hidden stocks – caches and cellars, 'n' such. Long overdue supplies owed to the city, this is – plus extra fees for being late. Ha! My fear is the damned Kanese will burn it all around our ears before we make it back.'

Silk thought he had a far greater chance of defending the wagons from the Kanese cavalry than from Ryllandaras and so he said, 'Don't worry about them.'

Buell chortled a laugh and spat out a stream of the chew. 'Ho! Rather take on them fancy lancers, hey?' And he laughed on and off for the rest of the afternoon, much to Silk's irritation.

The gathering proceeded much as Buell predicted, though after the first sad collection of farmers' hovels Silk couldn't call it gathering so much as outright raiding and pillaging. The Hengan soldiers, footsore and chilled to the bone, gladly ransacked the huts and barns, stripping them of all stores. Further, as a lesson to all those slow to respond to their demands, they set fire to one farmer's house.

Silk sat on a wagon bench, one foot up on the brake, feeling rather like the odd man out. He watched while farmers were beaten to reveal any further secret caches or cellars and deals struck for favours among both sexes. His one contribution was, when the soldiers began drinking, to send a look to Venaralan, as if to ask *Do we really have time for this?*

The lieutenant, belatedly roused to assert his control over the men, set to shouting commands and beating the worst offenders with the flat of his blade. Order – if the word can be applied to wholesale stealing – was restored and the column rumbled off to the next hamlet.

One enraged peasant yelled after them: 'We'd prefer a visit from the beast!'

The troops answered with rude gestures, heckling, and mocking laughter.

Once every hamlet and tiny clutch of farmers' huts within two days' travel had been visited, the column headed back towards Heng. Most of the wagons were full of barrels, crates and bales of staples such as barley, millet, preserves, and smoked or salted meat. The scouts had been out hunting as well; they trickled in through the day, in groups of three or four, carrying butchered haunches and sides wrapped in burlap that they heaved bodily on to the wagons.

Several of the scouts reported to Lieutenant Venaralan, who then ambled over to walk beside the lead wagon where Silk lounged. 'We're being shadowed,' he said.

Silk raised his hat, sitting up, 'Not . . .'

Venaralan shook his head. 'No, not him. Riders. Crimson Guard. They're hanging far back, but the scouts spotted them.'

'Hunh. Why shadow us?' Silk wondered aloud.

'Can't you guess?' Buell answered, spitting. 'They're waitin' for the beast to show, that's what. Then they'll pounce.'

Outraged, Silk sat up straighter, peering to the rear. 'Burn-damned bastards . . .'

Buell chortled anew. 'That's the spirit! Why don't you show 'em one of your fancy-pants tricks?'

Silk shot the fellow a glare. 'In any case,' Venaralan offered, 'it's nothing to us. All we can do is hope they're disappointed, yes?'

Silk sat back, sighing and adjusting the brim of his hat against the lowering sun. He waved to the mules. 'Can't these things go any faster?'

'Don't see you pushin',' Buell answered.

They were still more than a day's journey out when calls went up of glinting reflections to the east. Buell clambered up on to the tallest barrel and peered in that direction, shading his gaze. 'Damn it to the Taker . . .' he muttered.

'What is it?' Silk asked.

'Armoured cavalry. Looks like them Kanese lancers.'

Silk couldn't believe it. 'Here in the north?'

Buell thumped down and snapped his switch over the mules. 'East. Must be pickets guarding the trader road. Caught sight of us.' He flicked the switch furiously; the mules brayed their complaints, but Silk detected no increase in their speed – not that it would make any difference.

'No point in that,' he commented.

Buell spat, growling his frustration. Venaralan jogged up to their side. 'Circle the carts and wagons,' he ordered.

Watching the column of cavalry approaching, their bright mail winking and glittering in the sun, their long green pennants flying, Silk had an idea. 'No!' he said. 'Stay in line.'

The young lieutenant gaped at him. 'That's suicide! We must defend.'

'I want them coming at us straight in a charge.'

'They'll slaughter us!' Venaralan waved a negative. 'With all respect, you're not the military commander here.'

Silk stood up on the wagon, squinted out over the man to the closing column. 'With all respect, I speak for the Protectress – so do as I command!'

'Let the man shoot his bolt,' Buell drawled. 'I got ten Hengan rounds says he'll do them dirty.'

The young lieutenant regarded the wagon-master darkly. 'None of us will live to collect,' he said, and dashed off, shouting to his troop, 'Ready crossbows!'

Silk steadied his footing as the wagon bucked and rocked across the grassland. He threw off his wide hat and set to summoning his Warren. 'Do you really have ten rounds on me?' he asked Buell.

The old scout pushed more leaves into his cheek, grinning. 'Naw. I'm just sicka all your boasting an' big talk.'

'Thanks for your support.'

'No problem at all.' Buell drew a short hunting bow from under the seat and readied a bag of arrows.

Silk reached within, but not for the familiar and ready entry of his Thyr paths. He reached far beyond his usual territory, and

224

searched out instead that glimpse he'd been granted of the far heights of Liosan, or Thyrllan, as some sources name it. There, if he could but tap into it, resided far more potency than he would need. If he didn't destroy himself in the act of summoning it.

He kept an eye on the lancers; they were cantering now, closing, bringing their lances to bear. They'd swing past in line, he knew, each taking a thrust as they thundered past the train. He waited for the chance to catch them all in line, and as close as possible.

'Mage . . .' Buell warned, uneasy, 'time's a-wastin' . . .'

'Soon . . .' he murmured, fingertips on his forehead. *Gods! Dare I reach there? What will happen? Will I burn, as I've read of others foolish enough to push so far into the Warren? Well, dead is dead . . .*

As the column of Kanese cavalry swung close, dirt now flying from the charging hooves, their lances couched and lowered, Silk reached deeply into the churning puissance of raw power that was Thyr itself, searching for that brightness he'd glimpsed in the Protectress, and he touched something there far upon its distant boundary, something utterly alien to his mind.

He screamed at the awful rushing potency of it even as there came, muted, the answering shrill screams of horses, the crashing of huge bodies slamming into the dirt as the animals fell and tumbled. The cries of the troopers could hardly be heard above the impacts of the bodies, while above all came the bellowing roar of flames. He fell without sensation, his consciousness, his very awareness, frayed to threads by the astounding energies coursing across his mind.

'You broke 'em!' Buell yelled, triumphant.

Someone bellowed 'Rush 'em now!' and then the wagon jerked and bounced as it hit a hole or a rock and he felt himself flying upended. He hardly felt the jolting blow that was his uncontrolled tumble among the tall razor-sharp grasses.

Noise roused him. That and the stink of thick smoke. Muted and blurred, as if through a tunnel. The clash of sword-strokes, the yells, curses and desperate panting of melee. He blinked, found he was sitting up, his once fine clothes torn and dirt-smeared, one arm useless across his lap. He was leaning up against the bed of an overturned wagon, surrounded by a mix of Hengan soldiers and scouts. Buell stood next to him, an arrow nocked, scanning the field.

The lieutenant appeared, sword bared, his brown Hengan surcoat slashed, blood smearing a mailed sleeve. 'Guard the mage!' he shouted and turned, readying. Buell loosed his arrow while the soldiers surged forward to meet an equal charge of Kanese, now dismounted, swinging slim sabres. Beyond the melee smoke churned over a prairie fire where shapes lay blackened.

The fighting surged back and forth; Buell nocked another arrow. A female scout now stood over Silk, deadly twinned gutting knives out, obviously ready to defend him against the Kanese troopers.

Utter madness! Groggy, Silk struggled to rise. Buell pressed him down with a hand on his shoulder. 'You rest now, sir. Done for most, you did. Didn't think ya had it in ya. Havin' some trouble with the last of 'em, though,' and he grinned then spat aside the entire wedge of sodden leaves from his mouth, and raised his short bow.

The Kanese were clearly the better swordsmen as they over-powered one Hengan soldier after another. Venaralan went down, slashed across the face. The remaining few scouts and Hengan troopers charged. The last crossbows fired; a few thrown knives found their targets. The two forces, lines no longer, met in individual and group duels, hacking and thrusting, seeking to push the other back as they shuffled and danced, raising clouds of dust and tumbling among the tall stands of stiff grass. Thick white smoke blew in banners over all, obscuring half Silk's vision. Yet it appeared to him to be a close thing – and tragically unnecessary.

He struggled to rise once more. 'No!' he shouted. 'Yield! We yield!' But he was so very weak, his voice a hoarse croak.

A Kanese lancer broke through, rushing for Silk. Buell stood motionless, arrow tracking, as the man's leap brought him within arm's length. Buell's shot took him in the chest even as the man's sabre sliced down through shoulder and neck. Buell fell, his hot blood splashing across Silk's front as he collapsed across his legs. The lancer fell as well, tumbling backwards; at such close range the arrow had penetrated his mail shirt.

The last of the defending Hengan soldiers fell in a gurgle of pain, clutching at his stomach; five Kanese now remained. These mercilessly slashed through the lightly armoured scouts – even those who now threw down their weapons and called for quarter.

Two lancers closed on Silk. 'Yield!' Silk called, uselessly. The last scout, the girl, caught the first sabre cut on one short knife, and going to her knees slashed upwards through a high leather boot and leather trousers, and up under the hanging mail shirt, perhaps even to the groin, gutting the man, who sank in a waterfall of dark blood.

The second lancer took the girl's scalp off in one swing, then raised the bloodied blade over Silk who peered up unblinking, thinking *What a useless way to die . . .*

Something struck the lancer and he peered down, surprised; the wet triangular head of a crossbow bolt jutted from his chest. He fell to his knees before Silk, then toppled. Astonished, Silk grasped hold of the wagon's planking to pull himself erect. He peered about the field and saw it was strewn with fallen corpses, horses and men, all smoking. Beyond, a line of wildfire topped a distant hill sending a white band of smoke high into the clear blue sky.

More mounted troops now surrounded him. But these did not display the flowing verdant green of Itko Kan; they wore the deep red tabards of the Crimson Guard. One approached, a woman, her long flowing coat of scaled armour enamelled the same blood red. She held a crossbow negligently in one hand as she came. 'City mage Silk, I presume?' she offered, amusement on her wide, olive-hued features.

Silk ignored her; he peered about, watching stunned as those Hengan scouts and soldiers who could stand – a mere pitiful handful – began to labour to their feet, clutching their wounds.

'My command . . .' he breathed, horrified.

'Congratulations,' the woman said. 'You won.' And she hiked up the heavy weapon to rest it over her shoulder.

His appalled gaze swung to the callous mercenary. 'You stood by . . .' he breathed, almost choking, 'while my men and women . . .'

'We thought you had them after your display, mage.' She prodded a fallen lancer with a boot. 'But these Kan Elites fight like devils. And they wanted your wagons bad.' She squatted next to a scout, pulled off a glove, and pressed a hand to his neck. 'This one lives.' She raised her chin, shouting: 'Luthan!'

'Kinda busy!' a man yelled.

Cursing, the woman tucked her gloves up her sleeve and set to yanking the belt from the man's waist. Silk staggered to stand over

227

her. 'You step in now? So late? After all this slaughter? You watched . . .' He couldn't continue. Horror and outrage choked him. Acid bile strove to push up past his dry throat and his heart hammered as if he were in the grip of some sort of terror. His gaze shied away from the slashed corpses, the exposed viscera – it was all so different up close.

'We are not in the employ of the Protectress of Heng,' the woman calmly informed him as she tied the belt in a tourniquet high on the man's wounded leg.

'Yet you act now? So late?'

'Aye,' the woman answered with her first hint of temper. She moved on to another wounded Hengan. 'And be thankful we did. Else you'd be dead.'

Silk studied the field and his slaughtered command. 'I wish I was,' he murmured aloud, realizing that this was in fact true. These men and women had held little regard or respect for him, yet they died to protect him. That sacrifice was a burden he couldn't even begin to face.

The woman was studying him with a new expression – if not quite compassion, then perhaps understanding. 'We thought you'd hold,' she offered by way of explanation.

Silk sensed that this was all he could expect from her, or any other of these hard-hearted mercenaries. 'What is your name?'

'Auralas.'

He eyed her more closely, her olive skin, dark brown eyes and mane of long black hair, at present plaited and tucked down under her mail coat. 'You look Kanese yourself.'

She straightened. 'I am.'

He was taken aback. 'Yet you shoot down your own king's Elites?'

Standing so close, he realized that he was looking up at the woman, and that the breadth of her shoulders far exceeded his own. 'He's not my king,' she answered with something like disgust. Turning away, she called loudly: 'Load the wounded! Let's get these wagons moving.'

Silk stumbled after the officer as she moved about the battle-field, calling orders to the troop of Crimson Guard, checking dressings, and, oddly, casting quick worried glances to the horizon. He held his aching head with one hand, biting back groans; he was still mentally bludgeoned after reaching out beyond the limits of

228

his Warren. He feared that he'd never again be able to muster the determination to risk raising Thyr – had he permanently damaged his mind?

Speaking very slowly, blinking back tears from the hammering in his skull, he managed, 'These wagons are the property of the Protectress of Li Heng. They are not prizes of battle. You'll not interfere in our journey to the city.'

'You haven't the personnel to make it,' she answered, rather brutally.

He still held his head, grimacing in pain, his other arm numb and useless. 'Then . . . we'll come back for the rest.'

'We'll escort you,' she said, moving on. 'Fingers!' she called, pointing to a youth lounging atop one wagon. 'Watch the perimeter!'

The youth, skinny, pale, and freckled, his hair a wild shock of sandy brown, rolled his eyes and offered a mocking salute. Silk watched the lad, puzzled – this was a mercenary? He was suddenly aware of an active Warren. A mage?

Auralas had moved on; he tottered after her. She was now over-seeing the stripping of all the corpses, Hengan and Kan alike, and he was suddenly outraged. 'What are you doing?'

'Your gear will be piled on the wagons,' she answered, without even turning to acknowledge him. 'Plus half the Kanese armour and weapons.' She cast him a quick humourless smile. 'You will have need of it, yes?' She straightened and shouted to the youth: 'Anything?'

'Nothing yet,' Fingers drawled.

Silk was still blinking. He felt as if he were moving through a dense fog. 'More lancers?' he asked.

Her answer was a grim 'No'. She whistled then, piercingly, and raised an arm, signing something. 'Let's get moving!' Silk stood motionless, at a loss. What was going on? It was all happening too quickly.

Auralas pointed him to a wagon – the one holding the lad, Fingers. As it passed he stumbled to it and climbed aboard. Over the barrels and sacks of provisions lay several of his surviving Hengans, their wounds staunched with rough field dressings. Four Crimson Guard sat in the bed also, crossbows cocked and readied, scanning the surrounding plains. The bench bounced and rocked beneath him, bringing dark spots to his vision and blasts of agony that threatened to crack open his skull.

'Who is out there?' he asked the lad. 'Seti raiders?'

This youth cast him a contemptuous glance. 'No. And you a Hengan. Hood's mercy, man. All this spilt blood? *Him*. The beastie.'

Silk's gaze snapped to the horizon and he immediately winced in the stabbing slanting sunlight. 'I thought you lot were hunting him anyway.'

'We are. But it takes all of us to hold him off.'

Silk straightened, peering about, then stood in the rocking vehicle. 'This is not the way to Heng. We're going west. Why?'

'Someone wants to talk to you first,' Fingers said, sounding exhausted by the effort of explaining.

'Who?'

The lad cast him another look, studying him through half-closed eyes, as if he'd just said something incalculably stupid. 'Orders from our glorious leader. He would like a word.'

Silk sat heavily. Oh. Courian D'Avore, whom some named the Red Duke, commander of the Crimson Guard – *he* was here? What could he want with . . . although, given what had just happened, Silk could guess why the man might want a word.

He sat back, broken arm across his lap, and despite his best efforts to remain awake the exhaustion and mental strain pulled upon him and he faded, his eyelids falling, his wrung-out and over-whelmed mind seeking the oblivion of rest.

*

Silk blinked to awareness and stared into the darkness of night. At first he panicked, believing that he was now blind, for he remembered only a dazzling shaft of brilliant light. A light like liquid fire; a fire that seared as it pierced him and he smelled the terrible stomach-turning stink of burned flesh, heard the hiss . . . Then a soft amber glow bloomed in the dark and he saw that he lay in a tent, a clay lamp stuttering on a nearby side table. He raised a hand and rubbed his eyes, groaning.

A chair creaked in the dark and someone said, 'You are with us again, I see.' The speaker moved the lamp closer and Silk blinked upwards at a Dal Hon male, his kinked hair going to grey at the temples, his eyes a mesmerizing black and his gaze sharp, though a welcoming smile softened his expression at the moment. 'I am Cal-Brinn. And you, I understand, are the city mage Silk. We are honoured to host you.'

Silk cleared his throat and attempted to assemble his jumbled thoughts. Cal-Brinn, a mage of the Crimson Guard. And not just any mage, one of the premier adepts of Rashan, the Warren of Night. There could be no misunderstanding why he was here at his bedside. Not after the display earlier. Barely trusting himself to speak, Silk nodded and swung his feet over the side of the cot. He carefully raised himself to a sitting position, hands at his head as if to keep it from falling off. A memory came and he examined his right arm: healed. He flexed the arm and nodded once more to Cal-Brinn. 'Thank you for the healing – and for seeing to my wounded,' and his voice took on an edge, 'even if you arrived belatedly.'

The mage lowered his gaze. 'I am sorry. But we were . . . constrained.'

'Constrained,' Silk echoed, and left it at that – he had no wish to hang about debating: he had to get the wagons back to Heng. He rubbed his forehead, fully expecting to find great cracks in it, and drew a steadying breath. 'Auralas promised that you would escort us back to the city.'

Cal-Brinn nodded. 'Yes. We will honour that. But first the duke would like a word. If you would.'

Silk did not want to face the notoriously fierce and blunt Courian D'Avore, but knew that it would be both boorish and stupid of him to decline, given that he and his command were not only in the Guard's debt but also at their mercy. So he gestured to the tent's front. 'Very well – let's get this over with.'

Cal-Brinn's tight smile told Silk that the man was fully aware of the calculation that went into his assent. He held out a beige stoneware mug. 'Tea?' he offered. 'I find it very restorative, especially after particularly trying magery . . . ?'

Rising, Silk accepted the mug, but declined to pursue the other invitation. Cal-Brinn rose also and led the way, pushing aside the heavy canvas tent flap. Silk saw that the man was fully armed and armoured, wearing an ankle-length mail coat, complete with hood, now thrown back, and a longsword sheathed on either hip. Over the mail coat he wore the requisite blood-red tabard of the Crimson Guard. Silk followed, feeling even more dishevelled and worn in the presence of the mage mercenary's martial habit.

Without, it was the depth of night. The sky was clear, the moon a few finger-breadths above the horizon. Torches on poles lit the encampment of circled tents, with the horses staked in the centre of the ring. For an instant the idea of placing the horses in the protected middle puzzled Silk. Then he realized, of course: *him*. The man-beast, Ryllandaras. As he walked, Silk sipped the hot herbal tea and was surprised by just how immediately restorative it was. The after-taste was a pleasant hint of caramel. 'Where do you get this?' he asked.

'My personal recipe, I'm afraid,' the mage answered with a smile. He led the way to the largest of the field tents. Here two sentries guarded the half-open tent flap. Cal-Brinn nodded to them and held aside the flap for Silk, who stood blinking in the relatively bright glare of candles and lamps set about the wide open tent. It was also quite noisy, as the tables that stood all about the circumference were crowded with mercenaries.

'It is our guest!' a great voice boomed out, thunderous and welcoming, and Silk knew who the speaker must be. He started forward, Cal-Brinn at his side. The gathered soldiers, male and female, many of whom Silk knew by reputation, turned in their seats to watch.

The two mages passed a crackling fire-pit and stopped before a table of thick planks behind which sat the Crimson Guard commander, flanked by two youths.

The contrast between the older man and the two youngsters could not have been more complete. Courian D'Avore was a burly giant in a laced leather jerkin, his hair and beard a mass of tangled black curls going to grey, his hands and face burnished by wind and sun to the consistency of worn leather, one eye a dead white orb from a sword cut that left a scar from brow to cheek. He was digging at the dinner before him, a rack of fire-charred ribs, and waving Silk forward with one greasy paw. 'Come, come.'

The youth on the man's right Silk knew to be his son, K'azz D'Avore, whom some called the Red Prince, more because of his regal manner and bearing than a claim to any title. K'azz nodded him a greeting: thin, ascetic, he had the look of a scholar rather than a warrior. But Silk found the pale eyes, greyish in this light, calculating, their gaze piercing.

The other youth was pale, slim, all in black, his features long and somehow conveying a moroseness of character. He wore a thin gold band, like a circlet, over his straight sandy-brown hair, and with a start Silk realized that he was looking at Malkir

Herengar, heir designate to the Grisian throne. He gave Malkir a bow that the youth answered with the faintest of nods.

'You are Silk, city mage of Li Heng, and one of its rulers, yes?' Courian said as he gnawed on a rib.

Silk grasped the mug behind his back in both hands and smiled modestly. 'Shalmanat is the ruler of Li Heng.'

Courian's gaze – the living eye and the dead – narrowed. He held the bone in his teeth and growled, 'Do not dissemble with me, mage. You five are her voice, her hands. You rule the city as nothing more than a damned cabal of mages.'

Silk hadn't thought of it in such a way before but couldn't, on the spur of the moment, dispute the characterization. The youth K'azz spoke up, 'Perhaps we should offer our guest a seat, Father. He has had a trying experience.'

Courian snorted harshly. 'Listen to my son, mage. No doubt after a hot meal we'll all be best of friends, hey? Perhaps we could all sing songs together.'

The youth's features were strained as he lowered his voice. 'I merely—'

'That is your problem, son. You *merely*.' Courian pointed the stripped rib at Silk as if it were a spear. 'It is strange, the beast Ryllandaras malingering about Heng, yes?'

Silk brought the stoneware cup out from behind his back and blew upon it, sipping. 'The beast does as it will.'

'Indeed it does – to the Kanese mainly, these days. But they are gone now from these northern plains, yet it lingers.' The one good eye examined Silk, gauging him up and down. 'It is almost as if it were waiting for something.'

Silk sipped again, loudly. 'The walls to fall, no doubt. You ought to try hunting it.'

The mercenary commander scowled, his jaws bunching in anger. He tapped the rib to the plank table. 'It is fast, deadly, and cunning. A difficult quarry.' He cocked his head, the dead eye now on Silk. 'Some say the Protectress possesses some sort of hold over the beast. What say you to that, mage?'

Silk sipped the reviving tea, remembered Ryllandaras's pledge of love and devotion to Shalmanat given in his own inhuman growling voice. He was sorely tempted, but could not bring himself to leap into that abyss. He said, 'Is it so surprising that her beauty should conquer all?'

Courian snorted once more. Now he held the rib in both hands before his chin, his elbows on the table, and, almost smiling, asked, 'What is going on in your fair city, mage?'

Uncertain of the man's tack, Silk found that all he could do was banter, stalling: 'We're readying a victory banquet.'

The grizzled mercenary affected mock surprise. 'Really? I find that difficult to believe.' He pointed the rib to Cal-Brinn at Silk's side. 'My mages have been yowling like cats in a bag on fire. They say something very unusual is going on in Heng right now. We hear rumours of some sort of daemon stalking its streets.'

Silk glanced to Cal-Brinn, who raised his brows in a silent question. Now he understood. 'Citizens hear a barking dog and this becomes the roar of Ryllandaras next door. Stories always grow in the telling. That is all.'

Courian's answering smile was thin. 'Of course.' He flicked the rib aside. 'Since you are done talking, have a seat. Eat. Tomorrow we will escort you back to Heng.'

Silk bowed. 'You are most generous, m'lord Courian.' Cal-Brinn guided him to a seat where he could eat without having to answer any further questions, and sat down next to him. He peered about, naturally curious about the Guard, but wary as well. He spotted the hulking Petra who fought with a two-handed mace, and scanning the crowd of mercenaries found the man he wanted: the tall, lean figure of Oberl, black-haired, his long legs stretched out before him. Champions all were these men and women, drawn from across the face of the continent and beyond, yet reigning over all was Oberl of Purge, champion of champions.

Perhaps the man felt Silk's gaze upon him, for he rose and crossed to their table. He sat opposite and regarded Silk, his gaze lazy. Cal-Brinn waved a hand in introduction. 'Oberl of Purge . . . Silk of Heng.'

Silk offered a nod. 'I have heard much of you, of course.'

The man's answering nod seemed to say *Of course you have*. He leaned forward over the table and said, his voice soft, '*I've* heard that the Sword of Hood is in Heng. Do you know of this?'

Silk nodded. 'Yes. I've met the man. Young. Seemed . . . competent.'

A drawing down of the man's lips expressed what he thought of Silk's evaluation of any fighter's competence. But he did nod in thanks for the intelligence, and pushed away from the table. 'I

234
.

would break into your damned city just to test the fellow's claim . . . but I am sworn to my duke.'

Silk resisted commenting and nodded instead, in farewell. 'Perhaps sometime . . .' he offered, to be diplomatic.

The man gave a tight hungry grin and walked away.

Silk found Cal-Brinn eyeing him and raised an eyebrow in question. The older mage cleared his throat. 'You've met him? Is he really— that is, what do you think of his claim?'

Silk gnawed on the rib of roasted pig that had been set down before him and considered that dawn visit. In truth, he thought the claim wildly unrealistic. Mortal swords of the gods were few and far between. Those of Fener and Togg and such – the beast gods and war gods – were the most common. But for the hoary Elder hoarder of souls to grant such a dispensation . . . well, that was another thing entirely.

And yet. That morning, within that old neglected mausoleum, he'd felt *something*. They hadn't been alone. He was no priest, but he'd heard talk that the Elder Realms such as those of the Andii and others were no more than older versions of the Warrens, and that even Hood's own path was one such. It was quite esoteric research. Yet he'd felt something.

He shook his head. 'I don't know. I consider it unlikely but not impossible.'

Cal-Brinn nodded at that. 'Fair enough.' He turned his attention to his meal.

Silk sipped his watered wine and tried to relax as the evening lengthened. His exhaustion and the lingering ache in his arm pulled at him. He understood now that the older mage was here beside him less as his minder than for companionship. For the broad tent was crammed with martial figures – among them some of the most storied in the lands – and Cal-Brinn was very much the odd man out. Yet the Guard possessed a cadre of mages second to none. He knew of Gwyn of Lammath, Petal and Red just to name a few. Even – and he searched the tent to find that skinny spotty youth – Fingers, Auralas had called him. The lad was sitting at a table laughing and joking, surrounded by armoured mercenaries yet wearing no more than a leather jerkin and buff trousers.

The Guard welcomed mages, he knew. And he felt the pull of it; of belonging, of the respect of one's companions. But, somehow, he couldn't imagine himself joining for the pursuit of money, or fame, or honour. No, it would take something more than that to win him over. Something larger. He couldn't quite put a name to it, but it was there. In this company he felt it pulling at him.

He shook his head again, blinking, and set down his wine. He felt a hand on his shoulder – Cal-Brinn.

'You should sleep,' the mage was saying, and Silk nodded. *Yes, it has been quite the eventful journey.*

In the morning the Guard was good to its word. They supplied drivers and an escort of twenty cavalry. Cal-Brinn sat with Silk in the lead wagon, while a surviving Hengan muleteer handled the team. The elder mage was quiet, clearly willing to allow Silk all the time he needed to think.

As the wagon rocked and bucked along a track that was nothing more than twin overgrown depressions across the rolling hillsides and shallow valleys, Silk considered the mercenary company's interest in the ongoing siege. They were here for the beast, of course, but clearly their formidable mage cadre was also aware of the strange happenings within the walls. Were they angling for some sort of advantage?

In time, he cleared his throat and shot a sidelong glance to the man beside him who sat at ease, a hand resting on the thick iron pommel of one of his swords. 'You intervened because you think there is something going on in Heng, and you are curious.'

The mage turned to regard him. His age was hard to tell. Older, yes, but by how much was impossible to know. The scars and roughened features told of a long hard life. And he was, after all, an adept of Rashan, and had perhaps followed – or been allowed to follow – one of the rituals of High Denul that rejuvenated the body and forestalled its ageing. 'You may avoid the subject with Courian,' he said, 'but you cannot hide the truth from me. Four Guard mages are here, and we all felt the shudder in our Warrens. It was as plain as an earthquake. Yes?'

Silk nodded, uncomfortably. 'Yes.'

'I am most interested in the thoughts of Hothalar on the matter. What is his opinion?'

Silk was quite surprised. 'Ho? You know of him? Why would you care what he thinks?'

Now Cal-Brinn's brows rose in surprise. 'Hothalar is one of

the foremost scholars of thaumaturgy and the manipulation of the Warrens. His experimentation is unequalled.'

Silk's astonishment must have shown on his face, for the mage of Rashan went on, 'But I see that that is not your area of interest.'

Silk looked away, his face heating. Damn Ho for leaving him in the dark! He must look like an utter fool. 'No,' he managed, holding his voice flat, 'it is not.' He cleared his throat. 'Indeed, I am no scholar of the arts. I am more practical.'

'From what was reported of the engagement, indeed so,' Cal-Brinn said, and Silk chose to take that as an offering of peace.

They rode in silence for a time. Silk was now thinking of the other issue Courian raised, the matter of Ryllandaras; here was something he could address. The beast had done its job. The north was clear and winter was now with them. Any further Kanese incursion was unlikely. Surely Shalmanat had no further need for the vicious creature.

He turned to the wagon driver and motioned for the reins. 'I'll take over – get some rest.' The man nodded and clambered over to the rear. Cal-Brinn cocked an eyebrow in silent question. Lowering his voice, Silk began, 'As to Ryllandaras . . . if there *were* a way to trap him, how might I reach you?'

Cal-Brinn nodded long and slowly in consideration. At last: 'If that were found to be so . . . I could leave myself open to contact from the Warren of Thyr . . .'

* * *

On the wall of a choked-off, dust-filled subterranean chamber ice crystals came into being in a latticework of diamond glimmer. They met, coalesced into a solid layer that crackled and hissed, sending wisps of mist into the dusty air. Sister Night emerged from the wall of latticed ice. Frost limned her short dark hair. Her flat features held her usual severe frown, and she wore her customary old worn travelling leathers. She raised a hand and a glowing ball of illumination materialized to float in the air.

She turned about, examining the chamber. It was squat; a mass of fallen earth choked off its one exit. From this heap, close to its leading edge, a pale hand could just be seen, reaching, nails broken where it had clutched desperately at the stone flags. Fat brick pillars cluttered the room; evidently these restrained the arched roof from total collapse.

She turned to the nearest wall and her breath caught. She approached, one hand outstretched, reaching out to crude sketches that cluttered the dressed stone walls. As her hand brushed close to one drawing she yanked it away, her breath hissing. She brought the globe of cold white light nearer.

It was a landscape done in charcoal, flat and desolate, bearing one central figure: the crudely traced outline of a structure, a brooding squat thing, almost a tomb, perhaps built of stone monoliths.

The woman flinched back as if struck. Amazement suffused her harsh features. 'By the Elder Powers,' she breathed. 'How . . . how did he . . .'

Her dark gaze narrowed now on the tomb-like structure and she brought a finger to her lips. 'Greetings, cousins,' she murmured aloud. 'After all this time. What have you been up to?'

Chapter 13

D ORIN ALMOST DRAGGED HIMSELF TO ULLARA'S GARRET TO rest and recover. But Rheena's warning against bringing any more attention to the girl came to mind and so he did not head that way. He stole a cloak and threw it over his shoulders and made his way to his last rented room, where he fell on to the straw pallet and slept.

He awoke to noon sunlight shining in from the one small window high in the wall. Groaning against the intrusion, he draped an arm across his eyes and lay considering his rather bleak-looking future. It now seemed quite clear to him that he did not have the proper qualities for rising within any organization.

Attempting to murder the boss was not a recommendation for promotion.

Freelance, then. But he'd tried that from here to Tali with nothing to show for it. In his line of work one did not simply hang out a shingle and wait for the clients to walk in. Lines of communication were needed. Contacts. Words to the right people and coins crossing the right palms. The unspoken trust that comes from years of deals and exchanges. As a newcomer, he had none of that established history. Nor, it seemed, was anyone willing to take him seriously enough to start.

What he needed, he decided, as he lay wincing from the stings and aches of all the cuts and bruises across his body, was some sort of impressive, undeniable, extraordinary achievement that would bring everyone round. What he needed, he realized, was a reputation.

But how could he take credit without letting anyone know it was him? He pressed his hands to his face, covering his eyes, and felt a crust of dried blood and the sticky accumulation of old sweat and grime. It was a godsdamned puzzle worthy of Oponn, that's what it was.

There came a knock at his door.

He froze. No one should know he was here; he'd been damned careful about that. Was he behind in payment? Maybe it was that drunk who worked as the concierge. He rose from the pallet as silently as he could, reached under, and withdrew the military crossbow he kept there, set its blunt nose against the floor and straightened, cocking it.

The cheap room was so small that a mere two steps brought him to the door off the hallway. He raised the crossbow to chest height. 'Yes?'

'Lunch!' came the answer. 'I have satay of rat wrapped in boiled cabbage leaves. Delightful.'

Dorin let the weapon fall, unlatched the door. 'What in the Abyss do you want?'

Wu came bustling into the narrow room, shut the door behind him. He offered one leaf-wrapped package to Dorin, who declined. The Dal Hon mage took a bite of his rat on a stick. He held out the other once more: 'You're sure?'

Dorin limped to the pallet, sat. 'I'm not hungry.'

Wu leaned back against the shut door. He nibbled on the rat while he studied his host. 'You look awful.'

'Thanks.' With a heavy sigh Dorin rose to stand before the tiny table that supported a chipped ceramic basin and a jug of water.

He poured water into the basin and washed his face while Wu spoke. 'It's the talk of the town. Pung the child-stealer's compound collapsing. Pung himself nearly killed. Of course I had the lads spread word that he'd turned on his mage, who, enraged, had blasted the very ground beneath him.'

Dorin slammed his hands to the tabletop and Wu jumped, nearly dropping his rat. He blinked. 'Did I say something?'

Dorin, his head hanging, forced through clenched teeth, 'Nothing.'

The Dal Hon shrugged. 'Well, I didn't mean *quite* that large an effect. The lads and lasses a wee bit too eager in their undermining there. At least we didn't lose the main house.'

Dorin sat. He pulled his torn and bloodstained shirt over his head and used it to daub dry his face. He frowned at his baffling visitor. 'How did you find me?'

'I sought your shadow.'

'Very funny. Look . . . what do you want? Whatever your name is.'

The mage looked surprised. His greying brows rose on his wrinkled forehead. Dorin had to remind himself that he was in fact no older than he. 'Why – we should strike now. While they are disorganized and undermanned.'

'Strike? Strike who?' He started unlacing the stripped bone and boiled leather vest he wore beneath his outer garments.

'Who? Why, the child-stealer himself, of course!' Wu pointed the rat. 'Now is the time for us to make our move.'

Dorin stared, then laughed. He laughed so hard it hurt the cut at his neck. Make our move? What was this fool going on about? He hardly knew where to start. He gingerly peeled the vest from his sweaty torso, started daubing at the dried blood. 'There's no move to make. And anyway, we have no men – unless you mean those kids.'

Wu waved a negative. 'No, no. I mean our property. The box Pung stole from us.' He made walking motions with his fingers. 'Quick in and out. None the wiser. Quiet as mice.'

Dorin stared afresh. He thought of the odd way this mage always managed to disappear. He leaned back against the wall. 'You could get us in and out of Pung's quarters?'

'Absolutely. I can get us anywhere. Even the palace.'

'Prove it.'

The mage led him on a roundabout route to an apparently abandoned tenement, siege damaged, its roof fallen in. He appeared to be trying for a jaunty walk, with his stick once more tapping the cobbles, but to Dorin the fellow's posture was more reminiscent of the cramped crab-like scuttle of someone who surely must be up to no good.

Dorin also noted Pung's former lads and lasses themselves, keeping watch from rooftops and alleyways. Within the tenement they descended to a basement and here seemed to be the main base of operations for these runaways, with kitchens and rooms floored with blankets and strewn with bundles. However, the youths here were all the older boys and girls, some even

241

approaching his age. Of the many younger ones there was no sign.

'Where's the rest of your crew?' Dorin asked, even as a sudden new suspicion struck him and he froze in the dirt hallway. 'Not the . . .'

The mage waved his little stick. 'No, no. I sent most of them off to dig at the escarpment.' Continuing on, he asked over his shoulder, 'You have heard of the gem fields?'

Dorin nodded. They lay to the west. A free-for-all of pits and caves along the base of the escarpment. Youths were preferred because the tunnels could be smaller. 'Who will they be working for? Surely not—'

'No, no. Of course not.'

They entered a large cellar and Dorin had to duck beneath its low roof of dusty timber joists. Perched snug on one support was the nacht. It bared its fangs at Dorin, who waved it off.

Sighing his relief, Wu sat on the bare beaten-earth floor before a small banked fire of glowing embers. A hole in the roof above allowed the thin tendrils of smoke to escape. He motioned an invitation to sit, but Dorin frowned down at the preparations. 'What's this? Smoke and mesmerism? Going to tell my future?'

The mage was unconcerned: he poked the stick at the embers. He waved the remaining lads, armed with crossbows, from the room. They shut the flimsy door behind them.

Wu waved again. 'Sit, sit. Please. You are no doubt tired and stiff from your fight.'

Dorin remained standing. 'That was yesterday.'

The mage eyed him critically. 'Then you are fighting fit? Armed?'

Now Dorin's gaze narrowed, and he crouched down across the fire, opposite his host. 'Of course. Why?'

Wu fanned the embers to glowing life. 'Oh, just that there's a chance something might be . . . summoned.'

Dorin rested his knees on the dirt, then snorted a laugh and shook his head. 'You almost had me going there. Your beastie! Ha. More illusion and suggestion.'

The mage was pressing the stick into the ground so that it stood upright. 'Oh, it's not illusion. It's real. Well . . . half real. Half of this world.'

Dorin cut a hand through the tendrils of white smoke. 'Save it

242

for the gullible ones. I saw the door to your cell. It was hacked by blades.'

Wu's grey brows wrinkled in a wince. 'Ah, I see. Well, the, ah, *thing* was there. It just didn't leave by the door.'

'Anyway.' Dorin rested his hands at his belt, feeling quite disappointed – and rather cross with himself for the feeling. 'I think we're done here.'

The Dal Hon mage raised a finger. 'One last minute, please.' He motioned to the dirt wall where the shadow of the stick stood tall and narrow in the umber ruddiness of the embers. 'See the shadow?'

Dorin grunted his agreement.

'Imagine, if you would, that that thin shadow was in fact a slit. A narrow opening on to another place . . .'

Dorin grunted again, this time dubious. 'Hunh. Shadow play and finger-waving. Don't try your tricks on me.'

'But it is open now,' the mage said, his voice now hoarse and clipped. 'Look within.' Dorin glanced to him, saw his fists white on his lap, his dark face clenched, and sweat dripping down his furrowed brow. Whatever the mage was doing, it was costing him an immense degree of strain.

He turned to the wall, and started, rather alarmed: the shadow had widened, or appeared to have widened. It was textured now, shifting and rippling. He edged closer, yet remained poised on his toes, ready to flee. *Something* seemed to be moving within the murk, and, closer now, he could make out the flat, gently undulating lines of a barren landscape. It resembled a near desert bathed in moonlit monochrome. He heard the distant moaning of a weak wind, heard the sands hissing as they shifted. Heated dry air brushed his face – blowing from . . . *where*?

The shadow was now a good arm's width: a painting – or a window – into another place. He reached out to touch the wall and his hand pushed in beyond it, encountering nothing. He yanked it back and turned to the mage, wonder in his voice. 'Is this a dream?'

'It is a portal to a new Warren,' the mage said through lips clenched in effort. '*My* Warren. My—' He broke off as both their gazes snapped to the door.

Dorin thought he'd heard a sound. A muffled call? Yet all was now quiet. Both listened for a moment longer, each remaining completely still. Then the door burst inward in a rain of slivers and black-clad Nightblades came pouring into the cellar.

Dorin had time for only an instant's evaluation – *too many* – then, as blades and crossbow bolts came lancing through the smoky air, he made his decision. He grasped the mage's shoulders and threw himself backwards towards the wall.

They fell tumbling over and over, far beyond the distance of the cellar wall. The mage was shouting, 'No! *No! Not yet!*' Dorin's last image of the cellar was of the nacht launching itself, snarling, claws extended, upon the Nightblades. He spun head over heels through twilight, then his back impacted on a yielding, hissing slope and he lost his grip and he and Wu rolled over and over each other, entangling and sliding, until he struck something hard and had the breath punched from him.

He came to lying on his side on a rocky barren slope. He turned over and peered at the sky: a dimness like heavy clouds, yet not clouds; the sky itself the hue of churning pewter and onyx.

Someone groaned nearby and Dorin sprang to his feet, blades out. It was Wu. He sheathed the daggers and pulled the lad over. The fellow groaned even louder.

'Where are we? What happened?'

The mage was holding his side. 'I'm hit. Done for. Gods, what a waste! What a terrible waste!'

Dorin drew his smallest and sharpest blade and slit the man's jacket and shirt, yanked them open. He was mildly surprised to see dark brown flesh beneath – the fellow really was from Dal Hon. He'd been hit by a crossbow bolt – grazed, really, beneath his ribs. The bolt appeared to have passed right through. Dorin set to tearing up his cloak as a dressing. 'It's a flesh wound.'

The mage clutched at his side. 'No! I'm dying. I feel the cold breath of Hood coming for me!'

He slapped the man's hands away. 'You'll survive. Unless you take a fever; then you'll die.'

The mage now pressed the back of a hand to his brow. 'I'm burning up! I swear!'

'Oh, shut up. Now, where are we?'

'For the love of the gods, man . . . let me die in peace!'

Dorin shook him. 'Where . . . are . . . we?'

The fellow slipped into unconsciousness. Feigned, or not. Dorin threw him down. Wonderful! Just wonderful. He straightened and peered round. Plain rocky desert extended in all directions. And just how far he could see was uncertain, the light being so strange and eerie – more a diffuse suggestion of light. It tricked the eyes and made the judging of distances nearly impossible.

One direction, however, appeared different. He thought he saw there the suggestion of angular shapes amid the desert plain. He hitched up the unconscious mage, set him over his shoulder, and started walking.

After a time, an unknown amount of time, it occurred to Dorin that the plain was one huge rubbish midden. He was constantly kicking aside bits of broken bone, glazed ceramics, and stone chips. He stepped over or around larger fragments of worked stone – what looked like the friezes and pillars of demolished buildings.

He had no idea how much time had passed. The murky sky did not brighten or dim in the usual manner: rather, it flickered, sometimes lightening only to darken once more. It was as if unseen things were drifting about, occulting whatever diffuse light there was.

In time, however, he became certain that he was approaching the ruins of a city. But no city such as he'd ever known. Hollow metal frameworks rose like statues to the sky. Toothed gears as tall as him lay all about. Broken rusted metal littered the sands. He hitched up the unconscious mage, uneasy in the face of such alien machinery. Yet he felt the need for shelter, and open doorways beckoned. He selected the smallest of the surviving buildings and entered.

He laid the mage down amid the wind-blown dust within then selected a gaping window from which to keep an eye upon the approach. He wondered idly as he stood watch who had built the bizarre structures, and whether they were even human. The entrances, for example, were far too low and wide. As were the windows. They did not seem built for ordinary men and women.

A groan brought his head round. Wu was stirring. The mage clutched at his side, groaned anew. 'Dying,' he moaned.

'No you're not. You'll survive.'

The greying head rose. 'It was touch and go, then. A near thing.'

'I've had worse and kept fighting,' Dorin muttered, eyeing the plain again. He thought he'd glimpsed a thin shape walking in the far distance – a ragged limping figure, now crouched, as if it were . . . watching.

Without taking his eyes from the rock-pavement desert and its rippling, twisting scarves of sand, he asked once more, 'Where in the Abyss are we?'

'Our tomb,' the mage groaned.

Dorin raised his eyes to the ash-hued sky. Dark shapes were crossing it, their wings huge and rigid. Giant bats? 'No. Really. Where?'

'My realm.'

Dorin turned to him, his brows high. '*Your* realm?'

The fellow was staring off into the distance. 'Fitting that I should die here, I suppose. One more beguiling mystery among so many for later travellers to puzzle over. One more set of bleached bones for history to gnaw upon. One more—'

'The wound's not mortal.'

This roused the fellow enough to lever himself up upon his elbows. 'Not this wound!' Then he moaned and pressed a hand to the side of his wrapped torso.

'Then what?'

'You'll see soon enough.'

Dorin clenched his teeth. He crossed his arms over his chest and grasped hold of the grips of the medium-sized daggers sheathed high in his two baldrics. Movement far down the main way caught his eyes and he leaned out for a better glimpse.

He had to stare silently for a time in order to comprehend what he was looking at. Then, without taking his eyes from the apparition, he asked, 'You mean something like a giant floating house?'

In an instant the mage was at his side. His hands, caked in dried blood and sand, clutched the window sill. Dorin had no idea what the thing was, other than how he'd described it. It was a blockish structure, a dwelling perhaps, hanging, seemingly unsupported, at the end of the main way. And he was certain it hadn't been there before.

'By the gods!' Wu breathed, awed. 'It's true!' He was out the doorway before Dorin could grab his fluttering jacket where it hung slit and unbuttoned down his back.

'Don't . . . we don't know how many—' But the Dal Hon was off, limping as quickly as he could down the way. Cursing, Dorin

246

followed, blades drawn. When he caught up to the mage he kept his eyes scanning the crumbling building fronts and asked, his voice low, 'What is it?'

'I believe it may be something like the Moon's Child.'

'Bullshit.'

'You know the tales?' Wu asked.

'Of course! The song of Gemnal and Astodil – the doomed lovers whose souls fly to the Moon's Child. Apsalar's quest for the impossible night-blooming rose. Yes, yes. All the fantasy tales.'

'Not so fantastic,' the mage puffed, limping along, holding his side. 'I have read eye-witness accounts of the floating mountain. Seen sketches.'

'I'll believe it when I see it. And that's not it.'

'No, no. Something *like* it.'

Dorin could now see that the thing had in fact been part of a larger structure. It was as if a room in a building had torn itself free and floated away. A large ramp climbed to end over nothing; a half-wall of stone rose behind a section of stone floor that was no more than a jagged broken surface. And from this ruin hung a wide ladder of rope and wood slats that brushed the ground.

'What I want to know,' Wu murmured, 'is what is the damned thing doing in my realm?'

'This isn't your realm.'

The mage jabbed a finger at him. 'I found it. It's mine. Finders keepers. Mine! Well . . . there was this scholar whom I, ah, took some papers from. He'd done some pioneering research – but he'd never *seen* it!'

Dorin raised his hands open-palmed. 'Okay, okay. I'm just saying that there might be—' He broke off because someone – or thing – had just emerged from a building ahead, about mid-way towards the floating house. The thing froze and studied them as they in turn studied it.

It suggested to Dorin an upright lizard. It possessed a blunt lizard-like snout, now turned their way. Its legs were thick and powerful-looking, while its arms were thin and frail. It wore a vest of some sort of hide, and baldrics from which hung numerous bits of metal. It was holding one such piece of equipment in its long-fingered hands as it stared at them with unblinking black and amber eyes.

A long tongue emerged and flicked the air. The blunt snout

turned to the floating house, then back in their direction as if the creature were gauging the distance.

The tableau held, frozen, until out of the distance beyond the broken ruins, rising and falling across the rocky desert slopes, there came the brassy howl of a hound.

All of them broke into a run. The creature dropped the piece of metal, its gait half waddling, half hopping. Wu fell far behind as he puffed and gasped. Dorin was much faster than the thing, but it was far closer to its goal. It reached the ladder and clambered up, drawing the bottom slat up with it as it went. Dorin arrived, jumping. His fingers brushed the lowest wooden slat even as it was whipped up and out of sight. 'Let us up, damn you!' he called.

The saurian head peered down for a moment, the tongue flickering, then withdrew. The structure, which listed severely to one side, now began to edge away on a path that would take it just over the broken tops of the buildings on the right. Wu arrived, panting and wincing. He waved at the artefact. 'Come back!' Aside, to Dorin, he whispered, 'Why didn't you kill it?'

The suggestion annoyed Dorin immensely. 'Kill it? We don't even know what it is.'

The hunting cry renewed, measurably louder now.

'We are dead,' Wu stated flatly. He let his hands fall loose at his sides.

Dorin was eyeing the distance between the tallest of the ruins and the course of the broken canted fragment. He waved Wu onwards. 'Come! Run!' He started off without waiting or checking to see if his companion followed. He traced a route to a jagged multistorey edifice whose tallest thrusting point would intersect with the artefact's path if it did not alter. He heard Wu clattering after him through the broken rock and rusted metal litter.

The howl burst upon them once more. So loud was it that its bass impact shook the stone walls raising drifting scarves of dust. Dorin could not even imagine such a beast, and certainly did not want to face it armed only with close-quarter weapons. He entered the building's ground floor through one of the low wide windows, and was confronted by a maze of rusted mystifying machinery. He spotted a ramp rising to the first floor and made for it – Wu could easily follow his footsteps through the ages-old layer of dust and sand that covered the floor.

The ramp rose in a curve to the first floor and a second one started up leading to the next. These floors lay emptier than the ground; broad hallways led off to rooms accessed by large oval openings. The roof of the second had collapsed in places, and through the jagged gaps Dorin glimpsed standing remnants of the main supporting elements of the third. These were his goal. He clambered up a nearby slope of the broken rock and made the roof – such as it was.

The bottom of the floating fragment loomed overhead, drifting lazily. Dorin ran, picking his way carefully along the edge of a narrow standing wall. As he went he unwound a thin line from his waist. His path took him to a tall jutting angle of wall and he climbed this just as the artefact brushed over. Its shadow, as it fell across him, only slightly darkened the strange diffuse light that pervaded everything.

He released the grapnel's tangs and they locked, extended, even as he let it go to start whirling, spinning, as he let out more line. He threw. The grapnel arced up and outwards, reaching, only to strike the flat face of a stone wall and bounce away, falling to the street below.

He let his arm drop. The floating platform coasted onward. He heard the mage struggling among the wreckage of the slope behind. He started slowly re-looping the line.

Wu arrived, panting. 'I'm impressed,' he gasped. 'Nearly reached it.'

'I need a longer rope,' Dorin murmured. Watching the thing coast away it occurred to him that the unearthly construction, though ragged and broken, still possessed a strange sort of beauty as it silently floated off. He wondered whether it really was a fragment of that giant mountain many named the Moon's Spawn.

Wu peered round and clapped his hands together. 'Well. We can perch here like birds and hope they don't reach us.'

Dorin's gaze snapped to him. 'They? There's more than one?'

The mage's expression became pained and he wove his fingers together. 'Er, well, yes.'

'Wonderful.'

A new howl burst through the streets below and Dorin flinched despite his efforts to contain the reaction. He searched about, frantic for an escape, and his gaze fell on the structure next to them. Shorter than this one, it was in far worse shape; much of its interior flooring had collapsed. In fact, it looked as if all of the ramps to the higher floors were gone.

'We have to jump.' He pointed to the roof below.

The mage shrank from the edge. 'No. There is no way I can do that. I'll just sit here and think, thank you.'

'They can't reach us there. Come on.' He grasped a fistful of the mage's clothes at the shoulder and marched him along to where a section of roofing allowed for a run at the gap.

Wu batted at his grip. 'This is absurd. It matters not where we die!'

'Do you want me to fight or not?' Dorin snarled, shaking him.

The fellow threw out his arms to indicate their surroundings. 'Well, yes. I had hoped we could come to an arrangement. But that was before *this*! Thanks to you we're stranded in another realm and dead!'

'Thanks to me we're still alive,' Dorin muttered. He faced the neighbouring structure, renewed his grip on the man. 'We're going to run and jump, you hear? The gap is narrow. Not a street. It can be done.'

The mage suddenly clutched at his leg, hopping. 'Oh, a cramp! In my leg. An awful cramp. I get them, you know – damned inconvenient.'

Dorin fought to keep him upright. 'Would you stop—'

Both stilled then, as each heard it from below: the flinty scrabbling of huge nails or claws on stone, and a titanic beast's great bellows-like breathing and snuffling.

The mage broke free of Dorin's grip and took off for the ledge, yelling in wordless terror, his arms thrown wide. He disappeared from sight over the lip, his torn jacket flapping like failed wings. Dorin ran as well, not even daring to glance back to the open floor behind where even now a great shaggy monstrosity might be loping to close its jaws upon him. He flung himself out kicking as hard as he could.

He landed in a bone-rattling impact, tumbling and rolling, his breath punched from him. Shaken, he leaped up immediately to stagger to the edge where he'd glimpsed the mage lying prone, half dangling. He yanked the man away from the lip just as both legs slid over.

'You have to roll when you hit,' he explained. 'Roll. Don't just land like a sack of flour.'

From the building behind came a great howling bellow of rage that shook the air and they both flinched, hunching. A blow like a sledgehammer struck the wall where they'd been standing and loose stones fell to the alley below.

Covered in stone dust the mage stood blinking, dazed, blood running from his mouth. 'What? Roll . . . what?' Dorin led him to the middle of the tiny section of roof they now possessed and sat him down.

'Think here.'

Nodding, still quite shaken, the fellow sat. He pressed a hand to his side where fresh blood gleamed. Dorin drew his middle-weight blades, thin long-knives, and crossed to the nearest broken edge of roof. Cautiously, he peered over; a pile of rubble here. Tall enough? He hoped not.

He continued his investigation of their perimeter. What now? An anonymous death in some alien desert? Not what he'd imagined for himself. Not at all. He glanced back to the ridiculous mage: the fellow sat cross-legged. Thinking of a way out, he hoped. Still, if he got them in, why shouldn't he be able to get them out? He went to him, peering down. 'Do your magery, or whatever it was that you did before. Get us out of here.'

The fellow raised his gaze and offered a sad sort of lost smile. 'Yes. That's the idea, isn't it? Just not that easy. What a shame. I had such plans . . .'

Rocks clattered below. A grating rumble that might have been the growling of a giant vibrated the stones beneath their feet. Dorin went to the ledge to scan the clutter of the collapsed sections. A shape padded into view, a tawny, shaggy pelt of sandy brown. So huge was it Dorin thought for a moment it was a horse. That was until it raised its blunt muzzle, its pointed ears pricking up, and fixed bright amber eyes upon him.

The eyes captured him, and he stared fascinated and horrified, his blood congealing. What he glimpsed was not malevolence or evil, but hunger. A savage primal hunger that allowed no barrier or obstacle to stand between it and its goal. What shook Dorin was the sudden reversal of roles: prior to being caught by those eyes he'd always considered himself the hunter. Now he was prey – and it shook him to his core.

He blinked and shook his head as if coming out of a trance or a dream. Now he knew how the mouse felt, he realized.

The beast let go a great challenging roar and leaped. Its fore-paws scrabbled at the lip of the roof and Dorin sliced at them in a sudden panic. Stones were torn away as the beast fell back. He retreated from the edge, his heart hammering. Gods! What a brute.

A howl of frustration went up from below, the roof shaking beneath Dorin's feet. In its colossal rage and frustration the beast threw itself against a wall and the entire structure rocked, weaving. Another section of wall fell in a crash of stones.

'Do something!' Dorin yelled as he fought to keep his balance.

'No point,' the mage answered. 'Look.' Dorin shot him a desperate glance. The fellow was wiggling his fingers over the stones of the roof. 'No hard shadows here. None. Nothing to catch hold of.'

The beast battered the standing wall. Another section of roofing fell away. Stones clattered to the alleyway below and a great cloud of dust billowed up. Dorin backed up nearly to the mage. 'But I thought we were *in* shadow. Isn't that what this place is called?'

He gripped and re-gripped his knives. If he could leap on to the thing's back ... More howls rose then, brassy and eager, from the twisted ways of the surrounding city. Dorin raised his eyes to the smoky opalescent sky. Wonderful. More of them.

'I didn't call it that,' Wu answered, sounding maddeningly calm. Then he jerked to his feet, suddenly animated. 'Shadow. Could that be the answer? It is broken, shattered. But it is all shadow? One aspect?'

Both almost fell, tottering, as the beast threw itself against another wall and the roof canted. Stones crashed and tumbled. They were left with hardly enough room to stand.

'Do whatever you must now!' Dorin yelled.

'Very well. I will open a way but we must jump blind. I have no idea if it will work or not ...'

Dorin scuttled up the slope of the roof on his hands and knees. 'Never mind! Do it.'

'It is done.' Dorin turned; the mage was standing on the very lip of the roof, pointing out to the gap beyond. Peering past Dorin's shoulder, his eyes suddenly widened in terrified amazement. Dorin spared one glance back to see the monstrous hound's glaring eyes and slathering muzzle levered up above the roof, its forepaws scrabbling. The roof rocked even more steeply beneath its massive weight. Stones cracked and gave under their feet in a series of explosions. Dorin launched himself forward, taking hold of the mage's loose flapping shirting and jacket as he went.

The two arced outwards over nothing as with a buckling roar the remaining walls and ledge of roof collapsed completely. Dorin landed with a grunt and felt the sharp blows of falling broken stones. He held his head, stars in his eyes, and bit his lip to keep from bellowing out his pain.

Blinking back tears, he peered about. He almost stood in astonishment but caught himself in time: it was night and he was back – but not in the city. Outside its walls. He sat in a dried pigsty, covered in dust and caked mud, amid the litter of fallen stone. A groan and a stirring amid the mud betrayed that he was not alone.

'Where—' Wu began, before Dorin clamped a hand to his mouth.

'South of the city,' he hissed. 'In the Kanese lines.'

The mage's greying brows rose above Dorin's hand, and he nodded his understanding. Dorin removed his hand. 'Told you I could do it,' the mage whispered. Dorin just shot him a look of disbelief. He helped the wounded mage to his feet and together they limped to the cover of a hedgerow. Dorin led them northeast.

They passed by encampments of the besieging Kanese soldiery. They stilled as patrols marched past, then continued on. Dorin was puzzled by the ease with which they eluded detection until he noticed how the shadows seemed to cluster so very thickly about them; how the night appeared more monochromatic and dulled to his vision than ever before. It was as if he were peering out at the world through thick cloth. Then he noticed that while the mage clutched at him for support, his other hand was weaving and curling as if manipulating some unseen matter, and his lips moved silently in constant incantation.

One hilltop stood between them and the river. The burned ruins of a collapsed tower topped it. Pickets occupied the position, but they snaked between them. Here Dorin paused as the modest highland offered a view of the plains to the west. Campfires dotted the dark fields, along with countless tents. One gigantic multi-poled tent dominated the ground south of the lines. It glowed golden with many inner lights. The field command and residence of King Chulalorn the Third, he assumed.

On an impulse, he whispered to the mage, 'Could you get us in there – into Chulalorn's quarters?'

Wu did not even glance in that direction. 'Of course,' he answered, waving a hand dismissively. 'I have already done it.' He motioned to Heng's gigantic walls which cut off the view to the north in a great broad swath of darkness. 'What worries me is how we can possibly get into the city.'

Dorin did not answer. He continued to study the king's pavilion and its satellites of surrounding lesser tents – quarters for functionaries, bureaucrats, officers and guards, he assumed. It was like an entire mobile city, ringed and guarded by hundreds, no doubt.

An indisputable prize.

Wu was tugging at him. 'I said,' he hissed, 'how will we get into the city?'

'Can't you just magic us in?'

The mage rolled his eyes in exasperation. 'I can't walk through walls.'

'But we're outside the walls now . . .'

'We travelled through that other realm, didn't we? Through . . . Shadow itself. Do you wish to return?'

Dorin shuddered at the thought of confronting those beasts again. 'No.'

Wu nodded, fierce. 'Wise decision. So?'

Dorin motioned him onward and down to the riverbank. 'Tell me, son of the hot Dal Hon plains . . . can you swim?'

Chapter 14

IKO WAS DEEP INTO A PRACTICE DUEL – PART OF HER DAILY effort to exhaust herself mentally and physically – and so she did not notice the beginning of the commotion over by their compound's main doors.

When she and Sareh broke off from one another, both panting, their chests working, the noise and pleas finally reached through to Iko's consciousness and she glanced over. A crowd of her Sword-Dancer sisters blocked the entrance, all talking at once.

Without setting down the wooden practice blade she headed over and pushed her way to the front. Here she found tall Yuna gripping an old man, one of the palace servants. The girl was holding him by the neck just as one might squeeze a goose. The daily food delivery lay scattered on the stone floor – rice, bread, and some sort of boiled vegetable.

'What is this?' Iko asked.

'A damned insult is what this is,' Yuna growled, and she shook the man once again. The retainer's eyes bulged and he gurgled as he pulled at her clenched grip.

'Release him,' Iko said, and made it a request by sounding tired of the display.

Yuna's thin lips tightened as her mouth drew down, and she studied Iko carefully, obviously weighing whether or not this was worth a possible challenge. Grunting, she let him go and he stumbled back, bowing and rubbing his neck. She waved him off. 'Go back to your wretched masters and tell them we'll not tolerate this shit.' The gathered sisters all added their loud support to the demand. The servant ran out the doors.

Iko eyed the trampled food. 'And how does this help our hunger?'

Yuna gestured to the mess. 'This is all it deserves. Wormy rice, stale bread, and old tasteless roots. An insult! We are guards to kings! They dare offer us such filth?'

'The city's besieged, Yuna,' Iko observed. Unfortunately, she failed to keep all the sarcasm from her voice and the woman's gaze flared in anger.

She stepped close, leaning over Iko, and whispered, low, 'Do not think you'll dispense with me as easily as you dealt with Torral.'

Iko spent a fraction of an instant considering her options. Like Torral, Yuna respected strength. Any apologies or yielding now would be taken as a sign of fear and weakness. Even if she didn't want a confrontation, it was too late. So she crossed her arms, arched an eyebrow, and said, 'Don't make me go to all the effort now that you've ruined dinner.'

Yuna continued to study her, waiting for any betraying sign of fear, a tremble or a flinch, and with none forthcoming she leaned away, letting go a light snort. Brushing past, she commented, 'Who put you in charge?'

Iko bit back any hint of the fact that Hallens herself had made her second in command. Hallens did not want it divulged, and Iko would respect her wishes. She supposed it was a less than subtle hint that Iko would have to earn the respect of her sisters, almost all of whom far exceeded her in their length of service. She went to find her commander.

Directions from a few of the Sword-Dancers brought her out to the far westerly gardens of the palace grounds that were open to them. Here she found the woman standing meditatively, her hands clasped behind her back, staring off to the west. Iko approached and a change in the tension of Hallens' back told her that the captain was aware of her, probably even knew who it was.

'The natives are restless,' Iko murmured as she stepped up next to her.

The woman cast her a glance. A small smile played on her lips. 'I heard.'

'We can't take this much longer.'

'I know.'

'There will be blood next time.'

'Very probably.'

'Then why—' Iko clamped her lips shut against her own complaint; she knew full why: the king's orders. She said instead, 'We will lose our effectiveness.'

'Yes.' The woman reached out to a limp dead flower sagging on its brown stem and broke it off. 'A killing frost. I hear the local servants complaining of this cold. Very unusual.'

Iko had been shivering, but then she always did now when venturing outside to exercise. 'Yes? What of it?'

Hallens glanced to her and for an instant Iko thought her dark eyes looked haunted before she turned away. 'Word has come,' she said, the old familiar iron in her voice.

A thrill of tension shot up Iko's back. 'Yes?'

'It will be soon. We will be asked to take and hold a position in the city. The moment we hear where, we must move.'

'I understand.'

Her commander eyed her once more, let out an uneasy breath. 'The messenger was unusual ... it was a very low-ranked Nightblade. And his manner was almost ... fearful. I believe the Nightblades have been enduring punishing losses here in the city. The one I saw acted almost as if he were being hunted.'

Iko let out a snort of disbelief. 'Impossible.'

'In the south, yes. None there that can rival the Nightblades. But we are closer to the homeland of our old Talian overlords here. The servants of the Iron Crown kept all in line for decades.'

Iko shuddered at the mention of the assassins who slew at the command of the old hegemony. 'They were destroyed in the uprisings.'

'Perhaps. In any case, we must be careful.'

Though puzzled, and quite troubled, by her commander's manner, Iko nodded. 'Of course.'

Hallens hugged herself. 'It is very cold.' She glanced to Iko. 'You were not with us at the fall of Fedal, were you?'

That had been one of the most storied, and bloody, of all the subjugations of the city states of the south. Iko shook her head. 'No. That was before I was given permission to join a field command.'

'I see.' The woman paused, as if she had been about to go on but had reconsidered. Her mouth tightened and she nodded, curtly. She gestured, inviting Iko to return with her to their quarters. 'Well ... not long now.'

As they walked in silence, Iko uncomfortable, Hallens distracted, Iko considered her commander's last question. The fall of Fedal. Few had witnessed the death of the old ruling family in that ancient fortress. But Iko had heard strange stories and hushed whispered rumours. Sorcery had accomplished what the ranks of Chulalorn's soldiers could not. The stories were that the defence, up to that point so unassailable, had collapsed in one night. And that the few soldiers who had entered the private quarters of the ruling family before they were sealed off reported unbelievable sights. Whispers were of entire rooms engulfed in hoarfrost, with men and women sitting at table, frozen solid in the act of eating dinner.

Outrageous. But Hallens' concern over escalation came to mind, and Iko cast her a worried glance. So, with the stalemate in the field would the battle now shift to new ground? To where all their vaunted skills and training may prove useless? She recalled her disgust that Chulalorn should stoop to sending his Nightblades against the Protectress; with that failure he may be pressed to even more dangerous and desperate means.

The possibility troubled her just as much as it obviously troubled her commander. Oddly enough, her first concern was for Chulalorn himself. She was worried that he would stain his hands with such tools. It was unworthy of him, of his dynasty, that he should compromise so much to conquer.

She let out a long sigh. Yet perhaps this was all nothing more than a warrior's distaste for the ways of sorcery. She did not understand it; and so she was suspicious of it.

She glanced up to see the captain's eyes upon her, and there was an uncharacteristic softness and care in that gaze that made her realize that for all her own anxieties, Hallens was burdened far more by the terrible weight of fear for all the sisters under her command.

* * *

When Silk walked the palace halls and found them utterly deserted, he was rather put out. He was on his way to confer with Shalmanat. The inner palace guards still stood their posts, of course, but the usual messengers, pages, and bureaucratic functionaries were missing. Also absent was the usual crowd of city notables and aristocrats who gathered daily at court to see and be seen, and to gossip and make deals. It struck him that over the last month or so the day to day workings of the city had inexorably ground to a halt. Perhaps many of these paper-pushers were sick, weak, or too frightened to leave their families alone. The few functionaries he did pass hardly raised their eyes as they walked the halls listlessly, papers pressed to their chests, looking sadly dishevelled. Nothing, it appeared, was getting done.

Everyone's acting as if we've lost, he decided. And we haven't. At least not yet. But we will if this malaise takes hold.

He nodded to the guards before the Inner Sanctum, and entered. Within, as the heavy door swung shut behind, he halted, shocked and surprised. The room was completely empty. By the gods – surely not Shalmanat as well?

Then he mentally shook himself and walked on towards the chamber's centre. No, of course not. He was simply used to finding her here, if she was not out walking the private grounds. Before coming here he'd made certain she was not in the gardens, nor in her private apartments. Where else then could she be?

He reached the simple seat of power at the exact centre of the domed chamber – the camp stool of worn leather and wood – and stood peering down at it, a hand at his chin. Worry touched him then. The ruler of a city at siege, seemingly gone missing . . .

He did something then that he'd never dared do before; he sought her out. His fear of raising his Warren had faded, and now he reached out, feeling among the many auras for that unique one; non-human, tinted, as he now knew, by Kurald Liosan. Though it took a great deal of searching, he found it. And where he found it troubled him deeply. Far to the north it was. Well beyond the walls of the city.

He released his Warren and nearly allowed himself to thump down in the seat before him, but halted the motion at the last instant. He paced before the stool instead. What in the many realms was she up to? She never left the city. He paused in his pacing then, considering.

At least that he knew of . . .

He walked then, stiffly, and sat down against the wall next to the door, extending his legs straight out. He steepled his fingers together and pressed them to his lips, thinking, his gaze narrow. And he waited.

~

A small noise roused him from a doze – movement far across the domed chamber: Shalmanat entering through a door the existence of which Silk had had no hint. This also chagrined him; he knew of one concealed way into this room but that was not it.

He rose on aching stiff legs. Far across the way Shalmanat paused, nonplussed perhaps, then continued. She gave him a nod in greeting, calling, 'Silk, what is so pressing?'

'Nothing so pressing as your absence.' She was dressed for travel, in old worn leathers, her hair drawn up and scarved. 'And where have you been?'

Closer now, he saw a brow arch and her lips tighten as she considered his words. 'That is my concern, I think.'

'I – we – your bodyguard should know.'

'You are not my bodyguard, Silk.' Amusement now curled her lips. 'You are ill-suited for such duties, I should imagine.'

For an instant fury blazed across his vision, then he blinked, swallowing. He screamed within: *I would die for you!* Outwardly, he stammered, his fists clenching, and he damned the heat at his face. 'You were with him, weren't you? With Ryllandaras.'

She considered him again, her head tilting aside. The look she gave him made him think of the affection and pity one might feel for a distressed pet. 'As a matter of fact I was. He is old, you know. Very old. And has been witness to many of the great clashes of the past. I went to speak to him about these – troubling – manifestations in the city.' She sat then, slumping, upon the stool.

He peered down at her for a time before asking, 'And?'

She roused from her thoughts, blinking. 'He said that in the stench of the city he could smell the sands of a lost Hold . . . the Hold of the Tiste Edur.' She shook her head as she spoke, and appeared so troubled that he almost forgot his anger and resentment and threw himself at her feet to hug them – anything to ease her burdens.

'We will get to the bottom of it,' he assured her.

She nodded distractedly at his words, her gaze elsewhere, lost in her thoughts, seemingly having utterly forgotten his presence. He almost reached out then to smooth her silver hair but dared not, clenching his hot hands together at his back. And he bowed, briefly, and took his leave.

* * *

260

Dorin was sorting through a tabletop of rag-tag weapons brought together by the lads at Wu's orders. Outside it was nearing dusk, and having slept through most of the day he felt rested, though favouring his left leg from a deep cut sustained during his encounters on the roofs the night before.

This night would see more of the same, his hunting of the Nightblades. The first step in his plan, such as it was. He frowned at one rusted and pitted knife: would've been a fine weapon . . . a hundred years ago. He made his selection among them to replace lost blades and began easing them into his baldrics.

'Ah, here you are!' announced Wu as he came bustling into the cellar of their new hideout. He was rubbing his hands together and waggling his brows. 'Ready to get on with my plan, then?'

Dorin eyed him sidelong as he thumbed the edge of a hooked blade. '*Your* plan?'

The mage was unperturbed. 'Of course! Our assault upon Pung's headquarters!'

'He's nothing now.'

'Not *him*. The box, my friend. We must have that box.'

Dorin now sighted down the razor edge of a lethal stiletto. 'Why? What's in it?'

'Never mind. What I know is that it's important.'

Dorin peered down at the mage, who was hunched over like an old man. 'You don't know what's in it, do you?'

Wu screwed up his face in defiance. 'I don't have to know. My instincts assure me it's important.'

Pulling an old cloak about himself, Dorin headed to the door. 'Well, it can wait. I'm busy with my own plan.'

'And what plan is that? Hunt down all the Nightblades? Why? To what end? What are they to you?' He thrust high a wizened finger. 'Ah! Wait! I see. You are after what they ward. You would take a contract perhaps?' He waggled the finger in dismissal. 'She would never hire you.'

'Not a contract. Think of it as . . . credentials.'

Both greying shaggy eyebrows rose in exaggerated under-standing. 'Ah. I see.' The wrinkled lips pursed in regret and he shook his head. 'And you would expect my cooperation in this effort, no doubt.'

Dorin felt his shoulders tightening in the familiar irritation the

261

fellow could so easily summon in him. He looked to the ceiling a short hand-breadth above his head. 'Fine! When?'

The mage waved his hands in deference. 'Oh, there's time yet. The lads and lasses aren't finished clearing the tunnels. Do go on.' He shooed him from the room. 'I'll let you know.'

Dorin stared, his mouth open. *Gods!* Cracked as a heat-maddened rat. He considered a number of blistering replies only to snarl under his breath as he stormed out.

Much later, even as he knelt hunched in the cover of a brick chimney, he still couldn't rid himself of his anger at the jumped-up little fellow. Who did he think he was? Had that been an *order*? Why on earth did he put up with it? Stupid useless little prick!

Two dark shapes dropped on to the flat rooftop and readied crossbows as they studied the streets below. Dorin drew his knives and charged.

They were good enough to sense his silent approach across the dried clay roof. They spun, but he was too close: one shot missed and the other weapon he knocked aside to fire out across the roof. He sliced the tendons of one knee of each and they buckled. One he kicked to topple out into the alley below. The other he thrust in the groin, ripping up, just as one might slice a fish. This Nightblade fell curled round the mortal wound like a pinned bug.

Have to teach the little man a lesson, Dorin decided, as he straightened. Clarify the relationship.

Then he threw himself flat to the roof. Crossbow bolts cut the air above him, shot from behind. He rose in a charge. On the opposite lip of the roof two more Nightblades rose from cover. One threw aside his crossbow, advancing to meet him; the other reloaded.

Dorin and the Nightblade met close to the edge of the roof. Each fought with two knives. The fight was silent but for the sound of the weapons sliding across each other as the blades kissed and scraped in short staccato bursts.

The Nightblade sought to circle round to expose Dorin for a shot, while he counter-circled to keep his opponent in the way as they duelled. They shuffled, their soft leather moccasins brushing the dried clay, their arms extended, blades balanced in their grips ready to suddenly reverse or threaten a throw.

A quick series of feints brought Dorin in close. The Nightblade had to retreat and Dorin drove him back with constant rapid thrusts and cuts. The man regained his balance after a few shifts, but he was closer now to his brother. Dorin had him where he wanted him and he pressed again, closing.

The fellow managed to catch both blades on his and they balanced there, corpse-a-corpse, the blades scraping and grating, the Nightblade's breath hissing from him in explosive gusts. Dorin realized he'd made a mistake: not only was this fellow heavier and stronger than he, but the other Nightblade had shifted round and was now sighting down the stock of his weapon straight at him.

His acrobatic training served him well then as he kicked and twisted in the air, hammering the breath from his opponent and circling behind. The other Nightblade swung his weapon, cursing. Dorin was furious with himself for letting the game go on for as long as it had, but it was over now, for when the kick had landed, breaking ribs, he knew he'd won. Even as his feet touched the roof again he surged inwards once more, blocking a forearm, and stitched the fellow's torso in a series of short jabbing thrusts, driving him backwards into his partner. The two tumbled from the roof, arms flailing, to land with heavy wet thumps on the cobbles three storeys below.

'Impressive!' a man shouted. Dorin spun, crouching. A Nightblade stood far across the roof, his arms out, deliberately showing his empty hands. 'Such an aggressive style! Faruj was your teacher, yes?'

'Who?' Dorin felt behind him to ease down on the roof's edge – just in case.

The man wore loose black trousers and shirt, his hair black as well, cut short. He opened his arms wider in the sketch of a shrug. 'Well, I suppose he wouldn't have given his real name, would he? Wiry? Able to beat you with one hand?'

His old master *had* done just that – pinned or forced him to yield almost every day, usually with one hand.

But the old Talian Master of Assassins, Faruj? In truth? Some had whispered it, but the old man had always laughed off any such suggestion.

None of this Dorin showed on his face, which he held flat. 'I don't know what you're talking about.'

Another sketch of a shrug from the man. 'Of course you don't. How much?'

'How much what?'

'How much to work for us? We could use a man of your skills.'

'Work for Chulalorn? Really?'

The Nightblade waved a hand impatiently. 'Surely that does not matter. Think of it as self-advancement. Name your price. How much?'

Something in those words – their arrogant delivery, or their literal meaning perhaps – brushed Dorin with a strange affront. He knelt further, feeling with his toes for a brick lip along the wall. 'I suppose you're right. It shouldn't matter. But I'm not for sale.'

'Pity, that.'

Two screams erupted then, freezing him, and a crossbow bolt snapped the air over his head. One keen screech was that of a hunting bird – astoundingly loud. The other was torn from a human's throat, and it held unimaginable agony. Dorin unfroze to spin to his left, and saw a titanic bird of prey looming over another Nightblade. Its talons encircled his skull, their dagger lengths piercing the sockets of his eyes. The man had dropped his crossbow and was yanking futilely at the bird's grip.

Wings broader than the height of a man unfurled. They gave one mighty stroke and the predator lifted its victim from the roof, his legs kicking and spasming. They rose into the night air over the street, and then the creature released its grip and the man fell, a limp and silent form, dead already.

What on earth was that? Dorin glanced back across the roof; he was alone. He shuddered uncontrollably for an instant. It was an after-effect of that chilling call. No doubt the screech was meant to freeze prey, and in his case it had worked. He became mindful then of his exposed position and ducked down to find his way to the alley.

He walked from one patch of darkness to another through the empty mid-night ways, making for the north. He knew whom to see; twice now birds of prey had attacked his enemies and he did not know whether to be grateful or angry. He reached the side of the tall stable and climbed to the open gable of the garret above.

Within, he found the rafters crowded by the usual dozing day-time hunters. Beneath, perched on a box, sat Ullara, legs crossed, also apparently asleep. Her eyes, however, fluttered open as he approached, and she smiled, dreamily. 'Safe, I see,' she murmured.

'Thanks to you?'

'Thanks to my King of the Mountains.'

'King of the Mountains?'

She gave a weak shrug. 'One of my names for him. That is where he comes from. Far to the north. The Fenn mountains. He is lost and lonely here. Out of place among lesser hunters.' She tilted her head, studying him. 'Like you.'

'I am not lonely.'

'Yes you are – you just can't see it.'

He sat next to her, sighing. 'Well . . . my thanks regardless. You are better?'

She nodded, leaned against his side. 'Yes. Thank you for the coin. My brother is recovering.'

'Good . . . but I have to ask that you stop doing this. It is too dangerous for you. I have enemies. Feuds.'

'I know. I can help.'

'No. Stop. Do not involve yourself.'

She wrapped her arms round his. 'It is too late.'

'Ullara . . . no. This is no game.'

'I know. Hold me.'

'What?'

'Hold me. Stay and hold me. I don't want to be alone.'

Gingerly, reluctantly, he tucked his arm about her, pressed her closer. She felt very hot against his side. Her forehead burned where it pressed against his chest. Her eyes slipped closed and her light breathing eased into a slow steady rhythm.

He held her, rocking gently, until the flush of dawn came to the windows. Then he eased her down and covered her with an old horse blanket and made his way down the wooden slats of the wall before it was light enough to see.

* * *

Sister Night spent most of her time meditating. She sat cross-legged in the dirt cellar of a burned-out ruin safe from any interruption save from rats and cockroaches. And these, sensing a living being, always moved on after investigating. What she was attempting took an inhuman degree of patience, and it was therefore providential that she was, in fact, not human. She was engaged in a very gentle exploration of the borders of a Realm, or Hold, long sealed away from trespassers. Sealed by the mightiest of those active amid the material realms, such as her brother K'rul, and Kilmandaros, and Osserc. Care, therefore, was the order of the day.

After her first brush she had come to the conclusion that what she sensed was not so much a torn *gate* to the Realm, in the sense of a forced permanent access, but rather the true reaching out of an attuned practitioner, such as any manipulator of his or her natural source, or Warren.

This achievement was itself epochal. The discovery – or rather the reawakening – of a Hold lost to all. Powerful entities would take notice. Already during her investigations she'd had to shy away from the attention of the one left behind within Kurald Emurlahn, its champion.

She would most certainly not wish to be caught by *him*.

And yet the puzzling question remained: how was this done? She sensed no Tiste Edur blood or legacy. And Emurlahn was theirs just as Galain was of the Andii. She could only conclude that access was not achieved directly to Emurlahn. Rather, that reliable voluntary access to a halfway region, or bridge, had been forged. A human Warren. The wild chaotic half-realm named Shadow.

A dangerous non-place, this Shadow. Things were rarely as they seemed. Things were layered. What seemed reality was in fact . . . inconsistent. Even flagrant deception.

She sensed then that she was not alone, and as she identified her visitor she smiled at the poetry of it. She opened her eyes, blinking as she resurfaced from journeying so very far from herself, and said, 'I was just thinking of Galain and Emurlahn. It is therefore only fitting that Liosan should be present as well.'

The Protectress of Li Heng, Shalmanat, stood before her. Her hair shone silver in moonlight shafting down through the ruined floor above. Soot from the burned remains smeared her leathers at sleeve, thigh, and cuff. Sister Night inclined her head. 'Greetings, Lady.'

'Lady no longer. That was another life.'

'Regardless. What can I do for you?'

'Why are you here? What do you want?'

'I told you – I am investigating interesting theurgist phenomena.'

Shalmanat scowled sourly. 'There is more to it than that. I know

266

who you are, or more to the point: *what* you are. Your kind bring only destruction. I'll not have it. I want you gone.'

'I will go. When I am ready.'

The Protectress clenched her fists until her arms shook then let go a great gust of breath and raised her face to the moon in silent resignation. They both knew she did not have the power to force compliance. She sat then among the fallen brick, surprising Sister Night, and hung her arms limply over her knees, appearing utterly dejected. 'Will he come?' she asked.

Sister Night blinked. 'Who?'

'The Son of Darkness.' She gestured to the night sky. 'I do not think I could bear to face him. Will his Keep blot out the sun above and blast us into rubble?'

Face him, Sister Night wondered? There are few today who . . . *ah, I see.* Oh, Shalmanat. After all this time. And he probably does not even remember you. She shook her head. 'He does not guard the borders of Emurlahn.' *There is another who sees to that.*

'Yet he will be angered by this breach.'

'Will he? Who is to say? Times change. People . . . change.'

Shalmanat pressed her hands to her face. She whispered, nearly choking, 'So many dead – and for what?'

'A long time ago, Protectress.'

The hands whipped down and Shalmanat glared, her eyes swimming. 'Not to those who lived it! We can't just make it disappear!'

Sister Night had nothing to say to that.

They remained silent for a time; the wan silver light of the moon rippled down upon them among the fallen brick and burned timbers. Eventually, Sister Night cleared her throat, saying, 'If it comes to it, I will – do what I can.'

Hugging herself, Shalmanat nodded, openly relieved. 'My thanks.' Rising, she tottered, steadied herself at a fallen charcoal timber then ran her hand through her snowy hair, leaving a streak of black soot. She nodded a farewell and climbed the slope of fallen brick.

Sister Night remained, staring off into the dark. It was true, she had not considered that this breach, or development, might rekindle the old enmities – hardly any of those old players remained. Yet, obviously, there were many who could not let go of the past. It was how they had learned to define themselves. So many reflexively looked to the past rather than the future. She wondered, then, whether she had just tripped upon a fundamental division in what characterized approaches to life and to the world at large.

She tilted her head in the dark, her black hair brushing her shoulder, and considered what other things her own preoccupations might have blinded her to. It was a troubling thought. She resolved to broaden her attentions in the future and try to remain more open to wider potentialities when they were offered.

Perhaps this was what brother K'rul had meant when they spoke. It was not for nothing, after all, that he was known as the Opener of Ways.

Chapter 15

SILK WAITED IN THE NIGHT JUST NORTH OF THE CITY WALLS. The broken ground was hard, glinting with ice and crescents of wind-blown frost particles that could not yet be called a proper snowfall. The sky was clear and it was unusually chill. The cold bit at him and seemed to stab his very bones. He drew his thick fur cloak tighter about himself as his breath plumed.

To the west, across bare trampled fields and the broken black skeletons of burned trees, a battle raged on.

But it was not an engagement between the besieged Hengans and the invading Kanese forces. Rather, it was a running confrontation between the mercenary Crimson Guard and their quarry, the man-beast Ryllandaras.

A battle that began at sunset after he betrayed the creature's whereabouts to the Guard.

All for the eventual benefit of Li Heng, of course. After all, he reasoned, the monster had served its purpose – driven the Kanese from the north – yet the fiend remained a menace to any future peace and so one would be negligent to let such a moment pass.

At least that was how Silk had presented his case to his fellow city mages. And they had concurred. The future prosperity and safety of the city and its citizens had to be considered.

He rubbed his hands to warm them then nodded back to Smokey who stood at the black cave opening sunk at the base of the city wall; a hidden tunnel that would be sealed and never re-used after this night. Smokey raised an arm in acknowledgement and ducked back within.

Now it was up to him. He ran his hands over each other slowly, feeling the cold smooth flesh, then opened his Warren. Once more he reached not for the familiar paths of Thyr but beyond, searching for that trace – or flavour – of Elder Liosan. Not that he would dare try to summon such potency again. No, this night the mere suggestion of its presence should suffice. The merest scent upon the night air, so to speak.

It should be enough to bait the trap.

Finished, he headed back to the tunnel opening. For it was the opinion of Koroll and Ho that the Crimson Guard – for all their vaunted martial expertise – did not themselves possess the power necessary to slay the beast. It was an ancient piece of wisdom that only an Ascendant could slay another Ascendant. And while Silk had no idea as to the accuracy of the saying, having seen Ryllandaras up close he doubted that the Guard could finish the job.

Halfway there he stopped, turned back, and crouched, waiting. He did not have to sit long. Out of the dark came the thump of heavy footfalls. A pale shape emerged, crashing into broken trunks, half falling, loping onward.

The form resolved into a blood-streaked Ryllandaras. Chains snaked behind him. One trailed from a wrist, another from his neck.

'M'lady!' the creature bellowed, roaring, desperate. 'You are here?'

Silk straightened, waving. 'This way!'

The man-beast lumbered towards him. Behind came calls and the clatter of armour. Ryllandaras frowned down at Silk, blinking. Though slashed and bloodied he still emanated ferocious power and vitality. Silk considered the old saying that a wounded animal is the most dangerous. 'You?' the beast roared, pulling up short.

Silk pointed to the tunnel. 'She waits within – she offers sanctuary from your hunters.'

The man-beast examined the chain dangling from his wrist, shook it, and barked a rolling laugh. 'Sanctuary from my hunters! Ha! I was besting them!'

Appalled, Silk crossed his arms. 'Do you wish to see her or not?'

'This way!' came a distant shout from the dark.

The monster ducked, grunting his agreement. 'I will enter, little mage. But not in search of sanctuary from any foe. I go to see her.'

Silk waved him on. 'Very good.' The man-beast thumped past,

heading for the opening. Silk followed, walking backwards, his Warren of Thyr now raised.

Shapes in dark armour came running out of the night. Silk raised a bright flare of light, causing the closing mercenaries to halt and throw their arms up over their faces. Silk recognized Cal-Brinn among them, who blinked at him. 'Stand aside!' one of their number called.

'The hunt is over,' Silk answered.

'Just kill the bastard!' shouted another of the Guard, and he pushed forward.

Silk intensified his light into a sizzling white ball that he waved before him. 'Would you make war upon Li Heng as well?'

Cal-Brinn threw an arm before his companion and addressed Silk. 'You do not know what has happened.'

'Inform me.'

'The beast has slain Malkir, heir to the throne of Gris.'

Silk merely shrugged. 'He was a fool to have risked hunting him.'

Cal-Brinn gestured to the wall. 'And what is it you are risking?'

Silk dared a quick glance back: the aperture of the tunnel was even now closing as a great slab of dressed stone descended. He lowered his Warren and blinked in the dark. 'You could not have slain him – we'll finish the job.'

Another shape came lumbering out of the dark, the Guard's commander, Duke Courian D'Avore, together with some twenty more of his force. His iron cuirass was splashed with blood and he gripped his neck where fresh drops ran down his raised forearm. His son K'azz sought to support him but he shook him off. 'He's ours!' the man bellowed, spitting in rage. 'Paid for in blood! Yield him to us!'

Silk bowed to the Duke. 'The city mages of Heng will see to Ryllandaras.'

'Keep him as your pet, you mean!'

Silk felt far from confident, surrounded as he was by a maddened crowd of mercenaries who felt cheated of their quarry, but he crossed his arms nevertheless, hoping to convey complete indifference. He wished Koroll, Ho or Mara were here rather than he. But they no doubt had their hands full at the moment attempting to subdue the man-beast, wounded though he may be. Thinking on that, he reflected that perhaps he was better off here than closeted in a narrow tunnel with an enraged Ascendant.

Courian raised his bloodied blade. 'Yield him to me now, or by the beast gods I'll separate your smirking head from your slimy body.'

K'azz took hold of his parent's sword arm. 'We have made one enemy today, Father. Let us not make two.'

The duke glared down with his one good eye, scowling his confusion. 'An enemy? What do you mean? What enemy?'

'With Malkir dead his twin, Malle, is now heir,' said Cal-Brinn. 'She spoke against his coming and will not forgive us. I fear we will not be welcome in Gris.'

The duke grunted his assent, drew his blade across his already red cloak, and sheathed it. He peered at Silk through his one eye, slitted until it was almost closed. Silk had the impression of a bull squinting through a fence. 'You're lucky, little mage. If it were up to me alone I'd cut you in half just on general principles.' He motioned Cal-Brinn onward. 'We'll return the body. Come, we're moving out.'

The Guard backed away, covering their commander. All but the young K'azz, who remained behind. 'What will you do with him?' he asked Silk.

Silk studied the slender youth looking so very martial in his battered blood-red armour of overlapping iron bands, mailed sleeves and skirting, his bright pale eyes quite open and curious. Still to come into his full growth, yet already a good hand's breadth taller than he. So this was the Red Prince romantics sang of. He felt an unaccustomed sensation of envy and it was so new he almost savoured it. He shrugged again, his arms crossed. 'We cannot be certain of slaying him, so we will entomb him.'

The youth nodded, backing away. Silk turned to go.

'You betrayed us,' the youth called. 'You used us to weaken him and drive him to you.' Silk stilled, saying nothing. 'One good betrayal deserves another,' the lad called again from the dark, and disappeared into the gloom.

For a time Silk stood motionless, frowning at the night. Then he shook himself, shuddering with the chill, and hurried to the one remaining northern tunnel entryway to aid his fellow mages.

Finding his brethren together with the entrapped Ryllandaras was not difficult; the creature's bellows shook the catacombs' stone

272

walls. Clashing chains and angry, frustrated yells guided him to the site of the struggle. All the tunnels were far too low to allow the man-beast to stand, and so he lay flailing and lashing. The chains crashed and rattled against the walls.

Ho was shouting to Mara: 'Hold him still, dammit!'

'Don't you think I'm trying!' she snarled.

Koroll had two of the beast's chains in his hands and was struggling to drag the monster up the tunnel. Silk stepped over to where Smokey stood leaning against a wall. 'Took your damned time,' the mage of Telas murmured beneath the cacophony.

'How's it going – or need I ask?'

Smokey waved to indicate their lack of progress. 'The damned beast's not cooperating in his imprisonment. Rather like a drunken soldier.'

'How unreasonable of him.'

Ho threw down the end of one chain and backed away to draw a sleeve across his sweaty face. 'All right, you stubborn bastard. We tried being nice.' He nodded to Smokey.

Smokey cracked his knuckles. The man-beast turned his long head to glare up one-eyed at the mage. 'Don't make me burn you bald,' Smokey said with a smile.

Silk missed it; a telltale tensing of the muscles it must have been, or a slight drawing in of the limbs, but Mara caught it and even as the beast lunged forward, jaws agape, his head was smashed aside into the wall. Everyone cursed their surprise, ducking and backing off. Clouds of dust obscured the narrow tunnel. Silk slapped it from his fine blue shirt and black vest.

The dust settled, revealing a hole bashed through the wall to a neighbouring tunnel, and Ryllandaras, blinking, shaking the stone dust from his head.

'I'll twist your head off if I have to!' Mara called, her voice taut with anger, and perhaps a measure of fear.

The beast's lips drew back into something like a mockery of a smile, revealing black gums and canines the length of daggers. 'You can try,' he growled with a panting, jackal-like laugh.

Ho set a hand to his hip, ran the other over his brush-cut grey stubble, and looked to the ceiling. 'Not going to make it easy, are you?' He motioned to everyone. 'Grab a chain and pull . . .'

*

A sharp jab woke Iko. She opened one eye, fully aware, to see Hallens peering down at her, a fierce grin at her lips. 'Ready yourself, little sister. Word has come. We leave immediately.'

She jumped to her feet, pulled her quilted aketon over her head, asked, 'Where?'

But Hallens had already moved on.

Iko yanked on her mail coat, belted it, and threw her sheathed blade over her head and on to her back. All around, her fellow Sword-Dancers readied themselves. All was silent but for the soft tinkle of fine mail armour and the shush of leather sandals. At the doors, sisters signed commands: *double file, quick.*

They formed up and set out across the gardens. Two sisters waited there. Knotted ropes had already been secured over the wall. When Iko reached the top she glimpsed the sprawled shapes of palace guards among the bushes – unconscious only, she hoped, as she bore them no particular ill will.

Their route took them south through the empty night-time streets; the city's own strict curfew aided them in their passage. They were running in double file, as swiftly as was possible in potentially hostile territory. Sisters posted at turns, or forced-open posterns or minor gates, directed them on then joined the rear of the file as it passed. Soon, Iko knew, it would be her turn to be posted as they cycled through their number.

When she reached the fore, Hallens was there giving commands. At this point they had reached a section of the second-last of the ringed rounds, the Inner, and were next to the tallest building in sight. Its third-storey roof was pitched, which was unusual for the city, and allowed the easiest access to the parapets rearing above. A sister was already at the top straddling the ridge, readying ropes. Hallens nodded to Iko and another, Gisel, to make the climb. They started up the building's side, cat-walked up the steeply pitched roof, and took hold of the rope.

Iko went first. The ropes were knotted and she climbed by alternately raising hands and feet. So far their blazing speed had served them well; if any alarms were being sounded, they'd left them far behind. The climb was strenuous, and after the months of waiting she was in far from her best shape, but the adrenalin of action drove her on. She slid in through a crenel and fell to the catwalk to roll to a crouch, then froze.

A guard was approaching from less than thirty feet away;

perhaps he was on patrol, or the scraping of the iron grapnel had drawn him, but in any case her sudden appearance had shocked him as well. Only now did he begin to raise the crossbow in his hands.

She charged, eyes fixed on him, searching for the telltale signs of imminent firing. Luckily the lad gave them: a sharp inhale and that rise and tensing of the shoulders. She fell, rolling. The bolt cut the air above her. She came up but was still short of her target and had to roll once more, coming up with one arm to brush aside the weapon and the other jabbing, fingers straightened, up into the throat.

She caught both him and the weapon as he fell choking, hands clutching at his neck. She pressed a hand over his mouth and whispered, close: 'Hush now – it's all right. It's over. You did your best. Hush now . . .'

He strained for breath one last time. Terror of death filled his wild eyes as his gaze pleaded with her. Then they lost focus, easing into a fixed empty stare. She straightened from the corpse.

Behind, her sisters were descending the wall on the outside.

She continued to stare down at the body, studying the clean face. A boy. Just a lad. Perhaps forced into the watch, handed a weapon, and told to walk the walls. Hardly any training at all. It wasn't fair. Wasn't fair at all.

Steps behind and Hallens stood with her. She too studied the dead youth, then turned to her. 'That must have been a hard one.' She motioned to the sisters waiting their turn. 'Take the rear.'

Somehow unable to speak, Iko merely nodded.

They ran in double file along the streets of the Outer Round. To Iko's growing surprise and dismay she realized that they must be headed to one of the main city gates. If their mission was to take and hold the gate how could they hope to prevail against the city mages? It was plain suicide – they would be brushed from the position in an instant.

Being at the very rear she did not have to participate in the various skirmishes that accompanied the taking of the gate. All was over in a bare few minutes. She stepped over fallen Heng guards, found kicked-in doors and broken furniture. The counter-weights were released, initiating a great shuddering and groaning within the walls, and the enormous slabs of iron-plated wood – strong enough to withstand the beast Ryllandaras – began grinding open. Iko joined Hallens and five sisters waiting at the mouth of the entrance tunnel; the rest of the Sword-Dancers had spread out to hold the gatehouses and adjoining parapets. Without, the dark of mid-night betrayed no movement.

Iko looked to Hallens who stood with arms crossed, displaying no unease. 'Where are they?' she whispered. 'A city mage will be here soon.'

Hallens merely lifted her broad shoulders in a shrug. 'We will fulfil our mission.'

Then noise brought Iko's attention to the raised road outside. Dark shapes now rose from all sides. They seemed to swarm the road, advancing in a tide. Kan Elites, their tabards and gear smeared in soot, came jogging in. They parted, swerving to the right and left of the main way. One halted before Hallens and nodded. 'Hallens,' he said.

'Kuth.'

'You are relieved.'

Hallens inclined her assent. 'We'll hang about, if it's all the same to you.'

He answered the assent, gave a drawled, 'Always welcome,' then turned to ordering his troops.

Bells now clamoured all about the city and the sounds of fighting echoed from far down the main avenue. A long column of green-coated regulars was advancing up the south road. They must already have been on the move even as she and her sisters took the gate, Iko realized. 'Why have we decided to attack tonight?' she asked Hallens.

The captain considered, tilting her head in thought. 'Must have been a tip. A Hengan traitor sending word that now was a good time for some reason.'

Iko nodded at that. Yes, that was how most sieges ended. Betrayal from within. 'So it is over, then. The city taken.'

Hallens eyed her in tolerant amusement. 'This is only the first wall. Three more nested defences face us now. Each as strong as the first.'

As if on cue, crossbow bolts came arcing down among them, smacking into wood or skittering from stone. Everyone ducked behind cover even as the first ranks of the regulars came marching up the tunnel and followed directions to split to right and left.

'You see?' Hallens said from her side of the guard-post doorway where they'd taken cover. 'Each inner wall is taller than the outer. They can shoot us at will.'

'And where are the mages?'

Hallens' answering grin was knowing. 'Where indeed?'

Iko was shocked. 'You think it was they? Betrayed their mistress?'

'Chulalorn might have given them a better offer.' Hallens shrugged again. 'It's possible.'

As a trained warrior, Iko was raised to value honour and duty above all. But she was not naïve or some callow youth; she understood that others carried far looser interpretations of those words than she – and that some knew them not at all. Still, it was unsettling. What, then, of trust?

Eastward, up the avenue, the clash of battle rose. After a few moments Iko could see that a sudden press of Hengan defenders was pushing the Kanese regulars back. Hallens had also been studying the fray, and she stepped out, offering Iko a wink. 'Shall we—'

Something knocked the woman spinning and she staggered, peering down at her chest. Iko stared as well, horrified yet fascinated to see blood now spreading in a rich red bloom down the armour. Hallens fell to her knees. Iko and three other Sword-Dancers rushed out to drag her to the cover of a gatehouse.

She lay on her side, coughing up great mouthfuls of blood. The fletched butt of a crossbow bolt protruded from her back. She reached out to Sareh, kneeling before her, and strained to say something, but no words emerged. The effort seemed to take all her remaining strength and she sagged, her chest no longer heaving.

Sareh rose, still staring down. 'They've killed her.' She said it as if she couldn't believe it.

'The cowardly scum,' Yuna breathed, too stunned for rage.

Iko could not take her eyes from the corpse. Hallens, dead? The best of them? How could this be?

'We will exact such a blood price,' Yuna snarled. She snapped her gaze to Iko. 'And you? Still think they are worth any respect?'

Blinking, Iko looked to her, and saw that tears marked gleaming streaks down the woman's face. She raised a hand to the grip of her whipsword, clenched it there, fierce. She had to force open her jaws to answer, 'No. None.'

277

It was only Koroll's incredible Tartheno-Thelomen might, combined with Ho's own surprising display of strength, that allowed them to drag the chained Ryllandaras into his stone sarcophagus – that and the powerful pushing of Mara with her D'riss Warren. Silk and Smokey contributed little, it was true, other than to remain as additional hands should the beast break free.

Along the entire route the man-beast maddened them all with his constant panted chuckling and obvious mirth at their groaning and sweating to scrape him along. As they dragged him up and over the lip of the stone sarcophagus, Silk could contain his irritation no longer and he glared down at the bound beast, snapping: 'And what do you find so funny about this internment?'

Ryllandaras shrugged his monstrous shoulders as best he could, wrapped in chain and pressed within the carved stone depression as he was. 'I wish to thank you,' he panted. 'You, my enemies, deliver me to my love. Now she can come to me whenever she wishes. Many hours shall we while away in the dark.'

Silk flinched from the stone lip and it seemed to him that the beast's new bout of laughter was directed solely at him. Ho began drawing on the hanging chain and the thick granite lid of the sarcophagus suspended above began creeping down.

The stones grated as they met and Silk thought to hear some final threat or curse from the beast, but instead all that came to him was a last murmured, 'Fear only love, my little mage friend.'

Ho shook the chain, saying, 'If this is released, counterweights will lift the lid.'

Koroll nodded. 'Very good. For we are risking a feud.'

Silk eyed the half-giant. 'A feud? Who would fight for this one?'

Koroll appeared surprised. 'Why, his brothers, of course.'

Now Silk was surprised. 'Brothers? Who—' He cut the words off short as Ho threw up a hand for silence.

'Listen!'

Silk cocked his head but heard nothing untoward echoing up the empty tunnels.

'Fighting,' Koroll rumbled.

'They're in the city,' Ho breathed, astonished.

Mara's usual sour glower deepened even further. '*What?* How?'

Smokey was staring up at the ceiling. 'Never mind how. We must go – now.'

The four set off, raising their Warrens as they went. Silk, however, lingered. Swift movement – through streets or through his Warren – had never been his forte in any case. And he had further reason to hesitate. How had the Kanese known to attack now?

How indeed.

He brushed a hand over the dusty top of the crudely carved granite and remembered the last words from that damned lad the Red Prince. One betrayal deserves another. The bastard. He may have handed Li Heng to the Kanese – and all for what? A fit of pique? Just to get even?

He brushed his hands free of the dust and sighed. Well . . . it was only the death of the heir to the Grisian throne, after all. While in their charge.

He turned to go to join the fray, but paused as there came from within the great block of solid granite the definite tones of low panted laughter.

The mocking laugh followed him all the way up the tunnel.

*

Dorin stood on the roof of one of the towers that dotted the comparatively thin wall of the Palace Circle. It was long past midnight, coming on towards the first of the predawn light. He was facing south, where the fighting had entered a heightened pitch now that the city mages had finally thrown their weight into the battle.

He wondered what had taken them so long.

The streets below were heaving in what could only be described as plain chaotic panic. Never in living memory had any enemy penetrated the walls of Heng, and now its citizens were choking the streets. Half were determined to flee the various gates of the ring walls, while the other half were just as determined to squeeze their way in. The Hengan militia and reserves could only look in frustration at gates jammed open by wagons, carts, and a solid press of human flesh. The streets were equally impassable as hordes rushed from gate to gate.

Like a fire in an anthill, Dorin imagined.

For the first time in many nights he felt relatively at ease. The

Nightblades, he knew, were now quite busy elsewhere and he could relax. As for the fate of the city, a Hengan or a Kanese administration, it mattered not one whit to him.

The salmon and orange glow of the predawn gathered in the east while the deep purple of the night retreated to the west, and Dorin saw that he was not alone. Another solitary figure stood on a roof a little way off. He, or she, also appeared to be studying the battle. Curious, but wary, Dorin made his way towards this other watcher.

Gaining the same roof, he saw that it was a woman, though quite lacking in the curves that would normally proclaim the gender, and unusually tall. She wore old travelling clothes that had seen hard use, stained and a touch ragged. Her black hair was also a mess: unkempt and roughly hacked to a medium length.

She startled him by turning at his first steps; her face was pale and long, the eyes large and strangely luminous in the dark. She unnerved him further by inclining her head in greeting, as if she knew him, then turned her back to return her attention to the battle.

Dorin paused, rather uncertain how to proceed; her manner reminded him of various dangerous mages he'd seen. And various madmen, and women. He approached, but kept his distance, finding his own vantage where he could glimpse the streets of the Inner Round. Closer, he discovered that his instinct had been correct. His senses were highly trained, and though he was not a mage he could almost see the power sizzling the air about this one.

The woman's arms were crossed and she unlimbered one to point to the southeast. 'They have lost another toehold on the Inner.'

Dorin obligingly studied that quarter. Here the eruptions of power that rocked the night, accompanied by the occasional flash of energies, had been more concentrated. Now they were dying down.

'They should pull back,' he opined. 'Secure their gain of the Outer.'

'Yes,' the woman agreed. He noted her gaze sliding sidelong to him. 'But will they? Sometimes early success leads to overreach. Many campaigns – and careers – have been cut short by recklessness.'

'Recklessness,' he suggested, now feeling as if he were the new object of study, 'is sometimes just inexperience.'

'Agreed. The remedy, then, would be due caution and care, would it not?'

Dorin felt his chest tighten with a strange dread. He was now certain they'd left behind the topic of Heng's fate. He began, tentatively, 'Challenging the unknown requires the taking of risks . . .'

The strange woman's gaze hardened, almost in warning, he thought. 'Of course. But beware of recklessness.'

He inclined his head in acknowledgement. She turned her face away, asked, 'What is he like?'

Dorin did not need to ask who. He cleared his throat, considering. 'He is . . . odd.'

She nodded at that. 'Good.' And she added, half under her breath, 'Oddness is probably a requirement.'

For his part, Dorin was becoming rather curious about her. He asked, 'And who are you?'

'Just a curious observer.' She motioned to the streets once more. 'Barricading the gates. They are relinquishing the Outer.'

'A foregone conclusion. The mages are too few to roust the Kanese.'

The woman nodded. 'Shalmanat may lose the entire south. I wonder if she will cut all the bridges across the Idryn.'

'She will not see Heng destroyed. I believe she will sue for peace before then.'

The woman studied him anew, nodding. 'I believe you are right. And what is your name?'

'Mine to keep.'

A near smile tugged at her lips. 'You are learning.' She dropped her arms and inclined her head in farewell. 'We may meet again.'

Dorin answered her nod. She crossed to an open trapdoor and descended the ladder. Dorin sat, rather shakily. He knew that the Dal Hon mage had accessed *something*, some potential source of power, and now he understood that others had noticed and were interested as well. Some – like this one – might be content to watch and wait, but others might not. He and Wu would probably have to defend what they'd dug up.

An echoing bellow rolled from the tangled streets to the south. It announced Koroll in his battle glee as he waded into the Kanese once more. Smoke from countless spot fires plumed in an arc across the Outer Round. Some were no doubt set intentionally, others accidentally. They marked the worst of the engagements.

Dorin waited for the dawn to reveal who now controlled the south of the city.

*

Iko held open a door for her sister Rei, then slammed it shut, watching through its slit. She was panting with exertion, her chest shuddering. Numerous minor cuts and bruises pained her, but nothing incapacitating. She pushed loose hair aside, worked to steady her breathing.

She and her sisters had wreaked bloody murder among the Hengan defenders, taking one of the gates to the Inner Round only to lose it again when the city mages appeared in flames and blasts of Warren energies. It was their bad luck to have been stranded on the wrong side of the gate. She now regretted her weakness in yielding to her rage and lust for revenge. What had it gathered them? Other than fallen sisters and nothing to show for it. They should have marched away once their objective had been reached; their duty lay with the king.

She turned an eye on Rei, nearly as young as she. 'Well . . . it was good to finally stretch our limbs but it appears to be over. We will make for the nearest gate. No doubt the others are withdrawing as well.'

Rei's answer was to wince as she gripped her hacked arm, and nod.

'Stay behind me.' Rei nodded curtly once more. Their fine mail was proof against edges and piercing, but some Hengan had managed to strike her with a wood-axe – only banded armour could have withstood the blow. Iko gripped the door. 'There should be one near to the west, shouldn't there?'

Rei straightened, gripped her whipsword in one hand. She ground out, 'I will follow.'

'Very good.'

Iko yanked open the door and slipped out into the street. Two guards spotted them almost immediately. They charged and Iko answered, rushing as well. As always, the far greater reach of the whipsword saw them through. Both Hengan guards fell aside as the keen blade snapped out, slicing across their faces. Iko charged past.

Crossbow bolts ricocheted from the stone walls next to her. They were fired from rooftops and the north wall. She dodged round burning upturned carts and wagons, jumped over debris and sprawled corpses.

She drove off two more gangs of roving Hengan guard. For that was what the battle had degenerated into: disorganized street-fighting where packs sought to consolidate their small sections of buildings. She had no idea as to the larger drift of the attack, but it did seem that the Hengans were merely cleaning up the Inner, what with the arrival of their mages.

She led Rei out into the wreckage choking an intersection so that she could try to get a look up the street. Through black smoke boiling out of the doors of buildings she glimpsed a gate, now barricaded and hung with banners of Kanese verdant green. 'Almost home.'

A barrage of arrows fell about them and clattered from the stones. Rei grunted then, falling to one knee. An arrow had passed almost entirely through her thigh. Iko knelt to pick her up while searching for the source. A column of Hengans was advancing up the avenue, at their fore a black-robed Dal Hon woman bearing a wild mane of ropy kinky hair. Mara. Iko cursed her luck and turned to make for the gate, half-dragging a moaning Rei with her.

Crossbow bolts skittered from the cobbles all about her and snapped from the walls. Heavier answering fire cut through the air from the gate and the Hengans scattered for cover. A bellow of rage brought Iko's attention round: Mara, a raised hand clutching the air, her eyes on them.

The building next to Iko started groaning. Stones grated, sliding.

Iko ran, dragging Rei, as the entire shop front next to them tottered outward over the street. Dressed sandstone blocks rained around them. The cobbles beneath her feet juddered as the wall came crashing down. She threw Rei forward. Something cracked into the back of her leg, driving her to the road. Dust obscured her vision and she choked on it, coughing.

Figures moved like ghosts through the hanging particles. Iko tried to rise but her foot was pinned. She sought among the broken stones for her weapon, found its grip gritty with powdered rock.

'Sword-Dancer!' one figure called in a strong Kanese accent.

'Here!' The figures closed, revealing dusty surcoats of green. 'My leg—' she began.

'No time.' They heaved and she screamed as her foot seemed to snap off.

The next moment she knew she was being half-carried with each of her arms over a soldier to right and left. Crossbow fire continued to strike about them as they wove between barricades held by crouching Kanese regulars. Her feet dragged behind her and she felt as if she were in a delirium. 'Rei,' she called, suddenly remembering.

'We have the other,' one soldier said.

'Good.'

'You are the last, I think. That hellion Mara really wanted you.'

Iko wanted to answer, but her foot, knocking among stones and fallen timbers, twisted in a way it shouldn't, its bones grating, and she knew nothing more.

Chapter 16

ONCE THE BATTLE DIED DOWN INTO A SULLEN STARING match across barricades, Dorin returned to Wu's underground quarters. He knew he was no expert at sieges but it appeared to him that the two sides now had each other in a death grip and were determined to throttle one another.

He found Wu in his cellar 'chambers' sitting cross-legged and staring at a wall, a low fire burning behind him. He appeared to be doing nothing more than watching the shadows play across the surface as he sat chin in fist.

'Fight's over,' Dorin announced. A decanter of wine stood on the table and he poured himself a glass. Drinking it he gagged – still as sour as rat piss. More ancient looted grave offerings. He set the glass aside.

Wu turned to him, blinking, his face blank. 'The what?'

'The siege, you know? The Kanese have taken the south Outer Round.'

The Dal Hon mage waved the development aside. He returned to eyeing shadows. 'Well, that's good for us, yes?'

'How so?'

'Chulalorn is more likely to hang about, isn't he? We can move on Pung.'

Dorin peered at him. 'Or not. He may think it all in hand and give things over to his generals and return to the south. But anyway, Pung is nothing to me now.'

Wu rose, stretching his arms. 'Not Pung. Our rightful possession – stolen from us.'

'From you.' Wu poured himself a glass of the wine and Dorin watched him gulp it. 'How is it?'

285

Wu coughed, and with great effort managed to force the drink down. 'Oh, it's quite good,' he gasped. 'A unique aftertaste. You should get to know your wines. As to who or what Pung is – that is immaterial. We need that box.'

'You mean *you* want that box.'

'It's my price. As agreed, yes?'

'Exactly . . . as agreed. You help me reach Chulalorn and I will help you. Chulalorn may leave at any time but your box isn't going anywhere, is it?'

The youth appeared pained. 'Well, that's the problem. The object is disguised. It doesn't appear valuable at all. It may be thrown away.'

Dorin remembered Pung's lackey, Gren, saying that the mage had had nothing valuable on him. 'What does it look like, then?'

'Never mind. The point is it is just as urgent!'

'Chulalorn first – Pung's going nowhere.'

Wu glared for a time. He raised a brow as if attempting to give the evil eye, but Dorin did not change his own expression of placid scorn. Wu slumped, waving the matter aside. 'Oh, very well. I suppose we will be too busy once we have the item in any case.'

Dorin ignored the bait. 'I'll go to reconnoitre the site.'

Wu opened his arms in disbelief. 'There is no need. We were just out there – I got us away and I will get us back in just as easily.'

'We haven't agreed on routes. Or fallbacks. Or rendezvous sites in case we get separated.'

Wu's gaze darted about the dim cellar. 'On what?'

Dorin let his arms fall, utterly disheartened. 'Oh, great gods below! Let me organize this, all right?'

Recovering, Wu now held a lofty expression. 'If you must.' He reached for the wine but shied away at the last moment. 'The diggers have the tunnels ready to hit Pung's compound, you know. We need only dart in and out.'

'Later. First I'm going out to get a feel for the lie of the land out there.'

'Very well. Ah . . . need I come along?'

'No. I most certainly don't want you along.'

The Dal Hon's prematurely wrinkled face turned crafty and sly. 'If you insist.'

Dorin just gave him another hard look before he turned to the flimsy door. 'Later.'

'Yes, later.'

Dorin knew the damned mage was up to something but he let it go, hoping it wouldn't interfere with his reconnoitring. He headed into the warren of tunnels and catacombs. The nearest exit he found was guarded by a lad, one of the diggers, now armed with a crossbow and a wicked-looking long-knife. The lad gave him a deep nod, almost like a salute. 'Sir.'

Dorin was startled. 'Sir?'

'You're second in command.'

'Really?'

'Un-huh. And I want you to know we've pushed Pung's boys out of this quarter.'

Dorin was even more taken aback. 'You're *fighting* them?'

''Course! They'd wipe us out, wouldn't they?'

'Well, true enough.'

'Oh, and there's a message for you.'

'A message?'

'Yeah. From a girl. Came last night. Gave her name as Rheena. Says it's important she talk to you.'

Dorin nodded, considering. Rheena? Really? 'Well, when I get back, I guess. My thanks. What's your name anyway, lad?'

'Baudin, sir. Named for my father, and my father's father. All Baudin.'

Dorin examined the lean, hardened youth – barely twelve perhaps and already toughened by a life of privation and abuse that none should have to endure. 'Well, don't mount any major attacks without consulting me.'

'If you say so, sir.'

'Yeah. I say so.' He gave a nod of farewell and squirmed from the exit, concealed as it was beneath a pile of wreckage.

He made for the east and the water gate of the Inner Round. Here he slipped into the Idryn and swam out towards mid-stream, making for a piece of flotsam that he gripped as it drew him along. Once he was far enough from the city, and with dawn coming on, he made for the south shore, slid up among a stand of tall grasses and cattails and lay there, letting the sun dry him.

Mid-morning, he found a vantage among the meagre hills south of the city and kept a watch on the tent city that the Kanese had raised. The focus of his attention was the central ring of larger tents – the officials, court, and field command of King Chulalorn the Third. He watched the guards trading off. He timed their rounds and made a rough count of their numbers, then waited for night. He ate a small meal of smoked meat and a knuckle of hardened cheese, and emptied the one skin of water he'd brought.

When dusk came and the shadows deepened he rubbed dirt over his hands and face and set out crawling on his elbows and knees through the grass. He found the night uncommonly chill; he even encountered ice-covered pools of standing water, which he imagined must be unusual for the region.

His slow cautious approach paid off as he made it through the first two rings of pickets and guards to reach the tents of the military encampment itself. Now he moved from the deep shadows of one tent to another. He considered, momentarily, dressing in a Kanese surcoat but dispensed with that plan as he'd already blackened his face and hands. So he kept to the darkness, eluding roving guards until he reached the security ring surrounding the innermost tents of the royal command itself.

Up to this point the purpose of his approach had been merely to test the security. But now he was beginning to wonder whether he should actually make the attempt. When, after all, might he manage to come so close again? But that was not proper procedure, according to his teacher – *never rush anything* had been the old man's refrain. Still, so close . . .

He manoeuvred round the ring until he reached a point where the walking pickets crossed one another to leave a brief gap unwatched. He waited here for them to return on their route. For an instant, crouched as he was behind piled equipment, he had the definite sensation that he was being watched. The hair at the nape of his neck stirred, and he felt an eerie prickling down his back, yet he could see no one, and no alarm was raised. He shook off the sensation and readied himself.

As the guards crossed he darted out around them, utterly silent, and reached a narrow darkened lane between the glowing walls of the occupied tents. This had been his goal all along: this narrow twisting gap. Like a hidden passageway within walls. Now he had a chance to locate Chulalorn's private quarters.

Silent, crouched, he padded along, listening and sensing. Would it be one of the darkened ones? Surely the king wouldn't have retired for the night yet . . .

His only warning was a frigid iciness that gathered in the air.

Hoar frost blossomed on the canvas tent wall next to him and then a hand seemed to take hold of his neck like a giant seizing him from behind and he was slammed face first down into the frozen mud and trampled yellow grass.

Footsteps approached: heavy, uneven, limping perhaps. A real hand – larger than any human's – grasped his neck and lifted him bodily from the ground to hang free, his legs swinging. A twisted scarred face peered up into his and Dorin knew that whatever this being was, it wasn't human.

The man-like creature was hunched over near double as if its spine were bent. Its thick muscular limbs were twisted and seamed with deep scars. It snorted, eyeing Dorin closely with one strange amber eye, and set off carrying him as if he were a trapped rabbit.

The creature pushed into a tent that was empty but for guards and a small cage of iron bars. With a clawed hand the thing tore the baldrics from Dorin then threw him into the cage and slammed shut the door, locking it.

'Bring the lord,' the giant growled to a guard, who bowed and ducked outside. The creature, so very man-like, eased himself down into a saddle stool that creaked beneath his weight. Now Dorin had time to examine him more carefully and it seemed to him to bear a marked resemblance to the creature he'd encountered when he'd first met Wu; one the Dal Hon had named a Jaghut.

The creature winced, stretching his legs. He regarded Dorin with his alien eyes. 'So, little one,' he said, in a voice like rocks cracking, 'you are quite good. I almost missed you. And I would have, but for the one with you.'

Dorin had been rubbing the life back into the frozen flesh of his neck, and he stilled. One with him? 'I'm alone,' he managed, hoarse.

This brought an amused smile from his captor. He raised a crooked mangled hand. 'Quiet now, the king comes.'

Two Kanese elite guards entered the tent and held open the canvas flap. A man ducked within and straightened. He wore long robes of green silk, damasked in silver, and gleaming in swirls of precious stones. His features were classic dusky Kanese, lean and ascetic. Long midnight black hair was tied and thrown forward over one shoulder to hang down almost to his waist.

The man – King Chulalorn the Third, ruler of all south Quon, Dorin assumed – bent down to examine him with an expression of vexed irritation. 'What is this, Juage?' he asked, practically scolding. 'I am interrupted for this?'

'An assassin, m'lord.'

On his knees in the small cage, Dorin grasped the bars. 'I am no assassin!'

'Pray then what are you?' Chulalorn sniffed.

Dorin raised his chin, defiant. 'A spy, great king. Sent to gather intelligence.'

'An actor,' the giant Juage chuckled.

With a thumb and forefinger Chulalorn picked up the torn baldrics, each bristling with knives, loops of wire, and other equipment. 'For a spy you are uncommonly well armed.' In his cage, Dorin had nothing to say to that. Chulalorn let the broken belts fall. He waved to Juage. 'Squeeze what you can from him then get rid of him. I care not how.' He turned to go.

'It is not him I am interested in squeezing,' the creature rumbled. 'It is the one with him.'

Chulalorn paused, frowning. 'What nonsense are you speaking? He is alone.'

'To your eyes perhaps.' Juage waved the king onward. 'But do go, these are matters far beyond you.'

Chulalorn froze, his eyes flaring, outraged. 'Beyond *me*? Explain yourself.'

A satisfied smile revealed the creature's prominent jutting canines in full. 'Just that. Matters far beyond the names on any of these pathetic local thrones.'

Now the king glared, his hands clenching into fists. 'One day you will go too far, Juage.'

The creature waved him off again. 'Usefulness is a two-edged sword, little king.'

Chulalorn hesitated, searching for the proper retort, but failing to come up with anything he snorted his scorn and swept from the tent in a brushing of his thick dragging robes.

'Now you two,' Juage said, flicking his fingers at the remaining guards. 'Exit now, while you may. Secrets will be revealed here that may blast your souls to the Abyss.'

The guards' brows climbed in alarm, and, eyeing the creature in obvious unease, they edged towards the flap and hurried out.

Dorin also eyed the giant, at a loss. Quite mystified, he asked, 'What are you doing?'

Juage raised one hand for silence while with the other he made teasing 'come-hither' gestures about the tent. 'Come out, come out. I know you are here. Come out of' – the creature turned an eye to the darkest corner of the tent – 'the shadows.'

Dorin clenched his teeth in irritation. *Damn the gods. Is he really here?*

The light wavered within the deeper murk and a shape emerged, hunched, aged, leaning on a short walking stick. Wu, in his image of a wizened old mage. He nodded to Juage. 'How can I ignore such a charming invitation?'

Dorin glared at his erstwhile partner. 'What are you doing? Following me?'

A small moue from the mage. 'Of course.'

Dorin slammed the bars. 'You *idiot*! I was caught because of you! He sensed you!'

Completely unruffled, Wu gave a deprecatory wave. 'A small matter. But we are here now to discuss very great matters – is that not so, Juage?'

The giant gave his predatory smile once again, his yellowed canines showing. He reached a long arm out to a table and took up a handful of nuts that he cracked in one fist and began tossing the meat into his mouth. 'You two are fools. But first, let me tell you my own story – and it is a sad tale indeed.' He grimaced, reached into his mouth to pull something out, a bit of shell perhaps, and began. 'As you have no doubt deduced, I am of the Jaghut kind. Through foolishness of my own that is no business of yours I was enslaved generations ago to the Chulalorn dynasty. I have been forced to further their petty territorial ambitions. It is a humiliating servitude I would do anything to be free of.' He tossed the broken shells into the brazier burning at the centre of the tent. 'But that is neither here nor there. I offer my own example as a warning to the two of you. You who are yet able to walk away from a similar galling servitude.'

Wu had been studying his walking stick, but now he gave an airy flutter of one hand. 'Do go on.'

'I speak of course of your ignorant entanglement with the Azathani. I smell their influence upon you. I warn you – you are nothing more than pawns to them. Expendable pawns.'

'Azath, you mean,' Dorin said. He'd come to the conclusion long ago that the chamber he'd entered with Wu was one of those eerie haunted structures, the Houses of the Azath.

'As you will,' Juage answered, picking up more nuts. 'Azath, to your limited human understanding.'

Wu was now leaning forward, his walking stick firmly planted before him. 'What advice would you offer, then?'

Juage waved them off with the back of his hand the way one might shoo a fly. 'Walk away. Just walk away. The skeletons of your predecessors litter the path you have so foolishly set out upon. None have succeeded. None can succeed. Too many Ascendants stand against it. That realm must not be reawakened. All have agreed. The Son of Darkness especially.'

Dorin gripped the bars of the cage. The Son of Darkness? By the gods, what had they stumbled into? He noticed that his grip was next to the lock, and that the lock was a very old design that he knew inside out, having been trained to build and rebuild one much like it over and over again. He reached down and pulled a tool from his ankle.

His companion had been thoughtfully prodding the ground with his damned stick. 'Very well,' the young Dal Hon said. 'Thank you for your generous offer. Now, here is mine – you release my partner and promise not to interfere with us any more, and we will allow *you* to walk away.'

The Jag stared, quite taken aback, and then his eyes, sunk deep beneath his heavy brows, slit in irritation. 'Do not try me, little mage. I could break you. Take my advice. It is indeed generous. Take it . . . or you will not leave this tent alive.'

Wu tapped the stick to the ground, studying his handiwork. 'And I say – do not force me to summon my pets.'

For an instant Juage gaped, then he slapped a wide hand to his thigh, chortling. 'Ha! You are an amusing fellow, I give you that.' He tossed more nuts into his mouth. 'But not even a fool like you can be so deluded as to think those wild beasts are your pets! No one can compel them and they answer to no one.'

'There are hints,' Wu said, his gaze still on the ground, 'that there is one in Shadow they answer to.'

Juage grunted his understanding, chewed thoughtfully for a time. 'I doubt they answer even to him. In any case, it boots not. The choice stands. Move on – or die.'

Sighing, Wu jammed the stick into the ground so that it stood upright next to the brazier. 'Then I say . . . you had better start running,' and he swept his hand through the shadow cast by the stick.

Juage surged from his stool. 'You little fool! You'll be first down their gullets!' He threw the remaining nuts at Wu and charged from the tent, bellowing: 'Guards to the king! *All guards!*'

'Are they really coming?' Dorin asked, not quite believing that the fellow could actually have summoned those terrifying beasts.

Wu calmly kicked the torn baldrics to the cage, approached, and bent down. 'Open up please.'

Dorin pushed open the door, took up his equipment. 'Already done.'

'Excellent.' Wu ducked inside and pulled the door shut behind him, locking it.

Dorin stared at the skinny lad crouched next to him. 'What are you doing?'

'Saving our collective arses – as they say.'

Dorin opened his mouth to curse the fellow to the furthest reaches of Hood's paths but didn't hear a word he said as a titanic baying howl erupted right next to the cage. He clapped his hands to his ears. The brazier went flying in a cascade of embers that set the tent alight and *something* emerged from the smoke and churning flames. It towered over them, panting like a bellows. Twin brown paws thumped to either side of the barred cage. An enormous head lowered and eyes the brightness and colour of the golden setting sun regarded them, hot with hunger. Beneath, black wet lips drew back from jutting canine fangs.

Dorin and Wu jammed themselves to the rear of the cage. A small voice in the back of Dorin's mind wondered *Is this the same one I saw before?* He thought not.

Snarling like splitting stones, the beast lunged. Its maw crashed into the bars, pushing the cage backwards. Iron groaned, bending and creaking. The cage gouged the earth, sliding, tore through the tent canvas. They flailed and rolled as it tumbled, striking equipment and even knocking aside running soldiers.

Alarms split the air throughout the camp. Another enormous hound's call thundered in the night nearby and Dorin thought *Ah, at least two then.*

'As you see,' Wu said, a hand pressed to a bleeding nose, 'we are quite safe.'

'Quite—' A swipe of one huge paw sent them skittering onward, rolling and spinning and mowing down tents. Soldiers hacked at the beast but it appeared determined upon tearing them from their haven.

Dorin held his head and turned to his companion. 'It seems to really want you.' But the mage lay unconscious. Blood pouring from his nose smeared his face crimson.

Jaws clamped on to the cage once more. Iron bars snapped explosively. The beast ran with them, battering down tents and lines of soldiers. It flung its head, sending the cage soaring. They tumbled down a slope of tall grasses and splashed into the frigid dark waters of the Idryn. Dorin had one instant to steal a breath of air before the heavy iron cage carried them to the bottom.

*

Iko was on her cot trying to meditate to stave off the pain of her ankle when the alarms sounded. She lay with her leg bound in a splint of wooden slats wrapped in cloth. Her sister Sword-Dancers were up and out in an instant while she struggled to rise. Her immediate thought was for the king, of course, but then the deafening roars burst across the night like eruptions of thunder and she knew this was something else entirely: an attack upon the camp by the man-beast, Ryllandaras. Set upon them in retaliation for the ground they had gained, no doubt.

She limped out into the night, a hand at the grip of her whipsword. Soldiers ran past while officers bellowed orders. Iko made for the king's quarters. The level of panic she encountered was rather worrying: the regulars either milled about uselessly or stood frozen in terror. But much of the effectiveness of any sorcerous attack was in the broader fear it generated, or so it seemed to her.

Whatever was attacking the camp was rampaging about seemingly at random, as she heard the monstrous braying moving hither and thither. She crossed a trail of its destruction in a line of trampled tents, scattered equipment and torn corpses. One body she passed had been bitten in two across the torso, and she wondered what manner of horrific daemons had been loosed upon the camp.

She reached the pavilion that served as the king's private quarters and was waved through by her sister Sword-Dancers who held the perimeter. Within, she drew up short, as she saw next to Chulalorn a giant whose twisted body resembled the caricature of a man. She took the arm of Sareh nearby and hissed, 'What is this?'

Sareh's face echoed her own distaste. 'None other than Juage himself.'

She released her sister's arm in a flinch of disgust. Juage! The ogre of the southern mountains! He had ruled a kingdom high among the peaks until Chulalorn's grandfather had defeated him and chained him beneath the very mountains he had terrorized – or so it was said. In the south they named his kind Jaggen, or giant. Inhuman, in any case. This was a sorcerous escalation of the worst kind. Deals with devils. Hallens' warning appeared to be justified as the fear struck her that events were spiralling out of anyone's control.

While she and her sisters guarded the perimeter of the tent, Chulalorn argued with his pet fiend.

'Can you not dismiss them?' the king was demanding.

'They will go shortly, m'lord,' Juage answered in his rumbling bass. 'They cannot stay long from their . . . well, their native realm.'

'So there is nothing you can do.' Chulalorn's tone was sneering.

'There is nothing anyone can do against these particular . . . summonings.'

'I wonder then why I do not release you back to your internment.'

The ogre bowed obsequiously. 'I will defend you should they attack . . . m'lord.'

'Yet you say they are not sent by Shalmanat.'

'No, m'lord. A minor hedge-wizard only. A dabbler and a fool. No doubt dead now.'

Chulalorn snarled, outraged, 'Are you saying a minor wizard has destroyed my camp?'

Juage bowed again. 'Give an imbecile a torch and you will get a fire.'

Chulalorn exhaled noisily, mollified for the moment.

Sareh touched Iko's shoulder and motioned to the outside, tilting her head. Iko listened and heard only the yells of the soldiers, the crackling of flames, and the occasional bellowed command. The sisters about her all eased slightly in their stances, listening as well.

Juage raised a huge gnarled and misshapen hand. 'I believe they may be gone now.'

The king grunted his satisfaction. 'As you predicted.' He crossed his arms, regarding the creature. 'I am tired of this interminable siege, Juage. You said you would end it – do so.'

The ogre bowed once more. 'Soon, my king. Soon. It is almost cold enough.'

'Make it cold enough. Quickly.'

'As you order,' and the monster bowed, very low and unctuously.

Iko looked away in distaste. Disgusting! This was beneath Chulalorn, surely. Yet he would have his way – there was nothing new in that. The will of kings. Hallens had warned her of this as well.

Yuna, who with Hallens' death had been given command of the Sword-Dancers, came to Iko and looked her up and down in obvious disapproval. 'Get back in your cot. You're of no use here.'

And Iko bowed as low as she could with her splinted leg. 'As you order . . .'

*

On the north bank of the Idryn a bedraggled, mud-slathered shape drew another limp form up the mud bank and fell to the ground, gasping. All was dark but for the fires burning in the Kanese camp to the south. Dorin wiped the cold slick clay from his face and lay exhausted, luxuriating in the sensation of just being alive. Sleep pulled at him but he knew that the deep sleep of the cold was a slow sure death and so he roused himself, lifted the unconscious Wu over his shoulder, and staggered inland searching for cover.

In the ruins of a burned-out barn he started a meagre fire from leaf litter and sticks and huddled about it with the still unconscious Wu. The Dal Hon youth had taken quite a hit to the head from the bouncing of the cage, but at least his nosebleed had clotted over. He may wake up addled, as so many who take such strikes to the head did, but in his case how would one know?

He tucked the lad's ice-cold hands to his chest and patted his shoulder. *Well done, you crazy lunatic. You really did save our arses – even if it was you who endangered them in the first place.*

Dorin sat back against the charred wall and kept watch through the dawn.

The mage's eyes popped open a good while after sunlight slanted down to warm him. The eyes roved about the ruins, red and blood-shot, and then the fellow grunted, satisfied, and croaked, 'As I said. Quite safe.'

Dorin would have laughed had he the energy. He motioned him up. 'Let's go.'

'Not the river, I beg you.'

'No, not the river. The north is open. I know a number of ways in.'

Wu strained to rise, groaning and hissing. 'Thank the gods.'

Once inside the walls Dorin kept them to narrow back alleys, for they were alone, and much of the territory they had to pass through was held by either Urquart or Pung. Eventually they came limping back into Wu's domain; or, more accurately, his lads' and lasses' domain, for in truth they did all the organizing and fighting. All was merely done in his name.

When they came staggering down the chute of a tunnel a lass approached Dorin, motioning for his attention. Dorin allowed a gang of lads to take Wu from his hands.

'There is someone here to see you,' the girl said.

'Who?'

A shrug. 'I'll take you. This way.'

She led him to a block of quiet, near-abandoned disputed streets that lay between Wu's gang and Pung's. This long into the siege few citizens ever left their quarters, which were barricaded and barred. It was now just a matter of waiting it out. You either managed to survive with what you had, or you didn't, for there was no longer anything left to buy, barter, or steal.

The girl led him to a cellar, one open and known to all parties. Here he was surprised to find Rheena – much skinnier, paler, and looking markedly older, but unquestionably Rheena. The girl started from her chair when he entered, gasping, 'What happened?' and he realized that he must present an even worse appearance.

He tried to straighten his mud-streaked half-dried leathers. 'I was out . . . scouting. What are you doing here? Pung would kill you if he knew.'

She bit her lip, and pulled at her tangled red hair. 'I'm sorry, Dorin. I'm very sorry. I tried to warn you. I had nothing to do with it. I kept my mouth shut, but Loor knew. He talked. He's angry with you – he thinks you betrayed him. Please, don't kill him. Please. He's just a dumb kid. He doesn't understand . . .'

He took her cold hands in his. 'What's happened?'

She would not raise her eyes. 'I'm finished with Pung now,' she whispered, fierce. 'This isn't what I joined for. She wasn't even involved . . . I'm sorry . . .'

Dorin let her hands fall. He backed away shaking his head, then he turned and ran.

He did not remember his passage to the streets of the caravanserai staging area in the west Outer Round; it all passed in a blur. He refused to think of what might await him but the moment he entered the narrow alley next to Ullara's family barn he knew, for there among the rubbish lay two dead birds.

Proud predators both had been in life, a red falcon and a kestrel. They lay now broken and bloodied. Looking up he saw smears of blood at the ledge of the open gable far above. He climbed while refusing to allow himself to think at all – he held it all at bay, waiting until he reached the loft.

Within it was as he dreaded: scattered feathers and broken bodies of every single roosting bird that Ullara had taken in. All had died fighting to defend her; all had been slashed or crushed. And amidst all the corpses, Ullara lying on her side, her legs and arms trussed. Gently, he untied the rope, releasing her blue hands and feet, and turned her on to her back. When she rolled over he flinched away, for her eyes had been gouged out.

The next thing he knew he was vaguely aware that someone was saying sorry over and over again in a cracked broken voice while he held her pressed to his chest, rocking her. Her chemise was wet against his face. 'I'm so sorry,' that person was whispering, hoarse. 'It is my fault. All my fault.'

He kneaded her hands and feet, massaging the life back into them. She stirred with the pain of the blood returning. He found a rag and wrapped it about her head over the savaged holes that had once held her eyes.

He sat with her head cradled on his lap through the night. He arranged her skirts, set her hands on her chest and sat looking down at her. He studied her for a very long time before blinking heavily and coming back to himself. Ever so slowly, he drew up the rope that had bound her and coiled it as he did so.

298

A fine length of slim taut hemp. Pung's thugs must have brought it with them.

He had a use for it too.

He had no idea how long he sat there with a hand on her forehead. The beginnings of a penance, perhaps. Dawn came and still he sat. Once, far above, came the heart-wrenching keening of a great bird, and he knew that her King of the Mountains still lived.

With the warmth of the morning she stirred. Her hands rose to her eyes but he caught them and gently lowered them to her chest.

She tried to speak – cleared her throat, and tried again, 'They told me this was a warning.'

He nodded, then flinched inwardly with the realization that she could not see it. That she would never see again. He swallowed to wet his raw throat. 'I understand.'

'They offered me a choice, you know,' she said, her voice eerily flat. 'Hands or eyes . . . but I fooled them. I chose my eyes.'

A shudder took Dorin at her words. Something elemental and very dark seemed to move beneath them.

'Listen, Ullara. I will take you with me. I can hide you. I know where—'

'No.'

'Don't be a fool. I can hide you, truly I can. Keep you safe.'

'No.' She raised a hand to his face and gently brushed it down his features, caressing them. 'Find him,' she whispered through her sharp clenched teeth. 'Find him and kill him.'

Dorin shuddered again at the ferocity contained in this slim young form. She seemed to burn in his arms. No wonder the birds of prey came to her. They recognized the spirit of a sister.

'Yes. Yes. I will.'

She relaxed once more on to his lap. 'Good.' She pushed his hands away. 'Go, then.'

'Ullara! What of you?'

'I will be fine. My father is below – too frightened to come up, no doubt. Do not worry. I will call him.'

'But . . .'

'Go. Find him. He thought you and I could be frightened off but he made a mistake. He doesn't understand what we are.' She pushed herself from him and sat up. 'Go. Do not return until he is dead.'

Chastened by her fire, he took one of her bloodied hands and pressed it to his lips. 'Yes. And . . . I'm sorry. I did not understand you either.'

'No, you didn't. Now it is too late. Now all that is left to us is vengeance and the hunt. So go.'

He clambered to his feet. 'Ullara . . . I—'

'Go.'

He lowered his head. 'Yes. I will find him.' Bending down, he kissed her brow above the stained cloth then descended to the alleyway below.

The moment he set foot on the littered cobbles movement snapped him around. Some sort of vagrant stirred beneath a dirty blanket and rose, coughing. As the figure straightened it wavered into the familiar elderly shape of Wu. The mage peered up at the gable then lowered his head and clasped his hands before his stomach. 'I'm sorry,' he murmured. 'She was an innocent.'

'Yes.' Dorin nodded. 'Yes, she was.' He drew a long shuddering breath and released it feeling as if he were releasing everything with it – his every wish, every foolish grandiose ambition, and every childish dream. All his plans for any future. 'It was my fault.'

'Do not blame yourself.'

'If I had moved against Pung as you wished this would not have happened.'

'We cannot be certain.'

Now he frowned, vaguely irritated. 'Why are you here?'

'I am worried about what you're going to do.'

'You know exactly what I am going to do.'

'Ah, yes, well. Exactly my worry . . .'

'I thought you wanted Pung dead.'

'Of course. But not you. Please, Dorin, let's not be hasty . . .'

He thought of her slim frame – so tiny and frail – and shook his head. Blinding. A terrible, awful, cruel maiming. How could anyone do such a thing to an innocent soul? 'Things have changed.' *Dorin died in that loft.*

'Ah, I see. As you say. But let us take a moment to consider—'

'No. No more planning or considering. Look what my delaying has cost. I am finished with it. I'm going now.' He faced the Dal Hon mage directly. 'Are you with me or not?'

'Of course I am with you, as always. But please, for the love of the gods – wait for nightfall at the least, I beg of you.'

Dorin brushed past to the alley mouth. 'Dusk, then,' he allowed, grudgingly. Something among the litter caught his eye and he picked it up. A bird's leg and clawed foot, torn or severed from its owner. Blood still limned the black curved talons. He studied the grisly object for a time then slipped it down his shirt.

'Let us prepare,' said Wu, and his short walking stick appeared in his hand.

In the loft above, Ullara felt about the floor before her, patting the messed straw, feeling her way to the gable window. Reaching the wall, she pulled herself erect and felt at the window ledge. She raised her face to the warm morning breeze. 'Come,' she whispered to the breeze.

After a time the brazen call of a bird tore the sky and broad wings buffeted the air. A tall heavy shape perched upon the roof opposite.

Ullara raised her hands to the cloth at her eyes and unwound it. Once it fell away she studied her hands as if marvelling at them, then turned her attention to the roofscape of the city beyond.

'Go, my hunter,' she urged the wind.

* * *

'It is not as bad as it could have been,' Ho was saying to Shalmanat while he, Mara and Silk faced their mistress in her sanctum. 'We have them contained within the Outer Round. The river gates are sabotaged, and the arches broken. They have no way in but to take the walls or the gates, just as before.'

But Shalmanat would not look up. She sat slumped upon her camp stool, a shawl draped over her shoulders. 'The populace will have lost faith in me,' she whispered, staring at the floor.

Ho cast Silk a meaningful glare. Silk cleared his throat and knelt next to her. 'Not at all, m'lady. The populace holds firm. The Inner Round walls are defended. Holding one section does not give them the city entire.'

'I will not yield the south.'

'Of course not. There is no need.'

'Nor will I accept Dal Hon's offer,' she said.

Silk raised his head to look at Ho who grimaced, taking a heavy breath. 'They will come if we accept their authority.'

'I will not escape one tiger by putting my head into the jaws of another,' she snarled, pulling her shawl tight. 'And speaking of that,' she snapped, glaring at Ho, 'what is your excuse for Ryllandaras?'

Ho clasped his meaty hands behind his back, nodding. 'Think, Shalmanat. It is really for the best. This Kanese incursion is only temporary. It will pass. But he remains the eternal enemy. With him out of the way our trade will burgeon. We will be able to rebuild even stronger. And it is also a mercy; someone, eventually, would have killed him.'

The Protectress's gaze slid away, unfocused. 'I promised him I would keep the plains open . . .'

'And you did – for a time. But Tali and Purge are expanding in the west. They have made no such promises.'

'And Tali has made an offer of alliance,' Mara added. 'If we accept their aid.'

Shalmanat snorted. 'How it still rankles with them! They would like to finally march their Iron Legions through my streets!'

'They are too far off anyway,' Mara said. 'We must finish this ourselves.'

The Protectress raised her eyes and Silk was shocked to see them bloodshot, sunken, red-rimmed, and shining with a feverish light. 'Yes. Finish it. I hoped it wouldn't come to it – but it may. It may have to.'

Silk eyed her warily, troubled by her tone. 'What do you mean?'

'Warn me of any preparations for an attack,' she told Ho. 'Any massing of their numbers.'

Ho bowed. 'As you order.'

'And this attack in their camp?'

Ho waved the topic aside. 'The beasts appeared among them, rampaged, then disappeared once more. I dare say they did more damage to the Kanese than we have.'

'What are they anyway?' Silk asked Ho.

'Daemons summoned by a minor talent who could not control them.'

Shalmanat, Silk noted, tightened her lips against saying anything.

'We are done, then?' Mara asked. 'We must get back to the walls.'

The Protectress waved them off with a weak gesture.

Silk lingered, hoping to talk, but she kept urging them out and so he relented and backed away after Ho and Mara. The guards pulled shut the door. Silk hurried to catch Ho.

'What did she mean, finish it?' he asked.

The heavyset mage was lumbering through the palace halls with his sideways swinging walk. 'You know her only as the ruler of the city, but she is powerful in her own right.'

'She is afraid of that power.'

Ho nodded his dour agreement. 'As she should be. What troubles me is this unusual cold.'

'This winter? It has been a rare one, I understand. But they suffer just as much as we do.'

The sour mage grunted his half-agreement. Silk's thoughts turned to his own worries. He thought he understood Shalmanat now. She must see herself being driven into a corner. Forced to take up her worst nightmare – her powers. And these he knew as Liosan. Elder Light. The wellspring, he now knew, behind Thyr and Telas – neither of which drove him or Smokey unhinged with dread. It was more powerful, yes, but in the end it was just another Warren, was it not?

* * *

They gathered in a narrow tunnel recently dug out beneath Pung's quarters. Wu's urchin diggers bristled with weapons but their youth made Dorin uneasy, though in truth they were but a few years younger than he. Lowering his voice, he murmured to Wu, 'Only bring them up if they're needed.'

The mage nodded in his distracted, half-attending manner. Irritated by this, Dorin moved to the fore. 'I'll go first.' He took a small shovel from the hands of a girl and cut into the wall they faced. She winced in agony at his hacking.

'Careful,' she implored.

Dorin grunted his assent and slowed. Light shone through, dim, but enough for their starved vision. A portion of the dirt wall fell away revealing a root cellar. He stepped in and around old barrels and crates. The air stank of rot and damp. A short ladder led to a trapdoor.

He listened at the slats of the door, heard nothing. He pressed

303

against it until it rose a fraction and stilled, listening once more. He heard nothing – no footsteps, no breathing, no creak of leather or wood. He raised the door further until he could see up an empty hall then entered and crouched, knives ready. Wu poked his head through the trapdoor. Dorin beckoned him upward.

The absolute quiet sent Dorin's instincts blazing with dread. This was all wrong. It felt like a trap yet there was no one about. The house seemed deserted. How could it be a trap with no one here?

He motioned for Wu to pause then advanced to the main floor's centre and stood, listening. Again, he heard nothing – the house was indeed abandoned. Then it reached him. Distant, audible only because of the building's emptiness: someone walking far above, perhaps even on the roof.

Someone alone, pacing the roof. Waiting. Waiting for . . . *him.*

He straightened then, sheathing his knives in his new baldrics. He returned to Wu. 'Find your box, or whatever the damned thing is, if it's still here. I'll be above. I have an . . . appointment.'

The Dal Hon's gaze climbed to the ceiling. 'I see. You have my aid, of course.'

'No. This is personal. Don't interfere.'

Wu gave a slight lift of his brows. 'If you insist.'

He waved him off. 'Go and search.' He went to the stairs.

Another trapdoor opened on to the roof. Dorin knew it well. It was flat, the footing reliable. He straightened, drawing his best fighting knives.

Far across the breadth of the roof a dark shape straightened as well. It approached, resolved into a tall young man, cloaked, wearing a well-trimmed goatee. The fellow inclined his head in greeting. 'So, another student of Faruj, yes?'

'Where is Pung?'

The fellow's hands emerged holding similar fighting blades. He gestured widely. 'His location is immaterial to ones such as us, don't you think?'

'He's the only one I want.'

The fellow frowned an exaggerated disappointment. 'Really? You do not sound like a student of Faruj. Are you yet another poseur? I have found . . . well, killed so many. We cannot have people running about claiming to be our equals, can we?' He gave an apologetic shrug. 'It is bad for our rates.'

'Where did he bring you in from?'

'Unta, of course. It's where the money is, you know.'

'So much for Unta,' Dorin muttered.

'What? You said something?'

'I said, you came for nothing. I frankly don't give a shit about you.' He slid a foot back to the edge of the trapdoor.

'Leave and you die!' the assassin warned. He opened his arms once more, apologetic. 'It's just the way it is. Turn away and I will cut you down from behind.' He shrugged. 'Makes no difference to me.'

Dorin understood. He had known the moment he saw the man. But he had to give it a try. He nodded and eased into a ready stance, one blade low and forward, the other high over his head, but held point downward.

The assassin smiled hungrily and eased into an identical stance. 'What is your name?' he asked.

'Dorin.'

The smile broadened. He shifted, circling to the right. Dorin responded, circling to his right. 'My name is Stephan,' the assassin said. 'Did the old man mention my name?'

Dorin knew this for a trap – names had meant nothing to the old man – but he'd already sized up his opponent and had reached the conclusion that the fellow was damned vain. And so he said, 'He said he once tried to teach a cretin named Stephan how to throw a knife.'

The smile was whipped away. 'Don't make me mad, little boy. This could be quick – or it could be very slow. Agonizingly slow.'

Dorin relaxed completely into that loose awareness that was his state of mind for any duel. Nothing else mattered any longer – only the moment. There was no past or future. No plans or hopes or expectations.

Just this moment: the chill night air in his lungs; his breath pluming ever so lightly; the soft leather of his shoes gripping the bricks laid in a herringbone design across the roof; and the cool hard familiarity of the knives in his hands. He shifted into a new stance, warming up – and his partner responded, answering his rhythm. And with that he knew this Stephan had truly been a student of his mentor.

For the old man had taught knife-fighting as a dance.

It is a duet, he heard the old bastard say once more. *A duet, in which your goal is to kill your partner.*

Dorin allowed the ghost image of that old man, his sparring partner for years and years, to superimpose itself over the figure opposite. An entire childhood spent in a dusty cold barn shuffling in endless circles while this iron-faced skinny ancient struck him with his wooden knives on his arms, his legs, his head.

And lectured him interminably while doing so.

You must come to know your partner better than they know themselves, he'd snarl, and strike him across the bridge of the nose.

And he, his skinny bare arms a mass of purple-black bruises, struggling to organize a counter-attack.

Do not think of what you will do! A shocking blow to his temple that raised stars in his vision. *Watch what they are doing and think what they will do!*

And as the years passed his other training – his breaking and entering, his pickpocketing and rope-escaping – all became mere decoration next to his knife training. The bruises on his arms and legs became fewer and fewer. His duets with the old man lasted longer and longer there in the clouds of dust raised from the hard-packed floor of the barn.

You must come to know them as intimately as a lover. A thrust to his neck turned aside. A sweep evaded. Three false slashes with the blade hidden behind the wrist, high and low, followed by a spinning overhead slash that he intuited as show to cover a thrust to his side that he sidestepped, counter-attacking with what in sword-fencing would be considered a stop-thrust.

For when you know them so well you understand them – that is when you slip the knife in.

Stephan staggered back, yielding ground, a hand pressed to his side that came away wet and gleaming in the moonlight. He studied his fingers, then raised one blade to his forehead, acknowledging it. '*Touché.*'

Dorin eased into a more aggressive stance, both blades held out before him.

Stephan circled anew, weaving his knives. Dorin ignored the flash of the moonlight from the blades to watch the man's centre of weight instead. *He is leading – where are we going?*

The man refused to commit, dodging and circling, and Dorin

understood: his partner wouldn't be giving any more. He would have to be pressed. Dorin edged forward to begin the long chase that was cornering a partner. The man circled, again and again. But Dorin kept the pressure on, always working him towards a corner of the rooftop.

In the periphery of his attention, Dorin noted the moon sinking. This was his longest dance in years. A droplet from his brow struck his eyelid and he realized this was the first time he'd worked up a sweat in any fight since leaving Tali. Most bouts lasted a mere few heartbeats; a few traded slashes and parries. Yet he and Stephan already knew one another so well. Their stances echoed each other's precisely. He saw his own moves reflected perfectly in his partner's.

Reflected . . .

That thought saved Dorin's life.

Just as he assumed he had Stephan where he wanted him he realized that the opposite was true – that all along he'd been fed exactly what he'd expected to see. His reflexive rage at himself was a physical flinch that pulled him away the thumb's breadth necessary to save his life. The point that penetrated his shirt and the armoured plastron beneath passed between his ribs but didn't touch his heart.

Stephan's smile of victory froze as Dorin's blade slammed home in his neck.

Dorin clutched his chest, staggering backwards.

Stephan fell to his knees, both hands at his throat. Blood welled thickly between his fingers. One-handed, Dorin started tearing at his shirt and the lacing of the plastron beneath.

'Congratulations . . .' Stephan whispered, a ghastly smile on his lips.

Dorin fell to his own knees. He heaved the half-unlaced plastron over his head and threw it aside to thump to the roof. Blood smeared his hand at his chest.

'. . . you're the last . . .' Stephan fell to lie on his side with his eyes staring fixedly at nothing '. . . the last . . . student of Faruj . . .'

Dorin wavered, dizzy. There was a roaring in his ears. He blinked, thinking *No – this isn't what I came here for. This isn't what I want. I wanted . . . I wanted . . .*

He blinked more and more slowly, his sight darkening with each fall of the eyelids. Movement roused him: the crackling of footsteps in the grit of the roof. A murky wavering shape halted next to him, a stick set down to the bricks, tapping.

Dorin swallowed to wet his throat, croaked, 'You gonna . . . watch me . . . bleed out?'

'Not at all. The urchins are on their way.'

The thought of those kids poking at him almost got Dorin to his feet. Wu pressed him back down. 'Do not worry, I have everything in hand.'

That's what fucking worries me . . .

The youths arrived, eased him on to his back. Small hands pulled at his torn shirt. The pain was swept aside like a receding wave, and Dorin recognized the effects of the healing Warren, Denul.

'You have a healer?' he murmured to Wu, amazed.

'Almost every one of these youths is a talent of one sort or another. That's why I picked them from all the hundreds of kids.' The mage studied his walking stick, sniffed. 'Really, Dorin, give me *some* credit.'

And Dorin let himself relax, yielding to the probing fingers, thinking *Oponn's jest! An army of damned talents?*

Chapter 17

ALIGHT DRIFT OF WINDBLOWN ICE GRANULES COVERED THE body in the alley. Silk crouched next to it, reached a bare hand down the man's chest, stone cold. More than a day, at the least. And not just another starving victim of the siege, either. Shot through by crossbow bolts – and these subsequently torn from the body as supplies were short everywhere.

'Starved?' Smokey called from down the alley.

'No.' Silk rested his elbows on his knees, rubbed his hands to warm them. 'Looks like a gang war. This is one of Pung's or Urquart's.'

Smokey cocked his head. 'Could be a murder made to look like such. We got informers, saboteurs and spies crawling all over us like godsdamned lice.'

Silk studied the cobbled alleyway. Small footprints in the dusting of sleet. Very small. Sandals and shoes, worn, some with holes in the soles. No proper boots. He raised his head to call, 'It's that new gang. Expanding their territory.' He stood, brushed his trouser legs, then went to where Smokey, in a long woollen coat, leaned up against a wall. 'I hear Pung's in hiding.'

Smokey rolled his eyes. 'I don't give a shit. What I want to know is whether it's the work of any blasted insurgent or traitor.'

'In my opinion? No.'

Smokey grunted his satisfaction, pushed from the wall. 'Okay, leave it be. At least in this cold it won't rot.' They started up the street.

'It's going to be a messy spring this year.'

Smokey hunched further, shuddering. He tucked his hands deep within the coat. 'Don't care.' He added, muttering, 'So long as we live to see it.'

'Have faith, my dour friend. Burn's Turning has come and gone – we are in the season of rising light. Kan's thrown its best against us and been repulsed. They'll crawl away with the melt.'

'It's not Kan that worries me – it's malcontents here. Like at the Inner Gate.'

'Mara caught them before they took control and now their heads adorn it as warning to others. Everyone will think twice now.'

Smokey grunted sourly. 'We were lucky. We might not be next time.' He cocked an eye to Silk. 'What's got you in such a grand mood?'

Silk thought about that. He *was* in an inexplicably good mood this day and he wondered on its cause. He decided that it was as he'd said: Kan really did seem exhausted. It looked to him as though they truly had repulsed Chulalorn's overreach. And time was on their side. With every day that passed, the status quo solidified and opinion grudgingly shifted in their favour. In a siege, the mere survival of the defending party was itself success. It was up to Kan to prove otherwise.

'I do believe we've turned a corner, my friend.'

Smokey laughed his scepticism. 'Hunh! That'll be the day I offer good coin to Oponn.'

* * *

Dorin sat up in his narrow underground room, more of a cell, just wide enough for his cot. He rubbed his chest beneath his thin shirtings, and remembered the chill touch of the knifepoint when it slid past his ribs. Must have punctured a lung at the least.

The cloth hanging across the doorway was edged aside and a youth entered: one of Wu's lads. The boy's dirty face registered surprise and he sketched a quick half-bow. 'Wu wants to see you.'

Dorin sat up, blinked in dizziness. 'He does, does he?'

'Yes sir.'

'Sir?'

'Yes sir, Dorin sir.'

'I meant – you don't have to use "sir".'

'We decided to use it.'

'Oh. Well, that's all right, then.'

The lad was relieved. 'Thanks. You sit – I'll go and get Wu. Oh, is there anything you want?'

Dorin tried to swallow, failed. 'Food and drink. And not from any tomb!'

'Right.' The lad left, the cloth fell.

Shortly afterwards a girl arrived carrying a wooden tray supporting a small loaf and a steaming earthenware bowl. 'What's this?' he asked.

'Broth of onions and mushrooms. All we got left.'

Dorin picked up the fist-sized loaf – it was rock hard. 'How am I supposed to . . .'

'You dip it in the broth. Softens it.'

'Ah.' He ate. The girl crouched, watching him. From the edge of his vision he observed her. Finally, he asked, 'What is it?'

'Four of us watched your fight. They say it was the most amazing thing they ever saw. So fast it was. Like magic. Will you teach us?'

Dorin thought about that while he dipped the bread and gnawed it. The dissemination of specialized knowledge outside any guild was, of course, punishable by death. Assassins didn't really possess an organized guild, though – too much the loners. However, they tended to follow rules similar to those of the secretive brotherhood of architects, or the closed guild of the goldsmiths, or the mystical gem-cutter guild. His teacher had guarded his hard-won knowledge and skills jealously. They were, after all, his only bread and butter. He had to sell them as dearly as possible. He'd taken only one student at a time – not that Dorin had had any coin. He'd been a charity case, taken on only because of his demonstrated ability. Teaching these lads and lasses would be seen as a gross break with tradition; a potential cheapening of all that he'd struggled so hard to possess. A betrayal of trade secrets that carried the death penalty.

He considered this while he stirred the broth with the knot of bread. 'I'll teach anyone who wants to learn.'

The girl shot to her feet, her eyes huge, 'Thank you!' She ran from the room, presumably to spread the word.

The cloth was edged aside once more and Rheena entered. She leaned up against the wall next to the doorway. She rubbed her hands down her thighs, her gaze on the floor. 'I'm glad you're okay.'

'Thanks to these kids. Can you believe that?'

Rheena laughed, crossed her arms. 'Kids? I was no older when I ran away. And that one who just left? She's a talent of Rashan. Walks in the night like a ghost.' She shook her head, amazed. 'Seems your friend has an eye for talent.'

Dorin thought about that. 'Yeah. I suppose he does.'

The half-smile fled her face and she brushed back her loose curls of red hair. 'So, how is she?'

'Blinded.'

'Blinded? Gods – I'm sorry.'

He shrugged aside the apology. 'It's my fault. You were right. I shouldn't have involved her.'

She hugged herself, nodding. 'It's the innocents who get it in the neck, isn't it?'

Dorin eyed her anew. 'Where's Loor?'

She raised her gaze to the ceiling. 'Must you . . .'

'Where is he?'

'Promise not to kill him?'

'Yes.'

'Or blind him?'

He scowled, truly offended. 'I'd never maim anyone.'

'Just saying!' She raised a hand. 'All right. So long as you don't harm him. He was just mad at you, that's all.'

'Mad at me?'

'He thought we were a team. He thought he was finally going somewhere . . .' She let her shoulders fall. 'Never mind.' She took a steadying breath. 'The Wayside Inn.'

He knew it; one of the worst dives in the city. 'Thank you.'

Her answering nod was miserable. 'And me?'

'You?'

She rolled her eyes once more. 'Yes, me. What of me?'

He gestured to the hall. 'These kids need a firm hand. Wu and I are busy.'

She dropped her gaze, drew a circle in the dust with the toe of her shoe. 'I see . . . I suppose I should thank you.'

'Just don't prove me wrong.'

She jumped as if stung. 'I'll not disappoint you.'

'See that you don't.' He gestured once more to the hall.

Rheena inclined her chin and left. Dorin finished his thin soup. When he looked up Wu was standing in the doorway studying him with the air of a pleased parent. It occurred to him that the Dal Hon mage was the only one apart from Ullara who could sneak up on him. 'What do you want?' he growled, irritated by that fact.

'All hale and whole, yes? Thanks to me.'

'Thanks to your healers.'

A flutter of one hand from the mage seemed to say *A minor distinction*.

'So? What do you want?'

'I? Why, nothing. Only your well-being, of course. It gratifies me no end to see you quite recovered. You should have seen yourself. Hood's doorstep, as they say. Why, if it weren't for me—'

'No.'

The Dal Hon mage, as ever in his false façade of grey hair and wrinkled visage, faltered, blinking. 'I'm sorry? No? What do you mean, no?'

'No to whatever it is you want.'

'I? Why, nothing. Nothing at all. But,' and he raised a finger, 'now that you mention it, there is one small favour . . .'

'No. We're done. You have that damned box thing, don't you?'

Wu drew himself up looking smugly satisfied, like the cat that ate the mouse. 'Absolutely. I, that is *we*, have acquired the, ah, object.'

'Good. Then you will help me move on Chulalorn.'

The mage lowered his finger. He set to tapping the stick to the dirt, his gaze lowered. 'Ah. Well. About that. I was thinking . . .'

'You're not reneging on me, are you?'

Wu now fluttered the air with his fingers, the stick waving. 'Not a bit of it, my friend. I was just thinking that now may not be the best time, that is all.'

'What do you mean, not the best time?'

'Well. It's quite convenient having him out there, after all. Suits our purposes, yes?'

Dorin crossed his arms and winced at a twinge from his chest. 'What are you talking about?'

The mage waggled his brows as if trying to appear knowing. Dorin raised a forestalling hand. 'Don't do that – not to me, anyway.'

Wu's lips drew down in a pout but he seemed to recover quickly as he now stroked the scraggy hairs at his chin. 'Let Chulalorn and the Protectress exhaust their resources battling one another. Who knows, perhaps the king's forces will even account for a city mage or two . . . We will then have a much easier hand, will we not?'

'An easier hand? What are you—' Dorin stared at the smirking hunched gnome of a mage for a moment then pulled a hand down his face, sighing. 'You're completely insane.' He straightened from the cot, waved the fellow aside. 'If you won't help with Chulalorn, we're done. I'll go it alone from here on. Thank you for the healing.'

Wu was frowning his confusion. 'But we nearly have the streets tied up. Soon we'll be able to move on the palace itself.'

Dorin paused in the doorway. 'I hate this damned city.'

'Well, it does smell – but they say it's the river . . .'

Dorin pushed past, started up the tunnel. 'We're done.'

'But I have the box! It is vital!'

Dorin halted, marched back down to the short mage. 'All right. Let's see this amazing artefact.'

Wu clutched his chest, his eyes darting. 'That's not really necessary . . . You need only take my word, I assure you . . .'

Dorin extended a hand. 'You said it's ours.'

The fellow's brows shot up. 'Time's wasting. Must be off.' He turned to go, but Dorin gathered up a fistful of his shirt.

'Let's see it.'

'Very well – if you insist. But do not be hasty. Appearances are always deceiving.' He drew the flat wooden box from his shirt and handed it over.

Something hard clattered within. Dorin slid the top open and peered inside. He was still for a moment as he considered what confronted him. He had had no idea what to expect but this was not it: it was nothing more than a broken stone arrowhead, or spear-point. A childish souvenir. A common piece of old knapped weaponry such as littered riverbanks and coastlines.

He dropped the box to the ground and the point fell to the dirt. He pressed the heels of both palms to his eyes, took a long slow breath. Finally, he managed, slow and deliberate, 'You Queen-damned utter lunatic. We're done. Finished. Completely finished.'

The mage's eager grin fell away. 'What do you mean? Isn't it fascinating?'

'Stuff the damned thing!'

'Well . . . if you're going to be like that I won't include you in any of my future plans after all.'

314

Dorin stalked up the tunnel. 'What a loss.' He continued on, muttering under his breath, 'What a fucking terrible loss . . .'

*

The young derelict always sat alone in the common room of the Wayside Inn. And he cradled just the one glass of homebrew through the night. The proprietor would have chucked him out long ago if it weren't for the fact that these days the room was nearly empty – better a few sad souls than none at all.

Dorin watched the figure from the bar. The lad looked awful: pale and sweaty as if fevered, his eyes sunken and red-rimmed. His shirt and jacket were torn and dark with dirt, as if he'd been sleeping in the street. Dorin pushed a few coins to the barkeep and waited for him to amble into the back kitchens. After a moment a crash as of dropped bowls sounded and the four men in the room craned to look.

Dorin slipped forward and eased into the chair opposite the lad.

Loor brought his gaze back from the kitchen entrance and stiffened, paling even more. Then he let go his breath and took up the drink before him, swallowing all. He set down the glass and gave a sickly smile. 'Been waiting for you.'

Dorin almost started at that, his hands going to his waist. *I underestimated this lad.* But no – he'd checked out the other three already, and none carried anything larger than an eating knife. And the proprietor hadn't betrayed any nerves when he spoke to him. *Just a turn of phrase.* Yet he kept his hands on the knives at his waist all the same. 'Should've organized a welcome.'

A lift of the brows. 'Tried. No takers. Dead man walking they called me.'

'They're getting smart. Where is he?'

'You think he tells me?'

'Where do you think he is?'

'He moves around . . . a lot.' Loor touched his ear. 'Still got the scar. You're good. Why'd you miss?'

'I still hit the mark, but I was put off by Tran. He really got up my nose.'

The lad laughed, a touch maniacally. 'Yeah. He did that to everyone. Rheena finally got fed up with it and did for him.'

'She did?'

315

'Yeah. He was interfering with her chances. She's good too.' He leaned forward and Dorin would've been alarmed but the lad had both his hands on the table, scooting the glass back and forth. 'Why'd you do it?'

'Do what?'

'Fuck everything up, man! You 'n' me 'n' Rheena. We was a team. We could be fucking running the show by now!'

Dorin stared at the wretched figure before him. *Ye gods, he just doesn't see it, does he? Where to start?* Tell him that he, Dorin, *was* running things now – *his* show?

Now he felt only pity. Pity and disgust. He waved the lad off. 'Get out of town.'

Loor fell back in his seat. 'What? Leave? Leave town?' He laughed feverishly. 'If you haven't noticed, there's a siege on! The Kanese are closing the north.'

'There're still gaps. Head out tonight. Now. Before I change my mind.'

'What, and get captured by the Seti and sold as a slave? They've moved south, you know – want in on the fun.'

'Better chances than you'll get with me.'

Now the lad's lips started twitching and he threw the glass back, forgetting that it was empty. 'It's all your fault!' he yelled, his voice cracking, and heads turned.

Oh, Queen of Dreams. Not a blasted scene! 'Just go. Now. Don't make me knife you just to shut you up.'

Loor heaved the glass at Dorin but he edged his head aside and it missed to burst against the wall. He surged to his feet, wiping his eyes. 'You ruined everything!' he snarled, and staggered from the common room.

Dorin sat quietly for a time. The other patrons were wise enough to return to their drinks. He rocked in his chair while he tapped his thumbs together on his lap. Ruined everything. Perhaps he had. So far nothing he'd started had turned out the way he wanted.

Ullara could certainly attest to that.

Perhaps he was a jinx. Some people were. They were just . . . unlucky. People got hurt around them. Better for all concerned that he slipped away as well. After all, there was an opening in Unta.

If he could just find Pung and finish this. The bastard wasn't even showing his shadow.

Dorin stopped his thumbs. He leaned his chair forward with a crash of the legs.

That fucking little sneak-thief shit. He knows. He's known all along!

He stormed from the common room.

He found Wu in his 'quarters' – the large cellar where he kept a fire, busied himself with his charcoal drawings, and hoarded a fair bit of the gathered funerary offerings of gold and silver.

The diggers guarding him let Dorin in and Wu looked up placidly from where he sat at a table, a slip of parchment before him. He laced his fingertips together, elbows on the table, and began, 'Well now. Come to apologize for your ill-considered—'

Dorin gathered together the fellow's shirt and jacket collar at his throat, dragged him from behind the table, and slammed him against the dirt wall. 'Where is he?'

Wu pulled at Dorin's fists, his eyes bulging. 'Now, now. Don't let's be too hasty . . .'

'You know, don't you?'

'Well . . . yes. But please . . . he is irrelevant now. We have taken the streets. Let him hide. Everyone has deserted him.'

'He's not irrelevant to me.'

Wu raised a finger between them. 'I understand. But consider. There are more than just us in this matter.'

Dorin released him and the fellow straightened his linen shirt and fine jacket of lined black satin. 'What do you mean?'

Wu nodded to the doorway where a number of faces stared in, their eyes huge. Wu shooed them off and they withdrew. Dorin noticed the monkey-like familiar in the rafters where it yawned hugely revealing enormous fangs and a bright red tongue. He crossed his arms. 'Explain.'

'If you corner him there will be bloodshed. And I do not like bloodshed.'

Dorin arched a brow. 'Really. You don't like bloodshed.'

'No. It's messy and unsophisticated. There are better ways of doing things.'

'Such as?'

Wu brightened, flashed his yellowed crooked teeth. 'My ways. Lying, trickery, deceit, cheating, or just plain patience. He will come to us.'

Dorin remained unconvinced. 'Where is he, then?'

Wu wove his fingers together at his chest, paced before the wall. 'Well . . . he has sought refuge in a temple.'

Dorin felt a gathering tension in his stomach. 'Which temple?'

Wu faced him, raised his steepled fingers to his chin, almost wincing. 'The temple to Hood.'

Dorin looked to the ceiling. *Queen-damned should've known it.*

Two figures dressed in dark walk an empty street at night. Ice crystals of sleet swirl about them. One is short, his walk a side to side duck-like waddle, the other tall and slim, his walk smooth and gliding, utterly silent. The short one taps a walking stick as he goes; the other holds his arms hidden within his cloak. This section of the Street of the Gods lies to the east, just next to the shore of the Idryn. The only sound comes from the pancake ice-floes clacking and bumping on their way downriver.

The two stopped before a rundown nondescript old mausoleum, its dark entranceway gaping open. The burned stubs of candles layered the threshold here, along with clay cups of liquor, wilted flowers, parchment messages, and other offerings. The shorter of the two figures stepped forward and planted his walking stick in front of him, palms resting on its silver head.

'Greetings,' he called. 'We wish to speak.'

A tall shape moved within the murk of the doorway. 'Hood grants no special favours.'

Wu rolled his eyes. 'Not to Hood – to *you.*'

'I am a mere servant.'

'A studied pose to fool the gullible. But not me.'

'There are no false poses before Hood.'

Wu turned to Dorin, muttered, 'This is getting tiresome.'

'I know you're in there, Pung!' Dorin shouted. 'Come out!'

'He is a guest of Hood.'

Dorin pushed forward. 'Perhaps we'll just come in there and get him.'

The shape advanced as well, resolving into the youth Dassem, sword readied. 'Then you will meet Hood.'

Wu threw his hands up. 'You are determined to shelter this criminal, then?'

'All are equal before the Dark Taker.'

Wu pressed a hand to his forehead. 'Oh, do shut up.' He waved Dorin off. 'Come. As you can see, he is nothing now. Just a rat hiding in his hole.'

Dorin spat at the doorway. 'Rot in there, then, damn you to Poliel!'

Wu urged him away. 'Enough. Let's go.'

'What of the child?' Dorin called back. 'You would keep *him* with her?'

Dassem tilted his head to where an encampment lay a little way down the empty road. Tents and awnings had been raised among the shrines and stone crypts, and campfires were burning. 'She is safe with a family of adherents.'

Dorin allowed Wu to push him onward, but reluctantly, glancing back a number of times. When they rounded a turn both stopped and pressed themselves against the nearest wall. 'What is the purpose of this mummery?' Dorin hissed.

Wu raised a placating hand. 'You shall see.' He pointed the walking stick up the narrow alleyway between the squat shrines and crypts. 'Ah, here we are . . .'

Two figures approached through the gloom. One Dorin recognized as Rheena. She held the arm of a slim man, slumped, his jacket torn. When he lifted his head Dorin was surprised to see the dejected features of Gren, Pung's onetime lieutenant.

Wu jabbed the man's chest with his stick. 'Greetings, Gren. How the worm and the table have turned, though I don't understand how tables turn – but that is beside the point. You understand your job?'

The fellow shook off Rheena's grip, straightened his jacket. 'Yes. But I want half up front.'

'You have your life up front,' Dorin grated.

'Indeed.' Wu nodded. 'You'll get no payment until the job is done. The east Outer Round wall here, two nights hence. Yes?'

Gren jerked his assent. 'Fine.'

'And until then you will enjoy the hospitality of our friend Rheena here – and my lads and lasses.'

Gren paled, swallowing. 'Don't let them at me. I mean it! Please.'

Wu jabbed the stick again. 'Do your job. Don't betray us.'

Rheena took his arm and yanked him away. Dorin watched them go. 'Two days, then.'

Wu nodded once more. 'Yes.' He gestured, inviting Dorin onward. 'A glorious boundless future awaits, yet here I am seeing to such trivial matters.' He pointed the stick to the night sky. 'This alone is a crime!'

'Boundless in your imagination,' Dorin muttered.

The young mage nodded, utterly untroubled. 'Indeed. My imagination is boundless – and thus so my ambition and destiny.'

Dorin could only shake his head at such utter drivel.

* * *

Silk picked his way down the Idryn's treacherous shore of frozen mud and iced-over puddles of meltwater. If he ruined the finish on his fine leather boots while on this errand he would be very annoyed. Earlier that day on the street one of the shambling destitutes had reared up before him like a terrifying vision of the future and muttered drunkenly, or as if dreaming under the influence of the d'bayang poppy, 'Liss wishes to see you.'

He'd halted, flinching from the man's stench. 'What was that?'

But the human wreck slouched on. 'Liss,' he'd repeated over his shoulder, droning as if only half awake.

Now he found himself navigating the churned and frozen grey-green mudflats and cursing the witch thoroughly. Why couldn't she live in a nice cottage like any other self-respecting witch? No, she had to sleep on the river shore, like some common fish-wife. She was powerful, he knew, yet she insisted on living like the poorest of the poor. He couldn't understand it.

He ducked under the lip of a wharf and walked down the slope of pilings to the current shore. The Idryn, he noticed, was lower than he'd ever seen it. Two figures waited ahead, both facing away, over the river; one squat and draped in hanging layered skirts and shawls, which one might interpret as worn against the cold, though Silk knew she dressed this way even in the height of summer; the other towering and equally ragged, the giant Koroll.

Silk nodded to them. 'Greetings, Liss, Koroll.'

They glanced back to him. 'You were right,' Liss said to Koroll, 'he really would get his fine boots muddy.'

'Very funny, Liss. What, then, is so very pressing down here at the river? Are the fish plotting against us too?'

Koroll tilted his craggy, scarred and tattooed head in thought. 'Few fish left here,' he rumbled.

'The river is low,' Liss said.

Silk nodded patiently. 'Yes. Yes it is.'

'It is tainted.'

Silk frowned as he attempted to parse the comment. 'Tainted? You mean poisoned?'

'Tainted. Touched. I can taste it in the crayfish.'

Silk grimaced his disgust. *Gods. She actually eats the ghastly things?*

Koroll swept an enormous arm to the south. 'The Kanese have not left.'

'No, they haven't.'

'Why haven't they?'

Now Silk blew out a breath and hugged himself; it was damned cold here on the flats with the plains wind whipping him. 'Well,' he began, tentatively. 'I suppose they want to defeat us.'

'Exactly,' Koroll affirmed, pleased.

'There is ice on the flats and the frogs are sleeping,' Liss added. She shot a hard glance to Koroll. 'It has been a long time since the frogs slept this deeply.'

Silk looked from one to the other. *These are our mystical aids? Hood help us. What a damned waste of my time.* He clapped his hands together to warm them. 'Well, thank you for that state of the frogs report. We'll keep it in mind.'

'Yet the Kanese are not the real threat,' Koroll rumbled to Liss as if Silk hadn't spoken.

'That chance is shadow slim,' Liss answered. 'None would bet on that.'

'Yet clearly some have.'

The old woman's laugh was harsh. 'A standing wager that none have survived.'

'What are you two going on about?' Silk demanded, quite offended at being ignored – he was, after all, completely unused to it.

Liss turned her gaze directly upon him and he was almost shocked by the attractiveness of her deep brown eyes. *The eyes of a very lovely woman.*

She looked him up and down then pointed to Koroll. 'He speaks of the meddler in shadows. But I say that one's chances are too low to concern anyone.'

'Chances of what?'

'Survival.' She waved him off. 'Now go. Give our news to the Protectress.'

He set his hands to his hips. Who was she to send him scurrying off like a messenger boy? He shrugged; it was all too bizarre. Sleeping frogs and a taint in the water? 'Very well. I will go. But do not expect to see me again.'

'Really? How sad. You make my day, my pretty, pretty boy.'

Silk sighed, then bowed, sweeping an arm in a courtier's farewell. 'I would rather kiss the crayfish, Liss dear.'

She was cackling with laughter as he picked his way off the mudflats.

* * *

Two days later, at sunset, Dorin settled alone into the ruins of a burned-out cottage just east of the city walls. Kanese cavalry watched here during the day, while at night torch-bearing columns walked patrols. He waited and watched, hoping Pung would take the bait. Personally, he wouldn't if he were in a similar situation. But that was too easy to say – he wasn't the one who'd lost everything and gone on the run.

Far into the night, long after he'd given up hope, the golden predawn light revealed movement on the wall: a shape slowly descending. Dorin eased himself to his feet and carefully approached. From cover, he recognized the monochrome outline of Gren, now on the ground, shaking the rope and peering upwards.

Another shape descended. Dorin waited, tensed, glancing about – was there to be a double-cross? The second figure was the squat and powerful figure of Pung. When he touched the ground, Dorin straightened and approached. Both men stared, motionless: Gren sweaty and panting, his gaze restless; Pung's eyes slitted in calculation.

Dorin tossed a small pouch to Gren. 'For your trouble.' It struck his chest and fell to the ground. When he stooped to pick it up, Pung's hand darted out to his neck, jabbing, and the man collapsed. Pung ran, headed for the maze of outlying ruined cottages and farmhouses.

For a time Dorin peered down at the still form of Gren, stabbed through the neck, then he collected the pouch and turned to follow

Pung's trail. He jogged easily along, enjoying the chill clean air, so different from the city. It promised to be a clear day; good for a hunt.

He shook timbers and pushed tottering walls to chase the man out of two hiding holes and urged him out of the township. Dorin followed him east through the overrun fields, on towards copses of trees that lined the north shore of the Idryn. A famous ancient stone bridge, he'd heard, lay somewhere east of here. The Kanese probably had it garrisoned.

Best to get the fellow before he sought refuge. As he jogged along he eased his heaviest throwing blade from its sheath under his left arm.

His quarry was stumbling now, exhausted, his shirt dark with sweat down his back despite the cold. He was babbling and sobbing as he staggered along. The stiff grasses, laced with frost, sliced at both men's legs as they jogged.

Dorin adjusted the grip of the weapon, blade backwards up his wrist, and drew back his arm just as a keening shriek tore the air above, making him stumble in shock. Pung, too, nearly fell, staggering sideways. Yet the dark shape that lanced from above did not miss. Talons spread wider than any hand-width clenched on the man's head, tearing, and Pung howled, hands going to his face.

Immense wings buffeted the air and the huge predator opened its curved talons, rose. Pung tumbled to the ground and Dorin slowed, his arm falling.

Then Pung climbed to his feet, weaving and turning, and Dorin winced, looking away from the lacerated ruin of the man's face, the blood dripping down the front of his shirt. He staggered off, blindly, numb with shock no doubt, and the dark shape circled above, falling once more.

The King of the Mountains struck again, knocking his prey down with the force of his blow. The predator hunched above his fallen victim, wings spread, beak darting and tearing. Pung howled and fought, shrieking. Dorin slowed to a halt. He sheathed his knife.

How long Pung writhed and screamed Dorin did not know, but it seemed a long time. Bones snapped in sharp cracks and flesh tore, ripping. Eventually the prone shape stopped flinching with every jab of the knife-like beak, and the great predator settled down to feed.

323

Dorin stood for a while, his breathing easing. The cold wind chilled him. He reached under his collar and withdrew an object on a leather thong – a bird's foot complete with its talons. He studied it for a moment before tucking it back into his shirt, and then he turned away and started jogging back to the city.

Chapter 18

THE MID-WINTER HAD PASSED YET THE CENTRAL PLAINS OF Quon Tali still lay gripped within an unnatural frigid chill, which troubled the Sister of Cold Nights deeply. The glacial frost was not of her summoning. It reeked of another Realm, and another kind, one she knew well and considered her cause. The extravagant and unpredictable Jaghut.

The preternatural cold drew her to the wall of the Inner Round, to a section overlooking the Idryn. It was still the thick of night, just before the gathering of any predawn glow. A cloying mist had gathered in the low-lying quarters and now smothered the entire course of the river. It was no natural fog – it had been summoned from Omtose Phellack, the wellspring of Jaghut magery, and it hid things.

Even as she watched, the Li Heng guards next to her squinting at the mists, oblivious, shapes came easing down on to the river's surface and formed up into ranks, waiting.

Her breath hissed from her at the scale of the puissance expended to bring this about. The river's surface frozen overnight. A road to the entire city now open to the Kanese.

It was a bid to end the siege and it was unfolding before her eyes. A gambit she could counter now in the simplest of manners. A few words to any guard; a summons of one of the city mages; a call to arms. Any of these could end the throw before it could be made.

Yet she did none of them. She remained quiet, her breath pluming, her chest tense. For she had sworn a vow to K'rul not to interfere. And in return for that vow he had promised her that she may one day reach her goal – a goal that had eluded her for untold centuries. And so she waited, watching, while the fog coiled and thickened and the basso creaking and groaning of the ice increased.

* * *

Iko shuddered in her full-length mail coat. Despite the thick aketon underpadding, the surcoat and the fur cloak, the iron still bit where it happened to touch flesh. Not only was she frozen here on guard next to the river, she was also profoundly uneasy. They were nearly within bow range! It was outrageous. No prior king of this dynasty had so endangered himself. Yet here he was. Chulalorn the Third, encircled by his bodyguard, watching his plan unfold from the shore of the frozen Idryn.

When she had been told the river was iced over Iko had scoffed. Who could believe such a thing? Yet here it was beneath their feet, clear flat ice like a pond's still surface, while the river flowed onward unimpeded just what? Two feet beneath? It was sorcery, and the name connected with it made her flesh crawl.

She flexed her grip on the cold coiled wire of the whipsword and clenched the other fist to her belt. Wincing, she tested the state of her ankle yet again. Every sister had been gathered for this mission and she'd been granted a brusque session with a harried Denul healer. Around her, all the Sword-Dancers who'd travelled north with the king now scanned the thick scarves of fog about them, uneasy, while within their circle the king stood with his generals, relaying orders and receiving reports.

Not only did the name behind this sorcery trouble her; the very unleashing of the tactic worried her. For it was a truism of all the treatises on warfare and strategy that she'd read: just as the sword is answered by the sword, so too is sorcery answered by sorcery.

And the Protectress was a byword across the continent as a sorceress beyond measure.

What could Chulalorn be thinking? Was he discounting those old reports as lies, propaganda? And if Shalmanat should answer this in kind, what could she and her sisters possibly do to protect him?

The ranks she could just discern through the unnaturally thick mist now began moving forward. They were advancing along the river's course from the east and the west simultaneously, as she understood the king's plan. They would march onward, ignoring the Inner Round and the other nested circles, to lay claim to the palace itself. Once the palace and the inner sanctum were taken the city would, in effect, be theirs.

Unfortunately, this meant dealing with Shalmanat. And Iko had more than a suspicion of who would be handling that confrontation.

So long as Chulalorn remained here, as far from the fighting as they could keep him, she would breathe as easily as she could. And so she continued flexing her grip to warm her hands, shifting her feet, and scanning the damned blinding fogs.

*

Silk was walking a patrol of the north Central Round wall. He was checking on the installation of siege weapons, catapults and onagers mostly, on this second to last defence before the palace grounds. The commander of the section walked with him. She was an older career officer who, from her obvious familiarity with the requisite engineering, had no doubt come up through the ranks.

He felt at ease with this one: the woman was secure in her rank and competence and obviously cared nothing for Silk's own putative position in the hierarchy of influence surrounding Shalmanat. She was also far older, close to retirement age, and so treated Silk as the mild inconvenience of a visiting dignitary come to inspect the works.

Progress in said works, unfortunately, appeared painfully little. 'Few are fully installed,' he remarked to the captain.

She took it all in her stride, her hands clasped behind her back. 'We are short of everything, sir. Timber, rope, dressed stone, general supplies. Even labour. Especially labour.'

'The city is full of citizens.'

Quite heavy and squarely built, the woman pursed her thick lips. 'Starving citizens who can barely lift a hammer.'

'I understand. Do what you can.'

'Of course.'

Shouts sounded from the base of nearby stairs and the captain frowned her irritation. 'What's this?' she called down.

'Some drunkard full of fight, captain,' a trooper answered. 'We'll send him off to dry out.'

Silk stepped to the edge of the catwalk and squinted down

327

into the shadowed street below. 'Wait! What does he want?'

Silence. Silk looked to the captain who shrugged her apology. 'Answer the man!' she bellowed.

'Ah – he says he has a message, sir.'

Silk waved his acceptance. 'Let him up!' the captain called.

As far as Silk knew he'd never seen the disreputable fellow before. His hair and beard were tangled and wild, his clothes practically water-repellent in their greasiness, and he obviously hadn't washed in a decade. He leered soddenly at Silk. 'Pretty boy.'

The captain raised a thick arm as if to throw a back-handed blow. 'Show some respect.'

'Message for the pretty boy,' the derelict repeated, and he gave an exaggerated wink to Silk.

Silk eased the captain's arm down. 'From who?'

'Ah – that'd be from whom.'

The captain's arm came up again and Silk made no move to lower it. '*Whom*,' he sighed.

The man straightened, gave a mocking salute. 'Message from Liss for the pretty boy.'

Silk waited, then sighed again. 'And the message . . . ?'

'River's frozen over.'

Silk stared, nearly uncomprehending. The captain scoffed her disbelief. 'That's impossible. Never in living memory has it frozen over.'

Silk thought of all the warnings. The hints and the predictions. Utter certainty hit him like a wave of dizziness and he nearly toppled from the wall. He pointed to the captain. 'Ready barricades along the shore! Do it now!' And he pushed past the foul-smelling messenger for the stairs and took them two at a time.

The very quiet of the mist-choked predawn streets that he passed gnawed at Silk's impression of certainty. How could it all be so calm? Why hadn't he noticed any magery? Thinking of that, he raised his Warren as he jogged along then sent a portion of his awareness ahead, questing and sensing. He detected nothing. Nothing at all.

Yet this reaffirmed his impression of warning. For in the past, whenever he'd happened to have his Warren raised near the river, he'd always sensed the alien aura of Liss. That alone was the main reason he offered her any respect – though it was thin and dispersed, and ancient-seeming, it was yet strangely powerful, seemingly everywhere.

And now it was gone. Or hidden. Disguised by magics obscuring the river. Obscuring, more importantly, what was going on along the river. He slowed, listening. Had he heard something? He cocked an ear, straining.

Noises came wavering to him through the dense drifting fog. The sounds raised the hackles on his neck and sent chills down his arms. The clash of weaponry and the yells of fighting. He ran on.

*

Someone entering his room awoke Dorin. Keeping himself completely motionless he opened his eyes a slit then relaxed: it was one of Wu's lads. The boy lifted a foot to kick the cot but Dorin spoke up. 'I'm awake. What is it?'

The lad jumped backwards then swallowed, half bowing. 'The river's frozen, sir. And the Kanese are invading!'

Dorin leaped from the cot. '*What?*'

''S true! I swear it!'

Dorin was pulling his gear on. 'I believe you. Where's Wu?'

'In his rooms.'

'Good.' Dorin waved the youth off and ran for Wu's quarters.

He found the young mage engrossed as usual in his drawings and shadow-staring. He wondered, briefly, whether the fellow ever slept at all. 'The Kanese have frozen the river and are invading,' he announced. 'Heng might fall.'

Wu did not look up from his sketching. 'I know.'

Dorin halted. He rested his hands on the parchment-strewn table. 'What do you mean, you know?'

The mage continued brushing with his charcoal stylus. 'I mean I've been aware of their Warren manipulation for some time now.'

'And you said nothing?'

The young mage peered up, blinking. 'Should I have?'

'Well . . . yes.'

'Why so?'

'Well . . . because I'd like to know what's going on, dammit!'

'Ah. Very well. I shall endeavour to keep you informed in the future.'

'Thank you very much.' Dorin straightened from the table, adjusted his baldrics. He picked up a drawing. It appeared to be a study of some sort of squat angular structure. 'What is this, anyway?'

Wu snatched the parchment slip from his fingers, snapping, 'It's not finished yet.'

'Not finished yet? You've been at this all winter.'

The mage tapped the charcoal stick to his lips, refreshing a black stain there. 'I can't quite *see* it clearly enough yet.'

'See what?'

'Shadow, of course.'

'I figured that out. I mean what, exactly?'

'If you must know,' Wu began, loftily, 'these are things I have glimpsed within Shadow.'

'Hunh. Well, are you coming or not?'

The mage narrowed his already beady eyes even further. 'Coming? Coming where?'

Dorin couldn't believe the fellow's obtuseness. 'The invasion! The Kanese!'

Wu waved him off. 'It matters not to me. However,' and he raised a finger, 'it would serve us better if Chulalorn did win . . . all the easier to unseat a usurper, and so on.'

'Easier to—' Dorin studied the fellow as if he were mad. 'You're not still going on about taking the city, are you?' Now he raised a warning finger, which he quickly lowered. 'If you fill these kids' heads with such impossibilities and they get hurt . . . I swear, I'll come for you.'

Wu waved him off and returned to his sketching. 'I believe you were going . . . yes?'

Dorin picked up another drawing.

Wu tried to snatch the slip away but Dorin evaded his hand. This sketch was framed in a rectangular outline and featured a dense dark tangled mass of writhing shapes. Dorin turned it this way and that. 'I don't think much of your execution.'

Wu darted out from behind the table to yank the parchment from his fingers. He pinned it to a timber next to dozens of other such sketches.

'You sure you don't want to come?' Dorin asked.

Wu sat heavily, frowned at the page before him. 'Quite.'

'Suit yourself.'

Dorin left to search for Rheena. He found her in the main common room where many of the lads and lasses ate and slept. He waved her over. 'Keep everyone locked down. This has nothing to do with us.'

'Yes. I've called everyone in already.'

'Good.'

'And you?'

'I'm going to keep an eye on things.'

She tightened her lips in disapproval, but nodded. 'Careful. And Wu?'

'His head's up his arse. You'll have to organize a defence here in case troopers come looking for trouble.'

'Looks like someone will have to.'

'Thank you.' He dashed from the cellar as she was saying something else, and didn't quite catch it.

*

Silk came across Hengan troops defending a hastily raised barricade of overturned wagons and heaped warehouse bales and wooden crates thrown up across a major access to the riverfront. From the fallen and the wounded being treated it was obvious that they had seen some action, but there was no fighting at the moment. Silk called for the officer in charge and was joined by a young sergeant-at-arms.

'Why are you not attacking?' he demanded.

The young officer flinched at his tone. 'They are far too many, sir.'

'Then why aren't *they* attacking?'

'Don't know, sir.'

Silk climbed the barricade, squinted into the heavy layered fog. 'What's going on? What could you see?'

'They've formed shield walls defending the shore, sir.'

Defending? Holding the river? Why do that when the streets lay open before them? He fought to penetrate the hanging mists but couldn't be certain of anything. There was one way to illuminate the situation, but doing so would open him up to retaliation from whoever was behind this astonishing magery. He could get squashed for his trouble. Still, whoever was manipulating these forces on such a scale . . . he or she must have their hands more than full. It might be worth the risk. He readied his Warren. 'Keep your

331

eyes open,' he told the sergeant. 'Tell me what you see . . .'

He raised his hands, summoned his energies, and sent a stabbing shaft of light streaming down and across the width of the river. He was too busy concentrating on his manipulation to study what the flash revealed. It lasted one instant and he immediately grabbed the sergeant's arm and pulled him down with him. 'What was there? What did you see?'

The young fellow was blinking in the dark. He started, hesitantly, 'A series of defences assembled against major accesses. Like outposts. But the majority were on the move – ranks marching west past us.'

Past them? West? Deeper into the city? Why pass by unsecured sections? They could be cut off. It went against all military strategy that he knew of to expose one's forces like this.

His thoughts went to the city centre. The governing quarters, the palace and the Inner Sanctum, and his breath fled from him. Gods of the city! *Unless one were making a throw for the seat itself.* Why waste the lives of hundreds, nay thousands, in messy uncertain street-fighting when in one clean stroke one could take control of the city entire?

He staggered from the sergeant, horrified by the vision. They meant to take the palace. They mean to take . . . his gaze shot to the tall single spire of the one tower rising into the night sky above the sanctum. *Shalmanat!*

He turned and ran without any explanation, any word.

'Sir!' the sergeant called after him. 'What do we do? *Sir!*'

The clash of battle echoing through the streets as Silk approached the Inner Round both reassured and dismayed him. It reassured him that he was right in his guess, yet he wished he hadn't been. He did not even slow as he passed through fortified Hengan positions to enter a contested main thoroughfare that led to the nearest gate, which was held by Kanese infantry.

Even as he ran, crossbow bolts hissing about him, he raised his Warren and cast ahead of himself without restraint, without thought of what was to come. The infantrymen and women massed in the gate shouted their pain as they dropped weapons and pulled at their armour, falling and writhing. Smoke wafted up carrying with it the stink of burned flesh.

He ran over them where they lay crying in agony, the smoke

rising from them. In such an extravagant manner, flaying all about without any holding back or husbanding of his energies, he reached the palace grounds. Here city elites still held the main structure of the Inner Temple. These ranks let him through and he jogged for the throne room.

He found Shalmanat cloistered within, together with Ho. He halted, panting, exhausted and drained. 'Good,' he managed, hardly able to speak. 'I caught you before you withdrew. We can escort you from the city, of course.'

The Protectress wore a long cloak of thick wool that she drew up about herself at his words. 'I'm not going.'

Silk looked to Ho for support; the man shrugged his helplessness. He offered, 'We cannot hope to hold them all off . . .'

'How long until dawn?' she demanded.

'Perhaps an hour.'

She nodded at this. 'Until then. One hour. Can you do that?'

Ho and Silk shared a glance. 'We will try,' Ho answered.

Her nod turned fierce. 'Do that. Give me the dawn, gentlemen.' She backed away, waving them off. Ho bowed, and when Silk would not move he took his arm and drew him on.

'Where is she going?' Silk demanded.

'I believe she is withdrawing to the tower.'

Silk was appalled. 'There's no retreat from there!'

Ho would not release his arm. 'Then she will surrender – if she must. Now come with me. We have a great deal of work ahead of us.' Silk allowed himself to be led off. Not that he had any choice as Ho was immensely strong, but he did not resist. 'What does she mean, the dawn? What does she want with the dawn?'

The shaggy, unkempt fellow was grim. 'I'm afraid we'll find out. For now, we will hold, yes?'

Silk yanked his arm. 'Yes. You can count on me.'

Ho released him. His thick lips drew back from his blunt teeth in a humourless smile. 'We shall see.'

*

Fascinated, Dorin traced the route of the invading Kanese infantry along the Idryn's course, past river gates and on to the city centre itself. From rooftops he watched while hastily thrown up barricades and strongpoints were overrun by an irresistible Kanese advance

333

to the Inner Round. It was as if the Idryn itself had overflowed its banks, he reflected.

Here, resistance hardened. Elites with nowhere to retreat held out in narrow gates and chokepoints. Yet the overall current could not be held back. The Hengans were already outnumbered by the Kanese and more were flowing in from both the east and the west.

The end, it appeared to Dorin, could not be disputed.

And in consequence, it lost its interest for him. No need to linger here. What he wondered now was who was in charge of the operation. The slim possibility that Chulalorn himself might be down there somewhere directing the campaign was intriguing. That was worth investigating. And so he waited, and watched, and eventually he spotted a runner, a messenger, and shadowed the young woman as she jogged off along the river's length.

He lost sight of her a few times in the thick curling scarves of fog – burning off now with the coming dawn – until her trail led him to the river gate of the Inner Round. Here she joined a mass of Kan Elites, all picketed and readied, guarding a position in the shadowed murk of the gate.

Chulalorn himself, he was sure.

And he became certain when he glimpsed the bright shimmer of the fine mail coats of the Sword-Dancers, in double ranks, encircling the centre.

His target, come into the open. Yet now would be the worst time, with everyone alert and readied. The very opposite of the proper moment, in point of fact. And so he sat back in the shelter of a chimney on a tall building overlooking the Idryn, content to watch, and evaluate.

Shortly afterwards the crackle of grit on the rooftop alerted him that he was not alone. Knives readied, he peered round the brick chimney to see a lone figure standing on the roof's edge, also studying the secured position on the Idryn. He relaxed, lowering his weapons; it was that strange foreign female mage.

'Greetings,' she called without even turning.

He straightened and approached. 'We meet again.'

'Indeed. It would appear we are creatures of habit.'

'Why are you interested?'

'This . . .' she gestured airily to the night, 'manifestation interests me.'

'I know its author.'

She turned to face him directly, one brow arched, and again he was struck by her alien appearance: not obviously inhuman, but not quite right in the proportions of the eyes, cheekbones and chin either. 'In truth? Now you interest me. Who, or what?'

'A Jag. Named Juage.'

'Ah. He is here. We have met . . . long ago. Strange that he should lend himself to such an . . . errand.'

'He said he was compelled. That the Kanese kings have a hold over him.'

'Indeed.' Now her face hardened, the jaw tightening and the lips compressing into nonexistence.

'He is a friend?'

'Not as such. He is Jaghut. They are a strange kind, I admit. Alien to you, but admirable – in their own manner – to me. Their current . . . well, *situation* concerns me. It is something I have sworn to look into.'

'What will you do?'

'Nothing. As yet. But time is running out.'

Dorin eyed her, wary. 'What do you mean?'

'I mean that dawn is coming and these Kanese have yet to subdue the Protrectress.'

'And so?'

Her mouth drew down once more. 'There may be a confrontation that would be dangerous for everyone.'

Dorin was shaken by the strange woman's certainty, but there was little he could do at the moment. 'Well, thank you for the warning.'

The mage turned to the east and raised her chin to peer past the forest of roofs that lay all about them. 'We shall see soon enough.'

*

Silk used his forearm to push up the sword thrusting at him and drew the soldier's belt-knife with his other hand to thrust it straight up under the man's chin. He staggered backwards as the man fell. Ten of the Hengan palace elites remained standing with him in the corridor. A new wave of Kan infantry rounded the corridor to crash shields with the elites. Silk reached for one shield and took hold; with direct touch he easily heated the bronze to glowing and the fellow howled, falling away as he pawed at the burning piece. A javelin thrust at him but, as he had experienced only a few times before, with his Warren elevated to its fever pitch everything seemed to be happening in slow motion. He jerked his head aside and thrust in past the weapon to take the fellow in the eye. This brought him to the front and now he was forced to bat aside several short sword thrusts, turning one to break a wrist, slashing a forearm, and leaving the dagger in a last one's throat.

The rush ended with this last Kanese to fall; the elites were panting, seeing to minor slashes and cuts. Silk fell back as well, hands on knees, trying to catch his breath. 'That's all for now,' he managed.

'We'll hold,' a female elite said. 'What with you taking half of them.'

A mass of approaching footsteps announced another rush of Kanese.

He signalled for a withdrawal to the next inner set of doors.

Crossbow quarrels whisked past them and the Hengan elites ducked, holding their wide shields behind them. Silk merely backed away, dodging the missiles – as before, with his Warren sizzling about him he could see their paths the way a shaft of light crosses a darkened room. Yet he was past spent now, weaving, his grasp upon Thyr slipping. He ducked behind the palace guards to lean against a wall, his head spinning in exhaustion.

The bellowing and laughter of Koroll in full battle fury echoed up the corridor from another wing of the palace. Beneath that growled the constant low roar of Smokey's Telas flames and a kiln heat emanated from the main audience hall on the left.

Silk nodded to the surviving men and women of the guard to hold these doors. Only one last set remained behind: those that led to the throne room itself, their last retreat. He was worried that the Kanese may yet get behind them and cut them off, and wanted to check on all the other accesses and corridors. Yet he couldn't bring himself to leave these guards. Earlier this winter he knew he would have, without a moment's thought or misgiving, but something had changed. Men and women had died for him. They'd given up their lives. He'd seen it up close, felt their blood on him. And it had changed him.

He could admit that now. A damned late time in one's life to come to any sort of empathy with others, but there it was. Some never came to it at all.

He nodded encouragement to the female guard, who was clutching her leg where she'd been stabbed through. 'No need for much marching now anyway,' he told her with a wink.

She smiled through her pain and gestured up the hall. 'You needn't stay, sir.'

Sir. First time anyone in the palace had ever called him sir.

'We promised the Protectress the dawn, and we'll give it to her.'

'Yes, sir.'

'They're advancing as a solid column behind shields,' the forward guard warned everyone.

Silk roused himself, pushing from the wall. 'One more time . . . I will try to hit the shields again.'

'Thank you, sir.'

The elites readied themselves in ranks, two across. Silk, at the rear, reached for his Warren once more and found it frighteningly distant. In attempting to raise it he fell forward on to the rear of the soldiers ahead of him and they supported him, alarmed. Their mouths moved but he heard nothing above the roaring in his ears as he pushed himself further and harder than he ever had before. Finally, almost beyond conscious volition, he grasped it and lashed out at the shields and armour of the column now pushing against the elites before him.

When his vision returned he found himself being dragged backwards between two wounded palace guards. They sat him just inside the threshold of the throne room and swung closed the double doors and barred them. He struggled to his feet. 'What happened?'

'They bought us some time,' one told him.

Neither of these was the female guard he'd spoken to. He nodded, accepting this just as they had. 'Hold here,' he told them. 'I'll check on the others.'

In answer they saluted him as they would a commanding officer. He returned the salute then jogged, or rather staggered, to find the others. The main entranceway to the throne room he found choked with thick black smoke and radiating a deadly gasping heat – somewhere within that maelstrom Smokey appeared to still be holding.

The crash of stonework sounded from further along and here he came to Mara, panting and sweaty amid a cloud of dust. The hallway before her lay choked by a collapsed heap of fallen blocks and crushed masonry. In the east he found Ho and his contingent of guards retreating towards the throne room. Next to him, Koroll held a barred set of doors. From far off came a resounding booming, as of heavy blows. He headed back to his position.

The two guards were pressed against the doors, which jolted beneath a steady pounding. 'They've brought up a timber or something,' one shouted to him.

Mara joined them. 'Not long now,' she muttered, sourly.

Silk glanced back to the frail filigree door that led to the tower stairs. Hardly defensible, that.

The pounding stopped. Silk listened, wondering what was going on, and dreading some new stratagem.

'Hello inside!' a voice called, its south Itko Kan lilt quite strong. 'Is anyone there?'

'What do you want!' Silk bellowed with more defiance than he felt.

'You have fought well in defence of your ruler. Chulalorn sends his respect. But it is over now. Surrender and we will allow you to keep your lives.'

'And what of the Protectress?'

'Exile.'

The heavy stink of smoke wafted over them and Silk turned to see Smokey approaching. His clothes were scorched and blackened, his hair smoking.

'What guarantee can you offer?' Silk demanded.

'The word of our king. From one ruler to another.'

'I don't trust Chulalorn,' Smokey growled to Silk, his voice so hoarse as to be near soundless.

'Give us your answer,' the voice warned. 'If we must break in we will slay all we find within.'

'Give us time to put it to the Protectress,' Silk called. He whispered to Smokey, 'How long until the dawn?'

'About a quarter of the hour,' Smokey mouthed, near silent.

'Give us half the hour!' Silk called.

They waited in silence for the Kanese response. After a brief time the officer answered, 'Very well. The half-hour. But no more.'

Smokey offered Silk a wink, but Mara scowled, still dubious.

Dorin was crouched on his haunches on the rooftop, listening to the general panic gathering in the streets below. He'd heard some fighting up and down the river's shore, isolated pockets mostly; the majority of both sides appeared to be waiting. The Hengans were exhausted, numbed by the invasion, and too heavily outnumbered to mount a counter-attack. The Kanese infantry remained firmly in ranks, obviously under orders to defend their frozen highway through the city.

Yet as time passed the fog was lifting, and Dorin wondered whether the sorcerous ice would melt with it. The Kanese would have to get moving if that were to happen.

'It looks as if they've won,' he opined to the female mage with him. 'What is your name, if I may?'

'You may call me Nightchill. And do not be too hasty.'

'The Hengans aren't even fighting. They're beaten.'

'They are certainly shocked and demoralized, I agree.'

'What is everyone waiting for?'

'Word from the palace, I imagine.'

He grunted his understanding. They believed the palace taken, the Protectress fallen. Why fight and die when the cause was lost already?

The citizenry, however, was not quite so pragmatic. Panicked mobs surged through the predawn streets and the Hengan guards now found themselves embroiled in crowd control.

'It has taken too long,' Nightchill suddenly announced, and Dorin peered up at her. She was studying the one tall structure of the city – the tower that rose so very high over the palace. He straightened to examine it as well. Something strange was happening there at its peak. 'What . . .' He realized that what he was seeing was the dawn's oblique golden rays striking the parapet at the tower's viewing terrace. 'I don't see what . . .' He stopped again as an answering glow seemed to echo the rays. It was swelling, burgeoning, even as he watched. 'What—'

'Get down!' the woman yelled, and, displaying astonishing strength, she yanked him to the ground and bent over him.

Blazing ferocious radiance stabbed at his eyes and he groaned his pain, pressing his fists to his face. A deafening sizzling like the crackling of ten thousand fires erupted next to him and he howled, certain he was being burned alive. The very building shook and juddered beneath him as in an earthquake as something came grinding and thundering through the city. '*What is it?*' he yelled to be heard.

'Elder magics,' the woman shouted, next to his ear. 'Kurald Liosan, unveiled.'

'Who?'

'The Protectress, of course.'

The unveiling, or summoning, pounded onward in a sizzling growling as of a waterfall in flood rushing past his position. It went on and on, swelling, burgeoning until he was certain he was about to be consumed, then slowly, relentlessly, it passed, or faded, or he'd become deaf and blind from the punishment. He dared a glimpse by pressing the backs of both hands to his eyes and sliding them apart until he could glance between fingers. The vision dazzled and awed him. Twin sizzling firestorms of light each as tall as the sky. Each pounding its way along the river – one rolling to the east and the other to the west. Even as he watched, the westward one overran a huddled column of Kanese soldiery. Within the waterfall of brilliance they seemed to blur, dissolving, eroding. When the avalanche ground onward all that was left behind was a smear of ash and soot upon the rotting ice.

The power unleashed here appalled him. How could they counter such might? In short, they could not. No one could. Surely there must be an equivalent price to be paid for such expenditure. He was frankly rather overawed; he thought he'd known power before. But all he'd seen to date paled to insignificance next to this display. Nothing, it seemed to him, could ever be the same again.

Nightchill helped him up and he stood blinking as a glow filled his vision. The thundering roar scoured onward, but distant now. 'I can barely see.'

'It should pass.'

'What *was* that?'

'She has sent the fires of Liosan, or Thyrllan, down the river. Many are slain. I must go now.'

Dorin blinked his weeping eyes. 'If you must.' She did not answer – no doubt she'd left already. Blind, feeling as if he'd been roasted over a fire, he sat again then hissed, yanking his hands from the roof: the bricks had burned his palms and he could just hear them all about him, crackling and ticking with the radiated heat of the sorcerous onslaught.

*

The instant the brilliant light burst upon them Iko and her sister Sword-Dancers were blinded with everyone else. Blinking, hands extended, they encircled the king and began edging him back along the river, heading for the Outer Round. Panicked officers and messengers pulled and clutched to reach Chulalorn, but the Sword-Dancers, unable to tell who was who, fought everyone off.

Iko raised her forearms to her eyes and squinted through the narrow slit between. In this manner she could just make out some sort of towering pillar of pure white coruscating energy that appeared to be heading their way along the river. It was like a waterfall of light pouring down from the sky. It came pounding the surface, consuming all in its path. White flames licked its edges, turning blue and orange as they annihilated building fronts and wharves. The tumult was swelling to an unendurable howl.

She watched the approaching wave of brilliance wash over entire companies on the river. They dissolved in the fiery light like wisps of tinder in a furnace. Even wagons brought down on to the ice disappeared in the onslaught. It was as if they were ground to dust before her straining, aching eyes.

A closer company, an entire column, now sought shelter under wagons and she shouted to them to run but her voice was utterly inaudible even to her. The immense tower of light ground onward and the wagons disappeared even as the soldiers beneath squinted into the light as if seeking enemies. 'No!' she shrieked, but they vanished as if snatched away, blown to shreds of ash like leaves in a windstorm.

She tore her gaze away, blinking, dazzled by after-images. She set her lips to another Sword-Dancer's ear: 'We must flee the river! Now!'

This one nodded her understanding and passed along the order. Together they worked to redirect the shuffling protective circle, searching for any route up the shore. Feeling their way along, they came to a stone stairway leading up from the frozen surface. An access for washing perhaps, or collecting drinking water. They began slipping through two by two up the stairs. The king, held low among them, now struggled against such disrespectful

341

treatment. They held him down despite this, hands at his back and neck.

One of their number found a narrow alleyway bound by two tall brick buildings and they withdrew between, the king hidden.

The punishing roar had swollen to a landslide thunder and the stabbing radiance was somehow even brighter. Its intensity lanced Iko through her squeezed shut eyes. She imagined that this was what standing at the edge of an avalanche must feel like.

The crescendo roared up level with them. Tiles and bricks, shaken loose from above, came crashing down. A reflected kiln heat made her pull her hands from the brick wall as the stone burned too hot to touch. The waterfall thunder continued past like a mountain tumbling down a slope.

Eventually, in the relative silence, she straightened, tentatively. After a time, Yuna sent a sister off to investigate. A hot wind now blew from the river, heating Iko's face. It carried the stink of smoke, and of roasted flesh.

By the time the sister returned Iko's vision had half cleared, though floating dots of darkness obscured it. The sister was pale, her face strained, even sickened. She said nothing, only shook her head. Yuna gestured them onward to the west. They headed that way, restraining the king among them like a prisoner.

Luckily for them, Iko thought, no counter-offensive was in motion. The Hengans, guards and citizenry alike, appeared just as stunned by this unprecedented cataclysm as they. She and her sisters reached the inside of the Outer Round wall where it marched down into the Idryn and only then did it come to her that they were on the north shore. They would have to cross the river.

Mist obscured the wide expanse, but not the thick heavy fog of before. These hanging tendrils resembled more the steam of heated water. Yuna pointed a sister ahead and she eased out on to the frozen surface. It gave slightly beneath her feet, and water now coursed above the ice sheet, but it held. Yuna gestured two more to attempt to cross. They set out keeping a good few paces between them. Soon the mists swallowed both. Some tens of heartbeats later came a high whistle – one of their 'all-clear' signals. Yuna sent out two more.

In this manner, some few at a time, they crossed the river. Chulalorn went in the middle of the crossings, with guards established behind and before. Iko was among the last pairs to go.

It was unsettling in the extreme starting out. The ice sheet creaked and groaned beneath her feet. The mists obscured her vision – it was as if she were walking through clouds. Her footing was unsteady as the surface gave and yielded like soft clay. Her boots were sodden by the river water now coursing over the rotting ice.

Shapes emerged from the mists around her and she jerked her sword free, nearly falling as the ice rocked beneath her. They were Kanese regulars retreating from the city centre. They came as ghosts, some singly, some in groups, limping, supporting one another. All bore horrific wounds. Their surcoats and leather armour hung blackened and burned, some still smoking. Their faces and hands were cracked and scorched, their scalps bare, the skin broken and bleeding. The only sound was a low constant moaning as of intense agony dulled now by numbness.

Iko stood still as the army of near dead limped past her, sloshing and splashing through the shallow water above the ice. We've been destroyed, she realized. How many hundreds – nay, thousands – had they lost here this day? They no longer possessed a viable force. They had no choice but to retreat and hope to limit whatever damages may follow from this disaster.

It was as Hallens had feared. Sorcery had been answered by sorcery – power had drawn power. The sudden need to slap Chulalorn across the face for all these deaths washed over her like a physical force and she suppressed the urge with a shudder. He could not have known. Yet he should have.

She slogged onward, splashing, her feet now sinking into the softening dough-like ice sheet. She made the southern shore, pulled herself up the still frozen mud slope by yanking on tall grasses, and joined the waiting party. Here she dutifully took her place in the defensive circle about the king and they made their way south to the encampment.

Yuna was already giving orders to her sisters regarding the logistics of the retreat while the king said nothing. He staggered along at their centre, his brows crimped in complete incomprehension, his gaze on the ground, seemingly as stunned and numbed as his soldiers themselves.

*

The eruption of power that came with the dawn had knocked Silk and his fellow mages to the floor. He and Smokey had been

343

negotiating for more time with the Kanese officer; the man had had enough and his troops were once more pounding on the doors. The doors were yielding and he and Smokey were readying themselves though Silk knew he had nothing left to give – he'd exhausted himself drawing upon his Warren and could barely summon it.

All that changed, however, when the stupendous swelling of power blossomed from far above and all five mages dropped their own preparations to peer upwards in awed astonishment. Even when Silk couldn't imagine it possibly intensifying any further, the upwelling continued to grow and surge. It doubled, and redoubled again, utterly beyond any capacity he had dreamed any mage could possibly channel or sustain.

The unthinkable might drove him to clutch his head in agony; dimly, through blurring vision, he glimpsed Smokey falling to his knees. He fell as well, only just catching himself on one hand. His head hanging, he saw red droplets pattering to the polished white marble flags beneath him and he touched his nose to find warm wetness there as blood flowed freely. Somewhere, out of his vision, Mara screamed in wordless protest.

A renewed burst of puissance drove him to the floor where he lay, hardly able to hold on to his consciousness. He felt as if he were pinned beneath the mightiest cataract in the earth and all those tons of water were pounding down upon him. He lost awareness while holding his head to keep it from bursting and giving vent to his own soundless scream.

He awoke being shaken, and turned over to blink upwards at the giant Koroll. The other mage handed him a cloth rag. 'Thyrllan . . .' Silk groaned.

The giant nodded. 'A dose of the might of the Tiste-kind.'

Silk wiped the thickly caked blood from his nose, mouth, and chin. He slowly and carefully pushed himself to his feet. Dizzy, he peered about, squinting. Smokey and Mara were rousing themselves; Ho stood aside, waiting, appearing little the worse for their exposure to the cataclysmic power. Silk felt a surge of resentment for that.

He staggered over to the Hengan mage. 'We must go to her now.'

Ho nodded and headed for the tower door. The long climb up

the circular stairway was an agony for Silk, because of his weakened condition, and because Ho insisted upon leading the way, and lumbered like a dozing bear. He examined nearly every step as he went; Silk fumed, urging him on, hand cradling his head. 'Would you hurry?' he hissed for the twentieth time.

'She either lives or not,' the older mage answered gruffly. 'We must be careful – who knows what stresses this has placed upon the structure here.'

Indeed, the white marble of the tower was too hot to touch, and still seemed to glow, but all the more reason to reach Shalmanat. Silk growled and resisted beating his fists on the man's broad back.

After four more turns of the tight climb Ho announced, 'We are close.'

When Silk reached the step he found a stain of black flakes upon the polished white stone. He touched his fingertips to it and brought it to his nose. He smelled the iron tang of dried blood.

It was a thread of spilled blood descending the heated steps, drying as it came. Silk pushed the wary Ho onward with a hand on his back. They found the uppermost door open a fraction and Ho pushed it wider. His breath eased from him in shock and Silk pushed past him. The room was black with soot as from a ferocious fire; the furnishings lay as ash scattered about the floor; the very stone around them ticked and crackled with cooling; the radiating heat drove Silk to shield his face.

She lay half out upon the viewing parapet, naked, her clothes a mere dusting of white ash. Silk ran to her. A sickle blade of some white stone lay next to her. Silk was sickened to see blood still running from each wrist, a trickle now. She had slit both.

He tore his shirt and set to binding the wounds. Ho crouched next to him. 'Sacrifice . . .' the man murmured, awed. 'I'd thought it sorcery but I was wrong. This is a religious invocation. The cult of the Liosan. Elder Light.'

'Shut up and help me.'

'I will carry her.'

Silk acceded to that – the man was far stronger than he.

Gently, the burly mage eased her up to cradle her in his arms. Blood formed dried black trails from her nose and mouth. Perhaps the movement pained her for she stirred then, blinking, and Silk was shocked to see the orbs of her eyes all deep crimson – shot through entirely by blood.

Ho started down the stairs, but Silk lingered. He leaned out of the parapet, careful not to brush the steaming hissing stone, and peered over the city. Mist still obscured most of the river and streets, but from what he could see the ice sheet was breaking into slabs and these bumping their way down the flow. The streets remained empty, citizens and soldiers alike stunned and shocked by a demonstration of power utterly unprecedented in any living memory.

Of course now he understood. Now he could see her reluctance. Not only the awful weight of this loss of life, but the possible cost of her own.

And from this point onward she had certainly lost the love of the people here. In exchange she had won their fear.

Steps sounded behind and Smokey joined him at the viewing terrace. He too glanced down, then shifted his gaze to him. 'We have to salvage what we can.'

Silk nodded, his mouth dry. 'Yes.'

Smokey started down, gesturing him to join him.

*

She found him lying in the shallows. A steaming husk hardly recognizable as a human, or humanlike, form. Smoke still plumed from his pitted scorched flesh. When she lifted him up he whimpered like an animal in agony. She raised her aspect to cool him while she held him in her arms, and though he was twice her size she carried him easily, like a child.

His breathing slowed as her power worked upon him and his eyelids fluttered open. Recognition focused within his tawny gaze. 'Sister Night,' he whispered, his voice breaking. 'I sensed an Azathani near. I did not know it was you.'

'Quiet now, Juage. Do not strain yourself. I have you.'

His cracked bleeding lips spread in a wry smile. 'Still a friend of us foolish kind, are you?'

'Hush now.'

She carried him to an abandoned cottage and set him down within, then went to the gaping doorway to keep watch. They were on the south shore, not that distant from the Kanese encampment, but she did not think them at risk – not now, at any rate.

346

There ought not to be any more patrols or excursions coming out of that camp. Not any longer.

Instead they were no doubt breaking everything down in a panicked rush, loading their wagons, carts and mules and slogging off southward before any vengeful Hengan sally could be organized. Chulalorn himself had probably already departed, bundled into his personal carriage, surrounded by his cavalry elites and bodyguard.

If he'd survived, that was. Her impression was that he had. His kind usually did.

Perhaps it was the heat, but a light drifting rain began to fall across the landscape of trampled fields and burned-out crofts and sheds. It was a rain black with soot and smoke, as if the very sky had burned. Later in the day Juage stirred, groaning, and she came to sit cross-legged, studying him. The stink of roasted flesh had no effect upon her. His eyes opened once more and he turned his head to regard her. The light rain hissed down around them, dripping from gaps in the broken slate roofing.

'Why do you involve yourself in this stupidity?' she asked.

'Sadly, I have no choice. The grandfather found me and released me. In return he asked for service to his family. Unfortunately, I had no idea he possessed such an extremely large family.'

Sister Night eyed him, dubious. 'Come now, Juage. A Jaghut compelled by a human?'

Juage attempted a shrug, and hissed in pain. 'Well . . . very nearly. In truth I am here for the same reason as you. Power draws power, does it not? Something is going to happen here and I know you sense it also.'

Sister Night nodded, conceding the point. 'In any case, you were a fool to move against the Protectress.'

He shook his head, wincing as the burned flesh of his neck split apart. 'Come, come. You did not expect this either.'

She nodded again. 'True. But you must have known she was Liosan . . .'

'Yes, I sensed that, of course. But a priestess of the cult? Able to unveil true Kurald Thyrllan?' His tone turned chiding. 'Admit you were as shocked as I.'

The barest of smiles pulled at her severe mouth. 'I was . . . surprised by the . . . extravagance of it. I admit that. No doubt she is in even worse shape than you.'

He chuckled. 'No doubt.'

For a time she listened to the rain drifting down in thin sheets. 'And now?'

'Now I must play my role – and keep an eye on these lands.'

She pursed her thin lips. 'And if Chulalorn were not to have survived the attack . . . ?'

He shook his head once more. 'Now, now. Did you not swear not to involve yourself in such matters? And in any case, there is an heir.'

She gave the smallest of shrugs. '*I* made such a vow, yes.'

His amber eyes narrowed to slits as he regarded her. 'Sometimes I suspect you are even more devious than T'riss.'

She rose. 'I have no idea what you are talking about. But what I can say is that since you are so incapacitated I suggest you rest here for a day or two to recover.'

He nodded thoughtfully. 'I suppose I do need to recover my strength.'

'Indeed. Take care, then. Farewell – for now.'

'And fare you well, Sister Night.'

She bowed and stepped out into the thin misty rain.

Chapter 19

WHEN SILK AND SMOKEY PUSHED OPEN THE DOORS TO the entrance hall they found it deserted. The remaining Kanese troops had fled. Though exhausted, the two mages headed south. Down at street level the carnage was infinitely worse than appeared from the distance. A chain of fires burned all along the course of the Idryn, on both the south and north shores. The Protectress must have performed a miracle in containing the coruscating power of the river, but warehouses and tenements crowded its banks. Many of these now burned uncontrollably and threatened to engulf the city in a storm of fire and destruction far worse than anything Chulalorn had planned.

They made for the walls of the Inner Round overlooking the Kanese-held Outer. They imagined that any counter-offensive would originate from here. A focused assault on a certain gate, or section of the curtain wall. Koroll, Ho and Mara had headed for the worst of the blazes. Mara, Silk knew, would be invaluable in collapsing burning buildings and shifting wreckage, while Ho and Koroll could treat those caught in the flames.

He and Smokey would keep watch against any counter-offensive. Not that he personally expected to be much help as he couldn't do anything with his Warren until he'd had some rest. But he could stamp out panic and rally the Hengan troops. Not that he expected a counter-attack. Not after passing the burned human wrecks who had dragged themselves off the river and now wandered the streets begging for help, or simply mewling in unutterable agony.

Enemy soldiers would normally be cut down without hesitation, but most of the Hengans recoiled from these horribly wounded monstrosities. Silk, too, could do nothing to help when he passed them where they lay reaching to him, or standing motionless in the middle of streets and alleys, stunned by overwhelming pain.

When they reached the Inner Round wall they separated, he taking the right flank, and Smokey the left. Silk found the soldiers all gawking northward towards the Idryn, hidden now within billowing clouds of black smoke. Despite his own fatigue, he roused himself, barking, 'Watch the enemy!' then made a show of pacing off, as firm in his step as he could manage.

Once he had them back at their posts, he kept up a roving review, stopping to ask after any movement from the Kanese. As morning reached towards noon, he took the time to rest at each guard tower. He hoped to reassure them with his presence, though he was under no delusion regarding his usefulness in any assault when in fact he could barely remain on his feet.

He paused at one post for a ladle of water to wash the awful taste of the smoke from his mouth and here he noticed a young Hengan pikeman who kept craning his neck to the north. Silk gave him a look. The fellow touched his forehead. 'Sorry, sir. Did you see it?'

'See what?'

'The flames 'n' such.'

'No, I actually didn't. I was indoors.'

'Like the sun's own glare. The Wrath of the Goddess.'

'The what?'

The lad ducked, touching his forehead once more. 'That's what our sergeant called it.'

'Ah.'

The lad's hands, Silk noticed, were sweaty on the haft of the pike. 'Is she mad at us?'

Silk blinked, quite taken aback. 'I'm sorry . . . mad?'

'Angry, you know. 'Cause we lost the Outer.'

A band of tightness clenched Silk's chest and he had trouble drawing breath to answer. When he spoke there was a strange thickness to his voice. 'Not at all. She's proud. Proud of what you've done. Very proud.'

The lad's brows rose in surprise. 'Really? I don't think we've done so well.'

'Well, you have. That army out there has fought for decades. No city or principality has stood before them. They haven't lost a war yet. But we've held them back. And that's saying something. You can be sure of that.'

350

The young pikeman didn't look entirely convinced, but he smiled just the same. Silk gave him a nod and continued on. As he walked, his hands clasped behind his back, he wondered whether that was even true. And did he really believe it?

He decided that he did. Chulalorn's was a hardened professional army inherited from his father, while these Hengans relied mainly on citizen militia to guard their walls. The city's standing army was a paltry force; by far the majority were labourers, craftspeople, cobblers or shop-owners. They were terrified, out of their depth, yet brave enough to stand the wall. They were of course defending their own; their children, their loved ones, their property. But he would not discount their courage for all of that. What better reasons to fight?

Certainly not at the behest of some self-seeking king or prince. Though sadly that always seemed to be the case. He leaned into a crenel and watched the rooftops and streets of the Outer Round before him. All was quiet; deserted even. Of course the Kanese weren't organizing an attack. It would be outrageous. An insult even, given the sacrifices already made.

Yet he would keep watch. He had his duty as well. And perhaps these men and women would draw some measure of reassurance from his presence – given the horrors of the morning.

Though he was far from reassured.

The Wrath of the Goddess.

He shivered despite the heat of the day.

*

Dorin reached the main avenue leading to the western gate and slowed, short of breath, as he saw no large fires in this district. He walked now, stepping aside from rushing wagons and panicked families dragging their bundled possessions from the devastation. Once the female mage, Nightchill, had left him alone on the rooftop he saw all the many fires starting up along the river's shores, and his thoughts rushed to Ullara. He ran immediately for the western Gate of the Sunset.

The streets were a clamouring chaos of fleeing citizenry stampeding for the nearest gates, all convinced the city was about to be consumed in a raging firestorm. The solid press of their numbers impeded the militia as they attempted to reach the fires. City guards had to resort to beating them from their paths.

Confirming everyone's fears, black boiling smoke hung

351

everywhere and embers fell all about, causing spot fires that people either ran from or fought to extinguish. Through this nightmare of fearful yelling families, Dorin made his way to the caravanserai district. Here he found the buildings, far from the riverside, standing free of any major fires. At Ullara's family barn, Dorin saw what must be her father and brothers on the roof, wielding blankets as they beat out falling embers. The caravanserai district was of course close to the gate, and so the press was intense. But through the milling crowd Dorin spotted Ullara herself. She was sitting by the roadside with a dumpy woman who must be her mother, cloth bundles of their goods about their legs. She wore a wide-brimmed hat and a cloth about her eyes, and she had her arm wound through her mother's.

He did not approach; not when she was with her family. He watched instead from the vantage point of an alley mouth while the solid press of wagons, carts and families on foot shuffled by on their way to the gate.

All through the morning the father and brothers beat at the spot fires with blankets. At times the thick smoke from conflagrations raging closer to the river came boiling over the Inner Round wall to completely obscure them. Dorin tensed then, ready to rush in, but eventually they would emerge elsewhere on the roof, coughing and wiping at their eyes. They dared not let up as their roof was made of wooden shingles and was particularly at risk.

A neighbour's corral and barn caught fire and Dorin joined the helpers fighting that blaze. By noon the volunteers had managed to contain it, but the property itself was completely consumed. He rested with them, crouching, elbows on knees, as ladles of drinking water made the rounds. The afternoon sky above their heads glowed with leaping flickering orange and lurid red playing across the underside of the churning black smoke.

Ruefully, Dorin wondered whether the Protectress had just succeeded where Chulalorn hadn't despite all his efforts.

The informal firefighting crew Dorin had joined was called to another blaze in a block nearby and they ran there. Someone threw a bucket of water over him as he passed and the shock of the cooling water was a rejuvenation.

This building was a large rundown tenement. Dorin didn't give a damn for the property itself, but the fire could pass along to neighbouring buildings and become a menace to Ullara's barn. He and a few others helped clear the rooms. Dorin burned his hands badly doing this, opening one flame-ridden passage, but he wrapped his hands in rags and kept working. Again, the building was a total loss, but they managed to contain the blaze.

At dusk he sat on his haunches alongside the empty street – all those who wished to leave had long since gone – exhausted, his clothes blackened, sweat-stained and scorched. His crew laughed and joked among themselves. A flask and a pouch of snuff made the rounds.

He sat with his blistered hands outstretched, hardly able to clench them, and cursed himself. Look at what he'd done! His working tools, his hands, and now just look at them! And for what? Some rundown shithole whose owner had probably torched it on purpose?

He shook his head at his stupidity. An old woman passing down the line stopped before him and took hold of his hands. He tried to yank them away but she had an amazingly strong grip. She started kneading in some sort of stinking animal grease. He gazed up at her, startled, as the pain quickly subsided. She wore multiple layers of skirts, stank of the river, and puffed on a long-stemmed clay pipe as she worked on his hands.

She moved on to another wounded fellow down the way. This one had had the misfortune of catching an ember in his eye. Dorin held up his hands, staring at them in disbelief. The blistering had subsided and the raging crimson burning was fading even as he watched. He knew High Denul healing when he felt it and he snapped a look to her.

She was grinning behind her pipe as she worked on the next fellow, and she offered Dorin a wink.

'What's your name?' he called.

She grinned all the wider. 'Liss it is and that is my thanks. A favour for a favour.'

He sat back and flexed his hands, still bewildered.

The crew was breaking up as fresh volunteers arrived. Dorin pushed himself to his feet and staggered off, utterly spent.

*

Once they had escorted the king to his quarters, Iko looked round and saw that the full fifty of the current bodyguard were present now, all posted within and about the complex of tents, and she judged him more than secure. She sought out Yuna, their acting commander.

Once she had her attention she bowed and spoke. 'Perhaps a few of us could go to offer help.'

Yuna shook a negative. 'We have our duty here.'

'Just me, then.'

'No. We have our job and it is here.'

'With respect – the king will hardly be secure if the camp goes to the Abyss around him.'

Yuna scowled her irritation. She raised her voice to the gathered sisters: 'Anyone wish to accompany Iko?'

Rei stepped forward. 'I will go.'

Yuna snorted a breath. 'Very well. We can certainly spare you two.'

Iko clenched her lips, saying nothing. She nodded to Rei and they pushed through the tent flap. As they jogged north to the river, Iko could not help but watch her sword-sister curiously. Finally, she asked, 'Why did you come with me?'

'I didn't come with *you*. Help is needed – that is plain.'

Iko nodded, chastened. 'Of course. You're right. It's just that no one else . . .'

Rei sighed. 'Do not judge them. It is easier to remain in the pavilion. To use duty as an excuse to avoid all else.'

The stream of sufferers thickened as they neared the shore. Iko felt overwhelmed by the severity of their injuries. Where to start? How could she make any difference? Their cries tore at her heart. She knelt to one fellow sitting among the rushes, apparently catatonic, his back a great mass of seared flesh. 'Let me help you.' Rei, meanwhile, jogged on to another knot of wounded.

The soldier peered up at her, uncomprehending, blinking sleepily. She took his arm and raised him up. His breath hissed from him in an agony beyond words. She began walking him to the infirmary tents. 'This way. Almost there.' Tears ran from the man's eyes, so great was his pain.

She came across others – some fallen, others standing dazed – and urged them to go with her. More emerged from the darkness and coiling mists like wandering ghosts. She did her best to cajole them along towards the infirmary.

These tents she found to be a mass of humanity. One could hardly take a step without having to avoid some wounded trooper, and the awful stink of burned flesh almost drove her out. She laid her charges down and sought a healer. In one of the brighter lit tents she found a woman treating a soldier who was being held down by four burly assistants. This bonecutter, a mechanic rather than a Denul healer, was using a knife to dig away cloth and armour that the ferocious heat of the sorcerous attack had fused into the flesh of the man's neck and chest.

At Iko's entrance the woman snapped her an annoyed glance then shouted to soldiers nearby, 'Get her out of here!'

Iko pushed away a trooper's arm. 'I am here to help.'

The grey-haired woman snorted as she bent to her patient. 'There's a first. Earlier this night one of your sisters came charging in demanding I leave this work to attend to the king. You are not on a similar errand?'

'No.' Iko watched, fascinated despite her horror, because the man the healer was working on was still awake as she dug into the weeping bloody mess of his neck. He writhed in the grip of the assistants and clenched his jaws on a folded strip of leather jammed into his mouth. 'Is there nothing you can give him?' she asked. 'No palliative?'

'We are out of everything. The Denul talents are merely stopping the bleeding. This is salvage work. All we can do at this point.' The woman glanced up, gave her an evaluative look. 'You are quite skilled with a sharp edge, I assume?'

'Yes.'

The woman nodded curtly. 'Very good.' She looked to one of her assistants. 'Set her up on another table.'

An assistant came to her and gestured for her armour. He helped her expertly as she quickly undid her belts and ties, and she realized that he must have had a great deal of practice in getting soldiers out of their armour. He led her to a wooden table covered with fresh blood and pieces of cut cloth and leather. Next to the table stood a long tray on which lay a collection of bloodied tools, including wicked-looking saws and the sharpest, slimmest blades she had ever seen.

The woman came to her wiping her bloodied arms and hands on an equally bloody rag. 'Name's Haral.'

'Iko.'

'Okay. I'll be sending you the donkey work. Amputations, mostly. Frees me up for the more difficult stuff. Are you all right with that?'

Iko's mouth had suddenly gone stone dry. She nodded and managed a faint, 'I'll try.'

'Very good.' Haral nodded to the assistants at the door flap. They ducked out and returned carrying a wounded trooper. As Iko watched they slid him on to the table. His arms had been scoured to the bone by burns and Iko looked away, blinking back tears. Haral studied the patient while nodding to herself.

'Okay. Take the right at the elbow, wrap the left.' She returned to her own work.

Iko was still blinking back tears, trying to swallow to wet her throat. The assistants began cutting away the blackened cloth and the crisp burned leather armour from his arms. One handed her the blood-slick grip-end of one of the thin blades. 'Cut through down to the joint,' he murmured, 'then use a saw.'

She nodded her readiness and they tensed their grips on his arms, neck, and legs. She took hold of the right forearm and drew the blade across the pale inner flesh of the elbow.

The man convulsed in agony, screaming, arching his back and writhing. Iko flinched away, horrified, and dropped the knife. One of the assistants retrieved it and returned it to her. She cleaned it by wiping the blade down the edge of the table. 'Sorry,' she whispered, almost crushed with humiliation.

The assistants merely indicated their readiness and she bent to the trooper once more.

She froze, then, as she saw him staring up at her.

'Please don't,' he begged her in the barest of whispers. 'Don't . . .'

An assistant jammed a piece of leather into the patient's mouth, told Iko, 'There are many waiting . . .'

She swallowed, nodding, and set to work. The man screamed and howled behind the gag. He arched his back and writhed the entire time she cut at flesh and sinew. He sagged into unconsciousness only when she set the saw to the ligaments at the joint.

No sooner was she finished with the limb than the assistants slid this fellow away and replaced him with another – this one with a shattered leg. She pointed to the knee and one of them nodded an affirmative. She set to work again.

So it went through the rest of that day and on into the dusk. Iko had stopped thinking by noon and by the evening she was a mere automaton that could only wait, numb and exhausted, to be told where to cut and what to do. At twilight the bonecutter Haral came to her and said something. Iko merely stared, uncomprehending, her ears brutalized by all the screams. The older woman had to finally pull the knife from her hand and set the surgery assistants on to her. They steered her gently to a wash station and filled a ceramic bowl with warm water before returning to their work.

She stood staring down at the water for a time before she understood, and then she dipped her hands in up to her elbows and began to rub. She rubbed and scraped and scoured harder and harder. The water became so crimson and clouded she couldn't see her hands. When she drew them out they looked like someone else's. She was happy with that thought, and dried them on a rag.

Only now did she realize that her long loose shirtings hung from her heavy with blood and gore. She reached over her shoulder and carefully drew the shift over her head, then tossed it on to a pile of similarly bloodied discarded clothes. She stood in a thin chemise and linen trousers, which hung blood-bespattered from the knees down. She peered about and found her gear where it had been set aside, carefully folded. She picked it all up, the whipsword on top, and headed out.

Straightening from the tent flap she had to pause, dizzy. She drew in deep breaths of the cool night air. 'A moment!' someone called from within, and the bonecutter Haral emerged. She held a small cup in her hand. 'Tea.'

'Thank you, but I don't really drink—'

'This isn't your regular tea, child.' Haral extended it to her.

Iko accepted it. 'My thanks.' She sipped the hot drink and blinked immediately, her eyes widening. 'What is this?'

'A special recipe. Gets me through days and nights of straight work. Can't use it beyond that, though. You start seeing things.'

Iko downed it, grateful. 'My thanks.'

Haral nodded, her arms crossed. 'The lads say you're a wonder with a knife. Ever thought of training for a cutter?'

Iko shook her head. 'No. It is too . . . painful.'

The older woman nodded, acknowledging the point. 'You get used to it.'

Iko held out the empty cup. 'I must get back. I've been gone too long.'

Haral took the cup. 'Well, thank you. Really.'

Iko bowed her head and turned back to the royal pavilion.

Chapter 20

DORIN DRAGGED HIMSELF BACK TO THE ABANDONED HALF-ruined house Wu and his gang were currently using as their headquarters. He thumped down the steps to the cellars and entered Wu's rooms to find the fellow still puttering among his drawings.

He pressed a hand to his brow and shook his head at the other's seeming obliviousness. 'Did you even—'

'Feel it?' the Dal Hon interrupted without looking up from his work. 'Yes. Of course.'

'Well?'

Wu raised his head, blinking. 'Well what?'

'What are you going to do?'

The lad's appearance as an old man made him look gravely annoyed. 'Do? What is there to do? What is done is done.'

Dorin wanted to yell that there was a damned lot to do, but understood that this would be lost on the fellow. He shook his head instead, and peered about. 'Do you have any fresh wine here? I've been roasted alive.'

Wu pointed his charcoal stick to a table. 'You smell like it. Help yourself.'

There was water on the table but Dorin did not trust its freshness and so he poured a glass of wine and sniffed it, but couldn't detect anything beyond the smoke he carried on him. Shrugging, he sipped while leaning back against the table and studying the hunched mage. 'Where is everyone?'

'Looting what they can.'

Dorin nodded, then jerked, having nearly fallen asleep on his feet. 'Ah.' He drank the wine. 'What I mean is, doesn't this finish your stupid plan to take the city? You can hardly match that.'

Wu waved his dismissal. 'I doubt she can pull another one of those from her sleeve.'

Dorin raised a brow. Painfully glib, but probably accurate. He watched for a time while the fellow squinted at the fluttering shadows the single candle cast upon the bare wall. Then he asked: 'When will we go back?'

His back to Dorin, the little fellow stiffened as if caught in the act, and slowly turned. He was grinning, which only made his wrinkled face appear even more menacing and unpleasant. He winked. 'Soon. Those hounds remain a problem.'

'There must be a way past them.'

Wu pointed the charcoal stick at Dorin. 'I like the way you think, my friend. Yes, there must be a way. But what?' He added, muttering to himself, 'Oleg's notes held no hints . . .'

'What was that?'

Wu straightened, fluttered his hands among the papers. 'Nothing. Nothing at all. No.' He paused, eyed Dorin critically. 'The question is, what are *you* going to do.'

'Me? What do you mean?'

Wu gestured expansively. 'Now is the time to strike, is it not?'

Dorin felt his brows rise. Indeed. He hadn't considered . . . Still, kicking a man when he was down. It felt . . . dishonourable, although that was a sentiment his old teacher had worked hard to beat out of him. He considered the proposal then nodded. 'Now would seem the best time.'

'Exactly. Let us go, before he withdraws.'

Dorin glared. 'What, *you*? Not after last time!'

Wu held up his open hands. 'Not to fear. That assault flayed Juage alive. I felt it. He is no longer a threat.'

Dorin considered his wine, finished it. 'Very late tonight, then. I must rest first.' He sniffed at a soot-stained sleeve. 'And bathe.'

'Later, then.'

*

Though she was exhausted and strangely numb – almost as if she were sleepwalking – Iko cleaned herself further then dressed properly to check in on the king's command tent. She desperately needed a rest, but she really should report first. She entered the tent and was adjusting the hang of her mail coat and the

359

fold of her belt when Yuna called out, 'Where have you been?'

Iko raised her gaze and did not flinch from the other woman's haughty glare. 'Helping.'

Yuna grunted her indifference and turned away.

Iko joined her sisters at guard. The king was in conference with his generals round a table strewn with maps and parchment notes. As always she tried not to listen, but she could not help an ever-growing disbelief as it dawned upon her that the king was in the midst of organizing an attack.

'The easternmost gate on the north wall, then,' Chulalorn reaffirmed, and he pressed a finger to a map. 'They will not be expecting the attack.'

'No, they will certainly not,' one old general muttered, and the king eyed him for a time before he allowed a servant to pull a new shirt up one arm.

'The north shore, my king?' another enquired.

'The boats being built remain hidden in their buildings, do they not?'

'Yes. Some have been damaged. But most remain.'

'There are certainly enough now,' old Mosolan added, and the king glared once more.

Though outraged by what she was hearing, Iko hid a grin at the old campaigner's barbed comments. Mosolan had served the current king's grandfather and father, and now the third had no choice but to endure his censure.

They debated the details for some time before deciding upon a predawn launch. Chulalorn waved them out. 'You have your orders.' The generals bowed and withdrew.

Alone now but for her sisters and the servants fussing over the king, Iko felt no such devotion to service as Mosolan and the other generals. Perhaps it was her fatigue, or the memory of all the soldiers she'd just worked upon, but she could not stop herself from stepping forward and clearing her throat. 'My king ... surely enough has been done. We should withdraw.'

Outraged, Yuna hissed for silence.

Chulalorn turned to her; he was quite astonished at being addressed. He waved a ringed hand indulgently. 'My child, this is not your concern. Be still.'

Iko was appalled. '*Concern* . . . My king, haven't enough Kanese died serving you here? Perhaps if you were *concerned* you would see how high a price has been paid already.'

Chulalorn's hand fell from his beard. The servants froze, staring. The king snapped his fingers and Yuna appeared before Iko, glaring, furious. She pointed outside. 'You are confined to quarters,' she hissed, 'until I have dealt with you.'

Iko looked to her sisters for support but saw only disapproval from most, while a few showed a sad sort of mute sympathy. She bowed stiffly to Yuna, 'As you order,' and marched from the command tent.

In her quarters she threw herself down on her cot, pulled her writing tablet on to her knees, and considered her future. Her armour rested on its stand next to the cot, looking rather like a decapitated soldier. The image made her head swim and she rose to take down the armour and roll it up. No one she knew of had ever resigned from the royal guard before. It was unheard of. Tantamount to betrayal. What, then, could she do? Years of service to a man for whom she had lost all respect? Yet he was a king – it was not her place to judge. What if this new attack should succeed? Who was to know?

Returning to her cot, she slammed her stylus to the tablet and hung her head. She would request transfer to the teaching halls in the capital. She should be allowed to serve there, instructing new generations of sisters.

Yet could she stomach even that? Sending child after child into the service of men or women who without a thought would sacrifice them to their own overweening ambition?

No, she could not see herself meekly doing that.

She pressed her fists to her face, rocking for a time, and felt hot tears on her palms.

After sitting through the twilight she came to a decision. She reached up and drew a hidden blade from the rear of her jerkin just behind her neck. She examined the bright silver blade in the dimming light. The Short Blade. The last resort of honour – should there be no hope.

Well, she could see no hope now. She had lost the devotion that had been the foundation of her service and had sustained her all this time. She'd cut it away slice by slice in a bloody tent. She held the blade tight in both fists before her, considering its edge.

Yet he was the king, and she had been born into his dynasty, as

361

had her parents and their parents before them. She slipped the weapon home in its sheath. Very well. She would serve – but only because it was her place in the world. Gone was any blind devotion; hers would be a cynical eye cast upon the throne.

A gaze something like that certain light she'd seen in Hallens' eye. Only now was her old commander's tone clear to her. The stern cheerlessness that had mystified her before. Had she too experienced this sudden revelation – seen her world turned upside down in an instant?

Had she seen the possibility of it in her?

She set the writing tablet aside. If Hallens could endure such service, then so too would she. Let Yuna come and rage at her; let her sisters scorn and disapprove of her as they would.

She now had the strength not to care at all.

* * *

Slipping through the lines of the Kanese encampment this night was as nothing compared to the last time. In fact, Dorin was at first quite surprised to find these southerners making no effort to retreat. No defences or tents were being broken down, though the outermost ring of pickets had been abandoned. Probably they no longer possessed the troops to maintain it.

Of his companion's whereabouts on this run he had no idea. Which suited him fine. The young mage was somewhere out among the tents pursuing his own bizarre set of priorities. Thinking of that, Dorin realized this was his first work of any sort with a partner, if it could be called a partnership when he was still so uneasy with the informal arrangement. In truth, it didn't feel like any sort of arrangement at all.

More like a temporary alignment of aims and goals.

He didn't wholly trust the fellow, even now. He was just too erratic and unpredictable. Frankly, Dorin rather suspected the fellow was mentally unstable. He was glad not to have him underfoot while he pursued this mission.

The second ring of pickets Dorin eluded easily; these men and women were obviously still quite shocked and traumatized by the cataclysm that had taken so many of their brothers and sisters. He gained the complex of tents and pavilions that constituted the royal precincts. Here he padded between tents, listening. From his earlier visit, and from questioning Wu, he knew that the king's private pavilion lay to the rear of the main command tent. Having identified it, he was now manoeuvring to find a sheltered route to its side.

He moved in a crouch, knives readied, stopping and starting, constantly straining to listen and sense about him. The night was still quite chill and his breath plumed; he damned the odd crystals of ice that crackled beneath his soft leather shoes.

After some doubling back he settled upon a path to the hanging cloth side of the royal tent. He waited, crouched on his hams, listening. No guards appeared to be posted at this particular gap, but he would have to be wary, as a random patrol was always a possibility.

He padded forward and slit the nearest rope cinch of a peg then rolled beneath the lip of the heavy canvas cloth. Within, he froze, listening and peering about. He lay behind a travel chest and rolls of what appeared to be extra carpets or heavy blankets. He lifted his head a fraction to peer over the piled rolls of cloth, and saw that he occupied a room in the large pavilion given over to hanging rails of richly embroidered clothes, a gold-filigreed set of scaled armour on a stand, and several chests that presumably held more clothes. He had known he would have to explore to find the king, but he had not expected to find himself in the royal dressing room.

He rose and padded to the hanging of lighter cloth that served as a door. Peeping out, he saw that he was indeed next to the bedchamber, and here was a figure in a long loose shift of pale green silk, kneeling in prayer before an altar. His long midnight black hair was unbound and hung now down over his lowered face, but Dorin recognized Chulalorn.

He stepped out and the man stilled, revealing that he'd sensed him. He turned, slowly, looking up, and Dorin knew he had his target.

'So you have finally come,' the man said, nodding to himself.

Dorin moved to keep both the king and the entrance to the bedchamber in view. 'Finally?' he said.

Chulalorn lifted his shoulders in a shrug. 'Let us say no king or queen of Itko Kan has died in their sleep. It is either war, or treachery.'

Dorin edged to the hanging, listened, and heard nothing. 'So this is treachery,' he said.

'How much is she paying you?' Chulalorn asked. 'I'll double it.'

'You know I can't accept that.'

A twist of the man's lips. 'So, a professional.' He glanced aside, nodding as if to another party, but Dorin had heard nothing and so did not shift his gaze for that fraction of an instant as the king threw what he'd been concealing in his hand. Dorin twisted his shoulders aside and threw at the same moment.

The king's dagger missed but Dorin's did not. A single leap took him to the man to clamp a hand over his mouth to stop any scream or choking gurgle as he fought for breath. He held him there, hand over his mouth, and edged the blade sideways to widen the wound. He let the king down gently as he spasmed, then withdrew the blade. Bright heart's blood coursed down the front of the pale green shift in a thick wet stain.

Finally, the man stilled and Dorin drew his hand away. He straightened, reached beneath his jerkin and shirts and plastron to a leather thong about his neck and drew it out. He pulled off the object there, the bird's foot, and dropped it on to the crimson field spread across the king's chest.

Movement at the hanging spun him round: a woman in fine mail armour, kneeling, head down in deference. 'My king . . .'

As she lifted her head Dorin threw again. The fine thin blade took her in the eye and she jerked, slumping. Rapid movement beyond her revealed that she was not alone.

He shifted to the tent wall aside of the entrance as two more armoured women burst through. Long thin weapons sliced the air about them in a hum. He reached to his baldric and threw at both. One thin blade struck home in a throat, but the other woman flicked the dagger aside with a snap of her flexing longsword. 'Aid! Assassin!' the woman bellowed, and that keen blade now whipped out at him.

He threw himself down, sweeping, and caught the woman's lead foot, taking her down. When she hit the ground he fell on her with a dagger to the neck.

Yells now and more pounding footsteps. Cursing silently, he leaped to the tent wall and slit it open, running.

Guards were converging from all sides; he was at the centre of the entire damned encampment. He felled a number of closing troopers and ducked through more tents, but the circle was closing about him.

Then a great brassy animal howl brought him up short and he clamped a hand to his panicked heart – oh, by all the gods no! But for him, who had heard the titanic bellow so close, it was not quite as earth-shaking as it should be and he realized what he was hearing.

If there was alarm before it was a full-blown riot now. Dorin stepped out into a mass of functionaries, servants and courtiers, all running about to save goods or themselves. Tents were on fire – or looked to be – and thick black smoke coursed in the alleyways between the tents, obscuring everything. The night was also suddenly a good deal darker than he recalled it being.

A hand plucked at his sleeve. 'This way.'

Dorin yanked his arm free. 'I know the way!'

'Just helping.'

'I don't need your help.'

'It would appear that you did – getting caught and all.'

He ducked into a tent. 'I wasn't caught. And anyway, what were you up to then?' A chest was thrust at him, which he took. 'What's this?'

'A war chest . . . literally.'

'Chulalorn's?'

'Ours now.'

Dorin could just make out the shifting shadowy figure of Wu at the rear of the tent. 'Could you cut through here?' the mage asked, pointing.

Dorin tucked the rather heavy chest under one arm. 'What, you don't have a knife?'

'Have to keep my hands free. And you have more than enough for both of us.'

Dorin slit the canvas. 'What about that stick of yours? Where's that?'

'Comes and goes.'

Wu slipped through and Dorin heard him say 'Oh dear'.

A patrol of armoured Kanese troopers occupied the intersection of alleyways. They squinted at them through the smoke.

Another of the great brassy hound's bellows now burst forth, erupting from the gap to the left where a dark shape could be seen advancing through the coils of black smoke, slathering, eyes at a man's height, glowing a golden amber.

The troopers charged the beast.

Wu took off running in the opposite direction, his robes hiked up over his skinny dark shins. Dorin followed, covering the rear. Together they reached the outer picket line and Dorin was fascinated to watch how shadows now swirled about them in obscuring snaking banners.

'We are not in Shadow?' he asked, a touch alarmed.

Wu puffed as he jogged along, obviously not used to such exertion. 'No. I am using it – but we haven't entered the Warren.' The mage drew out a handkerchief and daubed his sweaty brow. 'It is done, I assume?'

'Yes.'

'Very good.'

'Good?'

'Your reputation shall grow now, my friend.'

'A poor reason to kill a man,' Dorin mused.

Wu fluttered a hand. 'He let his pride rule him and suffered the consequences.'

'His pride?'

Wu halted, a hand at his chest, blowing out great breaths. 'Well, he should have withdrawn.'

'Now you're some sort of military tactician?'

'Oh, no. Just much more . . . indirect.' He pointed north with his walking stick, which had suddenly appeared in his hand. 'Not the river again. I absolutely refuse.'

Dorin headed east. 'Don't worry. There are boats here that the Kanese have abandoned.'

Wu pressed a hand to his chest once more. 'Well, thank Togg for that, my friend. Dunking in water is bad for your health, you know.' He looked Dorin up and down, frowning at what he saw. 'Though you could use a wash . . .'

*

When the alarms sounded Iko leaped from her cot, pausing only to jam on her boots and yank her sword free. She burst from her tent wearing her linen trousers and shirtings to find the encampment in an uproar of confusion, and immediately made for the king's quarters. Soldiers ran to and fro seeking any enemy; servants and court functionaries ran past her, intent on escape.

A blood-chilling howl burst forth then from the quarters nearby and after halting, stunned, she ran in that direction. She found many who had seen the beast, but none had caught it as it rampaged about the alleyways and tents. She gave up the pursuit and ran back to the king's quarters.

Here her sisters were turning away all but the highest of commanders and court officers. She pushed through to Chulalorn's private quarters to find the king laid on his bed, bloodstained and quite obviously dead. So too were three of her sisters, Yuna among them.

Iko searched among her feelings and found that she mourned the loss of her sisters far more than that of her king.

Next to the bed stood Mosolan in a loose cotton shirt, his long iron-grey hair unkempt about his shoulders. The man was studying something small that he turned this way and that in his fingers. Iko nodded to her assembled sisters and crossed to him. 'What is this, sir?'

He extended it to her. 'This was set upon his breast by his killer.'

It was a bird's foot, but not just any bird: a large bird of prey, complete with talons, now stained in blood. 'What does it mean?'

'A badge, or sigil. An announcement. A warning. All at the same time.'

'I did not think the Protectress would have dared.'

'Neither did I.' The general set the foot on to a slip of white silk then rolled it up and placed it in a wooden box. 'You and your sisters will head immediately to the heir.'

Iko nodded. 'Of course. I will inform our new commander.'

The old general raised a greying eyebrow. 'That is you.'

Iko swallowed hard; her glance went to Torral, who glared her resentment. 'With respect, m'lord, that is for the heir . . .'

'As acting regent until the heir's investment, I so order it.'

Iko bowed her head. 'Very good, m'lord.'

'You and your sisters are dismissed. The elites will escort the king to Kan for his funeral. You must go with all speed.'

Iko bowed. 'As you order, sir.' She gestured her sisters out and left with them.

When they reached an outer chamber, Torral turned upon her as she had known she would. 'Since when do outsiders dictate our officers?' she demanded.

'Just until the heir decides,' Iko answered calmly.

'The heir? The heir? Do not talk to me of him!' Torral stabbed her fingers to her chest. '*We* decide. Us.'

Iko merely shrugged. 'Very well.' She raised her chin to the gathered sisters. 'Are we fine with things for now, or need we organize some sort of vote?'

There was silence among them until Rei waved to the exit, saying, 'Now is not the time, Torral – let's just get going.'

Iko raised her open hands to Torral. 'Then let us go.' She headed out with her sisters leaving Torral behind. The Sword-Dancer remained staring after them, her jaws working.

* * *

Word of the tumult within the Kanese camp came to Silk by a messenger, and he returned to the palace. Here he waited with Mara, Smokey and Koroll in the empty audience chamber, their steps echoing hollowly from the white marble pillars and walls. All they knew was that Shalmanat yet lived. They waited for Ho to come out of her quarters, for they had news for him and things to discuss.

Such as the future of Heng itself.

As the night passed, Silk dealt with messengers from the various quarters of the city, all with urgent details of organization. Between times he tried to doze on the marble throne. Heavy footsteps finally woke him and he straightened on the tall chair. Smokey roused himself where he was lying down on one of the stone benches that those seeking audience occupied during court business and nudged Mara to wake her. Koroll emerged from the far shadows.

Ho nodded to them. 'She sleeps. I have numbed the pain. But she is weak – very weak. Too much blood lost. I have done all I can.'

'We have Denul talents here in the city,' Silk objected. 'Summon them.'

Ho blinked at him, appearing completely drained. 'None is as skilled in such matters as I.'

Silk was amazed – he hadn't known that. He inclined his head. 'My apologies.'

Mara cleared her throat. 'We have news. Chulalorn has been assassinated. His army is retreating. The siege is over. The question for us is . . . do we pursue?'

368

Ho absorbed the news with his typical stone-faced calm. He frowned. 'Pursue? Whatever for?'

'They are in complete disarray,' Smokey said. 'We could eradicate their remaining force. Punish them further.'

Ho was shaking his head. 'No need. Who killed the king?'

Koroll spoke up. 'I believe it was our young friend.'

'We don't know that,' Mara objected. 'Why do you say that?'

'Who else?'

Mara threw open her arms. 'It's a wide world . . . Dal Hon wouldn't mind.'

'Why don't we pursue?' Smokey asked, gesturing to the south. 'They have stores, equipment. We need it. We could capture it.'

Ho waved off the idea. 'On the contrary, we should offer help. Perhaps they need more carts and wagons . . .'

Silk barked a sudden laugh at that. '*Touché*, Ho! What a supremely galling insult.'

The burly mage frowned his confusion. 'I was only trying to help.'

'So what are we going to do?' Smokey demanded. 'Let them go freely, without any further cost? Look what they've done to us.'

'Their king is dead,' Koroll rumbled. 'Let them go. It is Heng that needs our attention, not Kan.'

Mara slapped a hand to her palm. 'We have to decide, now. Either way.'

'Ignore them,' Ho said. Koroll grunted his agreement.

'I say we pursue,' Smokey said. Mara pointed to him, nodding. She eyed Silk. 'Well?'

Silk realized that they were all now peering up at him – except Koroll – as he was still occupying the throne. He cleared his throat, rather self-conscious, and considered. Did he really give a damn about the Kanese? He decided that he didn't. 'Let them go.'

Mara glowered, muttering, but didn't challenge him.

'It is this assassination that troubles me,' Ho said. 'She will be blamed. Representatives from the other states will denounce it.'

'What of it?' Mara asked, now pacing in circles, obviously eager to go. 'That and this demonstration of her powers leave her unassailable. No one will ever dare attack us now. We rule the centre of this entire continent unopposed.'

'It is a troubling precedent.'

'We could capture the assassin,' Koroll suggested. 'Put him on trial and execute him for regicide.'

Mara laughed her scorn. 'Oh please. Are you telling me this is something to be upset about? Sons strangle their own fathers for a throne. Daughters poison their mothers.' She threw up her hands. 'If a prince doesn't have paid agents in place to kill his brothers then he isn't fit to rule!'

'All is not so dark as you say, Mara,' Ho objected. He pointed to the throne. 'There it is. Shalmanat is weak. I'm sure Silk is willing to give it up. Take it.'

Silk started, half rising from the seat. Mara laughed nervously. 'Well, I wouldn't take on all four of you . . . Besides, I have no formal claim.'

'Since when has that been necessary?' Ho asked. 'Go ahead – take it.'

She raised her hand in an obscene gesture. 'Go to Hood's path, Ho,' she said, and stormed from the audience chamber. Silk felt a buffet of Warren power and the tall stone doors boomed shut in a crash. Pieces of broken marble facing clattered to the floor.

In the long silence that followed, Koroll offered, 'So . . . do we track this fellow down?'

Ho was staring after Mara. 'Yes,' he answered, distracted. 'We will execute him for regicide to placate the other states.'

Chapter 21

A KNOCK AT THE DOOR WOKE DORIN. HE PRESSED A HAND TO his eyes and groaned. 'What time is it?'

'Afternoon,' answered one of the digger lads.

'Gods! The afternoon? Orders were to let me sleep till dusk.'

'Yes, I know. But Wu's called a meeting. Wants you there.'

Dorin let the hand fall. 'All right. I'll be there.'

'Want tea?'

'Hood yes.'

'Okay. We'll get you some.'

'Thank you.' Dorin swung his legs from the cot and sat up. He rubbed his face then examined his cut and bruised hands. Did he have to personally defeat every dumb thug in the city before they'd come round? He wasn't trained for this sort of fighting; he was a knife-fighter, not a grappler. How many would it take before they'd just wise up? It would all be so much easier if he could just kill them. But that would rather defeat the object of assembling a gang, wouldn't it?

Sighing, he pulled on his low soft shoes and went out to find the meeting. He was handed a tiny glass of tepid tea and directed to Wu's rooms, where the mage kept a sort of unofficial underworld court. Here he found Rheena standing up against the wall. She was in charge of their troop and all the day-to-day running of the territory. She operated out of Pung's old quarters; Wu had obviously called her in for this get-together.

Dorin noticed that she was now dressed in a fine engraved leather jerkin over a loose-sleeved white cotton shirt with black trousers. She gave him a smile and a wink and he nodded in answer, leaning back and crossing his arms.

'Business is good,' Wu called to him. 'And we have most of it.'

He gave the barest of shrugs. Wu's lips pursed and he glanced about to the ten or so hand-picked lieutenants and bodyguards. 'Yes, well . . .' He set his elbows on the table and meshed his fingers. 'I have decided on a plan . . .'

'What is it?' Dorin demanded, wearily.

Wu let his hands fall and shot a quick glare. 'Our problem is that we lack street muscle and enforcers. We can't defeat Urquart one to one. Dorin here can't be everywhere.'

'I agree,' Rheena added.

Dorin agreed as well, but wasn't certain of any alternative. 'So? What's your plan, then?'

Wu raised his hands and steepled the fingers again, then noticed what he was doing and whipped them from sight. 'I've assembled quite the war chest. I'm sure we have far more coin on hand than any other gang. Therefore, I suggest bribery, price-hiking, kickbacks and outbidding. We'll take the market out from under all of them and squeeze them dry. Then we'll bribe or outright buy their followers and muscle.'

'Beat them with gold,' Dorin said.

'I like it,' Rheena said, and offered Dorin a nod of agreement.

Dorin considered, tilting his head and thinking. He had to admit the plan had a real elegance. What he liked was the logic: why subdue everyone when you could just offer to pay them twice as much? Once word got out they'd start trickling in on their own. And when Urquart couldn't meet his payroll . . . well, everyone would just melt away.

He gave his own nod of assent. 'Okay. Give it a shot.'

Wu was obviously disappointed by Dorin's reaction. He raised his brows. 'Well, with that enthusiastic endorsement we are in agreement.' He waved everyone out. 'Enough for now. My partner and I need to talk.'

Rheena jerked a thumb to the doorway. 'You heard the man. Get going.'

'You too,' Wu said, shooing her out. She shot a glance at Dorin who inclined his head to the doorway and she straightened her shirt. 'Fine. I'll be outside, then.'

Once the door was shut Wu turned his attention to Dorin and studied him for a time. He knitted his fingers across his stomach, twiddling his thumbs, and cleared his throat. 'I know how you feel,' he began.

'Oh? You do?'

'Absolutely. This work bores you. You are thinking . . . what now? Is this all there is? What possible challenge remains?'

Dorin raised a brow. 'Really?'

'Of course. And I understand. Really, I do.'

'You do.'

'Certainly. And I have been thinking. Other challenges beckon.' He reached into his shirt and withdrew a flat wooden box.

Dorin jabbed a warning finger. 'Do not talk to me about the godsdamned box.'

Wu quickly slipped it back within his shirt. 'Okay.' He drummed his fingertips on the table before him. His brows rose. 'About Shadow. I think I may have a solution . . . We could return, as you say.'

Dorin, his arms crossed, leaned forward. 'You *think* . . . you *think* you have a solution? You'll have to do better than that.'

'Well, we have to test it. How else will we find out?'

'And this testing . . . it involves us dangling ourselves in front of these daemon dogs, I suppose?'

'Hounds. They're referred to as hounds.'

Dorin looked to the ceiling. 'Whatever you say. No. Not good enough. Go dangle yourself.'

Wu ducked his head and fluttered his fingers among the papers piled on his desk. 'I think we have a greater chance for success together.'

'You mean you have a better chance with me.'

'Let's not get bigheaded,' Wu observed loftily.

'No, let's not.'

Wu stared; Dorin returned the stare. Wu held his glower, his brows lowering. Dorin tilted his head a touch to one side, drew a long slow breath. The silence lengthened between them. He could hear the murmured voices of their crew in adjacent rooms and halls. He waited.

Wu finally pressed a hand to his brow, sighing. 'You are so *infantile*. So be it! Shalmanat, then. We move against her.'

'From what I hear we only have to wait.'

'No. She is recovering.' Dorin lifted a brow. Wu opened his hands as if insulted. 'What? I have paid sources in the

373

palace.' Dorin grunted his satisfaction. 'So, we are agreed, then?'

He was shaking his head, tapping his thumbs to his biceps. 'I don't know. I'm really developing a strong dislike for this place.'

Wu's grey brows wrinkled in confusion. 'Well, where then?'

'I've been thinking about Unta . . .'

'Unta!' The mage threw his hands in the air. 'As I've said: we'd just have to start all over again.'

Dorin sent him a glare. 'We? What do you mean *we*? I can do just fine on my own!'

Wu now held his palms out, soothing, 'Of course, of course. No one disputes that. That is not the question. The question is – what should *we* do?'

'Exactly.' He pushed himself from the wall. 'What should we do?'

Wu merely stared from beneath his wrinkled brows. His tiny ferret eyes darted right and left. Dorin sighed and let his arms fall. 'I'm going to take a walk.' He pulled open the door and headed down the tunnel hall. As he passed Rheena he said, 'I need some air.' She drew breath to say something, but perhaps noted his expression and reconsidered, and nodded him out instead.

He walked aimlessly through the late afternoon, until an errand he'd been considering for some time brought him to the caravan-serai district of the western Gate of the Dusk. He was now slightly anxious, which was almost funny, given what his errand here was, but he felt it just the same. The district was booming now with the end of hostilities; travellers were thick in the streets, and the first of the traders' caravans had arrived from the nearest cities, such as Ifaran and Ipras. Produce was finally out on the stalls and shops. And people had money now that work was easy to find, what with all the rebuilding to be done. The delayed spring rains, now arrived with a vengeance, were cleansing away the lingering stink of smoke. It seemed surprising to him how quickly people could put hard times out of mind and look ahead to future plans. He supposed it was both a strength and a weakness.

Eventually, after much idling and delaying, he arrived at the wide doors of one of the larger stables in the district; that of Ullara's family. In time, the portly fellow he assumed to be her father came to him, harried and busy now with all his new business. 'Yes, sir?' he asked. 'What can I do for you?'

374

'You have a daughter blinded in an attack during the siege?'

The proprietor's brow crimped, troubled, and he frowned. 'What of it?'

'She is well?'

'As can be. She works with the animals. Seems to have a way with them.'

Dorin cleared his throat. The proprietor waited, looking him up and down, and Dorin saw him eyeing his new soft leather shoes and new charcoal-grey cloak. 'I am touched by her handicap,' he managed, and held out a small bag. 'This is to help with her upkeep. You are kind to have kept her on.'

The proprietor did not reach for the bag. 'As I said . . . she has a way with the animals.'

'Please take it. I do not wish her to be any burden to you.'

'If you insist. My thanks. Who shall I say came by?'

'No one. No one came.'

The man frowned anew, but nodded. 'Very well.'

Dorin inclined his head and left. Ullara's father was hailed by other patrons, and Dorin's last view of him was of the man tying the pouch to his belt.

He turned a corner and pressed his back to a wall. He cleared his throat, blinking. He hoped the father would say nothing; he was sure she'd be angry with him. Perhaps the bribe would be enough to prevent the father from tossing her out to beg on the streets. But he had to do what he could. At least until he was certain all this infighting between gangs was over. Then it would be safe to return; then he need not worry about what risk he might be bringing to her.

Once they'd made certain of their grip on the city, of course.

He returned to walking the streets. The curfew had been raised and people were in a celebratory mood, though not nearly as exuberant as Dorin imagined they might have been, given the price paid. The taverns and brothels were doing a booming trade, and he and Wu had a cut of that action.

He did not share the mood.

Frankly, he did not know what to think. Assassins didn't work with partners. You never heard of such things. Yes, there was a tradition of schools and crews, such as the Nightblades; but those were groups, not partnerships.

He frowned as he walked along – it just didn't seem workable.

Who would be in charge? Him, of course. But the crazy mage would always head off and do whatever he wanted. He didn't listen to reason, couldn't follow orders. Had no discipline, no training. How could it possibly work?

As always, his wanderings took him up to the rooftops. He sat on the ledge of a three-storey brick building looking to the south, overlooking the Inner Round. The night was very black as heavy clouds promised more rain on the morrow, but the city was alight with celebration of the end of the siege, and victory.

Though bought with sorcerous devastation such as had not been seen in generations.

Dorin tapped his thumbs together at his lap. Perhaps they could go far together, after all. Yes, the lad's manner and habits drove him to distraction. But there did seem to be a real genius hidden behind all the nonsense. Who else had solved this mystery of Shadow? At least that he knew of. There must be some potential in it. If they could just figure out how to exploit it properly . . .

A light step behind him stilled his thumbs. He drew back his hands, letting the hilts of throwing daggers slip from his wrists into his palms, and slowly glanced over his shoulder. It was that fop, the city mage, the one named Silk.

'There you are,' the fellow called from across the roof. 'Been looking for you.'

The other city mage he'd faced before, Ho, also stepped out from cover, while a Dal Honese woman with a great mane of thick hair rose up from an alley, alighting on the roof. 'What for?' Dorin murmured and glanced down to the narrow cobbled way three storeys below, where an enormous giant of a fellow now came shambling out and peered up at him. His toothy grin was bright in the gloom.

Dorin carefully rose to his feet and faced Silk. The fellow adjusted the wide frills on his dark blue silk shirt. 'Oh, just the matter of a murder.'

'What of it?'

The mage waggled a finger at him. 'Can't have you going round killing people. Not on. We'd like you to come with us peacefully. As you can see, you have no chance.'

'You don't really think I'm going to come quietly, do you?'

'We'd rather you—'

Dorin snapped two throws and the slim blades would have

flown true had not the black woman waved at that instant, sending the two missiles awry. As it was, the mage Silk broke off to peer down at his side where his shirt was sliced open. Dorin was gratified to see him pale to a ghostly white. 'Get the bastard,' the mage snarled, outraged.

Dorin turned and jumped the alley, but even as he was in the air something slapped him aside and he tumbled, arms flailing, to slam into the brick ledge of the lower roof opposite. He gripped it, winded, his chest screaming its pain. *Damned mages.*

Heavy steps thumped to the brick roof and the wide frowning mage, Ho, appeared and stared down at him. He took hold of Dorin's shirts and lifted him on to the roof. The pain was excruciating as Dorin's torso stabbed into him. *Damned mages broke my ribs!*

All that lay between him and freedom now was this heavyset mage who held him conveniently at arm's length. 'Sorry, old man,' he murmured, and thrust him in the heart. The hand released him. He fell, almost losing his balance, and ran free to escape.

Something yanked him back by an arm. He turned, and was stunned to see the burly mage still standing – even managing to grip his arm. He stared, absolutely astounded. He could not help but state the obvious: 'You should be dead.'

The mage pulled the blade from his chest, nodding. 'Yes, I should be.' He punched the pommel of the weapon into Dorin's chest and he collapsed in a sizzling blaze of agony, hugging himself.

Yet he would not give up. He imposed his rigid self-control over the torture of his broken ribs and managed to rise to stagger on. But after only a few steps that formless power took hold of him again and crushed him flat to the roof like an insect.

'I have him!' Mara called from the far roof.

Ho lumbered for him once more. The entire area darkened, however, and shadows were now flitting all about like tatters of storm clouds. Ho batted at them and squinted about – he seemed to have lost sight of him. 'Where is he?' the big fellow called.

'I still have him!' Mara answered.

'Will someone do something?' The mage grumbled.

Flames burst to life all about the circumference of the rooftop. Someone yelped in pain and Wu hopped into view batting at his trousers and sleeves. Ho reached out and grasped him by the neck, lifting him from his feet. Dorin strove to throw a weapon but

Mara's grip had him pressed so firmly he found he could not even draw breath. His vision was darkening and a roaring now filled his ears.

The shadows drifted away to nothing and the flames snapped from existence. Ho lumbered to the roof's edge and held Wu out over the open space. The little mage struggled in Ho's wide hand. 'Now let's not be too hasty . . .' he gasped.

'He'll fall!' Dorin warned even as Ho opened his grip and Wu slipped from view. 'No!' Dorin yelled with the last of his breath. Ho stood peering down and pressing a hand to his chest, rubbing and frowning to himself.

Disbelieving, Dorin managed to drag himself in a crawl to the roof's lip. He peered down to see the crumpled form of the mage lying twisted amid a pool of blood spreading from his split skull.

He's faking again, Dorin told himself. He must be. Faking it.

'It was only two storeys,' Ho rumbled above his head. 'Not much of a mage, then.'

It's false.

Then a dog emerged from the murk, sniffed at the still form, and started lapping up the blood.

Dorin rolled over to peer up at Ho. *It's not – the poor fellow couldn't fly*. He knew that for certain.

Ho drew a short wooden truncheon from his belt and swung at him. He tried desperately to shift his head but Mara still held him in too tight a grip. The baton crashed into his skull and starry darkness swallowed him.

*

He awoke in a dark cell. He immediately felt at his chest and found his ribs had been healed. So, they wanted him alive. Then he remembered, and a great rage swelled over him making him feel all about himself for a weapon – any weapon. But they'd taken everything. All his equipment, all his belts. Even his shoes were gone.

He rested his head back against the cold stone wall. They didn't have to kill the poor fellow! Still, maybe he wasn't dead, only badly wounded. Or he'd faked it. But it had seemed so *real*. How had he done it?

Well, it was of no help to him now. He rose and found on the floor a plate covered by a wooden bowl. Within lay bread and a cold porridge of boiled barley. He ate and banged on the stout wooden door. 'Hello! Anybody there? Hello?' After he'd waited a long time footsteps sounded in the hall beyond. 'Hello?' he called again.

'So you are awake,' a man answered. It was one of the city mages. That fire mage, Smokey. 'What do you want?'

'What are you going to do with me?'

'You will be tried and executed for the murder of Chulalorn the Third.'

'It was a favour.'

'Regicide is no joke. The kings of Tali and Unta and all the others are outraged. They demand someone be punished.'

'Didn't most of them come to the throne over the bodies of their predecessors?'

'That's different. They're of noble blood. You're a nobody. A commoner.'

'Ah! I understand it now. That justifies all they've done.'

He heard Smokey's answering sigh. 'I didn't come to debate questions of social justice. Things are as they are. Get comfortable, because you're going to be here for a while. Representatives are coming from all across the lands. They demand justice be done.'

'Justice? Don't make me laugh.'

He heard footsteps walking away. 'Hello? You hear me? Hello . . . ?' He banged a fist to the door. 'Bastard!'

He spent time trying the door, but without any of his equipment it was beyond him. He exercised, ate, and slept again. When he next awoke he exercised again. After a long period of stretching, he sat back on the cot of stuffed straw and pondered once more on Wu's death. Had it truly been real? It had seemed so convincing . . . Yet he'd been taken in by the bastard, what, twice before? Perhaps he should just assume that nothing was as it seemed.

Then it came to him and he sat there chuckling in the dark. The solution. It seemed so obvious now that he'd seen it. 'Are you there?' he asked. 'Because I figured it out.'

The tap of a stick striking stone sounded. Dorin sat up to see the hunched fellow standing in the far corner. 'Figured it out? It was quite flawless.'

Dorin shook his head, surprised by how . . . well . . . relieved he felt. 'How did you do it?'

The mage waved the question aside. 'What tipped you off?'

'The dog. There are no dogs left in Heng.'

Wu raised a finger, nodding. 'Ah. And I thought it was such a nice touch.' He shook his head. 'Just goes to show – simplicity. Don't get fancy.'

'But how did you do it? I *know* you can't fly.'

The lad shrugged. 'He didn't have hold of me in the first place, did he.'

It occurred to Dorin that it might be that when he saw this Dal Hon mage he wasn't really seeing him. He stood, then frowned, thinking. 'How long were you going to let me rot? Were you here all this time?'

Wu gave an airy wave of his walking stick. 'Oh, I checked in once or twice. Just wanted to see if you'd figured it out.'

Dorin wasn't at all satisfied but knew that was all he was going to get out of the fellow, so he subsided, scowling. 'So, now what?'

'Yes. That is the question.' Wu toyed with the walking stick. 'I believe we have the edge on most of these five individually. Other than Koroll, whom I suggest we simply avoid. However, Ho's demonstration troubles me. There is much more to him than meets the eye. You are right – he really should've died.'

Dorin sat back on the cot. 'Ah . . . Well, there's always Unta.'

'No, we're almost there, my friend.'

Dorin shrugged. 'I really don't care where I – or we – go.'

'Exactly! So it might as well be here.'

Dorin frowned, scratching his forehead. 'I really wonder about your so-called logic here.'

'Immaterial, my friend. Consider it situational. I am a great admirer of that Talian tradition of philosophy called the Convenience School.' He tapped a thumb to his lips, squinting in thought. 'Otherwise known as the Rationalizationists. Very popular among their noble patrons, they are.'

Dorin waved aside the man's foggy meanderings. 'What do you propose?'

'I suggest we look into this Hengan mage. Get to the bottom of things, as it were.'

'And how do you propose we do that?'

The mage opened wide his rather short arms. 'Why, right here, of course. You have been brought to the man's research quarters, conveniently enough.'

Dorin pressed his hand to his forehead. 'And the cell we are in . . . ?'

'Oh, the door is very secure. Can't be opened from inside. Quite impossible.'

Dorin let his hand fall. 'So . . . ?'

Wu pointed the stick to the back of the cell. 'Not so the rear wall.'

'So . . . you can get in and out?'

'Yes. Pop in and out.'

'Not in Shadow, surely? What of the dogs?'

Wu winced. '*Hounds*, please.' He pinched the bridge of his nose, pacing. 'Think of the border between this realm and Shadow proper as a thick curtain. You can sort of hug the curtain, so to speak. Travel along it without really committing to either. See what I mean?'

Dorin shook his head. 'I have no idea what you're talking about.'

Wu looked to the ceiling. 'The unwashed masses . . . what can one do?'

Dorin crossed his arms and sat back on the cot. 'You're saying we're in Ho's private section of the catacombs here?'

'Yes.'

'The very ones you've been trying to enter all this time but claimed they were too well protected?'

Wu made a show of studying his walking stick. 'What of it?'

'Did you allow me to be captured so that you could get in?'

Wu pointed to the rear wall. 'Shall I pop round and let you out, then?'

Dorin studied the fellow through narrowed eyes. 'Yeah. You do that.'

Wu waved cheerily. 'Won't be a mo.'

It was far longer than just a moment before Dorin heard rattling and fussing at the cell door. The struggle continued for some time, followed by cursing and more rattling and banging. Dorin looked to the ceiling and tapped his fingertips on his lap. The banging became a long drawn out screeching as of rusted metal. After that the door began edging open. It gaped wide enough to allow a sweaty Wu to put his head inside. He pointed to the thick door. 'A touch stiff . . . the damp an' all . . .'

Dorin slid out past him. 'Right. All I need now is . . .' He broke off as Wu held out his baldrics and other gear, including his coils of wire and fine rope.

Wu slapped his hands together. 'Fine. Good. This way,' and he motioned Dorin onward.

'You first.'

Wu pursed his lips. 'Right.' He clasped his hands behind his back and ambled off, peering about like a gawking bumpkin.

This section of tunnels consisted of large dressed limestone blocks, vaulted, with sconces holding the occasional torch, most of which had burned out. Wu listened at then tried each door they passed. Most opened on to mundane rooms. One chamber proved to be a library of scrolls and parchment in floor to ceiling nooks. A table was strewn with sheets covered in notes and diagrams.

Wu pushed aside a few sheets while making tisking noises to himself. Dorin leaned in the doorway, arms crossed. Wu raised one sheet. 'Oh my . . .' Dorin rolled his eyes. Wu looked to him. 'If this work was known of, our friend Ho would be run from the continent.'

'You can understand those scratchings?'

'The general drift.'

'Which is?'

'High Denul. Life researches. But twisted. Corrupted.'

Another chamber was a laboratory of sorts. Boxes lined the walls containing ingredients in powder and leaf form. Tables held large glass bowls and globes. Mice, spiders, and lizards occupied the globes. Bizarrely, on a shelf high along one wall sat a row of crude stringed wooden puppets.

Upon peering up at the puppets Wu's comment was 'Oh dear . . .'.

One globe as broad across as a man held a heap of dirt and leaves and sticks. Dorin tapped it, curious as to what sort of creature might live here. Moles, perhaps? He flinched away when a tiny creature hidden amid the leaves and twigs pressed its face against the dirty glass. The thing was shaped like a human in miniature, only twisted and deformed, its face obscenely reminiscent of a baby. It glared at him and bared tiny dagger teeth.

'A daemon,' Dorin hissed to Wu.

Wu bustled over to tap the glass. 'A homunculus.' He cast a surveying glance round the chamber and nodded to himself. 'Yes . . . it is all making sense.'

Dorin glared back at the little beast, which stuck out its tongue. 'Stop making vague knowing sounds. What's making sense?'

'Why Ho didn't die.' Wu motioned them out. 'Let's keep going.'

The vaulted damp tunnel led on to a series of cells such as the one that had held Dorin, but these were far older, and stronger, with doors of solid iron. Wu checked each cell as they passed. They came to a locked door. Wu rattled it then jumped as a gruff voice within bellowed: 'Lar. *Lar!*' Whoever was inside now bashed on the door, which resounded beneath the heavy blows.

Wu gingerly slipped a slim viewing port open and peered inside. He flinched away as the prisoner punched the door. Dorin eyed him. 'Well?'

The mage was stroking his chin thoughtfully, looking quite impressed.

'Who – or what – is in there?'

Wu blinked, coming to himself. 'Ah. Well . . . I suppose you could say that Ho is in there.'

'What?'

'Yes. An exact twin. Which means . . .' He pulled on another door that proved locked as well. He peered in this cell also, and nodded to himself. 'Amazing.'

Dorin peered in as well but saw nothing as the cell was black as night. 'I can't see anything. How can you see?'

Distracted, Wu murmured, 'Darkness is no impediment to my vision now.' He tried the door across the way; it too was locked. He looked in then slid shut the viewing port and returned his attention to Dorin. 'We should go now. It is dangerous to remain.'

'What? All of a sudden it's dangerous?'

'In light of our current understanding of the situation.'

Wu hurried down the tunnel and Dorin, annoyed, kept pace. 'Perhaps you'd like to share this understanding?' he whispered, fierce.

Wu waved his walking stick. 'Certainly. Ho did not die – it is especially difficult to kill him – because there is more than one Ho.'

Dorin squinted at him, now even more irritated. 'That's not an explanation.'

Wu paused, his brows rising. 'It's not?' He shrugged and continued. 'Very well. Our friend Ho has been a very naughty fellow indeed. He has researched and replicated – with only partial success, it would seem – an ancient and forbidden theurgist ritual. One I have only read of as legend. The ritual of D'ivers. He has split himself into many.'

'You mean like a twin?'

'Something even more intimate. True copies. Three at least. Any one of them extremely difficult to kill, having thrice the life-force, so to speak. Beheading or burning is perhaps the only way to be sure of killing these things.'

'That is . . . a perversion of life.'

'Exactly. And as is to be expected, the products are flawed. And here they remain, locked away for ever.'

'Dear gods. Merciless . . .'

'Quite. Our friend is not to be underestimated.'

Wu led them down smaller side tunnels until they entered low-roofed dusty catacombs that were quite obviously rarely travelled. He slowed his pace here, thoughtfully tapping the head of his walking stick to his chin.

Dorin too was thinking. If the fellow couldn't be killed then they'd have to subdue him somehow. Tie him up, or chain him. But he was so damned strong. 'So what do we do, then?' he asked.

'If the events of a few days ago proved anything, it is that we are outnumbered. As we are on the streets. I suggest we recruit. I pride myself that I have something of an eye for talent and so I have someone in mind.'

Dorin gave the little fellow a sidelong glance. 'An eye for talent? You're not suggesting you recruited me? Because you didn't.' Wu just paced along, now humming to himself. 'Really, that's not what happened.' Wu swung his walking stick about, knocking cobwebs aside as he went. Dorin halted. 'Let's get this straight.' Wu continued on up the tunnel. 'You didn't!' Dorin yelled after him, his voice echoing in the passage.

Wu headed to the Street of the Gods and Dorin trailed after. Long before they got there he realized whom the fellow had in mind and he sighed his distaste. Gods, *him*. The self-righteous, holier-than-thou prick himself. They found the old mausoleum; it was now at the centre of a larger section of occupied temples and yards all thronged with what appeared to be adherents or refugees. Families squatted beneath canopies in the street. The mausoleum itself was now more of a shrine. Burning votive candles crowded the doorway and a horde of kneeling worshippers choked any access.

Wu planted his walking stick and addressed a shawled woman nearby. 'We are looking for the acolyte of Hood here. Dassem. Have you—'

'The holy Sword of Hood?'

Wu and Dorin shared a glance, and Dorin looked to the sky. 'Ah, yes . . . *that* Sword of Hood.'

'He is out in the fields sending off the dead.'

'Why of course he is,' Wu said, offering a smile. 'Thank you.'

They headed for the west Gate of the Sunset, now thrown open, its siege damage being repaired by carpenters and stonemasons. The heavyset Hengan female masons appeared to be just as husky as their male counterparts. A large crowd filled the fields to the immediate west. Here had been opened a mass grave for all the fallen of the siege, Kanese and Hengan alike. City bureaucrats might have initiated it, but the citizens followed the orders of one man overseeing the mass interment, the acolyte of Hood.

Wu wended his way through the crowd to where Dassem was leading hundreds of kneeling mourners in a prayer for the dead. Wu bowed his head, tapping his walking stick to the ground. Dorin lowered his gaze in deference.

When it was over, and the mourners clambered to their feet, Wu approached Dassem. The Sword of Hood spared them one glance then turned away to give instructions to a crowd of workers. Once this was done the young man headed off, ignoring them.

Somehow Wu managed to slip up to his side, Dorin kicking along in his wake, hands on his belt. 'What can you possibly want?' Dassem asked Wu. 'I doubt you've come to offer up your respects,' and he shot Dorin a glare. Dorin offered a tight smile.

'It is not what I want,' Wu began, 'but what I can offer.'

'And that is?' Dassem stopped suddenly. He bent to an old woman on her knees, overcome by grief. 'Take my arm, mother.'

The old woman grasped hold of his arm and rose unsteadily. 'He is gone!' she cried.

'So too shall we all,' Dassem said gently.

'This is reassuring?' Wu murmured to Dorin.

But the old woman nodded, 'Yes, yes. It is just so hard . . .'

'They do not suffer. It is we who suffer.'

The old woman patted Dassem's arm as he helped her along.

Dorin could not help rolling his eyes. The acolyte sat her in the shade of a hedgerow then straightened to the unwelcome intruders. 'You are still here?'

'Yes,' Wu said. 'How would you like all the funds you wish to glorify your god?'

'Hood cares nothing for coin.'

'No, but he might like a roof over his head. Say, a very large one trimmed in gold?'

'You cannot bribe death,' Dassem answered, and walked past them.

Wu pulled a hand down his face and threw an exasperated look to Dorin, who mouthed, *I know* . . .

Dassem was now in conversation with the young girl Dorin had seen sleeping in the mausoleum. She obviously bore Dal Hon blood in her wild kinky hair and dark nut-brown hue. She was saying, 'The farmer refuses to allow us to open the new pit.'

Dassem nodded. 'Tell him that the Sword of Hood says he should be honoured.'

She bowed. 'I will tell him so.'

When the girl jogged off Wu pushed forward once more. 'We offer to acknowledge the worship of Hood in Heng.'

Dassem paused, turned to them. 'How can you make such assurances?'

Wu opened his arms. 'Well, when you help us take the city we will do so.'

Dassem shook his head. 'I will not help you.' He turned to go.

'Even to further the worship of Hood?'

Dassem halted once more. He looked Wu up and down. 'A god needs your help, does he? Rather arrogant, don't you think?'

'You should know,' Dorin snapped.

Dassem pursed his lips, eyeing him. Behind the fellow's back, Wu frantically gestured for Dorin's silence.

'I am busy with my true work,' the Sword said, and walked off.

Wu came to Dorin's side. 'Thank you very much.'

Dorin watched the crowd part for the man; how many reached out to touch him as he passed; how some even fell to their knees before him and how he set his hand on the heads of these, as if in blessing. The sight of it sickened him. 'Condescending prick.'

'With reason, perhaps.'

'What now?'

Wu started for the city. As he walked along he used his walking stick to flick clots of dirt from his path. 'I am of the opinion that we steal a turn from Chulalorn's generals. I believe they had the right idea in bypassing all obstacles and striking straight for the head, so to speak.'

Dorin nodded. 'I agree.'

'If we succeed, then there remains nothing to argue over.'

'Agreed. When?'

'Soon. Within the morrow?'

'Two days. I need to rest and ready myself.'

'Very good. I will work on our approach. I understand there are various hidden ways into the temple precincts.'

'Done. I assume you are hiding us now?'

'Yes. We should stay hidden from now on – the obvious assumption will be that we've fled. As any sane fugitives would.'

'So you weren't hiding me that night?'

'Well, you walked out, didn't you?'

Dorin scratched his chin. 'Well . . . I suppose I did, didn't I?'

Chapter 22

THEY TIMED THEIR ENTRANCE FOR DUSK. DORIN HAD SLEPT most of the day; when the time came to set out he felt fully rested and recuperated. He – and, he assumed, Wu – had given no one any word of their plans or intent. They merely set out. They said nothing to Rheena, or the troop of followers, not even letting them know where they were going. Dorin assumed that she'd simply taken charge, as she should. After all, neither he nor Wu had any particular interest in running the actual day-to-day operations anyway.

Wu led the way, and Dorin was content to let him do so. Truth was, he now knew that any time the fellow appeared to be leading the way he was actually following at a safe distance. Dorin kept an eye on the streets and surroundings, scanning for threats. He assumed Wu was actively hiding their location. He now understood it was second nature for the shifty fellow, hunted or not.

The route took them by a roundabout way to the rich central precincts, close by the grounds of the inner temple, which stood next to the palace and shared its privileged position. The entrance was a lesser-travelled access of servants and the lowest ranked functionaries. Dorin waited while Wu scouted ahead, cloaked in shadow. By this means they steadily penetrated into the palace grounds. The wreckage of the recent fighting was still impressive. It must have been a ferocious battle here for the throne room itself. Yet Wu's route bypassed that main part of the palace, and it became clear to Dorin that they were headed for the Protectress's personal sanctum, the city's domed cynosure.

'Why here?' he whispered to the mage as they hid in a side gallery.

'She rests within.'

'Says who?'

'My sources.'

'You trust them?'

'I trust their greed.'

Dorin grunted his agreement. 'Very well. Now?'

'Now we wait.'

Dorin sat back, crossing his arms. This he understood. He had been trained in resting readiness. 'When?'

'When I sense it is all clear.'

'Why can't you just take a look?'

The Dal Hon youth, in his charade of an elder, drew together his already wrinkled grey brows. 'I cannot. There is only light inside that dome.'

Dorin snorted at that. Amazing. Some sort of Temple of Light, he imagined. Or a temple to the Protectress herself, as after her demonstration of might she was now quite openly worshipped as the patron deity of Heng. Much to the priests of Burn's outrage. Yet something of that troubled him, annoyingly.

They waited while night patrols passed by. Finally, Wu nodded to him and he uncrossed his arms, knives already in his hands. Wu crossed to a corridor that led to a small door that opened on to the temple. The scars of the past fighting marred the walls here, but much less so than in the administrative wing.

Wu was still for a moment, then he cast Dorin a significant look, and nodded. Dorin pushed open the door and the two entered.

It was a broad empty domed chamber, dimly lit by a sort of formless glow that covered the entire room. At its centre someone sat hunched beneath a blanket. Dorin paused; this was not right. He had been convinced of it the moment they entered the temple. But Wu glanced back at him, sending him a silent question. He raised his hands, uneasy, yet unable to say exactly why.

Was it because this was just too easy? But that was a ridiculous cliché. Assassinations that are properly planned should unfold easily. Proper preparation and all that . . .

Wu, however, obviously shared nothing of his disquiet. The mage sauntered onward, drawing a walking stick from within his belt – a real walking stick of wood this time – and swinging it about. Dorin was beginning to get a feel for the fellow: the stick appeared whenever he felt at ease, or confident. Perhaps, dared he say . . . cocky?

He had no choice but to follow along, hunched, craning his neck, knives in hand.

It was the Protectress after all – Dorin had seen her a few times. He'd been half dreading that it was Ho waiting for them, wrapped in the thick robes.

But it was she. Shalmanat. In the flesh. Hunched beneath thick enfolding layers of cloth. For warmth, he imagined. She stirred as they approached, straightening and blinking. She looked quite ill to him, even more pale than before, her eyes sunken and bruised.

'So,' she said, her voice hoarse and faint. 'You have come.'

Wu bowed. 'Good evening, Protectress.'

She drew a heavy breath, obviously still quite weak. 'What is it to be?'

'Exile, m'lady,' Wu said. 'If you would be so kind.'

'Exile?' She cast a questioning look to Dorin. 'Is this your answer? After slaying a king I should think you would consider it nothing to remove me.'

Dorin considered the question. He felt no urge to slay her. Quite the opposite, in fact. And if their objective could be achieved without the necessity of it, so much the better. He answered her look. 'Will you go?'

'You would let me? What if I returned, what then?'

Wu pursed his lips as he examined his walking stick. 'Then we would have to kill you.'

She nodded, accepting this. 'And the mages – what of them?'

Wu shrugged. 'They serve the city, do they not?'

Shalmanat nodded again, obviously relieved. 'Yes. As do I . . .' Something in her delivery of these last words raised Dorin's hackles and he drew breath to act. '. . . while you I think would not.'

The dome blazed to that familiar eye-searing brightness. Dorin could not help but bring the backs of his hands to his face, hunching against the agonizing punishment. The knives blazed to glowing brands in his hands and he flinched, dropping them. All his equipment sizzled now and he danced about, tearing it all from him. He heard Wu curse and the stick clatter to the stone flags.

'Do something!' he called.

'There are no shadows . . .' Then the mage laughed, almost giggling: 'No darkness. No shadows! I am a fool!'

A door opened and Dorin swung to the noise. He tore a strip of cloth from his shirt and tied it around his eyes then let his hands fall loose at his sides, waiting and listening.

Heavy flat footsteps approached. Ho. Two other lighter sets followed. Silk and the Dal Hon woman – Mara? Someone was stumbling about to his left – Wu, damn him.

Mentally, he retraced his position then took two quick steps to his right. His shin barked the stool, knocking it flying – she'd moved. No fool she. He waited then, listening once more.

'Well,' Wu suddenly announced to the room at large, 'I suppose I shall have to summon my daemon now.'

'Oh, shut up,' the Dal Hon woman snarled.

The heavy steps approached close, so very close. Just as one last footfall came in arm's reach Dorin edged aside, blocking the hands reaching for him. Ho grunted, his feet shifting.

'Just grab him, Ho,' the fop mage said. 'We don't have all night.'

Thank you. Dorin hadn't quite located that one; quiet, the fop. He circled, his course taking him that way.

Ho came lumbering after.

'I do possess a daemon,' Wu asserted, quite affronted. 'He is coming now and you are all in grave danger. I suggest you flee.'

'Shut up, fool!' Mara warned again.

'No killing here!' Shalmanat called suddenly from a good distance off.

This time, as Ho's last step brought him within arm's reach, Dorin knocked aside the arms and counter-attacked with a kick to the chest that sent the burly mage stumbling backwards.

Dorin also stumbled. He staggered back towards the fop mage's location. He heard the fellow step aside to avoid him. That was enough, and he spun, catching hold of the mage to clench the man's throat. 'Nobody move!'

Shocked silence followed for several heartbeats. 'I hear anything and I'll crush this one's throat. What of that, Shalmanat?'

'Please,' the Protectress answered, 'please . . . do not desecrate this place.'

Dorin heard true anguish in her voice. 'What of it, Ho?' he asked.

'Let's take this outside,' Mara snarled, and a door slammed open.

Dorin realized his vision was returning as he noticed he could

391

see the cloth pressed against his eyes. He used his shoulder to strip it from his head, all the while careful to keep a tight grip on the mage, Silk. He saw Mara marching Wu towards an exit.

'Wait!' Ho called, and he crossed to Mara and began tying Wu up. Dorin was chagrined to see that Ho was using his own wire to do so. He bound Wu's hands behind his back and wound the length round his neck as well. Then he tore Wu's jacket and wrapped it over the mage's eyes. 'You'll not slip away this time,' he said, satisfied, and urged Mara onward.

Dorin followed, hands at Silk's neck, his thumbs pressed into the man's larynx. 'Where are the other two,' he demanded. 'The fire mage and Koroll?'

'They are following the Kan retreat,' Ho answered behind him, helping Shalmanat.

'This way leads to the river,' the Protectress said as the little procession slowly shuffled along. 'You two offered me exile and so I return the offer. Go with your lives and never return.'

Wu mumbled something hoarsely and Mara shook him. 'What was that? Where is your daemon now, fool?'

'It's rather late,' Wu gurgled.

Mara shook him again.

They reached a tunnel exit and Mara pushed it open. It led to the mud shore beneath a set of piers. It was the depth of night. 'Get a boat,' Shalmanat told Ho and he lumbered off through the mud. 'We have a city to rebuild,' the Protectress continued, hugging herself. She pulled her thick robes tighter. 'We cannot waste any more time on you two.' She peered aside. 'Ah . . .'

Ho returned towing a blackened, half-burned old rowboat that he drew up before Mara and Wu. Mara pushed Wu in to fall on his back, where he writhed mumbling curses through the wire at his neck.

Ho waved Dorin in. 'Leave Silk here.'

Dorin set one foot into the shallow boat. 'I think not.' He forced Silk in with him. The mage reluctantly submitted.

'You haven't escaped yet,' Shalmanat warned.

'Exactly. I'll release him when we've passed the Outer Round.'

'We will be watching,' Ho warned.

Dorin pushed off and the boat began drifting downriver. He pointed to the oars and urged Silk down. 'Row.'

The mage appeared ready to say something – to curse him

perhaps – but he bit his tongue, subsiding. He set to mounting the oars. Dorin worked on releasing Wu, careful not to turn his back on Silk as he did so.

Wu sat up, rubbing his wrists and neck. 'Well,' he said, peering about. He slapped his hands to his thighs. 'It is night. I am free. I suggest we return to . . .'

'No,' Dorin said.

Wu blinked at him. 'What? No? Whatever do you mean?'

'I mean no.'

'We're not beaten, you know. That was a stand-off.'

Silk laughed at this as he rowed.

Dorin shot him a glance, shook his head. 'No. There are too many of them. Six if you count the Protectress.' He sat back, but kept one eye on the mage. 'Overreach. We're not ready.' And he surprised himself as, unbidden, there arose in his thoughts, a silent *yet*. He recalled the warning given him by that female mage – what had been her name? Something like Nightcold? 'We were reckless.'

'You're lucky to be alive,' Silk muttered.

'Shut up and row. The same could be said for you. We're alive because we offered exile to Shalmanat and she responded in kind.' He glanced to Wu. 'Your instincts saved us there.'

Wu inclined his head in acknowledgement. He drummed his fingers on the blackened wood of the gunnel. 'Where is he!'

'Who?'

'My daemon, of course.'

At the oars Silk snorted a laugh. Dorin looked Wu up and down. 'You don't have a daemon.'

Wu appeared quite offended as he drew himself tall and tried to straighten his jacket only to discover that it was gone. 'I do so. He just doesn't come when I call. He's not well trained.'

Silk was shaking his head.

The river gate of the eastern Outer Round was approaching. Teams of labourers were arriving for the day's work even as Silk rowed them between its wrecked stone arches. Dorin gestured the city mage over. 'Okay, get out.' Silk headed the bows for the shore. Dorin shook a finger. 'No. Now. Jump.'

'What? Into the water?'

'That's what's in the river. Go on.'

'But my silks . . .'

Dorin pointed again, rising.

Silk sighed and stood. 'Very well. Just so you know, you two are the stupidest—'

Dorin pushed him over and he fell with a great awkward splash. He flailed in the water, perhaps trying to swim, or giving them an obscene gesture. Dorin took the oars. Wu sat at the stern plate, peering back at the receding walls of Heng, lit now in dawn's pink and gold glow. 'Farewell, poor city. You will never know what you missed.'

'Wretched dung-heap,' Dorin muttered.

'What lies ahead?' Wu asked.

'The Idryn meets the Bay of Nap at Cawn.'

Wu tapped a finger to his nose. 'Ah, Cawn. City of merchants – sorry, I mean thieves, gougers, frauds and those who fatten themselves on the misery of others. We should do well there . . .'

The rowboat passed beneath the overhanging branches of a copse and Dorin started as something thumped down from a tree limb into the boat. It was that tiny monkey-creature, the nacht, baring its fangs in what he hoped was a grin.

Wu threw open his arms. 'There you are! What took you so long?'

'That's your daemon?'

The creature climbed Wu and tried to sit on his head; Wu fought with it to keep it from doing so. 'Indeed. That's its name – Demon. He's quite the troublemaker.'

Dorin corrected the boat's path by rowing gently. 'Give it another, please.'

The nacht hissed at Dorin and made gestures that vaguely resembled obscene signs. Wu pulled its hands down. 'Now, now. Bad Demon. Bad.'

'I'm beginning to think this is going to be a long journey,' Dorin muttered.

The nacht reached its quick hands into Wu's shirt and tossed a box to the bottom of the rowboat. It spilled open to reveal the broken piece of worked stone. Dorin hung his head in disbelief. 'We lose everything and that's all you come away with?'

'It's important,' Wu huffed. He shook a finger at the nacht. 'Bad Demon.'

Dorin picked up the flint shard and shoved it back into the box. For an instant he was tempted to toss the damn thing into the water, but that would hurt the poor fellow's feelings needlessly, so he threw the ridiculous object to Wu. The mage tucked it back into his shirt. As he did so, the nacht snatched his stick and threw it overboard. Wu swung a punch at the creature but it ducked. He pointed out over the water. 'Fetch! Get the stick, Demon!'

The nacht yawned, showing a pink mouth and enormous fangs, then curled up at the bottom of the boat and shut its eyes. Wu sat grumbling and fussing impotently at the stern.

Dorin decided that maybe he could come round to taking a liking to the ugly beast. He raised his gaze to the tall walls of Heng slowly diminishing into the distance behind them, and pondered on all he was leaving behind.

He regretted not having a chance to say farewell to Rheena. But the moment hadn't arisen. He also knew that she wanted far more than a partnership and that he wasn't prepared to offer – not yet, anyway.

As for Ullara . . . He paused in his rowing, resting his hands on the oars. Ullara . . . He hung his head and pressed a hand to his brow for a time.

He'd taken so much from her – and she'd given him so much. Even more than she knew, perhaps. She'd given him his true identity. It was terrible that she'd lost her vision when she'd seen his true self right away. And named him.

So he was finished with Dorin. He was not the lad he'd been when he'd entered the city. Not that he'd been some green farmhand, but he'd been untested, unbloodied . . . unready.

Not so now. Dorin was done.

Hard lessons luckily survived had put an end to that lad and his dreams. A transition from which a good few do not emerge alive. But necessary, if hard. The city had cut away the untried Dorin and trampled his dreams into the mud and the mire.

He was Dancer now, and Dancer from now on.

But he would not regret it or hold a grudge. Perhaps he no longer had dreams. He didn't need them. Now he had plans.

* * *

With the long delayed spring already giving way to summer, Silk walked the walls of Li Heng. The warmth of the sun was welcome on his new white silk shirt and new Untan olive-green silk pantaloons. Construction was moving along swiftly on most of the wall repairs. And since the siege he'd been enjoying far more respect from the Hengan militia, and among the citizens in general.

He stopped at a view over the river, but did not lean out of the crenel as the stone would dirty his shirt. He watched the muddy ochre-red waters course along and pondered once more on the fate of those two bold-faced would-be usurpers. The utter audaciousness of their ambition still made him shake his head in wonder. Were they simply criminals with arrogance far outstripping their abilities, or had he come within a hair's breadth of having to bow down to a psychopathic sorcerer? He still wasn't sure.

Mara still wanted them dead. But Shalmanat would have none of it. And in any case, it appeared they were gone for good. Lying in a ditch in Cawn with their throats slit, no doubt. As befitted a couple of common criminals.

The good news was that Shalmanat was recovering. He thought he'd actually seen a spot of colour come to her cheeks with the returning warmth.

But it was different now. It could never be the same after her . . . cleansing. Palace bureaucrats and functionaries who had treated her as a chief administrator before now bowed before her. Some even feared to address her. In the streets her ascendance was unavoidable. Shrines to her now stood on almost every corner. Temples openly worshipped her as the patron goddess of Heng. And the priests of Burn no longer dared object.

Yet all the while something else tinged the reverence. Something far less welcome to his senses. The populace had watched while the Protectress slaughtered thousands and now they laid garlands and burned incense to her in worship. But, sometimes, Silk noticed the taint of propitiation in their offerings. They venerated her, yes. But now they also dreaded her. For she was a goddess. And goddesses acted capriciously – they were not like normal people, nor even nobles. They were accountable to no one but themselves.

It saddened and worried him. For worshippers had been known to turn upon their idols.

The words of that young soldier returned to him and he shivered. *The Wrath of the Goddess.* They had seen her wrath and it terrified them.

It saddened him because – more than anyone – he did not want a goddess in Shalmanat.

Epilogue

IT WAS NIGHT ON THE FIELDS SOUTH OF HENG, AND SISTER OF Cold Nights crouched before a pile of kindling and dry moss. The sparks she struck flamed to life and she blew upon the fire for a time before sitting back on her heels. The fire's glow played over her tall husky form and reflected brightly in her pale hazel eyes.

She fed sticks into the flames as she waited. The firelight revealed that she sat not far from the croft where she'd brought Juage, but the Jaghut was gone now, journeying south to return to his pretended servitude. She rocked on her haunches, continuing her vigil.

It was long into the night before she sensed someone with her and blinked, drawing her thoughts from the far reaches where she had ventured – a place of low granite hills scoured bare. A cloaked and cowled figure sat opposite, studying the fire.

'Brother K'rul,' she greeted.

'Sister of Cold Nights.'

'He's left Heng.'

Beneath its thick cloak the figure raised and lowered its shoulders. 'Did I say he would stay?'

'You said I would find him here.'

'And you found him.'

She tossed a stick on to the fire. 'He can't be the one to succeed.'

'Why not?'

She scowled her distaste. 'He is incompetent. Dishonest. Nothing more than a self-seeking opportunist. How can he succeed where so many others have failed?'

'So, because he does not conform to your expectations . . . this means he cannot succeed?'

She let out a long hissed breath and threw another stick on to the fire, raising a shower of sparks into the night sky. 'Very well. I shall see it through.'

'Only then may you see where it might take you.'

She nodded. 'So you say. I am trusting you in this, brother.'

'And I you.'

She eyed him warily. 'How so?'

'Fate has plans for me as well. They are bound up with your actions. We are all entwined in the skein of events now.'

She nodded, accepting this. 'That I should have foreseen.' She held up a hand, rubbing the palm. 'I remain bound to the flesh and no longer have our old vision. It is . . . frustrating.'

'Trust sister T'riss in this.'

She barked a laugh. 'No.'

'You should make up, you two.'

She shook her head. 'Never.'

K'rul sighed. 'You are one to hold a grudge.'

'We all are. It is our curse. We never forget.'

'Indeed, we do not. Fare you well, sister.' The figure faded away.

'Fare you well, brother.'

*　*　*

Ullara rose from her straw pallet in the family kitchen that was an open-walled addition behind the barn. A cloth was wrapped tightly about her eyes and she crossed the beaten dirt floor carefully, hands extended, to where a cage hung from a rafter. She found the cage and drew the cloth blind from it.

Within, a small songbird chirped and fluttered about the bars. Ullara pulled the cloth from her head revealing the empty scarred pits of gouged-out eyes. She opened a small door on the cage and held up a finger. The tiny yellow and black bird alighted on the tip, singing happily.

The girl set the bird on her shoulder and turned to a counter, picked up a knife, and began cutting vegetables for the day's meal.

All morning the bird kept up a constant cheery song, though it quietened whenever anyone else entered the kitchen. Chores finished, Ullara went to the stables, the bird clutching her shoulder. Here, any strangers or patrons she met glanced away, or made warding gestures against evil. She headed to a set of stairs, hearing behind her murmured references to witchery and pacts – all of which she had learned long ago to ignore. She climbed a ladder to the attic and threw open the trapdoor to clamber up. The songbird now fluttered about her.

In the large open space of the loft the bird chirped happily as it explored the rafters. Ullara crossed the dark empty space to a gable. She threw open the shutters at the window. The songbird alighted on her shoulder.

The red brick rooftops of Heng lay before her. Smoke rose from countless cooking fires. The traffic of carts and wagons rumbled from the streets. Vendors touted their wares and the commingled talk and shouted bartering of the markets was a low constant tumult.

She crossed her arms, sighing.

The tiny bird kept up its constant cheery song, though, at one point, it chirped *Dancer!*

The girl rubbed a finger on its head and murmured, 'Shush, you.'

* * *

In the royal pleasure garden of the kings of Kan, Iko sought her hidden quarry. It was a warm night, and she stalked her target in her full fine mail coat, her whipsword at her back. Torches stood on tall poles at the many crossings of the paths about her. She edged aside the broad flat leaves of the rhododendron bushes; she peered into thick verges of white and pink rose bushes. She squinted up at the invitingly low limbs of the monkey-tail trees, and quietly crept round to peep behind the wide boles of the fat baobab trees, yet she failed to flush him out.

He was canny, this one. Sharp. He never used the same approach twice.

She did not take the marble-flagged path that forked into the flower garden wing, as cover would be too scarce there; instead, she turned to the path that led to the hedge maze. He thought he could lose her in there.

She entered the narrow lanes of the maze, shaking a bush now and again. At one point she thought she heard a muffled giggle from a lane that shadowed hers and she carried on, harrumphing her frustration.

Shortly thereafter she halted, peering round. 'Where is he?' she exclaimed loudly, vexed. 'Well – I can't find him!' She headed for the exit.

Just before she reached the opening, the bushes behind her shook and something poked her back. She spun, throwing up her hands. 'What!'

A boy danced in circles waving his stick, chanting, 'I won, I won, I won!'

Iko knelt, chuckling. 'Indeed you did.'

Four liveried servants approached and surrounded them. All bore lanterns on tall poles. The lad pointed the stick at her, now all serious. 'Did you hear me?'

Iko pressed a hand to her chest. 'I swear that I did not.'

The lad did not appear convinced. 'Well . . .' He played with the stick, eyed her sideways. 'Is it true?'

'Is what true?'

'What they say . . . about the killing. The assassination.'

Iko fought to keep her expression light. She nodded. 'Yes. It is true.'

'You'll not let that happen, though, will you?' And the lad peered up at her with his soft brown eyes, suddenly anxious.

Iko swallowed hard, her throat so tight and hot she was unable to speak for a moment. She put a hand on the lad's shoulder and brought her face to his. Her voice was low and thick as she managed, 'I swear upon my life that I will never let any harm come to you, my king.'

The lad scampered off, slashing his stick at the bushes as he ran. All four servants raced after, struggling to light his way as he charged about the many paths of the garden.

Iko straightened. She dabbed her eyes with a sleeve of her royal green jupon. The lad's route brought him back to her and he jabbed now at the tree trunks. He turned to her, suddenly. 'Do you know the name the guards at the palace have for you?'

Iko paused, wondering whether she wanted to know it or not. She inclined her head. 'No, sire, I do not.'

'Well, you always wear your mail coat. Always. No one's ever seen you out of it and so they call you Shimmer.' And the boy raced off again, the servants puffing as they chased after him through the trails, their lanterns bobbing in the darkness.

She arched a brow. *Hunh. Shimmer.* Well, it could've been far worse, that was for certain. She started walking after him, hands at her belt, pacing. Chulalorn the Fourth was a handful, that was for certain. But he was her charge. And Mosolan was regent until he reached adulthood.

Until then, she swore to all the gods above and below – that had ever been and would ever be – that no harm should ever come to him under her wardship. She had lost one king and would not lose another.

So did she vow.

ABOUT THE AUTHOR

Born in Winnipeg, Ian Cameron Esslemont has studied and worked as an archaeologist, travelled extensively in South-East Asia and lived in Thailand and Japan for several years. He now lives in Fairbanks, Alaska, with his wife and children. He has a creative writing degree and his novels *Night of Knives*, *Return of the Crimson Guard*, *Stonewielder*, *Orb Sceptre Throne*, *Blood and Bone* and *Assail* are all set in the fantasy world of Malaz that he co-created with Steven Erikson. His latest novel, *Dancer's Lament*, begins an exciting new series that is set in the same extraordinarily imagined world.